Elladur — The Awakening

Imprint©Delazi
ELLADUR — The Awakening

Angie Delazi
c/o Autorenservice.de
Birch avenue 24
36037 Fulda/Germany

Cover design: Giusy Ame/Magicalcover
Image source: Depositphoto
Map: Nishi Wadhwani,
www.instagram.com/craftedofstarlight/
Publisher: Independently published

For all dreamers.
For Eli and Isi — never stop dreaming.
For Miri — who dreamed with me.

PROLOGUE

His footsteps echoed in the empty hallway. Although it was only late afternoon, there was darkness outside the windows. *How appropriate for the day's events*, he thought. The door to the meeting room was directly in front of him. His heart pounded in an unsteady rhythm as he walked towards the closed door.

"Ready?" Kalden, his friend and advisor, said looking at him in anticipation.

"Could we ever be ready for what's coming?"

Without waiting for an answer, Alron strode past Kalden and opened the door. Four of the rulers were gathered in the hall. Beltan had not come, but this wasn't a surprise. Alron had counted on that. His gray eyes wandered across the long table before he moved to take his seat. Laron immediately started the conversation.

"Alron, we should reconsider our decision."

Alron managed to stifle a contemptuous snort. He knew Laron, with his thin body, felt uneasy because of Beltan had not shown up. Laron's manner annoyed him as much as Beltan's absence . What gnawed at those two men most was the fear of losing power. The devastating effects of war were the least of their concerns. He would have preferred to rebuke Laron sharply, but he needed him. He could not afford to lose a retainer. Beltan's disloyalty had caused him enough headaches.

"We've done nothing but discuss this for months. The war has already been lost," Crayna declared leaning forward, causing a few strands of silver hair to fall on her face. "I see it as Alron does. We have lost almost every important military base. The time to act has come."

Alron let out a sigh despite himself.

"Laron, rejoice in the fact that you will survive the night. Many others will not be granted this happiness."

Laron gave a contemptuous growl. "We don't know what will happen. We might destroy more than we save. And what about Beltan? We can't do anything about him. We don't even know if we can stop him. Even if we manage to lock him down in the device, we can never be sure how long it will take him to escape. Our decision is based on mere conjecture."

"What's the alternative? Letting Beltan win? He will lose con- trol of that energy! Do we really want to bear the risk of enslaving humanity?" Kalden laughed coldly.

Laron's eyes darkened. "You think I don't know that? All I want is more time. Have we really thought through all the options?"

Alron waved Kalden over. Hesitantly Kalden handed him the book.

"There is nothing left to discuss. This war must end. And the only way to do that is to wipe out the technology that we have relied on for far too long. We were aware of the risk from the beginning," he said his fingers reverently stroking the jade-green dragon mark on the cover of the book.

The Book of the Heavens, a work filled with all the knowledge in the world, and as such full of hidden clues and warnings. If they survived that night, their world would be a very different one, one without the technology on which their very civilization was based. Only this book would still exist—and the gifted children, as well as the children of the current rulers. They were all safe in one of the devices, deep underground. Alron flipped the book open and placed his thumb on the jade dragon engraving. He felt a sharp sting before a droplet of crimson blood was absorbed. The stone lit up briefly, a sign of successful transmission.

This process was a ritual that the rulers performed at every meeting. At the very first ritual the key for decoding the magical covers of the book had been stored in the memory of the rulers. This knowledge was then passed on to their children immediately after birth. Only the descendants of the rulers in that room would be able to access it. For anyone else, it would just be a book with empty pages.

He passed the book to Laron and waited patiently, picking at the wood grain of the table. He shifted in his chair as guilt overcame him. He doubted he would leave the room alive. The candlelight flickered, echoing his sentiment.

He'd consulted with Kalden and the scientists, but nothing had changed. They had no choice. If only they had never found that cursed rock! A new age had been ushered in, but at what cost? He still remembered exactly that day ten years ago, when the ethics council was dismissed. There had been riots at the university and massive demonstrations everywhere, but the development could no longer be held back. Laron returned the book, his face fiery red. Alron suspected his condition was a mixture of fear and anger.

"We cannot erase all progress," Laron hissed.

"That is clear. However, it doesn't change the decision," he replied, taking the book and handing it to his faithful friend. "Take it to the secret place! Hurry!"

No one except Alron and Kalden knew the secret place, though it was nearby. In moments, a viscous, black liquid gushed forth and spread over the table's surface. A section lit up in front of each ruler. Alron held his hand in the indentation provided for him.

"Let's finish it. Enter your codes," he ordered, and everyone followed.

When he heard the last sound in the sequence for the successful entries, Alron closed his eyes. The hall shook violently, but he no longer felt anything. When he heard the last sound in the sequence for the successful entries, Alron closed his eyes. The hall shook violently, but he no longer felt anything.

Five hundred years later

"It is not to defeat the enemies of my people that I seek strength, but to defeat my greatest enemy, myself."

—King Tharyos in the Temple of the World God

Chapter 1

She gasped, inhaling intermittently despite her burning lungs. Her muscles ached, but she kept running. As if through a veil, Liya saw shabby wooden huts, holes gaping through the roofs of many. An acrid, sulfur smell entered her nose, nauseating her. The same had happened a few minutes ago when she and Ewan were still in front of the enormous Qilonian wall. A shudder skittered down her spine; she felt that they were being watched. She'd felt this way since she arrived in Qilon.

Ewan stopped abruptly, and Liya bumped against his back. She heard him swear softly and followed his gaze. Six men came towards them. They split into groups of two to cut off Liya and Ewan's escape route.

"I'm afraid they're after whatever you picked up earlier," Liya hissed.

Ewan had not forewarned her, so she was unarmed except for her black-bladed dagger. Thankfully, she always kept it on her. She had found it in the cave by Lake Smutny. It was ancient and unique.

Her friend looked at her and whispered, "No one knew. Honestly!"

"Doesn't look like it, though."

"These are not the men from the cabin."

Before Liya could reply, one of the men came closer. "Give it to us, and we'll let you live," he said.

Liya drew her dagger, and Ewan followed suit, both of them getting into position to defend themselves.

"We are putting our lives on the line for a scroll. I hope it's worth it," she said softly.

"It is!" Ewan replied, just as quietly. "As soon as we break through , we run."

She focused on the two men who had stopped less than five steps away. Ewan eyed them contemptuously, just as they rushed for- ward. Liya slashed at the first man with the dagger, but he parried her swing skillfully and moved to attack. The moment he raised his sword, she spun and plunged the dagger into the man's left side. She rammed her knee into his stomach, then whirled around adeptly dodging the attacker behind her. Out of the corner of her eye, she could see Ewan strike down another of their adversaries with his knife, then grab the fallen man's sword to attack another. Obviously, the strangers had not expected them to fight back. How unfortunate for them!

"Run!" shouted Ewan.

He pulled a bottle the size of his palm from inside his coat, then threw it to the ground. The glass shattered, and a mist rose, obscuring Liya's sight. She felt Ewan pull at her arm, and they rushed out of the mist, back to the slums, the curses of their attackers echoing in her ears. Ewan held her hand tightly, running once to the right, then to the left. She quickly lost her bearings in this unfamiliar section of Qilon.

This was not the first time she'd helped Ewan, mainly because she usually had access to shady people, who sometimes worked for the nobles. But this time, the mission must be bigger than she expected. She'd clearly underestimated the situation.

With a little luck, we can reach the craftsmen's quarter unharmed, she prayed silently. She knew the men were still following them. Their voices rang out as they stumbled down the narrow street full of garbage.

"We're almost there," Ewan assured her quietly.

Dusk broke on the horizon. Lanterns shimmered in the alleys of the craft stores. They left the narrow dirt road and entered the wide stone street, slowing their pace to blend in with the early morning crowds. Nevertheless, they strode briskly toward the marketplace, hopeful that they would be able to disappear in the crowd.

Ewan turned around. "I don't see them," he said, keenly scanning the area.

"Do you think they've given up?"

"Maybe?"

They reached their destination shortly before the market closed. The sentries stationed every dozen feet kept them on constant guard. The marketplace was a hub of activity . Enthusiastic merchants, unconcerned with their surroundings, offered their goods loudly, as if it was the last ever opportunity for them to sell, while customers tried to push down the prices. The pungent, spiced smells of marjoram and caraway made Liya uncomfortable. She broke away from Ewan, gasping for air. He followed, also breathing heavily.

"That was close," she said between gasps.

"I'm sorry. That shouldn't have happened," Ewan said, regarding her with concern.

"What are you going to do now?" she asked, straightening up. "Surely they won't give up so easily."

"The danger isn't over. Let's move on." The pair made their way through the crowd as Ewan reflected on what went wrong. "Nobody knew about this meeting. I don't understand."

"Maybe the seller intended to take the goods back?" she suggested.

Ewan shook his head. "Bast is a smuggler. He wouldn't jeopardize his business and reputation like that."

Liya looked at him questioningly.

"Our people are a good source of income for Bast. That's all you need to know," he explained evasively as he ran his fingers through his black hair. "I'm really sorry, Liya. I didn't mean to put you in danger."

Ewan didn't usually take risks, and something like this wasn't his style either. Once they had crossed the market, Liya grabbed him by the arm and pulled him aside. She was immediately taken aback when she realized how battered he looked.

"Ewan, something is very wrong here."

"What do you mean?"

"For several days now, this feeling has hit me again and again. It's even stronger since we arrived here, and I'm not sure what's going on. It's a tugging in my stomach like a storm front approaching." She sighed deeply. "I can't explain it any better than that."

He looked at her with a furrowed brow, worry shining in his deep black eyes. He'd trusted her since childhood, but probably was surprised seeing her like this.

Gently, he led her along the narrow aisles between the stalls until they left the market behind. They walked in silence the rest of the way to the boarding house. Before he opened the front door, she held him back by the arm.

"Whatever you bought back there, you need to get rid of it," she said sternly.

"I know."

The house was not well attended at that time of the day. The air in the nearly empty parlor was filled with the sharp scent of meat stew. Liya's stomach growled. A few figures sat at the bar, chatting with the landlord. Ewan waved at the man behind the bar as they passed, then they walked up the stairs.

On the second floor, they said goodbye. Liya opened the door to her room, inhaling the scent of lavender. The bath she had ordered before leaving for the city was waiting. The water called to her, as she felt all the dirt and grime from her travels. Wall lanterns glowed radiantly, and gray curtains covered the windows. The wide four-poster bed looked tempting too, but she quickly slipped out of her dusty robe and got into the tub.

Relieved, she enjoyed the bath despite its lukewarm water. Her tension eased, and her muscles relaxed, but her thoughts continued to circle. If only she had been able to talk to Ewan undisturbed. What had happened?

He'd hired the smugglers to get a document, probably off the blackmarket. Presumably, there were several interested parties since after the drop, they had been followed and attacked. Ewan was convinced that Bast had nothing to do with the assault, which begged the question: Who else knew about this job?

Reluctantly, she got out of the tub. After drying herself, she slipped into a dress, brushed her hair, and gazed at herself in the standing mirror. The deep burgundy of her evening gown complemented her fair complexion and blonde hair. The silky fabric softly flowed around her slender figure. One of her shoulders was covered and embroidered with pearls, while the other remained free, showing her shapely but not too muscular arms. She wrapped a belt of the same fabric around her waist. Finally, she put on a red mask. As she glanced into the mirror for the final time, she noticed that her eyes glowed blue green. Then there was her necklace with the black crystal. It didn't really match, but Liya couldn't bear to part with it, so she kept it around her neck. She left the room and descended the stairs. Ewan waited her for her downstairs. He wore a white mask with golden ornaments. The golden collar of his black dress uniform shimmered dully in the weak light.

"You look adorable," he said with a smile.

"Very funny." She elbowed him in the ribs.

"I mean it. Rarely do I see you in beautiful clothes. And this looks great on you."

"Thank you, but I still don't feel like going to a ball. You'll have your friends to talk with, but I'll have to listen to the latest gossip from the women of Qilon. They tolerate me because of my position, but I am not one of them."

The only reason Liya had agreed to become the king's emissary was to gain access to the information available to the nobility. Events like these offered opportunities to obtain that information, but they required her participation in balls and other frivolous events.

"At least you will be spared the discussion with Jadmar tomorrow. It's about our troops. I expect he will want to renegotiate the levies again, without reducing the number of men," Ewan said.

"There haven't been any incidents on the Dar'Angaar border for a while. Maybe you can convince him to leave fewer soldiers deployed."

"In any case, tomorrow will definitely be more pleasant for you. The trade contracts should be extended without any problems."

Liya nodded in agreement. At eighteen, she was the youngest emissary of the King of Namoor. Recently, the king had promoted her to first envoy. Most of the time, she reported to general Adesson who gave her the orders. Other times Ewan was her contact. Rarely, she spoke with the king himself. The fact that she did not come from any of the noble houses didn't mean much to King Louis; her father had been a captain, and her position as emissary gave her access to the nobility for gathering relevant information.

As Liya entered the waiting carriage, she felt Ewan's breath close to her ear.

"Rhos is taking care of our business in the meantime. He's on his way home," he whispered.

Ewan and Rhos—what unequal brothers! Ewan was a tall man with a prominent face and eyes as black as night. Despite his young age, he was a captain in the Royal Army of Namoor. He was not only Liya's best friend, but also the brother she very much would have liked to have had. Rhos, on the other hand, was short, stocky, and blond. He was an officer but had no interest in further responsibility. Instead, he preferred to spend his time with his wife.

Rhos would surely take good care of the parchment and take it safely to Namoor.

Chapter 2

Qilon, Eryon's capital, was the largest arable area in the country with lush greenery, fields, and meadows. It stood in the middle of a vast oasis in the desert.

Although political decisions related to Eryon still rested with the Grand Duke and his council, they followed Namoor's recommendations. The former enemies were close allies, and, as a result, peace had reigned between Namoor and Eryon for a hundred years.

Liya enjoyed the light breeze during the short carriage ride. It was much warmer here than at home, although spring had arrived only a few days ago. The breath-taking beauty of Qilon had never ceased to amaze her. The main street, paved with large white stones, stretched out before them, leading directly to the palace. At just under twenty meters, it was as wide as the main gate. In the front garden of the castle, a number of ball-goers milled about.

Liya and Ewan got out of the carriage and strolled through the side entrance, which was reserved for high-ranking military members. She looked at the fascinating, elongated banquet hall. She liked the festively laid out tables, covered with crisp white tablecloths and adorned with assortments of roses. Dazzling light from a gigantic chandelier, lit by hundreds of candles, flickered on the polished cutlery.

They were welcomed at the entrance and led to their seats. The first thing that caught Liya's eye was a magnificent table set on a pedestal in the center of the room. The Grand Duke Jadmar posed pompously on the table and let his gaze wander around the room. The older Jadmar got, the more he flaunted his position. Two years ago, he had changed the seating arrangements for the grand balls. Since then, the women kept to themselves at dinner.

Not unlike what was expected, Liya approached a table with some duchesses from Eryon. Among them was Lady Amalia, whom she found to be quite nice. She belonged to the House of Sayen, and her family owned scores of land in the east. The duchess only stayed in Qilon from time to time.

"My dear Liya, how happy I am to see you again. How was your trip?" Amalia asked, beaming at Liya with big, brown eyes.

Her dark blue silk dress emphasized her slim figure, and bright pearls shone in her hair. Her high cheekbones stood out clearly. Liya thought she looked a little thinner than the year before.

"Good on the whole. How are you?" Liya replied.

"My school for gifted girls needs a lot of attention. To my regret, therefore, I had to skip some significant commitments," Amalia said with a smile.

She grinned. Unlike other women, Amalia was very particular about the social engagements she attended.

Liya took a seat and greeted the other ladies at the table with a smile. As usual, they did not react. Her presence did not matter to these ladies. In the past, she had been offended by this behavior, but now she was indifferent to it. Being invisible in this way had its advantages.

Despite the mask, she recognized Lady Marie immediately. The duchess wore a shimmering, dark green dress, which emphasized her breasts extraordinarily. An emerald necklace adorned her neck, and her lips glowed orange. Her red hair was pinned up, and her green mask matched her dress perfectly. Lady Marie was considered one of the most influential duchesses in this country. As a member of one of the oldest noble families of Qilon, she'd had access to political circles since early childhood. Not only did she know all the nobles and their relations to each other, but she could also influence the social standing of each one.

Liya suspected that Marie had learned quite a few secrets over the years and used this knowledge purposefully. She was sure that the lady got information not only through the wives of the nobles. She must have another network at her disposal. As Marie adjusted her mask, Liya caught a glimpse of a few eye wrinkles, revealing Marie's true age. In the presence of the duchess, this topic was taboo. She was in her early forties, but denied it, and liked to compare herself to Amalia, who had recently celebrated her thirtieth birthday.

Although Liya deeply detested these ladies' conversations, Marie's knowledge was invaluable to her. Through the intercession of the duchesses, she had met a count last year who now occasionally supplied her with information from Qilon, mostly about disputes among the nobles. A few days ago, this same count had sent Liya a message, suggesting that she attend the ball.

The banquet hall was already bustling with activity when the Grand Duke began his speech. She suppressed a yawn. Jadmar praised his lords, flattered them, dropped compliments about their wives, and mentioned his allies. He received polite applause for his speech. After that, dinner was served.

"Have you heard the latest rumors yet?" asked Lady Kare, Liya's seatmate, while sipping some wine.

Her pitch-black hair framed her oval face. She pursed her mouth, visibly enjoying being the center of attention. Her husband, Lord Rawnye, sat on the Council of Lords and was considered one of Jadmar's closest advisors.

Marie raised an eyebrow as she shoved a small piece of salad into her mouth.

"Supposedly, the Grand Duke's eldest daughter is being married off," Kare revealed, taking another sip. "It's all top secret because it involves a significant personage. The groom is said to be very wealthy and in possession of considerable lands. Supposedly, he is not from Qilon. Unfortunately, I have not been able to find out more." She sighed theatrically.

"There are not many lords in our country willing to marry that would take Lady Beth as their wife," Marie hissed.

"Marie, how can you be so mean?" Lady Sara giggled.

Sara, Marie's protégé, looked like a younger version of Marie. *Surely Marie has already chosen a suitable marriage candidate for you,* Liya wondered.

"We all know the truth. It's always about politics and power, isn't it? The question to ask is, what are the agreements attached to this marriage arrangement?" Marie remarked.

Liya was listening intently, even though—as she knew—her expression looked calm and disinterested. During her training at the military academy, she had learned to keep her emotions to herself.

"What did you hear?" inquired Kare excitedly.

"This is an enormously powerful person. Our dear Grand Duke was all too quick to agree to the deal. Why do you think? It's not just about the marriage of his daughter. You can take my word for that."

Sara shrugged. "Is that any more surprising? He's been trying to marry Lady Beth off for years. I probably would have agreed to anything, too, if I were in his place."

Liya suppressed a sigh. In everything, Sara emulated her role model, but she was only half as smart as Marie and had not understood the meaning of her words. For Liya, however, it was clear that something bigger was going on here. Marie's husband, Lord Ginald, sat on the council. Marie knew the background, and Liya wanted to hear more.

Kare chuckled. "I think Sara has a point there. Have you seen Lady Beth recently? That short hair!" She rolled her eyes exaggeratedly.

The ladies began a heated conversation about social duties and noble behavior. Apparently, Lady Beth, regardless of her indisputable appearance, did not take her responsibilities very seriously in the eyes of the duchesses. Bored, Liya poked at the salad with her fork while letting her gaze wander around the banquet hall. When the main course was served, the ladies devoted themselves to the meal and changed the subject.

"The wine is excellent, isn't it, my dear?" Amalia turned to Liya.

"Just the thing tonight," she commented.

"I see it the same way. How long are you going to be in town?" Amalia said, smiling mildly.

"Tomorrow, I will attend the council meeting, and the day after tomorrow, we'll hit the road again. Every night in a comfortable bed must be savored," Liya replied.

"I would love it if you could visit me—if you can find the time," Amalia murmured.

This surprised Liya. Until now, she had never received an invitation from a duchess of Eryon.

"With pleasure," she replied.

Contented, Amalia turned her attention back to the table conversation. Liya knew she could not appreciate Amalia's gesture as a merely courteous invitation. Amalia seemed nicer than the other duchesses, but she still pursued her political and social goals. The ladies of the nobility were trained since early childhood to conceal their true feelings and views so as never to find themselves in a political quandary.

While Liya was still thinking about it, the first gentleman asked her to dance. A welcome distraction! Dancing gave her the opportunity to disappear briefly. She politely declined, then slipped away to the terrace. She already felt the influence of the wine, and a pleasant warmth spread through her body. Her eyes fell on the White Tree in the garden of the palace. A few lights glimmered from the direction of the city. The stars shone, and a pleasantly cool breeze blew across her face. She closed her eyes, breathing in the beautiful moment.

"Are you enjoying the fresh air?" A somewhat familiar voice shook her from her reverie.

Startled, she whipped around. A man stood in front of her, wearing a black mask that left only his mouth and chin uncovered. Red outlined the eye holes. *As if blood trickled from his eyes*, Liya thought. To look up at him, she had to stretch her head back. He was almost two heads taller than her and had strikingly broad shoulders.

"Yes, it is very pleasant," she replied hesitantly, fixing his eyes, which shimmered dark blue in the dim light.

His gaze was as clear as the starry sky that night, but even more breathtaking was the sparkle that danced in it. She couldn't turn away from him. In the next moment, fear crept into every fiber of her body and froze her, like a warning. The stranger stood there, watching her.

"May I ask for the next dance?" He smiled.

She shook her head. "Maybe later, I just got out," she said softly.

He grinned, flawless white teeth flashing. Small dimples formed on his chin.

"That's not a problem. We can dance out here," he said as he took her hand.

He pulled her to him and turned with her, first slowly, then faster to match the music. Liya felt a brief, electrifying spark when his warm hands gently enclosed hers. Anxiety spread through her. Her gut warned her of the danger this man posed. She pulled away a bit, but fascination and curiosity kept her dancing. Her heart beat wildly when he pulled her closer, and she felt his warm breath on her skin. Hesitantly, she lifted her head. When he noticed her gaze, he smirked. She tensed but maintained eye contact. For a moment, everything else faded into the background. Even the music seemed to grow quieter. The applause came from far away. She could almost remember feeling like this before.

Smiling, he leaned down to her, murmuring in her ear, "Would you like to go for a walk? I don't think we're missing much here."

She wasn't sure why it happened, but with these words, the magic of the moment vanished. Dazed, she returned to the present.

Thinking of her table with the duchesses, she allowed herself to say, "That is indeed true."

Was he part of the delegation of Lady Beth's future husband? Against her usual caution, she decided to use this moment to learn more about the stranger. The many colorful lanterns emitted sparse light, bathing the garden in a soft glow. Liya ran her fingers over the trimmed bushes that lined the narrow stone path.

"What brings you to Qilon?" the stranger asked.

"I'll attend the council meeting tomorrow. I'm guessing you're not from Qilon either."

"No, I'm just attending the ball."

So, she was right. The spy in her came out to take up the game, despite the stranger's familiarity. Who was he?

They walked toward the White Tree. She thought of the stories about the magic that the tree had, supposedly, once possessed.

"It is said that people have forgotten how to listen. That is why the white giant no longer speaks. His magic has fallen silent." She closed her mouth, surprised she had said these words.

They stopped and looked at the oak tree, the thick trunk shimmering in the moonlight, its long branches stretching far into the sky.

"A slightly different story was told to me by my mother," he replied. "The magic of the tree was said to be so mysterious that the chief magicians decided to silence the tree forever. Too many people tried to use the magic to become more powerful."

"I like my story better."

"That's what I thought," he murmured.

The sound of his voice gave Liya goosebumps. The magic returned. *Where did this feeling come from?* she asked herself. Her heart pounded against her chest.

Slowly, he raised his hands to reach for her mask. As he loosened the fastener and removed it, his fingers touched her cheeks. She held her breath, not wanting him to stop, then immediately shook off the thought. In the sparse light, his eyes shone like gems.

"I've been wondering the last few years what happened to you."

Her body tensed. Her thoughts got caught in a fog as soon as she tried to focus on him. This whole thing was going completely wrong. She was supposed to be taking the lead, not him. *We know each other. But how?*

"Who are you?" she whispered, swallowing hard.

"I know you feel it too," he murmured. His hand brushed back a loose strand of her hair as he drew closer to her. His chest rose and fell as he took a deep breath. "I expected a lot from this evening, but not this. I have to admit, I'm a little surprised," he smirked.

At that moment, she hated the meager light in the garden. Who was he? She would have liked to touch his face, but she didn't dare. Her mind seemed to stop working near him, and that frightened her. As if suspecting what was going on inside her, he bent down to touch his forehead to hers. A tingling sensation ran through her. She inhaled his scent: the forest after rain. Confused and dazed, she shook her head, pressed both hands against his chest, and pushed him a little away from her. He frowned. His gaze threatened to pierce her. She felt as if he could see her true self behind the façade, almost like he had gained access to her soul. Fear crept through her again, and she backed away, frightened.

he felt as if he could see her true self behind the façade, almost like he had gained access to her soul. Fear crept through her again, and she backed away, frightened.

"You have the gift," she breathed.

"Interesting," he replied without taking his eyes off her.

What was he thinking? Angrily, she put her hands on her hips.

"You are responsible for the fog in my head. Did you use magic against me?"

"No. You would have felt that, and you know it."

"I don't know anything." A tiny part of her felt indignant. How she would have loved to blame it all on magic. But, somehow, she was relieved.

"Oh yes!" He took a step back.

"Anyway. I want to go back to the hall. Give me my mask, please," she replied, holding out her hand.

As he handed the mask back to her, he stroked the underside of her wrist with his index finger. She winced. That tingling sensation again! When his mouth twisted into a grin, she knew he'd noticed her reaction.

With a jerk, she tried to snatch her hand away, but he pulled her closer. Before she knew what was happening to her, his hands were around her neck. He lifted her head, and his lips gently brushed over her mouth, to her cheek, until she felt his breath on her ear.

"You can deny it, but your protective wall is crumbling," he whispered.

She felt his smile on her face and got annoyed.

"Says the man with the gift! Which one of us needs the wall?" she groaned, breaking free of him.

Without waiting for an answer, she turned away and fled. She felt his gaze on her back, but he didn't follow.

Laughter and dancing rang from the ballroom. The tables were empty, and most of the ball-goers stood together in small groups.

"Liya!" Ewan sauntered toward her. "Where were you? I've been looking for you."

What had come over her? Those eyes, so penetrating, as if he could look directly into her soul. Her lips and cheeks still burned from his touch. She felt blush rise in her face as she bit her lower lip, took a deep breath, and looked firmly at Ewan.

"What about our dance for tonight?" she asked.

He took her hand. "I hope you had a good time. What were the ladies talking about?" He sounded amused.

Instead of responding, she gave him a gentle nudge with her elbow. He had already drunk too much wine; his face was red. While they danced, they exchanged the gossip of the evening.

"I think you're going to go home without me tonight," he said with a mischievous grin as the music faded.

"Ewan, you're incorrigible." She rolled her eyes.

He shrugged and pointed to a busty brunette who was furtively looking over at them.

"Ah, I see. Who is she?"

He shrugged.

"You don't know?" she asked with amusement.

"Her name is Felicia. That's good enough for me."

"You're impossible sometimes."

After the dance, Ewan pressed a kiss to her cheek. "Good night, my dear, sleep well!" he said good-humoredly before staggering to the girl.

Sighing, Liya watched him leave. For a while, she chatted with other delegates. Shortly before midnight, she said goodbye and left the banquet hall. Once in the carriage, tiredness overcame her. She was looking forward to a good night's sleep, so she suppressed her thoughts of the stranger and the feelings he had triggered in her.

Chapter 3

The next morning, Ewan was already waiting for Liya in front of the guesthouse. He looked tired, and his hair was disheveled. When he greeted Liya, a grin spread across his face.

"Did you sleep at all?" she asked.

"A little," he laughed.

"You look like it." Liya smiled while she arranged his wild hair.

"Was everything all right with you yesterday?" he asked.

Surprised, she looked up. "Yeah, why?"

"You seemed upset," he said.

"Amalia invited me to her place," she answered lightly, changing the subject. There was no way she wanted to talk about the stranger now.

"A ladies' club!" he said, mockingly twisting his mouth.

She rolled her eyes. "I'm taking this seriously. Amalia acted all secretive, and my gut tells me there is more going on here than a social invitation. Jadmar is planning something, and I am sure Amalia knows something. This 'ladies' club' is my chance to find out more."

"Hmm, strange things have been happening lately," he agreed.

"Indeed. It's also strange about this scroll."

"That order came from the highest authority," he whispered. "But more about that later. The walls have ears."

With these words, he took her arm. Although she was burst- ing with curiosity, she stayed quiet. The highest authority could only mean the king.

The first rays of the sun warmed Qilon. Market traders had set up their stalls. Carts loaded with vegetables, fruits, and spic- es ambled past them. The streets of the city gradually filled up with people. The wind blew through Liya's loose, wavy hair with a gentle touch. Involuntarily, the stranger came to mind, but she immediately pushed away those thoughts. Instead, she focused on the hustle and bustle around her.

Soon, they left the simple white houses behind and entered the inner part of the city. Here, the white houses were larger and more ornate. They stood in spacious, lush gardens enclosed by iron fences. As she walked by, she smiled at children playing in front of the Magic School. Their happiness and laughter were contagious. The healing hand above the school's entrance glowed golden-brown. Qilon was famous for its sorcerers of the healing arts; in no other place in Eryon were better ones to be found. In recent years, however, the number of magic students had declined. No one knew the rea- son. The gift of magic was inherited by blood, but it wasn't always guaranteed.

Unlike Namoor, the magicians in Eryon did not live behind thick walls, but in the middle of the city, sharing their library and knowledge. In Namoor, the guild kept to itself; the legacy of the past, to live and share magic openly, had been forbidden.

When they reached the noble district , a brilliant blue sky replaced the violet-orange of the early morning. Gardeners drove carts of fresh flowers, reflecting the brilliant colors of the sky, to the Grand Duke's Palace. Among the passersby, the predominantly black-haired Qilonian women wore their hair down as was the fashion. Feathers, flowers, and wreaths decorated their hair, combined with gold necklaces, ornaments, and amulets around the neck, to show what a noble life they led. Their dark skin was considered the height of beauty. To blend in, Liya also let her hair down, but refused the fancy headdresses. She grinned at the astonished looks thrown her way. Her dress captivated with simple elegance; her pale skin, blond hair, and lack of jewelry caught every eye.

The gentlemen walked in fine pants and jackets, none carrying a sword or bow. Ewan stood out among them because of his height. He towered over most of the men by at least a head. His dark eyes stared into the distance, ignoring the admiring glances of the ladies. As they approached the Duke's palace, Liya saw a low stone wall surrounding it. The main gate stood open.

Ewan leaned down toward Liya. "Please, be more attentive today," he whispered.

That stung her. She felt her pulse quicken and her heart pounded violently against her ribs. What Ewan didn't know, nor anyone but Liya for that matter, was that her intuition was more than just a good gut feeling. She had been born with the gift and could wield magic.

The use of magic in Namoor was allowed only to members of the guild and as such anyone with the gift was required to join. Anyone who hid their gift was considered a rebel and accused of reason. Her position as emissary of the king protected her to some extent, her duties providing her the opportunity to conceal her gift. Nevertheless, she walked a tight rope.

Fortunately, no one would recognize her momentary restlessness. She owed that to her years of practice of looking expressionless, even when her pulse raced! She was always careful not to use too much of her gift. No one could ever know about it, especially not Ewan. She had often thought about letting him in on it, but she'd never dared. With her silence, she protected her friend and herself. She would rather die than belong to the guild.

Sometimes, she wondered how strong her gift actually was. Long ago, her mother had cast a surpressing spell on her magic with the help of a witch . Only few of them lived in Namoor, outside the guild, with no access to the four elements, but being able to use spells as their gift. The spell held back the limits of her gift. According to the witch, it would not be possible to eliminate entirely. The witch had also explained that she'd need to practice suppressing her gift until it became second nature. These days Liya could suppress her power without thinking. Nevertheless, this kind of energy had to be released from time to time. She did so safely as a spy.

Ewan announced Liya's arrival to the guards, and they entered the palace. A soldier led them up a lush staircase to the second floor. As they followed, the runner on the stairs swallowed their footsteps. The the lifeless eyes from the portraits on the gloomy ancestral gallery walls gave Liya goosebumps.

"Please, place your sword on the table there," said the young soldier who was guarding the entrance door to the hall.

The council members sat in a semicircle around Grand Duke Jadmar. Purple curtains on the fulminate floor-to-ceiling windows lent very little warmth to the otherwise cool room, despite the muted sunlight.

Liya noted that the water glasses of the council members were half full. Liya and Ewan had arrived on time, but clearly the meeting had started long ago. She hid her surprise, though the queasy feeling tugged at her more intensely. Her fingers tingled slightly as she gently opened the way to her magic and accessed the emotions around her.

In her mind's eye, the white ash tree appeared, with glowing branches that grew longer, spreading through the room, trying to catch the feelings of the dukes. Strangely, she couldn't. It was as though the emotions were lost in a fog her magic could not penetrate.

Jadmar rose and beckoned to them. He seemed pleased, a grin widening his chin, but his stress did not escape her—even without her magic.

"My dear Captain Ewan, I am glad to see you again," he said. He turned to Liya. "My lady, I hope you had a pleasant evening."

Liya and Ewan greeted the Grand Duke as he seated himself, before they in turn sat in their designated seats nodding to the round of council members. Behind Jadmar hung a life-sized portrait of the Grand Duke, framed in gold. Liya shuddered at the sight of the somber image against a wine-red background .

"Before we begin the session, I have some wonderful news for you." Jadmar stroked his hand over his sternly combed-back, gray-black hair and paused meaningfully. "I am pleased to announce that a wedding is coming to our house. My eldest daughter, Lady Beth, is to be married later this year."

The assembled lords applauded; some regarded the Duke sympathetically. It did not escape Liya that Mattern clenched his teeth while Jadmar spoke. The usually calm husband of Lady Amalia seemed to be displeased. Whatever was behind the marriage, Mattern was certainly not enthusiastic about it.

Someone on the table asked who the chosen one was, she believed it was Lord Mattern.

Jadmar cleared his throat. "The preparations have already begun. The wedding will take place on Lady Beth's birthday, in six months."

Jadmar clearly avoided the question to Liya's surprised. On top of that she wondered why the wedding should take place so soon. Among the nobility, preparations usually took at least a year.

Undeterred, Jadmar continued, "I know it's pretty quick."

Lord Mattern repeated the question about the groom. She watched small beads of sweat form on Jadmar's high forehead. Color rose to his cheeks.

"Through this connection, two countries are united." A tiny smile flitting across his face and he rose. "Our neighbor Dar'Angaar is in transition. The young Prince Amaar has taken over the leadership, and in three weeks, he will be crowned. With this, Dar'Angaar is returning to the old ways. Dar'Angaar is once again ruled by a King, not a Grand Duke. And this future king has asked for my daughter's hand in marriage. Isn't that wonderful?"

Liya felt sick. She couldn't believe what she had just heard. Out of the corner of her eye, she watched Ewan's expression darken.

"Wonderful for our downfall," growled the Lord of Loron.

Jadmar studied him with narrowed eyes. His anger was unmistakable. "Spare us your pessimism, Julius. The older you get, the gloomier you become."

She observed the Lord of Loron, his gaunt face reddening with anger. He clenched his broad hands into fists but said nothing more. This probably wasn't his first confrontation with Jadmar.

"I ask you, Captain Ewan and Lady Liya, to convey our invita- tion to the Royal House of Namoor. I hope our allies will welcome the union and celebrate this joyous occasion with us," Jadmar said.

"Of course, Grand Duke Jadmar," Ewan replied reservedly, bowing his head slightly.

"Excellent!" Jadmar said, clapping his hands. Liya watched as Lord Ginald, known for his loyalty to Jadmar, stand up, quietly walk to his Grand Duke, and whispered something in his ear. Jadmar shook his head vigorously.

"Right! Right! I almost forgot. My dear Ewan, could you prepare your retreat from the border with Dar'Angaar? We don't want to upset the young ruler; we want him to feel welcomed. For years, our people have lived in peace, and the wedding will seal this. Therefore, we no longer need the border guard." He quickly lowered his gaze.

The room silently buzzed. The Grand Duke had just utterly overturned the balance of power. Yet he sounded as if he was extending an invitation to the next ball. Ewan's gaze darkened further. Liya heard his jaw muscles crack from across the table. She could see how much effort he needed to control himself. In the past, Eryon had been dependent on Namoor; the king deployed Namoor's soldiers to protect Eryon's borders. Nevertheless, Eryon was allowed to exist independently, and Namoor made no claim.

"Eryon and its people wish your daughter a glorious matrimony and are pleased that she has found such a match. However, I would like to point out that Dar'Angaar has never been favorable to Eryon. We should take that fact into account and wait before we withdraw. Perhaps young Amaar is not like his father, but we do not know that just yet," Ewan said.

Jadmar waved off his concern. "No, my dear Ewan, I cannot agree to that. I have met the future king and have held numerous conversations with him. He is completely different from his father, believe me. It is time to leave the past behind and look to the future."

Gradually, the implications of what had just happened dawned on Liya. Only a few decades ago, the Grand Duke of Eryon would not have dared to go it alone. At that time, the King of Namoor would have sent his troops immediately to stop any kind of independent activities, which are not aligned with the policy of Namoor.

"Why the rush to withdraw? Can't it wait until after the wedding?" questioned Ewan.

A little impatiently, Jadmar shook his head. "Didn't you, dear captain, suggest at our last meeting that we reduce the number of troops? There have been no incidents on the border for the last fifty years. The protection is no longer necessary."

"If we reduce the troops even by half, then we won't be able to stop an invasion. We can't ignore the possible risks. We know nothing about Dar'Angaar's army. The danger of an invasion still exists. Eryon does not have the resources to defend itself on its own." Ewan sounded calm, but a threatening undertone lurked in his voice.

Of course, he had hit the nail on the head. Eryon would still be dependent on the Namooran army in case of emergency. Liya did not miss the tension in Ewan's voice. Tentatively, she tried sending her magic out. For a brief moment her power managed to sense emotions. Jadmar suppressed his anger; everyone else was afraid. What were they afraid of? She didn't dare use more of her gift to find out.

Ewan has a point," Mattern interjected, his voice brittle. "We shouldn't rush into anything."

Now Ginald leaned down to Jadmar. "If the son is indeed sympathetic to us and has peaceful intentions, he will understand our caution."

Liya eyed Ginald attentively. His thinning white hair made him look much older than his early forties. He would never stand up to Jadmar, yet he spoke with nervous conviction.

The Grand Duke rose. "We have heard your objection, Ewan. Nevertheless, there is no cause for concern. Prepare to withdraw the troops."

Although barely noticeable, the Duke had raised his voice ever so slightly, and he let his scowl roam the room. Liya wondered how it could have come to this, that the Grand Duke of Eryon was rebelling against his protector this way. Ewan let out an annoyed growl.

The rest of the council meeting proceeded as usual. There were no major decisions to be made, and the atmosphere remained cool. After the vote on extending the market hours by an hour, Ginald ended the meeting at a signal from his lord. Jadmar rushed out, followed by two servants.

Liya breathed a sigh of relief as she left the room with her friend. Restrained murmurs surrounded them. With clenched fists, Ewan asked her to be quiet and follow him. As soon as they left the palace, he took her hand and led her into a side alley. He wrapped his arm around her waist as he leaned down to her.

"We're being watched," he whispered.

She understood immediately. It was not the first time they had played a couple. She threw her arms around his neck.

"Where are they?"

"On the opposite side. What do you think?"

"It was very strange; I could not grasp their emotions properly. I am not sure whether it's Jadmar they fear or something else."

"Strange." Ewan sighed against her ear. "Did you notice anything else?"

"Yes, and that's what worries me the most. Jadmar is hiding something, and he had help concealing it during the session. I wouldn't rule out mages."

Surprised, he leaned back and looked at her, then immediate- ly returned to position. "All right, we'll go to the boarding house together. After that, I'll disappear for a moment to instruct our spies." He grinned mischievously. "Now pretend you're infatuated with me."

That was her cue. Suppressing an eye roll, she gave him her sweetest smile and pulled him closer. "I always have to do this," she whispered. "I see our pursuers. The two guards who were outside the meeting hall. They're hiding behind the flower stand."

"A truly resourceful hiding place," he murmured.

"Oh yes!" She smiled. "Do we wait until they give up?" she added, snuggling closer to him.

No. Let them follow us. If we disappear into your room, they'll think their piece. From your window, I can make a run for it across the roof." He cleared his throat noticeably, took her hand, and led her back to the main street.

A few blocks later, he continued, "I don't be lieve it! All these years, we have protected Eryon against invasion from Dar'Angaar. Dar'Angaar shouldn't be allowed to incorporate Eryon into its sphere of influence. That would change everything."

Liya resisted the temptation to look around for Jadmar's spies and thought more about the situation. Jadmar was acting like an autocrat. He was the Grand Duke, but all political matters had to be discussed and voted on in council. Liya didn't know what worried her more: Jadmar's behavior or the inaction of the other lords. Then there was the fact that he had essentially rebelled against the King of Namoor. And this coronation? She didn't know when a king had ruled Dar'Angaar last. It had to have been long before the Great War.

Ewan sighed deeply. "The preparations for this action began long ago, of that, I am sure. Jadmar did not consult with us, nor did he let us know. Certainly there were representatives from Dar'Angaar at the ball last night. Jadmar did not consult with us, nor did he let us know. The preparations for this action began long ago, of that I am sure."

He sank into his thoughts. Liya didn't mind; the stranger from the ball popped into her thoughts. A storm raged inside her, and her heartbeat accelerated. His name was Haydn. She had last seen him three years ago, the magic he used last night, was finally gone. She remembered! He had been looking for her at the ball yesterday; she was sure of it. But why? Perhaps he was more than just a soldier. Maybe he was an emissary, too. .

She'd never asked about his family back then, and he hadn't asked about her. She shook the thoughts from her mind. Haydn belonged to a past she had erased from her life. She instinctively sensed the threat hovering like a dark cloud over Namoor. Before long, they reached the guest house and Ewan left through Liya's window. Liya then sent a message to Lady Amalia. Unfortunately, she would have to cancel their meeting. She packed her things and disappeared through the window as well.

Chapter 4

At last, Liya caught sight of the fields outside the palace city. Dew shone on the meadows, and the cool night air chilled the atmosphere. The early morning sun dipped the sky in violet and yellow, occasional gray clouds interrupting the colors' play.

The palace city, formerly also called the Silver City, was in the east of Namoor. It was majestically enthroned on a hill in front of a forested mountain range. A broad view of fields and forests surrounded the city; beyond the wall in the northeast was the enchanted forest. There were, of course, many legends about the forest dealing with magic and enchantment, but it owed its name primarily to the fact that the magicians spent much of their time there. They searched for herbs and trained their students there.

The road to the city ran through flowering fields. The entrance was much wider than in Qilon, but not as ostentatious. A massive rock gate, with its iron grate, stood wide open so that two wagons could easily pass-through side by side. Stone lions towered on the right and left, and guards in shining armor patrolled the top of the wall.

Liya was exhausted from riding the horses all the way home. Ewan probably felt the same way. ven their horses showed signs of fatigue. They said goodbye to the small troop of soldiers that belonged to Rhos' unit. Ewan had contacted the men in an attempt to appear less conspicuous during their journey. Groups of soldiers from Namoor were nothing unusual on the streets of Eryon. On their way back, they had avoided the villages and camped in the forests. Although they'd only stopped for a few hours of sleep each night, it took them almost two weeks to reach their destination.

"We should convene the council right away to tell them the news," Ewan said quietly. "Could you inform the General? I have something to do first."

"Is this related to our little adventure in Qilon?" she asked.

"I want to have the authenticity of the parchment checked before I show it to the King," he confirmed, sighing.

He turned his horse and directed it to a path that led into the mountains. Liya, on the other hand, passed through the iron gate, happy to be home, even though she bore disturbing news. Within the city walls, time stood still—in a way. Things were as they had been for hundreds of years. There were farms with generous pastures where cows and sheep grazed. Archers completed their exercises in the open air. Children stopped on their way to school and watched the arrows fly with interest. Between the pastures, the wide path continued to the city proper. Beyond the farms, the first houses were built into the hill.

In the inner city, a maze of narrow streets led to inns, boarding houses, and numerous residential buildings. Intermittent were green plots waited to be developed. The center of the city, with its white houses and gray walls, housed the Mages' Guild. It seemed eerie and tense. Guards stood outside the gates, noting each visit. As she rode past, a shiver ran down her spine.

She moved the end of a long, wide street, lined with elegant two-story houses—a marked contrast to the jumble of homes and stores of the other neighborhoods. Nobility lived here. And, at the end of the street, the King.

As she approached the steps to the palace, she sighed and got off the horse. A stable boy hurried toward her, and she handed the reins to him. Her joints ached, her eyes burned, and she felt faint. Nevertheless, she dragged herself up to the observation platform . A gleaming stone floor welcomed her. Only the fountain, which featured two lions standing upright, mouths wide open, cast a shadow on the spacious square. To the right was the cuboid building that housed General Adesson's office. She quickened her steps.

Although few people were out and about, she didn't want to run the risk of being drawn into conversation, not when she had such strange and dire news to deliver. When she reached the ground-level building, the guards opened the double doors. She crossed the foy er to the end of the hallway and knocked on a plain door.

"Come in!" a voice rang out.

"Good morning, Mali. Is William in?" she asked as she entered. "Good morning, Liya. You're back already? Go on in," Mali chirped.

She knocked on the door of the duty room and stepped in.

William Adesson, an old, graying man, sat in a padded leather chair at his desk, studying documents. Even though the window was wideopen, the smell of his pipe lingered in the air. He looked up, stroked his red beard, and took off his round glasses.

"Liya, my dear, I didn't expect you back so soon. You look rather worn out." He stood up heavily and hugged her warmly.

His dark blue uniform, with its many silver buttons, looked crisp and new. He wasn't wearing the wide sword belt that usually adorned his round belly. He motioned for Liya to sit down.

"You look pretty serious. Should I be worried?" Thick brows shadowed his haunting brown eyes as he looked at Liya curiously.

"William, we must convene the Council of the Wise. I have news that cannot wait." Liya took a deep breath before she briefly described the events in Qilon. After, William stared at her, stunned.

Deep wrinkles dug into his face as he tapped his fingers on the arm of his chair. She could imagine how he felt. In six months, he was supposed to retire after nearly half a century of service. And now this!

"This is, indeed, not good news," he grumbled.

"I will ask Mali to notify everyone. We will meet in the King's Hall in half an hour." He took his pipe out of a drawer and leaned back. "We live in bad times," he added quietly.

"I'm afraid you are right," she agreed, just as quietly.

Quickly, Liya said goodbye, told Mali about the council meeting, and headed for the palace.

In the shadow of the massive mountain, the rocks to the side of the gray staircase seemed larger than usual. Back on the viewing platform, she allowed herself a glimpse of the palace's forecourt where stone effigies of the first king and his grand lords formed a circle. The gray statues were at least ten meters high. They'd probably been white, once upon a time. Their hands clasped the hilts of their swords as they gazed into the distance. As she walked past the inner circle of sculptures, she felt the past hovering over her like a gentle cloud.

She walked briskly across the square. A double row of white stone columns supported the canopy of the palace, where several birds sat, chirping and welcoming the spring. When the guards saw Liya approach, they paused their conversation and resumed their position by the front door. That made her smile.

"The general has called a council meeting," she said formally.

"I will notify the king's first counselor," one of the guards replied.

She followed him into the entrance hall, where she stopped for a moment to collect herself before heading for the hearing room. The wind whistled in her ears as she entered. Dark blue flags waved on a banner, giving life to the white lions on them. The hall was as cool as the slabs of the marble benches in the center of the room. They were arranged in a semicircle in three rows, creating the effect of a small amphitheater. The king's chair, with its soft, red cover, looked much more inviting.

Liya closed the glass windows that lined the far wall and rubbed her arms. The lions came to rest majestically. She looked out the win- dow and lost herself in the sight of the depths. She would have preferred to talk with the king alone, but news from Qilon had to be conveyed to the Council of the Wise if it concerned the safety of Namoor.

The current council consisted of three lieutenant generals, the general, and the three lords of the palace city. She doubted that any decisions would be made today. Sighing, she took a seat in the second row, planted her feet firmly on the floor, and held her knees with her arms, resting her head on her forearms and then closed her eyes.

"Liya, you're already here."

"Hm," she replied without looking up. She hadn't even heard Ewan enter the room.

"Have you reported to William about our trip?" he asked, sitting down beside her.

She raised her head and leaned back. "Yeah. You can probably imagine his reaction."

Movement at the entrance to the hall caught Liya's attention. With scowls on their faces, the commanders of the three legions strode toward the benches, while the lords stopped at the door, engaged in an animated discussion. Liya had expected them, but not the six mages who now entered the room. She nudged Ewan and gestured toward the door. *Their noble robes are only surpassed by their arrogance*, she thought.

"I asked that the magicians be brought in. There is much more at stake than Jadmar would have us believe," he whispered.

"As if the unworldly mages would help us," she snorted contemptuously.

"You don't trust them, and I have my reservations too. Still, we'll need their support if we're right about the level of this threat."

Bitterness spread through her, but what could she possibly say? That magic had destroyed her family? Her mother had insisted on teaching Liya magic. *Our gift sometimes demands much of us. It is our duty to accept that responsibility. It is your inheritance, Liya. Embrace it.* Her words still echoed in her ears. Then, her mother left. For a long time, Liya had passionately believed that she would return, but she never did. Liya hated magic, stopped practicing it, and used her gift less and less. Her mother could no longer force her to do so.

Her dull thoughts were interrupted when the mages placed themselves across the room. All but one wore the black robes of the members of the Mage Council. The lone mage dressed in claret adjusted his hood, she noticed his thick eyebrows. The other faces remained shrouded.

William joined them shortly after, a worried expression on his face. Before they could speak to each other, a murmur went through the room, and all heads turned to the center of the room.

Standing next to the ruler's chair, the first counselor announced, "Honored guests, a meeting has been called today for a special occasion. Rise for King Louis."

Everyone stood up and looked in the direction of the open door behind the throne. With quick steps, King Louis came in, followed by, a tall slender youth with blotchy skin, his eldest son Philipp.

Liya marveled at the king's graying temples. The last time she'd met him, she hadn't noticed any gray at all. He was only forty years old, yet he looked tired beyond those years. His combed-back, brown hair was longer than usual. His gray eyes studied the people present, his hands resting on the arms of his chair.

The blond prince resembled his mother. He scowled and pressed his mouth into a thin line.

The king cleared his throat. "Seeing as an extraordinary session has been called, I assume the matter is of great importance. I suggest we spare ourselves the opening ceremony and get straight to the point."

Zain Clove, the lieutenant-general of the Third Legion, rolled his eyes, unwrapped his knife, and began scraping the dirt out from under his nails.

Ewan stood up and gave a short bow. "My king!"

With a curt gesture, Louis urged him to continue. "As you know, Your Majesty, Emissary Liya and I have traveled to Qilon to attend the council meeting." His gaze darkened, his features hardened, and he clenched his fists. "Lord Jadmar' daughter, Lady Beth is to be wed. The wedding will take place in six months."

Louis frowned. Some of those present looked astonished, others disinterested.

Ewan took a deep breath. "The groom of Lady Beth...," he said, looking the king firmly in the eye, "...is none other than the son of the Duke of Dar'Angaar, soon to be crowned king."

Silence filled the room, then gave way to disbelieving murmurs.

Zain's knife clattered on the stone floor.

"That's impossible!" someone shouted.

"What does our vassal think he's doing?" another man exclaimed, as a general commotion arose in the hall.

Louis stood up and thundered, "Silence!" Turning to Ewan, he added, "Keep talking!"

"Lord Jadmar asked me to bring you an invitation."

The king fixed his eyes on him. "There is something else. Speak up, Ewan!"

"Jadmar demands the withdrawal of our soldiers from the border with Dar'Angaar. I expect sooner or later, he will demand the withdrawal of all our troops from Eryon."

"Traitor," someone yelled, and others loudly agreed.

"This is against the treaties!" shouted another.

"Silence!" The king's voice was ice-cold.

Zain stood up and raised his hand. "Our legions should take position on the border with Eryon."

William shook his head. "Jadmar would interpret that as a declaration of war."

"Even so. We should have taken Eryon a long time ago. It's long overdue," Zain replied.

"This wouldn't have happened under King Richard. He had a better grip on Eryon. That's what you get when your former vassal takes more and more liberties, and you let him," someone murmured.

William pressed his lips together.

Louis rose, paced to the front row, then turned to Zain. "We will not take a bellicose attitude toward Eryon."

Liya was sure that he had heard the criticism of his rule and the comparison with his father.

"Is it not a warlike act on Jadmar's part to ally himself with our enemy?" retorted Zain. "Amaar is having himself crowned king! The ruling family refused further coronations after the war. When was the last time there was a king in Dar'Angaar?" Zain's face turned red and he looked around for someone to answer. His question was met with awkward silence.

" When we were at war," Zain said, answering his own question. "We should think about that."

King Louis raised his hand. "We know too little to draw any conclusions. I don't make decisions based on vague assumptions."

His gaze slid over the restless lords and stoic mages before returning back to Zain and William. "We know nothing about Dar'Angaar's troop strength. I will not risk the lives of our soldiers merely for vanity. Before we risk a war, we need reliable information, not conjecture. "

Zain barely contained himself. "What about Dar'Angaar's magic? That poses a real threat."

The king looked at his captain. "Any intelligence in this regard?"

Ewan shook his head. "No, we can only speculate. Our people are following up on other leads."

Louis paused briefly. "We need to prepare for an emergency." He turned to his general and three lieutenant generals. "Get me an overview. I want to know exactly where troops are stationed and how many of them are near the border. I expect a report and an analysis of the situation, including suggestions on how we should proceed."

TThe men appeared content. The king had given them something to do. Liya thought that was a good move. That way, the military wouldn't get any strange ideas, especially the third legion known for its rash actions. Unlike the first and second legions, it consisted of a ragtag bunch of mercenaries and thieves. Criminals served their punishment in the third.

"What happens to the trade contracts?" someone inquired.

"Until further notice, we leave everything unchanged."

Whispers sounded; the king raised his hand. "I don't like this development any more than you do. But no one is helped if we act hastily. Sometimes, it is wise to keep quiet, and observe."

Zain frowned. "Sire, is it that you wish to lull Jadmar into safety?"

"Let him believe that we approve of the marriage, for now. Get me the necessary information in the meantime."

"By your command, Your Majesty," said Zain seemingly satisfied with the king's response.

"Ewan!" Louis took a deep breath. "We will withdraw our troops from the border between Eryon and Dar'Angaar. Establish a military base at Averin."

Averin was located toward the southeast of the border with Eryon. Surrounded by forests and mountains, the city offered a good hiding place. Relerin and Kapilar would have been strategically better, but they were too close to the border to avoid notice.

"Will we inform the lords of the other cities?" asked Lord Nekoda.

"I will call a meeting. Rumors spread quickly. We should get ahead of that."

"What about the wedding?" asked Lord Baldin.

"Gerard will convey our congratulations to Jadmar and confirm our attendence. My recommendation to you is to accept the invitation as well, but I will not impose my decision on you."

The mage in the claret robe rose. "One of our mages should accompany you, your majesty."

Liya listened cautiously. The mages never acted selflessly. She was sure they wanted to investigate Qilon to learn more about the Dar'Angaar mages.

The king approved. "Then everything is settled. We'll meet in three weeks to discuss how to proceed." He turned to the lords of the palace city.

"Gerard will inform you of the meeting with the lords of the other cities in due time."

Louis hurried out, followed by the prince and his guards. At first, silence reigned. Ending a meeting so abruptly was not usually the king's style. Quiet conversations rose around the hall.

Liya stood up. "There's nothing left for us. Let's get some rest before checking with the other lords and ambassadors."

Ewan held her by the arm. "Wait."

Somewhat confused, she retook her seat. The tension worsened, and she felt the fatigue more clearly than before. The king had calmed the council members to some extent, but for how long? Eryon's decision to form an alliance with Dar'Angaar changed everything.

Ewan talked to a few more people. When the last of them had left the hall, her friend took her arm and led her to the back door.

"We're going to the King's Fireside Room," he whispered.

Why is the king asking us to meet him now? They passed through a long, unadorned corridor and an oval room. Ewan knocked on a nondescript door and opened it. The two slipped into the fireplace room where the king stood at the window with his back to them.

"Your Majesty!" She and Ewan bowed their heads.

Louis turned to face them. "Ah, there you are. Did anyone see you?" Ewan shook his head.

Louis circled the small table and motioned for them to join him at the fireplace. "There's a lot going on, isn't there?" he sighed. The dark circles under his eyes stood out, and he looked paler than usual. His posture, however, showed strength and determination.

Liya's eyes roamed the pale yellow room, lingering on the pictres of mountain ranges and the city, then finding the bookshelf standing next to the door. The works appeared to be old, most of them bound in fine leather.

She longed to take a closer look. She looked at the display case with several ornate bottles and glasses until she noticed the king's concentrated gaze out of the corner of her eye. She knew that expression.

You know, don't you, Liya?"

You have the gift, your majesty." Embarrassed, she lowered her head, feeling herself blush.

Louis looked thoughtful. "The mages keep quiet about it. No one else can know about it. In this room, we are protected. A dampening field prevents unwanted listeners. The walls have ears, even in my palace." He turned to Ewan. "What did you find out?"

Ewan's face showed no emotion, but Liya knew that what Louis had just revealed bothered him. Magic was frowned upon in Namoor. His royal lineage would protect Louis from reprisals if it came out, but it would be a catastrophe for the kingdom's stability. "You were right. The Red Brotherhood has planted spies in Namoor. We'll take care of it." He pulled the scroll from his cloak. "This map is written in the ancient language. I can't decipher it. The planets are marked, all lined up." In one fluid motion, he unrolled the parchment on the wooden table in front of them.

It took Liya a moment to realize what it was all about. "Who is backing the Red Brotherhood?" she inquired.

"It's a long and complicated story. Supposedly, they existed in the time of the Elders. But what matters is that now they serve Dar'Angaar," Ewan replied, grinning.

What was that about? Was he just pleased that he knew something that had escaped her?

Normally, Ewan did not deal with history the way she did, and he'd counted on her ever since their time in the military academy.

She knew the legends, of course. Supposedly, the Elders were a group of leaders who, centuries ago, had determined the fate of mankind. It was said that they had access to extraordinary inventions. No one knew exactly what had happened back then. In a single day, entire cities disappeared; vast areas were shattered. TThe various ruins in the northeast were silent witnesses of that by the acient era. Liya's mother had told her how achievements and conveniences, such as the water pipe and the production of special clothing, came from the Elders. Liya herself had a thin chain mail shirt that was more durable than any armor. It was barely noticeable under her leather clothing and clung to her body beautifully. Her father had given it to her. Even more important than the remarkable knowledge of the Elders, however, was the fact that they had used magic.

"Could the magicians say anything about it?" the king asked.

"No. I invited them to the meeting to talk to them about the scroll, but no opportunity presented itself. I am aware, however, that they are looking for the stone tablets from the Ancient Era."

"The past seems to be catching up with us," the king murmured. After a pause, he added, "We can assume that the Red Brotherhood is responsible for another king being crowned in Dar'Angaar. They probably engineered this marriage." He sighed.

Ewan nodded. "My sources assume that all this is happening now because a certain planetary alignment is expected. That's exactly what we need to ask the mages about."

A queasy feeling creeper over Liya. Under no circumstances did she want to work with the mages. The danger of being discovered was too great. Even now, she had to use all her powers of persuasion to make it clear to the king and others that her skills were based solely on intuition and empathy. That included Ewan, even if she trusted him with her life.

Louis continued, "We don't know who we can trust. Not only are the events in Eryon and Dar'Angaar disturbing, but there is also a situation in our country. Ewan, you know best what our scouts and spies have been reporting for two months. Political unrest is rampant. My kingdom is not as solid as it seems. Groups are plotting against me. And, we have not yet been able to find their leaders." He closed his eyes briefly, then looked directly at her. "Liya, I require your services for a special mission. You will travel to Dar'Angaar to gather information."

Her heart stopped for a moment. "You want me to go there?" she asked in disbelief.

Before she could ask any further, Ewan jumped in. "That's too dangerous. No resident of Namoor can enter Dar'Angaar without special permission. To smuggle yourself in is almost impossible. If Liya is caught, she'll be sentenced to death."

She cleared her throat and hoped that her inner turmoil would go unnoticed. "We can assume that the borders will be more closely guarded now that we know about the marriage. "

Louis watched her intently. "You've succeeded before."

"It was summer; I took the path over the mountains. And I got very lucky," she argued.

She did not mention her encounter with Haydn, who had saved her from the icy beasts in the mountains. At the time, they had been surprised by an unusual storm. A shiver ran through her at the thought of Haydn.

"Ask your friends, the Nirm, for help," the king said sternly. Ewan folded his arms. "How will the swamp people help her?" Louis looked at her. "They are far more adept than you give them credit for. Aren't they, Liya?"

Her pulse quickened. Only a few knew the secret of the Nirm. "You know about this, your majesty?" Liya asked.

She was on thin ice, and it was beginning to crack. She had to concentrate. After witnessing the transformation of the Nirm, she had confided in Ewan. He had sworn not to tell anyone, and, as far as she knew, he had kept his word. The Nirm lived in seclusion in the swamp, but their villages served only as a front. Aside from their unnaturally white skin, they looked like any other humans, during the day. At night, they retreated into the mountains to assume their true form. They were much larger and stronger than humans, their skin was much harder and more resistant, and enormous wings grew from their backs. When they stood still, they appeared to be made of stone. They blended in so well with the mountainous surroundings that the few who spotted them were never sure they had.

"What kind of king would I be if I didn't know the people in my kingdom?"

She felt sick. She pressed her lips together, took a deep breath, and leaned forward. "What do you expect from me?"

"If the Nirm help you, you can enter and leave Dar'Angaar secretly. The stone shifters can fly, can't they!?"

Sensing Ewan's tension, she brushed his arm, calming him, before he said something rash. "I can ask them," she replied, turning to the king. "But they don't usually get involved in human affairs."

"In war, the Nirm would also suffer. You will find a way, Liya, as you always have. You are my best spy. Everyone underestimates you, and that's exactly what we're going to take advantage of. This mission is top priority; no one should know about it."

Ewan snorted. "I'll go with Liya."

Louis shook his head. "That's impossible. It's better if Liya goes alone. The Nirm don't trust outsiders. Besides, I'll be holding talks with the mages because we need to involve them regarding the Red Brotherhood and find out what they know. In this, I will need your assistance. Do you have a copy of the map?"

wan shook his head. "Not yet, but it's already been commissioned."

"Once its authenticity is confirmed, we'll meet again," the king said.

He then disappeared just as quickly as he had at the council meeting. Silently, Liya and Ewan left the fireside room and made their way out of the palace. When they descended the steps to the city, it was already past noon.

"I don't believe it. He can't expose you to that kind of danger," Ewan groaned angrily.

"Who else is he going to send? This isn't my first tricky assignment."

"We're talking about Dar'Angaar! I trust you are capable, but if anything goes wrong, no one can help you. No one!" he shouted angrily. "I'll talk to the king again. There must be another way."

"He's not going to change his mind. He seemed determined."

"Well, we'll see," Ewan replied. "Are you hungry?"

As if on cue, her stomach growled.

He grinned. "I'll take that as a yes. Let's get something to eat."

Even though she understood Ewan's concern, she agreed with the king. It was urgent to act. Each one of them was called upon to contribute what they could. Ewan's task was to find out more about the Red Brotherhood and the meaning of this planetary constellation. Her task was to gather information and feel things out. At the thought of a trip to Dar'Angaar, her chest tightened. She was afraid, but there was no alternative. They were entirely in the dark about the conditions in that country, and they needed the information before the wedding. Even if Zain reacted emotionally, he was right. With this marriage, the power shifted, and war was only a matter of time. She had no clue about how she would proceed in Dar'Angaar, assuming she made it there. How would she manage to convince the Nirm to help her? She sighed. Somehow, she had to succeed. The future of her world was at stake.

Chapter 5

Liya knocked briefly on the door before entering the room. Ewan sat at his desk. He did not look up. Two weeks had passed since their return from Eryon. News about the marriage and upcoming coronation in Dar'Angaar and had spread in no time. Unrest and rumors overshadowed the peace and tranquility of the Silver City. With this news already stirring up people's attention, she was deeply relieved that nothing about the withdrawal of the troops had leaked.

"Have you received feedback from the dukes of the other cities?" She smiled at him.

Sighing, Ewan folded up the parchment. He leaned back in the wide, dark green leather chair and folded his arms behind his head. Two swords that had belonged to his grandfather hung on the wall behind him. Liya trotted over to the large window next to the desk and pushed aside the airy yellow curtain.

"This room needs fresh air. I'm surprised you can work like this. What's the matter, anyway? This mess doesn't suit you at all."

"I don't know what you mean," he said indignantly.

She pointed toward the pile of papers on his desk. "That! You cannot even find a place to work," she said. "Maybe you should put those stacks away."

Impatiently, he clicked his tongue. "There are some important documents lying around here."

His suppressed anger surprised her, but she said nothing. Instead, she pointed to the paper he held in his hands. "What's this?"

With a grim face, he threw it back on the table. "Eliseus has written to the king saying he strongly condemns what has happened. However, it is not possible for him to come to the palace city. He says the journey from Ralaren is too arduous." He ran his hand through his hair. "I didn't expect him to carry his bulging body through the mountains, but he neither professes loyalty nor sends troops. Not even through the count will he represent himself."

"Hmm... I've never felt any feelings of dislike toward the king from him," she replied.

The reaction of the short, fat man astonished her. His principality lay high in the north, in the middle of the mountains. He may be lazy, but Eliseus was loyal to the king.

"I don't assume that either. I do think the lord of Ralaren is a coward. He has a small force and wants to have his army around him during these times. In case of emergency, he will not send us soldiers."

On this point, she agreed with him. Although the king ruled over Namoor, the large cities and lands were governed by lords who enjoyed relative independence. The first advisors to the lords were traditionally counts. Political decisions that affected the entire country were made in the High Council. The council also enacted the laws. While the king needed only a simple majority for his projects and draft laws, it was not possible for the lords to obtain decrees without the king's explicit consent.

In the councils, only the votes of the lords were counted as valid. They could send their counts to the meetings, but the counts did not get to vote. Usually, the meetings were held three or four times a year.

"We should go to the banquet hall. The lords of Kapilar, Relerin, and Averin have sent their counts; the other cities are represented by the lords themselves," she said.

"I was expecting Prem not to come," Ewan replied, tapped his fingers on the arm of the chair.

"Prem is taking advantage of the current political situation to weaken Louis. He is one of the king's greatest adversaries and leaves no stone unturned. His large army and proximity to Eryon's border puts him in an extraordinary position. He has always been difficult. Surely the lords of Relerin and Arun, like everyone else, know that the king would send soldiers to protect them."

"Of course they know that. But the king is far away. Kapilar, on the other hand, is close enough to react quickly. Besides, in case of emergency, Louis will need most of his troops himself. Prem probably threatened them too—with something," Ewan replied angrily. "Let's go and face the pack. Let's see how much damage Prem has actually done." He stood up.

An animated discussion was going on in the crowded King's Hall when Ewan and Liya entered. They crossed the room with quick steps. Liya sat down in the front row. Ewan stepped in front of those present and raised his hands. The voices became quieter.

"Welcome. The king will join us in a few minutes. In the meantime, I'll summarize the news from Qilon."

While he reported, she concentrated on gently releasing her magic. In her mind's eye, the white tree appeared, woven with light and magic. From its branches, her power poured into the hall. Unlike in Qilon, she had no trouble sensing the emotions in the room. She received a mixture of worry, fear, anger, and disappointment.

Ewan did his best to reassure those present. "Currently, there is no army advancing on our land. In less than six months, the wedding will take place. The royal family, as well as all the princes, have been invited. Grand Duke Jadmar of Eryon is convinced that the future king of Dar'Angaar does not want war."

"Are we stupid enough to believe that?" someone croaked from the third row.

The small Count Mergar rose. He represented Aquilia, the lord of the city of Relerin. Liya couldn't help but notice the prominent nose dominating his pale face.

"Why don't you speak out what is obvious to everyone? Perhaps the tyrant's son is not as bloodthirsty as his father, but are we not seriously going to assume that he is marrying with an intention to keep the peace?" Mergar shouted with a raised forefinger.

Exasperated, Ewan continued, "Of course, we remain vigilant. Protecting our land is the king's top priority." He looked directly at Mergar. "If Lord Aquilia is so full of concern, perhaps he should appear in person next time."

Although he spoke in a low, almost friendly voice, the threat sounded as sharp as a blade. Mergar snorted angrily and sat down. Liya suppressed a smile.

Count Rintal rose, nervously plucking at his white beard. "Ewan, Lord Prem cannot be present today. Nevertheless, he takes his duty to the council seriously."

Ewan's eyebrows drew together.

Rintal cleared his throat. "Also, he is very concerned about the safety of Namoor. From his point of view, there are doubts as to whether the king can protect us all. He did not foresee the current situation, and the alliance with Eryon is apparently not as solid as the king would have us believe." He paused. "Lord Prem, therefore, chose to instruct his soldiers and take precautions."

"Precautions for what?" If Ewan was surprised or angry, it didn't show. Liya never tried to read Ewan's emotions with her magic, as that would be a breach of trust, even if Ewan wouldn't know.

"In case of emergency," the count replied, continuing to pluck his beard.

"Exactly what emergency is Lord Prem preparing for?"

"Hm... Well, in case there is a war after all," Rintal answered hesitantly.

"Is that supposed to mean Lord Prem has information that we don't?"

"N-no, of course not."

A murmur went through the hall. She registered that those present were following the exchange of words intently. Some seemed amused by the course of events, others a little gleeful. But she noticed that the count's words had not failed to have an effect. Many now seemed unsettled.

"Unless the king issues any instructions, no action is to be taken. If Lord Prem is indeed concerned about his safety, he should grace the meeting with his presence next time. Or it may be that the responsibility of Kapilar is too burdensome for the lord."

This time Ewan's threat was abundantly clear. Even the faintest whisper fell silent.

"N-no, Ewan," Rintal stammered, "of course the lord performs his duties without any problems. There is no doubt about that. Perhaps my remarks have been misleading."

"A misunderstanding?" asked the king, who had reached the entrance of the hall.

Everyone stood up and bowed as King Louis walked in. She stopped using her magic. Now that she knew about his gift, she was even more careful.

Ewan grinned cautiously. "Lord Prem is making preparations for war instead of consulting with us. Apparently, responsibility for his city is a burden for the lord."

Louis stared at Count Rintal, his expression betraying nothing. "Are we at war, then, Count?"

Rintal bowed. "No, your majesty. As I explained to your captain, it was a misunderstanding. My choice of words was flawed. My lord is not in presence because he is very busy."

"What is more important than a council meeting with your king?" asked Louis.

"Well, I can't say for sure, I'm afraid." Rintal began to sweat. "I don't know all the details. My lord only asked me to convey his apologies to you."

Louis sat down on his chair. "Now, Count Rintal, tell Lord Prem that I expect his presence in the future. He is in charge of the city of Kapilar and serves our country. I will not tolerate independent plans. Have I made myself clear?"

Rintal wiped the sweat from his forehead. "Of course, Your Majesty, I beg your pardon. It was really just a misunderstanding, nothing more."

Liya perceived that many in the hall were as surprised as she was. Seldom did the king speak so clearly. In the past, the kings of Namoor had only rarely made use of their right to transfer the leadership of a city and its lands to another princely family. However, it was always possible. Although the right of inheritance was applied, it was not enshrined in law. Prem had pleaded several times to pass a law to this effect, but the king had always rejected his plea.

Louis turned to the other two counts. "What I said about the responsibility for our country and my expectations of the lords also applies to Lord Cenric and Lord Aquilia."

The two men acknowledged his command wordlessly.

"Now that we've cleared that up, I suggest we move on."

Liya looked at the king more closely. He appeared very tired. He had taken over the regency at the age of sixteen, shortly after his brother had died. The early responsibility must have been an enormous burden. King Louis was known to adhere strictly to protocols and to fulfill his duties responsibly.

She averted her eyes and turned to the conversation in the hall. It was her turn to explain the trade agreements with Eryon. Short and sweet, she told him that there would be no changes.

After she had finished, Rintal stood up. His face was still red. "If we assume that the future king of Dar'Angaar is indeed seeking peace, will there be a trade agreement between our countries?"

"Before we talk about agreements, we need to find out his true intentions," she replied.

The king rose. "Liya is absolutely right. I understand your concern, but we must all exercise patience."

Before the voting that followed, the counts left the hall. All the lords voted in favor of 'not making any changes for the time being and waiting.' With that, the king ended the meeting. He signaled to Liya and Ewan, bidding them to wait. After the hall had emptied, Louis told them to follow him. He headed toward a small garden at the back of the palace, which was mostly used by the royal children to play. Louis liked to retreat there to have confidential conversations. It was clear to Liya that he could protect this area well, thanks to his magic.

"What did you perceive?" asked the king.

"Hm… Count Rintal was visibly nervous, but his words were true. I didn't detect a lie. Most of those present were not enthusiastic about Prem's actions, and only occasionally did I sense sympathy for him. Nevertheless, some doubt you. This could become a serious problem."

He expected this kind of report based on her empathy skills and intuition; she left out the emotions she'd felt in the room.

"It's possible I underestimated Prem." Louis sighed and ran his fingers through his hair. He turned to Ewan. "Try to find out what exactly Prem is up to. Without evidence, I can't convict him. I need to have something concrete. My threat will only anger him, nothing more."

"Do you think Prem is in league with the Red Brotherhood?" she asked.

The king shook his head. "No, Prem would not betray Namoor. But I fear we are fighting on two fronts. Dar'Angaar is forming up at our gates, and Prem is putting out feelers for the palace city." He sighed, then looked at her. "When will you set out for the Nirm?"

"In a few days. I still have to receive the other emissaries."

"I understand. Try to get some information. That's all I expect. Don't take unnecessary risks."

She agreed. "Any restrictions?"

"None. You have absolutely free rein." The king gently squeezed her hands. "I trust you will return safely. After all, I promised your father I would watch over his little hawk. And I will. Sometimes, though, you have to let them fly, and the little hawks have to trust in their abilities."

In his eyes, she found only warmth. She realized how much she had missed talking to him lately.

Without waiting for a reply, Louis left the garden. As usual, they waited a moment before following him. In tacit agreement, they walked to the observation deck.

"I know you have a special relationship with the king. He took care of you when your father disappeared. You feel indebted to him, and he knows that, but he shouldn't ask this of you." Ewan exhaled loudly.

"We can do this together. Have faith!" she whispered, suppressing her own worries.

For a while, they were silent, each of them indulging in their own thoughts.

"What are you planning until you leave next week?" he inquired.

"I'll receive the emissaries from our cities and discuss the events in Qilon with them. You know how quickly news spreads and rumors start. I want to calm things down a bit in advance."

"You want to find out how the lords feel about the king and who we can rely on in case of emergency."

"That too!"

"The master spy in action!" He grinned.

She rolled her eyes. "Don't call me that. You know it's not quite true."

"Of course not." He raised his eyebrows mockingly.

"What can I say? I'm a natural!"

"Yes, with a considerable amount of self-confidence."

"And that's from your mouth!" She laughed.

"I guess we're both special." His eyes sparkled. That made her smile.

"Let's go see Rhos," he said after a while. "My brother is traveling to Qilon next week. The two of you can leave together."

"Are you ever going to stop worrying about me?"

"Someone has to take over. The word 'caution' doesn't exist in your vocabulary."

Her heart warmed. "I'm glad to have you. You're my brother."

He pressed a kiss to her temple. "Yes, I am, little hawk. And my sister I will always protect."

Chapter 6

Liya dismounted and carefully led her horse through the mud and reeds. The sun was high in the sky, and sweat ran down her back. It was much warmer in the swamp than in the palace city. She had been on the road for a week, and yesterday she had reached the swamp area. She was looking forward to seeing the Nirm. The people of Namoor found the swamp people strange, and that's why they left them alone. Despite their long friendship, Liya did not know exactly what the Nirm were capable of. She was certain they had considerable magical abilities. They guarded their secrets, and, except for Liya and a few others, no one knew that they turned into stone creatures, living in the mountains.

She heard children's laughter, pushed the reeds aside, and entered a wide clearing. The children skipped toward her.

"Miakoda, Miakoda, did you bring us something?" they shouted excitedly in Eriyok, the language spoken by the Nirm.

Miakoda meant *power of the moon*.

"Laixiishuhah," she replied with a smile.

"What's in there?" a little boy inquired, pointing to the large sack on her saddle.

Not understanding what they meant, she shrugged playfully, leaving the children puzzled. Together they walked to the open area where the Nirm's horses grazed. Occasionally, they traveled to nearby towns to go shopping. Liya unsaddled her horse and let it free. The village, hidden in the tall reeds, consisted of a collection of wooden dwellings. Most of the huts had two or three rooms, save for the communal houses that consisted of a single large room. The wooden windows were all open. A second frame with shutters was covered with fur to provide protection against wind and cold in winter. Long ago, the Nirm had built this village to keep their secret. Sometimes they stayed longer, mostly when people were around or to celebrate festive occasions.

Women in plain, light-colored clothes squatted in half-open pile-dwellings under grass roofs, preparing lunch. A sweet aroma hung over the hearth. Excitedly, the children pranced around Liya.

The leader of the Nirm approached her.

"Iishuhah, Sakima, wisdom on your way," Liya greeted him.

"Iishuhah, Miakoda, wisdom on your way," he replied, hugging her warmly as a wide smile spread across his white face and crooked nose.

Sakima looked the same as always. A wide cotton headband, decorated with various symbols, covered his high forehead. In the center was a circle with the face of a bird that resembled an eagle. His white shirt hung casually over his brown leather pants. His muscles moved underneath the thin fabric. White hair fell to his shoulders, and although many wrinkles ran through his face, his black eyes sparkled with energy. Liya always found it amazing how much the Nirm resembled humans during the day.

"How was your trip?" he inquired.

"Good, how are you and your people? How was the winter?"

While they strolled to the center of the village, Sakima reported that the harsh winter had been particularly hard on them, especially the elderly.

Many were still suffering from high fever, and some had already lost their lives. Sakima's wife, Pohawe, the healer of the Nirm, had not been able to find a cure.

"But what do we call it?" Sakima smiled. "Every day is a good day because you live."

Even though her request was of the utmost urgency, Liya knew that there was no point in addressing Sakima straight on. The Spring Festival, which was sacred to the Nirm, was coming up. Talking about politics during the preparations or even at the festival was considered an act of utmost rudeness. For now, she must be patient. She chatted with Sakima about the harvest and the upcoming festival. Again and again, she stopped to greet someone.

The evening highlight of the festival was planned on the central square. The festivities would last three days. The Nirm enjoyed games and competitions during the day, while the evenings were spent in cheerful company. Wood for the big fire was stacked in the middle of the square. Young women scattered colorful flowers while men skinned freshly killed game. She spotted Isi, Sakima's daughter. Isi looked up, returning her gaze, then ran towards them. Her black hair flew through the air as she hugged Liya wildly.

Isi grabbed her hand and pulled her away from Sakima. "I am so happy to see you! This time the spring festival will be special." Her brown eyes twinkled. "But first, we have to survive the storming gang here." She laughed and pointed to the children, who were eagerly waiting for the distribution of gifts. They spent the entire afternoon distributing gifts and chatting with people. In the evening, Isi took Liya to her house.

"You can stay in my room," she offered.

"Thanks, I hope it's not too much trouble for you."

"Of course not," Isi replied warmly.

The light of the setting sun flooded the largest room, where the dining table stood. The scent of flowers rose to her nose; she spotted a colorful vase of bright yellow marigolds on the table. She instantly felt at ease, thoughts of a possible war receding into the background.

Isi picked up a beige dress from the back of a chair. "This is for you—a traditional dress for tonight."

Even if the stone shifters spent most of the nights in the mountains, they loved festivals and their human form. Liya's heart warmed. "It's so nice, thank you. You always make me feel like part of your family." The dress was an expression of that; normally, the Nirm wouldn't bother.

"You *are* part of our family, Liya. You should never doubt that."

Liya took the dress and looked at the little pink orchids and tiny green leaves snaking along the seam on the sleeves and side.

"Thank you," she replied, smiling.

They went to Isi's room and changed. Isi shared the latest gossip while she put lavender flowers in Liya's hair.

"You can go to the festival like that. You look almost like a Nirm. Only your skin is not quite pale enough," Isi explained with satisfaction.

The sun could not harm the snow-white skin of the Nirm—another mystery about these people that awed her.

As they approached the site of the festival, she heard loud drums. Men danced in a circle as they welcomed spring with traditional songs.

"Looks like we're late," Liya whispered.

Isi grinned. "Believe me, you are never too late. It's gonna be a long night." Isi's friends approached them with drinks. The Nirm brewed drinks from various herbs, some of which contained more alcohol than Liya was used to.

"Did Isi already tell you about the festival?"one of the women asked with a broad grin.

"No?" Now she was really curious about it.

"Taimaaaaaaa," another friend sang softly, spreading air kisses.

Isi rolled her eyes playfully, but her face shone. "If Taima wins, he might ask me to marry him," she whispered.

Liya hugged Isi. "That's wonderful, Isi! I'm so happy for you."

"So, ladies, we're gonna celebrate tonight. As a fiancée, Isi won't have as much time to party with us, and besides, who knows when Liya will join us again!"

They toasted each other and drank the cup.

"Come on, let's dance," Liya said and pulled Isi to the dance floor, where quite a few Nirm were already dancing joyfully. She loved the exuberant atmosphere, enjoyed the happy people around her, and, for a moment, she forgot her worries. And Isi was right—the night had just started.

❦

Liya yawned heartily as she and Isi joined the others. The sun glowed red in the late afternoon sky. The men were about to play tewaraathon. Two teams competed against each other, and the aim was to get a wooden ball into the opponent's goal. The goal was the space between two columns, as tall as a man. A rope was stretched across the top quarter of the columns, which the players had to hit the ball over. Each player had a bat that ended in a braided ladle. To be able to tell the teams apart, the torsos of some of the men were painted gray. Sakima was the referee.

The Nirm loved this game. The whole village was watching. As soon as Sakima raised his hand, it happened! A crack announced the transformation. The ground shook, and slowly, the players' bodies stretched until they were twice the size of full-grown men. A wave ran through each of them from foot to forehead. Startled, she looked at the flawless white marble that gleamed in the sun. Like a finely crafted sculpture, their muscles were clearly visible, but these sculptures moved smoothly and quickly. Wings grew out of their backs, but the players immediately folded them. Liya knew that in the transformation, the wings appeared only when they were really needed or, like now, to present the full figure. After the game, the Nirm changed back into their human form.

"Where is Pohawe?" asked Liya once the game was over, and the music started to play.

"Siyaahn will come later," Isi replied. Siyaahn meant mama. Isi leaned toward her. "I think she is sewing a dress for me. Tomorrow is the third day of the festival, and so far, it looks good that Taima wins."

Liya hugged Isi. "He's one of the best; he'll win."

"You think so?" Isi asked sheepishly.

"I'm sure," she replied, patting her friend's hand. A distant memory jolted her mind. A few years ago, on her way back from Dar'Angaar, she had come across a group of Nirm girls surrounded by wolves. Since the Nirm's ability to transform didn't develop until between the ages of sixteen and eighteen, the girls were at the mercy of the animals. In short order, Liya had killed two wolves and chased the others away. Thereupon, against all odds, Taima's father had succeeded in getting her accepted as the first stranger in the Nirm community. She had lived with them for several months, learning their language, rituals, and traditions.

Her gaze swiveled to Taima. A tall, black-haired man about her age— slim, with narrow shoulders, but well-trained. Numerous scars adorned his torso. Like most young Nirm, he wore no shirt—only thin, brown cloth pants. Although his features appeared hard, his gray eyes reflected mildness. Taima's father had died last spring from a bear wound. Pohawe had not been able to save him, and the Nirm refused medical help from humans, lest they risk revealing their secrets.

Liya looked at Isi. "I'm really glad to be here."

"Me too. I asked my father to invite you, but he refused to send a message." She imitated her father. "Patience is a virtue, my child. If it is to be, Liya will come."

Liya chuckled. "You're really good at that."

Isi nodded. "Yeah. And apparently, he was right, but we'll keep that to ourselves."

"As usual," Liya whispered. Sakima always radiated a pleasant calm, and he chose his words wisely. His people trusted him.

She felt the warmth of the campfire on her face and enjoyed watching her friends sing and dance.

Sakima sat down with her and handed her a cup. "Drink, Miakoda."

"What's this?" she asked, sipping the bitter liquid carefully.

"Drink more!" Sakima demanded. "Every year, young warriors set out into the desert to seek the potion of the gods. From the sap of the peyote, we make an elixir that allows us to become one with Mother Nature. The gods give us visions."

Liya remembered the drink. A few years ago, she'd wanted to try it with Isi, but Sakima wouldn't allow it.

"Looks like you changed your opinion, Sakima." She knew that the Nirm drank peyote juice for the spring festival in order to be close to their ancestors and the gods.

He winked at her. "Now's a good time. Back then, both of you were too young."

"Your drinks are much stronger, so no complaints later."

Sakima toasted her with a grin. "No worries, most of us are seeking visions tonight. You won't be alone."

She felt a little sick to her stomach. "Sakima, I don't know if your gods will give me visions too."

"Our gods bestow visions on those who are ready for them," he replied with a smile.

Liya grabbed Sakima's forearm. She saw Taima walking toward Isi out of the corner of her eye.

"He's going to ask her," she whispered.

"Yes, I gave my permission—even if he doesn't really need it. My daughter decides who she marries, not tradition. But we honor our ancestors with this."

"I thought he needed to win first."

"The games will finish tomorrow, but I think it's more appropriate for them tonight, when they have more privacy, than tomorrow, when all attention will be on them. Tradition is important to us, but our kids are more important."

"I am really glad to share this moment with all of you."

After a while, everything around her began to spin. She would have liked to get up, but the earth beneath her moved, and the stars in the sky danced. Without thinking about it, she began to sing and move to the drums. She felt as light as a feather, connected to the moon and the stars.

When Liya awoke, she looked directly into Pohawe's brown eyes, which regarded her with concern. Her warm, slightly rough hand clasped hers. Confused, she looked around. She was lying in a simple wooden bed. Isi sat on the lower part at her feet. The room was barely lit by sparse sunlight that shone in through the windows. Although a green wool blanket surrounded her, she felt cold, and her head was pounding.

"What happened?" she asked, dazed.

"You were not yourself. You were speaking in another language; your body was shaking. Taima carried you to bed," Isi whispered.

"Sakima gave me this cactus potion. I already thought I wouldn't be able to handle it," she croaked.

Pohawe shook her head. "No, Miakoda, you had a vision!"

She sat up and felt her forehead. "Ow... My head!"

Pohawe handed her a cup. "Drink this tea."

She took a sip and scrunched her face in disgust. "What's in it? It tastes awful."

"Do you want to get better or not? Drink!" Pohawe urged her.

Even though she feared she would throw up, she obeyed. "What is it? You are looking at me so strangely."

Pohawe took the empty cup from her. "Miakoda," she said earnestly, "your crystal began to glow."

"My what?" she asked, puzzled. "And why do you speak Eryonic?"

"The villagers are curious. I don't want them to understand what we're saying. It's one of those things with us, about magic. Not always easy."

"I know you do. But I don't understand what you mean. What crystal?"

Pohawe pointed to Liya's neck. "That stone."

She looked down at her silver necklace and studied the oval black stone that hung from it. The necklace had belonged to her mother. Liya had worn it ever since she could remember. The piece of jewelry was the only thing she had left of her mother. She stroked its uneven surface with her finger. The stone felt warm to the touch.

"It's not at all clear to me what this is about. I mean, creatures have abilities, but ornaments don't," she marveled.

"Can you remember anything from last night?" asked Pohawe.

She shook her head. "There was singing and dancing. How I got into the house… I don't remember."

"You ran to the water with Isi to cool down. I was looking for both of you, and fortunately, no one but me saw that your crystal was glowing. You were speaking in another language. Sakima realized that you had a vision. The potion gives it to us, we detach ourselves from our thoughts, and we are free. He and Taima acted quickly. After we got you into the house, we darkened everything. Sakima told the others that you couldn't take the potion and were suffering from a terrible headache."

What exactly happened to me? "Did I do anything else besides speak in another language?"

Pohawe shook her head. "Your eyes shone brightly. That's all that happened. And now your eyes are more blue than green."

"Then I guess I've made a fool of myself," she muttered.

"It doesn't matter," Isi comforted. " The first time, many people feel the same way you did. Believe me, there's nothing to be ashamed of."

"Besides, no one caught on because we took you straight to the hut," Pohawe added. "Most Nirm don't like it when people take our peyote potion. They like it even less when people have visions as a result."

Liya knew that. Why had Sakima insisted that she drink the stuff? Worried, she looked around the room. "Is this yours, Isi?" She pointed to a white dress lying on the high rocking chair.

"Yes!" Isi said, beaming. "It's beautiful. Wait until you see it in daylight."

"You'll look pretty in it."

Grateful for the distraction, she talked with Isi and Pohawe for a while about the competition that was to take place in the afternoon. Then she fell asleep again.

When she woke up, it was already light. She still felt a little dull, but much better than before. Pohawe's tea was working. Suddenly, a strange smell rose to her nose. *Is something burning?* Without hesitation, she threw the blanket aside and hurried out of the room. No one was around, and there was no fire burning in the stove. The fireplace was untouched, too. The smell must have come from outside. The women must be preparing lunch for the feast. Curious, she glanced out the window, but she didn't see anyone or hear anything. An uneasy feeling came over her; her pulse quickened. Something was wrong. She slipped into her tunic and left the house. She followed the smell, which came from the clearing. Then she saw something. What was it? It couldn't be. Houses were burning on the outskirts of the village! She ran, calling for Sakima and the others, but she received no answer. She ran on, out of the village, across the clearing, to the road.

"Sakima, Pohawe, Isi, where are you?"

No answer.

She followed the path. Her muscles ached, and her head was pounding. Her heart beat wildly against her ribs. Again and again, she smelled ashes.

Abruptly, the environment changed; she was in the palace city, which was ablaze. People screamed desperately, jostling against Liya as they fled to the north gate.

"What happened?" she cried.

But the fearful townspeople did not answer. Tears welled up in her eyes, and her head throbbed like crazy.

"Liya!" Someone called to her from far away.

The voice sounded familiar. She searched for a familiar face as she pushed toward the palace. When the next attack of pain hit her, she cried out, fell to her knees, and took her head in both hands. But nothing helped against the pounding.

"Liya!" The voice was still faint.

Through a veil of tears, she noticed a shadow. In the middle of the palace city, in front of a wall of flames, stood a tall figure reaching out to her, but no matter how hard she tried to get up, she could not. It was as if someone held her down. She fought against it, but she was too weak.

"I can't do it," she whispered through her tears.

The fire continued to spread in her direction while the figure remained in the middle of it, calling her name over and over again.

She cried out in despair as the flames reached her...

...and woke up in a cold sweat. Confused, she looked around. She was in Sakima's house, in her room, in her bed. She took several deep breaths until her pulse calmed down. A dream—only a dream!

There was a knock at the door. Pohawe entered and paused. "Looks like you had a further vision, or?"

"I'm...not sure," she answered hesitantly.

Liya looked thoughtfully at Sakima's wife. A snow-white braid reached far down her back. Although Pohawe appeared petite, she radiated enormous strength.

"What do you want to ask me, Miakoda?" Pohawe asked.

"Let's talk after the party." She sighed. "Has the competition started yet?" she asked in an attempt to distract her.

"No, don't worry." She brushed a strand of hair from her face. "Take your time. I'll meet you outside." With those words, she left the room.

Liya forced herself out of bed and opened the small window to let fresh air into the room. She had to blink a few times before her eyes got used to the bright light. She freshened up and followed the others to the main square.

Young warriors participated in archery, arrow running, and spear throwing. There were three rounds each, and the hunt was final. She joined

Isi, who looked especially pretty today. Her long black hair was decorated with a wreath of flowers. Her hands and ankles were painted with roses two fingers wide. Her big brown eyes looked hopefully at Taima, who, as if sensing her gaze, looked up and smiled at her.

The drummers began to play while the children clapped the beat. When Sakima walked to the center of the square, the music stopped.

"Today is a great day for the Nirm. We welcome not only spring, but also our young warriors. Only yesterday they were boys; after the competitions they will return as men. What lies ahead will demand courage, ambition, and strength. Only when body, mind, and soul are one does a young Nirm succeed in becoming a warrior. It fills me with great pride to open the competitions."

Then the elders escorted the young warriors to the clearing near the big reeds, and the games began.

Chapter 7

Dusk bathed the sky in pinkish-purple shades of light. Isi grinned as Liya stepped through the door. In the faint sunlight that filled the room, Isi's dress glimmered pink.

"I have a dress for you too," Isi said, pointing towards the bed.

Liya followed her gaze. "I can't accept that." Touched by her generosity, she shook her head. "This was your grandmother's."

Pohawe entered the room. "You are not ready yet?" she remarked.

"Please talk to Liya." Isi sighed theatrically and pointed to the dress. "Tell her to wear that."

Smiling, Pohawe hugged her daughter and gave her a kiss on the cheek. "My little girl has grown up. I am so proud of you."

"Thank you, Mama, thank you for everything," Isi whispered in a choked voice.

Pohawe's eyes shone, and she swallowed. Mother and daughter stood for a while, head to head.

Pohawe turned to Liya. "So, why won't you put on the dress?" Stealthily, she wiped tears from her face.

"It's too precious," she replied softly.

"Get changed already and hurry up," Isi said, disappearing through the door.

Pohawe winked at her. "It's just a dress, Miakoda. If it gets damaged, so be it." She left to get dressed.

When the three of them departed the house, they could hear the sound of beating drums. Arriving at the fairground, Liya observed Sakima talking to Taima. The men embraced, the old man patting the younger one on the shoulder. Taima came over to Isi and put a wreath of flowers around her neck. The fiancée beamed. Out of the corner of her eye, Liya saw Pohawe crying. She took her hand and squeezed it gently.

After the opening dance, Sakima stepped forward and announced the engagement. Isi came running and embraced her stormily.

"I'm very happy for you," Liya whispered.

"Thank you, Miakoda; without you, this day would not exist." Isi laughed and proceeded to hug her mother before running back to her fiancé.

She wished Isi happiness with all her heart.

When Sakima snapped her out of her thoughts, she cringed. "Let's go somewhere quiet so we can talk."

Finally, she thought as she looked at him gratefully.

The ancestral home, a simple wooden hut larger than the others, lay on the outskirts of the village. They took off their sandals and placed them on a light blue cloth in front of the entrance. The few steps leading to the door were strewn with flowers, and the intense scent of incense wafted toward them through the open door.

Silently, they entered the house. The glow of the dimly lit lanterns grazed the tapestries, whose rich colors made the room seem mystical and ancient. Liya felt that she sensed the presence of the ancestors. They sat down on the cushions, which were arranged on the floor in a circle.

Sakima smiled. "It's been a long time since you last visited us."

"I know, almost half a year. I had planned to come earlier." She sighed. "Unfortunately, this is not just a visit between friends. I bring news. We may be facing a war with Dar'Angaar, and perhaps even Eryon."

"For several months now, we've been sensing changes. Something that has been prepared for a long time is starting to move."

"What do you know about it?"

"Many legends predict the change of the world. What has long been forgotten is returning." Sakima's thick eyebrows formed a line as he frowned.

"Do the planets play a role in this?"

"That's possible." He swayed his head back and forth. "Who can say with certainty what the people of the past age were capable of doing?"

She pondered this. She had heard that there were vast research facilities before the Great War—the legacy of the Elders.

"What do you know about the world before the Great War?" she asked.

"To understand things, you have to go back to the time of advanced civilization, five hundred years ago. We don't know much about it anymore. Ancient writings tell us that back then, they had not only invented weapons, but also things that made life more comfortable. With the aim to improve their abilities, they did research on people—until one day, it all disappeared. It is believed that a group of people was chosen to receive the gift. But how they ensured that the chosen group survived the annihilation is beyond me."

Instinctively, Liya reached for her dagger. "What happened to the people who survived the sinking?"

"That's an interesting question. For all we know, they had no memories of what happened, but they retained their magical abilities in relation to the four elements: fire, water, air, and earth. Most of them were able to control one element. Some could probably summon and use the power of two or even three elements. Very few, however, were able to access all four elements with the same degree of success. Those people built a new life for themselves. Peace reigned among them for four hundred years until the *Great War.*"

"The survivors... You mean the desert people of the Darlam Plain, don't you?" Liya remembered the story about them. The region was surrounded by dunes; only near the mountains were there rivers and green areas. "I never understood why they didn't share their knowledge with everyone else. Maybe that could have prevented the war."

"Scrolls are dubious," Sakima replied. "Sometimes you can't believe everything that's written there."

"Maybe, but this is one of the most important historical parts of Namoor. Keldor asked them for help—his wife was seriously sick. Scrolls or not, they refused to help him." Immediately after that event, he was crowned king.

"The truth always has two sides, Liya."

"He returned empty-handed, and a few weeks later, he mourned the death of his wife. That was the reason why he formed an alliance with Dar'Angaar—to weaken Elladur's position. I would say the facts are quite clear."

"Knowledge in the wrong hands is dangerous. Perhaps Elladur served a higher purpose."

Liya looked at him in disbelief. "You think Elladur's stubbornness wasn't the catalyst for the war?"

"I can't say. However, this explanation seems too simple. The connections are more complicated, but magic, for sure, has a big role. We believe that magic has no natural origin. Rather, it arose and remained in the *Ancient Era.* The downfall of this highly developed culture has something to do with magic. Whatever happened must have been horrible! We know that a group of the gifted were chosen by *the Elders* to take the role of the Guardians. They were endowed with additional magical abilities, and thus able to protect the bond between the worlds. That was their main task. They were also responsible for preserving the knowledge of the Elders and keeping it secret. These Guardians lived in Elladur."

"I've never heard of that." She frowned. "What do you mean by worlds? What other world are you talking about?" Her stomach rolled inside her.

"The world behind the tape. It is said that something lurks there. The Guardians protected the gates to prevent contact between the worlds."

"What happened to the Guardians?"

"Elladur lost the war—there were hardly any survivors."

"This war..." She pondered it. Something didn't make sense. "What interest could anyone have in killing the Guardians?" An almost unbelievable thought occurred to her. Surely this could not be true. "Do you think it's possible that someone wanted to gain access to the other world?"

For a moment, Sakima looked at her fixedly. "Keldor may have been looking for a cure at first, but he came across clues in Elladur from the Ancient Era. The trail led deep into the Darlam Plain."

She couldn't believe her ears. "Are you trying to tell me that Namoor's history is built on lies?" She heard how brittle her voice sounded.

He shook his head. "No. I'm just saying that the scriptures don't tell the whole story. However, there is no doubt that Elladur's leaders denied help to Keldor."

"But why?"

"Possibly because there was no cure for his wife. Keldor didn't want to believe it."

"How do you know so much about it?"

"My ancestors served the ruling family of Elladur a long time ago. Their task was to protect the capital and the royal family. When the Guardians realized they would lose the war, they sent two dozen of our people to the mountains."

Despite the warm air, she shivered. "I really don't know what to say. He wasn't alone back then. He didn't act alone. That would mean either he lied to all of Namoor's lords, or they knew about the real background."

"Sometimes people do not want to see the truth."

"But it's more than that. It means the entire history of Namoor is based on a lie. He propagated the danger from Elladur and made his people believe that he wanted to protect them. Only because of that would they accept the coronation. In truth, he aimed at the destruction of the Guardians to get access to something more powerful, right?"

She looked at Sakima in horror. Judging by his expression, she gathered that he believed it rock-solidly. She closed her eyes to organize her thoughts. Breathe—breathe slowly.

"Did it do him any good to take out the Guardians?" she asked.

"He managed to open the gates with his allies from Dar'Angaar, but the Guardians prevented him from going through. For some reason, Dar'Angaar turned on Namoor at the last moment, and the entrance was closed."

"What happens if the gates open again?"

"We don't know, and it would be better if we never found out."

"What is kept beyond the tape?"

"*The first seer found the hidden light. He brought the truth and the downfall at the same time.*"

"You're talking about Elladur, aren't you?"

Sakima nodded. "Our ancestors left us ancient scrolls with quotations from the Book of Heaven. He will unite the worlds and split off magic. Darkness rules his power. "

"He?"

"We do not know who 'he' is. Could be someone from this world or another. Much knowledge has been lost."

"Why didn't you tell me this before?"

"Today, you informed me about the latest developments and the possibility of war. Things are happening at the right time, stories told at the right time."

"Yeah, but I feel strange now. I was so happy when I was able to take the exam at the academy after all. I made an oath to Keldor and Louis."

"It was your way." Sakima took her hand and patted it. "You were sixteen and full of euphoria about your new assignment as the king's emissary." He waved his hands theatrically. "*To be allowed to serve a country with a great history... Heroes from a bygone era...*"

She grimaced. That was exactly what she had said.

"I don't think you would have believed me then." He grinned.

"What makes you so sure I will today?"

"Instead of leaving, you are still here, listening to me. That gives me hope."

"It's still unbelievable. Keldor is revered as a hero. It is to him that Namoor owes its greatness and wealth." She found it hard to push back her disappointment. "Any other secrets I should know about?"

Solemnly, he put his right hand on his chest. "I am an old man; I have a right to secrets. Everything..."

"Yes, I know," she interrupted him, rolling her eyes playfully. "All in good time!"

"We are very happy about your visit," he said kindly.

"I, too, am delighted to be here. Isi is thrilled."

"Yes, she is. And now for you? What news do you bring?"

"There will soon be another king in Dar'Angaar. Jadmar plans to marry his daughter to this future king. An alliance will form between Dar'Angaar and Eryon, which cannot be in our interest. Perhaps war will ensue."

"What will King Louis do?"

"He is having information gathered to find out if we are in danger. There's a problem, though. We have spies in Eryon, but not in Dar'Angaar."

"I wish there was something I could do for you. People rarely stray here, and we avoid the other side of the mountains."

"I understand. But maybe there is a way to help me."

He first looked surprised, then worried, and that did not escape her. His dark brows drew together. "The king has given you a mission, hasn't he? And I probably won't like it."

"I want to ask you a favor. I need to get to Dar'Angaar undetected."

"I don't understand this man. You just turned eighteen. This is irresponsible and way too dangerous."

The deep apprehension in his voice touched her. "I can take care of myself. You know that. I've been trained since I was five years old."

"You can handle a sword and bow, I agree. But in Dar'Angaar, magic is practiced openly. Are you ready for that?"

"I'm used to playing roles. I'm just going to listen around for a bit and then return. They won't discover me, so they won't use magic against me."

"I still don't like the whole thing."

"Please, Sakima, we must do everything in our power to prevent a war."

"Very well!" He sighed. "I will consult with the elders. This is not a decision I can make alone."

Before she could say anything else, they heard voices from outside.

"Let's go back to the feast," he said, standing up.

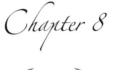

Raindrops tapped steadily on the wood. Liya suppressed the urge to pace around the ancestral home. Waiting was not for her, and she struggled to pull herself together. She saw Sakima casually carrying the teapot into the room, radiating a very calm aura. Her eyes wandered toward the door once again. She spotted Taima, who was also waiting. Upon meeting her gaze, he nodded to her.

Moments later, the four elders entered, followed by several women who brought in various dishes. The delicious-smelling fresh cornbread reminded her that she hadn't eaten yet. Sakima waited until everyone was seated in the circle, then pushed back his cushion and sat down next to Liya.

"I greet you, tribal leader of the Nirm," he said.

Ahiga scowled at Liya and muttered something unintelligible. She sensed his anger at her presence all too clearly.

Sakima took a few pulls on the hookah before passing it on. "Tribes of Nirm, Miakoda brings us news," he said solemnly.

She looked into the petrified expressions.

Ahiga took the floor aggressively. "We don't interfere in human affairs!"

She looked at him more closely. His shoulder-length gray hair was down. His harsh, black eyes were fixed on Sakima, and his white eyebrows scrunched together. He had an angular chin and a thin upper lip that disappeared behind his huge lower lip.

Seemingly undeterred, Sakima asked her to speak. She reported everything she had already told her friend.

Mojak, which meant 'never quiet,' said softly, "Demons sometimes haunt me in my dreams. They have red eyes."

Mojak seemed much older than the others. His fragile, slender figure led up to a narrow face with a small nose that radiated friendliness. Some of his teeth were missing. His short hair stood up in all directions, and a bald circle formed at the back of his head. His long white beard pointed downward.

"I came here to warn you about a possible war," Liya continued. "We don't know what to expect, and we have to expect the worst."

The elders remained in fearful silence.

She let her gaze roam over each one's face before continuing. "The king's ambition is to protect the people of Namoor."

Ahiga regarded her indifferently. "Miakoda, we thank you for your candor. However, first and foremost, we think of *our* people—the Nirm."

He had never attempted to conceal the fact that he did not accept her as one of their own. He believed strangers brought bad luck, which is why he had voted against Liya's admission to the Nirm community.

Gently, she put out feelers for her gift—just a little. Whatever the Nirm had in common with the desert people of old, the story Sakima had told her was more than a legend. She realized that. She had delivered bad news, but except for Ahiga's anger, she felt neither fear nor skepticism—as if the elders had expected it!

She turned to Ahiga. "I understand your doubts. However, your rejection and distrust of me do not change the facts."

She noticed the slight smile playing around Sakima's mouth.

"What do you suggest, Miakoda? What should we do?" inquired Mojak.

"I need your help to get to Dar'Angaar unseen. I ask that one of you fly me across the border."

"We thank you for your words and will consult," Sakima said.

She was dismissed. She rose, went outside, and sat down on the steps. As she put her shoes back on, Taima took a seat next to her.

"It's not looking so good for you."

"I figured as much, but it was worth a shot."

The wind blew harder now, and thunder growled in the distance. The moment the rumbling died away, Sakima joined them. He looked down at Liya and shook his head regretfully.

"We can't risk being seen in our true form," he said.

She understood it was a massive risk. The danger for the Nirm was huge, but she couldn't hide her disappointment. They all had to take *some* risks to prevent war. She would need to spend more time with the Nirm, trying to convince the members of the council by increasing the worry among their people. In that case, they might be forced to act. She didn't want to resort to that, but the danger of Dar'Angaar would hit them, too. There was only one other option to get to Dar'Angaar: either by boat or over the mountains, which would take more time. Time that she didn't have.

Someone shook her shoulders violently. She opened her eyes and found herself looking into Mojak's face.

"Come on, get up, girl!" he whispered.

"What are you doing here?" she hissed.

"Do you want to go to Dar'Angaar or not?"

"I thought the council—"

"I will not ask you again. We have little time. Get dressed. Leave your sword and bow. I'll wait for you at the jetty." He left the hut hastily.

She threw on her leather armor and stowed the dagger and throwing stars on her belt. In her bundle, she packed another robe and her dark green cloak. A few minutes later, she spotted Mojak by one of the rowboats, which he was pushing into the water.

"You took off in this boat! No one will suspect me," he said softly, grinning.

"You're going against the council's decision. Why?"

"I agree with you and Sakima. We have to prevent war. Some of us have forgotten the stories of our ancestors. It is important to know what is going on in Dar'Angaar."

"Thank you, Mojak." She grasped his forearm. "This means a lot to me."

"I do what I must for my people," he replied simply.

He moved a few steps away, and she heard a low rumble. Fascinated, she watched Mojak's scrawny figure stretch. His skin, which had been dull just a short while ago, shimmered like marble in the moonlight. His wrinkled face stiffened. Enormous wings grew out of his back, and she found herself face to face with a dragon-like creature, nearly three meters tall, standing on two legs and leaning down toward her.

The rumbling stopped, and his black eyes looked at her in amusement. "Do you want to keep admiring me, or do we want to fly off?"

Slowly, she approached him. "I've never flown before."

Mojak lifted her with ease and held her tightly in his arms. She felt like an infant. The next moment, he took off. Her stomach tingled. She clenched her eyelids and concentrated on breathing.

"Open your eyes, little one. You're going to love it."

Cautiously, she opened her eyes. The vast sea spread out beneath her, sparkling spectacularly. The sound of gentle waves interrupted the silence of the night. Above her, stars twinkled. Mojak flew higher and higher. She felt the cool air on her face, inhaled, and gradually relaxed. She laughed. A feeling of giddy joy warmed her from the inside, and she forgot all her worries.

"Indescribable!" she breathed in awe.

"That's it," he agreed.

She didn't know how long they had been flying when land spread below them. He must have used his gift to go that fast, even if she didn't feel it. She was grateful he took the seaside instead of flying over the mountains. This way, she could walk to the port city.

Mojak reduced their altitude, and steadily, the earth came closer. Her stomach heaved as they landed. If he had not continued to hold her, her knees would have given way. The Nirm let go of her and walked to a tree. The earth vibrated under his steps. He ran his index finger over the bark, and a white bird glowed on the spot.

"In two weeks, the full moon rises. I'll be waiting for you here. As soon as the moon wanes, the sign will fade," he said.

"I am indebted to you," she said, wondering what other abilities the Nirm possessed.

"Follow the path. At daybreak, you will reach a small village."

"I'd rather not know exactly how you know your way around this area," she replied with a grin.

When Mojak laughed, she heard the rumble again. "We were all young once," he said, spreading his wings. "We'll meet again in two weeks." He lifted himself into the air.

Fascinated, she gazed after him and took a deep breath as the black sky swallowed him up. Then she straightened her shoulders and went on her way.

I made it, she silently congratulated herself. *I am in Dar'Angaar.*

By sunrise, Liya felt exhausted and flabby. Hours of marching, with only a few short rest breaks, took its toll. She was not used to walking long distances. Mojak was proved right when, in the distance, she spotted an arrangement of houses. Finally, she would be able to look for an inn and have breakfast. Her stomach growled audibly at the thought of food. With renewed vigor, she quickened her steps. Her muscles throbbed, but she ignored the pain.

She heard something. As she listened carefully, she discerned muffled, threatening voices. The hair on the back of her neck stood up. Her body tensed, her mind raced, and her stomach tightened.

Thinking that the fields could provide sufficient cover to sneak by unnoticed, she left the road and walked into the ankle-high grass. The earth swallowed her steps. As she got nearer, the voices that grew louder.

"I'm not going to tell you anything. I'd rather die," a voice said.

A loud bang startled her. "No one is going to help you. You can either die slow and agonizing or the exact opposite. I promise you a quick death if you tell me where to find the crystal."

The deep voice sent a cold shiver down her spine. *What on earth is going on here? Who are these men?* She took off her leather bag, lay flat on the ground, and carefully crawled on.

A hoarse laugh rang out. "Do I look like I know anything about a crystal? I'm a sailor. You've got the wrong guy. I was on my way to the village to hire men for my ship."

A crack and a groan followed a blow. "I am aware of who you are, Captain."

The man gasped.

"Just tell us what we want to know."

Peering through the grass, she saw three men, one of whom was kneeling on the ground. By the gods, the two who stood measured at least two meters. One of them held the captain by the throat and shook him violently. She watched in disbelief. They would kill him, there was no doubt about that. What should she do? Wait and see? Try to help him and risk her own life? *I should leave as soon as possible. This is none of my business,* she thought. When the prisoner cried out, she winced. Why did her decision feel wrong, even though it was reasonable?

Damn it! Quietly, she crawled back to her leather bundle, fished out the green cloak, and threw it over her shoulders. Pulling the hood over to cover her face, she reached for her dagger in her boot and tucked it into the belt at her hip. With the leather bag in her left hand, the throwing star in her right, she set off. Just before reaching the spot where the men were, she bent forward and began to limp.

"Someone's coming!" said one of the men.

Even when she heard heavy footsteps, she kept her gaze lowered.

"This is where the road ends for you," the stranger's voice boomed above her.

"Have the sheep escaped again?" she croaked, shaking her head. "Hurry up! You useless son of a bastard! I have to go to town to set up the market stall."

"Who is that?" roared the other giant.

"An old, confused woman."

"Bring her!"

"Come, I'll lead you to the flock of sheep," the stranger whispered derisively and took the bag from her. The sharp smell of herbs and alcohol touched her nose.

"Thank you," she murmured, grabbing his arm.

Under the cloak, she put the throwing star back on her belt but kept her hand on the handle of the dagger. When they reached the place where the captain was being maltreated, the mixture of urine, alcohol, and herbs nauseated her.

"Surely you don't want this woman's blood on your hands, Captain!" said the guy bending over the prisoner.

She cleared her throat. "I'm not hurt, don't worry," she said, her gaze still directed to the ground.

The torturers laughed. "Let me see her face. Maybe it's prettier than the rest."

The man moved closer to her, turning his back on the captain. Her grip on the dagger tightened, and she raised her head slightly, suppressing a cry. The moment the giant pushed her hood back, she jerked the dagger up and rammed it into his chest. The sharp blade dug deep into his flesh. Before the other could react, she ducked and grabbed the sword at his hip. Someone kicked the side of her knee. She fell, struggled back up, pulled the sword in front, and parried a hard blow.

"Watch out behind you!" the captain shouted.

She whirled around, throwing herself forward, and plunged the sword into her opponent's chest. With her other hand, she pulled out her dagger. The attacker fell to the ground with a thud. At the same moment, the captain rammed into the guy who had been leading Liya. Without hesitation, she pulled the sword from the chest of the torturer she had struck down and parried the other's attack. She dodged, thrust, and ducked as metal met metal. She rapidly charged forward and delivered the death blow to the second giant. Warm liquid ran down her hand, and her opponent fell to the ground. It was over. She blinked. Hopefully, she would eventually forget the horrible sight of the dead. Panting, she fell to her knees beside the captain.

"The sword," he stammered.

It was still stuck in his shoulder. With trembling hands, she grasped the handle.

"Pull it out slowly!" the man muttered.

She did. He held his breath, cursed, and held his breath again. After she pulled the sword out, he groaned. He looked as if he might topple forward, but he turned to face her.

"You saved my life," he said softly. "I am Aval."

"Liya." *Had she really said that?* Her tongue had been faster than her mind. She shouldn't have told him her real name. Now it was too late.

Aval rose slowly. "We have to get out of here. Those two were just the vanguard."

Faced with the corpses, she could no longer suppress the urge to vomit. She got to her feet, stumbled to the side of the path, and threw up. She put her hands on her thighs and took a deep breath.

"Here, rinse your mouth out with water," Aval said, handing her the water bottle. "I need your help to pull the bodies to the side."

As they moved the heavy bodies, Liya suppressed another urge to vomit. They leaned against a tree for a while, breathing heavily.

Her eyes fell on the blood-soaked spot on Aval's jacket. "We should clean your wound."

"There's no time for that. We have to hurry."

Aval got up and marched down the path, Liya trotting behind.

The houses of the nearby settlement got closer and closer. After about half an hour, Aval's condition worsened. His arm hung limply, and his feet dragged on the ground.

"Let me help you," she said and put his arm around her shoulders, clasping his waist with her arm.

"Thank you." He shifted his weight, and they swayed.

He breathed heavily, and Liya had to slow down, even though she would have preferred walking faster. She looked around to make sure they were not being followed.

When they arrived in the village, Aval headed for a house with a huge door, on which hung an old sign with a duck painted on it. She figured it was an inn. In the early hours of the morning, there was little activity on the streets, for which she was grateful.

Before she could open the door, Aval held her back. "Let me do the talking—stay in the background!"

With a pain-distorted face, he pushed the door open. She breathed a sigh of relief when she realized that only one present was the host.

"Good morning. My sister and I need a room for two nights," Aval said.

"Have you also come for the wedding?" asked the host.

"Yes!"

"The rooms are all booked."

"We'll take the barn, too."

"Also occupied. I can only offer you the attic. The room is big. There is a bathtub, but no beds, only mattresses. For that, I'll charge you half the usual rate for a room."

"Agreed."

Aval took silver coins out of his jacket and threw them on the counter. "Is there breakfast yet? We'd like to eat in the room. We traveled all night."

The host turned his powerful body and yelled, "Mavie, make some breakfast and take it to the garret."

He handed Aval a key. To their relief, if he noticed the blood on his jacket, he said nothing. Liya followed Aval up the stairs. Once they were out of sight, she supported him. At the top, she unlocked the door and looked around the garret. The room was spacious, if barren. On the right side were several large bowls of water, a pitcher, and a square bathtub. Under the window were two mattresses. Next to them was a closet. *It will do*, she told herself. Carefully, she hoisted Aval onto a mattress and helped him out of his jacket. She looked into the closet and found a piece of cloth. Aval unbuttoned and removed his shirt with a restrained groan. His body was covered with blood-encrusted welts and bruises.

"I can imagine what it looks like," he said hoarsely.

"How long were you their prisoner?"

"They caught me two days ago. I managed to escape from them last night, but they caught me again at dawn."

When she touched his shoulder to clean the wound, he flinched. There was a knock at the door.

"Help me up! Let me do it!"

Frowning, she supported him so he could crack open the door.

"Breakfast, my lord," she heard the maid say.

"Thank you, put the tray outside the door."

After a few seconds, Liya brought in the board and carried it to the mattress. Aval closed the door. When she turned to him, he had already slid down the wall, and now he lay motionless. Concerned, she rushed to him. His chest barely rose and fell. Hectically, she searched his wrist. There! She felt his heartbeat, slow but steady. She had to stop the bleeding from his shoulder. *Damn!* That was not planned at all. She didn't want to use her gift. Apart from that, exploring the moods of people with her gift was way different than healing someone. She hadn't accessed that ability in a long time. But what else could she do? She was a stranger here, and they'd seen her and Aval. They would accuse her if something happened to him. *Nobody will know*, she told herself. She sighed and closed her eyes, calming her breathing, and concentrated. Power surged through her body as the gift stirred. The energy pulsed gently against the limits from her ban, but there was no need to push it.

Her breathing quickened. She had to act now. Comforting warmth spread through her. Her hand touched his shoulder, and energy pulsed through her fingertips. His shoulder appeared in her inner eye: red and blue threads following a stream. One spot, however, was black, and dark clouds of smoke hung over it. That was where the sword had pierced him.

She took another deep breath, drew strength from within herself, and sent out her magic, which shone like rays of light. The glow intensified. She watched the wound shrink until the clouds disappeared.

When she opened her eyes, the air shimmered. Weakness threatened to overwhelm her. She hadn't done any healing for ages, and she'd gone deeper into her magic than ever before. What bothered her, though, was that she had enjoyed the power. She shook off this thought and devoted herself to her task: moving Aval. She had to hold on a little longer. With the last of her strength, she dragged Aval to the mattress and covered him.

When she stood up, she felt dizzy. *Not now*, she thought, but the darkness pulled Liya into the abyss.

Chapter 10

Warm rays tickled Liya's face. As she woke from a deep sleep, it took her a second to become conscious of her surroundings. She heard men's voices.

"She saved my life," Aval was saying.

"I don't care. She's our enemy, and we're taking her with us." This voice was foreign to her. She kept her eyes closed and tried to concentrate.

"What's the point? We're not going back to the city at all. The search for the damn crystal goes on."

"We know where the crystal is. When you didn't show up, some of us stayed at the meeting place in case you did. The rest of us kept asking people and following, well, the magic trails."

Interesting, Liya thought. *They're able to follow the trails of mages.* The magicians of Namoor had a similar approach when searching for gifted people. She needed more information.

"It was close. I thought I was going to die yesterday. I don't understand why I'm doing so well today."

"The gods have been merciful, my friend."

She felt a tap on her shoulder. Carefully she reached for her dagger, but it was no longer on her belt.

"Is this what you're looking for?" the stranger asked.

She blinked a few times and found herself looking into sparkling green eyes. He waved the dagger in front of her. Quickly, she sat up.

"Who sent you?" the man asked.

"What do you mean?"

He pointed at her body. "Your clothes, sweetheart. There are no warrior women in Dar'Angaar. Here, women wear nice dresses, not leather pants. So where are you from, and how the hell did you make it across the border?"

Damn it! How could she have known that? Besides, she had not intended to take off her cloak on the way. One thing was clear: she would never betray anything!

Aval stepped closer. "Maverick, you're scaring her."

"That's what I'm trying to do," Maverick said urgently. "We'll get you talking, but first, we're getting out of here." He tossed the cloak towards her. "Put this on!"

As she rose, black dots danced before her eyes, and she swayed slightly. Aval moved forward, but Maverick stopped him.

"She saved your life, fair enough! Still, she is an enemy, Sonaris."

Aval shook off his arm. Hastily, she threw on the cloak and put on the hood.

Maverick grabbed her upper arm roughly. "What happens now is up to you. We'll go down together. You don't make a fuss, everything is fine. If you try to escape, I'll kill you. You try to scream, I'll kill you. Behave, and you'll stay alive—for now. Your choice, sweetheart."

She glared angrily at him but refrained from answering. She was too weak to fight back. She had to regain her strength, then she would come up with a plan to flee. Barely able to stand on her feet, she let Maverick drag her to the door and down the stairs. That healing had done her in.

Aval followed. The innkeeper watched with indifference as they left the inn. Although the street was teeming with people, no one paid them any attention. Tables and benches were already set up, and women were scattering flowers on the ground. *Ah yes—the wedding*, she recalled. If only she hadn't been so dazed!

Maverick headed for the stable. "You will ride with me," he determined.

Inside, he took out a rope from his leather bag. "Even though you saved Sonaris' life, I don't trust you. Give me your hands," he demanded.

Without resistance, she stretched her hands out. Grinning, he grasped her wrists and tied them up.

With an arrogant look on his face, he leaned towards her and whispered, "That's a good boy. Maybe you'll live longer than I thought after all."

His nose was close enough. She let her head shoot forward.

"Damn it!" he roared.

A dangerous glint decked his eyes, and she braced herself for a blow, but nothing happened. Aval came in. Concerned, he looked at his comrade and shook his head. Cursing softly, Maverick effortlessly lifted her onto his colossal horse before mounting himself.

They rode all day. By sunset, Liya was at the end of her rope, her eyelids drooping. Fear usually sharpened her attention, but not now. Her thoughts buzzed around those corpses. Her body gave up its rigid posture, and she leaned against Maverick's chest.

When someone tampered with her bonds, she woke up. With difficulty, she opened an eye, straightened up from her slouching position, and saw Aval. The morning was approaching. She was still on the horse, but alone. This was a favorable time for escape.

"Have a drink," Aval said.

She winced, her thoughts quickly shifting. Gratefully, she took the bottle and enjoyed the cool liquid. She gulped greedily. When was the last time she'd had something to drink? Or eat? She didn't know.

Maverick stepped out of a bush.

"You slept like a dead woman," he said, mounting the horse. "It's amazing you didn't fall off."

When he turned to her with a grin, she gave him a dirty look. He actually thought it was funny. They rode on. Aval stayed close behind them.

Liya's hackles stood up, and she tensed her muscles. She sensed danger—not far from them.

Maverick's noticed. "What's wrong?"

"Danger," she breathed.

He stopped and looked around cautiously. Silence filled the twilight, and nothing seemed out of the ordinary.

"There's nothing there," he said.

Moments later, Aval joined them. "What's up?" He looked at them with confusion.

"She thinks we're in danger." Maverick tilted his head towards her.

Aval jumped off his horse and put one hand on the ground. "We're being followed," he said and promptly remounted. "How much farther is it?"

"We'll reach the meeting point around noon."

"The animals are exhausted. We should ride into the forest. Fleeing is futile—the pursuers have already picked up our scent."

As they galloped in the direction of the forest, they heard their pursuers approaching fast. Maverick uttered several curses, knowing they would not make it in time.

"We'll stop here," Maverick shouted to Aval when they reached the first thicket of trees, jumping off his horse.

"Untie me. I can fight," Liya hissed.

"No way!" Maverick snorted contemptuously.

"I promise not to flee and to fight alongside you."

"What is the word of an enemy worth?" roared Maverick.

"What's your life worth to you?" she countered. "A dozen riders are coming at us. How long do you think you'll survive? Aval is hurt; he won't last long."

He pressed his lips together. His eyes positively glowed.

"She's right. Even with three of us, our chances aren't too good," Aval said with a groan as he got off his horse.

Growling, Maverick untied the knot. "If I so much as *suspect* you might escape, I'll kill you. Then I won't give a damn what our chances are."

She let herself slide off the horse and held her hand out. "My dagger!"

He handed it to her. "You won't get far with that, and we only have two swords."

"What about that bow?" She pointed to Aval's saddle.

"Yours," Maverick growled.

There were two dozen arrows in the quiver. The hooves of their pursuers thundered loudly. They were getting closer. Hastily, she looked around. The lowest branches of the tree above them were out of reach.

"Maverick, help me up the tree! Quick!" she said.

Using a robber's ladder, she climbed up and squatted on a thick branch. Leaves swirled through the air as the horses dashed to the edge of the forest. Maverick and Aval quickly hid behind the trees. The riders in the front leaped from their horses. Flashing their weapons, they ran to where Aval and Maverick were hiding while one of their companions rode after them.

The attackers resembled the giants that had mauled Aval, but something about them was different. Somehow, they looked less human with their broad shoulders, their pronounced neck muscles, and their extremely muscular physique. Liya could not put her finger on it, but they seemed more threatening. Without hesitation, she nocked an arrow, drew her bow, took a deep breath, and let go as she exhaled. It was a direct hit! Right in the head. But the rider did not topple from his horse. A roar of rage rang out, and red eyes looked in her direction. She did not think for long. The next arrow pierced his neck. This time, the huge body fell to the ground.

Hastily, she looked around to get a grasp on the situation. Maverick and Aval were defending themselves furiously; Maverick was clearly the better fighter. Metal clanked and sparks flew as she fired arrow after arrow. To finish off one of the monsters, she had to shoot two or three times. She was about to notch the last arrow when she noticed a shadow under her tree. This one was bigger and more terrifying than the others. All she had left to defend herself with was an arrow and her dagger.

Desperately, she looked around. Aval was lying on the ground, bleeding from a large wound in his thigh. With difficulty, he tried to pull himself up. Maverick yelled something that she could not understand over the clashing of swords. The giant beneath her kicked the tree violently. She barely managed to hold on.

"Come down, girl! And I will kill you quickly. If I have to come for you, you will die in agony." His voice sounded cruel, metallic, and dark. His eyes glinted insanely.

"Why does everyone always threaten me with death?" she muttered.

She made a decision. She clutched her dagger with her left hand and the arrow with her right. How grateful she was to Brath, her teacher, for making her practice using weapons with both hands for countless, excruciating hours.

"You have killed my brothers," rumbled the creature. "You will pay for this."

She assumed a sitting position with her legs dangling on one side, took a deep breath, and let herself fall. The creature had the nerve to look surprised before she thrust the arrow into the monster's red eye and drilled the dagger into its body. With a casual flick of its wrist, the beast flung her away, slamming her into the trunk of a nearby tree. The impact pressed the air out of her lungs, and her stomach heaved. The next attack came quicker than she had anticipated—she had no chance. The giant snatched at her and dragged her up. Claws as long as her entire hand squeezed her throat shut, and she began gasping for breath.

With the last bit of her strength, she struck his upper arms. He did not move. She choked frantically, fighting for air. *No! I will not die today.* Her hands glowed. Fire burned inside her. Concentrated energy coursed through her veins, rushing to her head and giving her boundless euphoria. Never before had her magic felt like this.

She curled her fingers deeper into his arm. The red eyes widened in disbelief. He let go of her throat, staggering backward, and crouched. She lunged at him, pressing her hands against his chest. Power surged through her. Intoxicating! Dark haze emanated from his body, and the monster could move no longer. A scream ripped through the smoke, fading her elation and clearing her vision.

Aval roared at her. The beast in front of her collapsed, dead. Aval and Maverick were surrounded by six beasts. The auras of the two men shimmered with bright light, while the attackers were shrouded in dark swaths.

She blanked everything out: the clash of swords, the stench of blood, the pool of red that formed beneath her feet. The world dissolved, leaving intertwined threads of light in every color. Her ears ached, but the euphoria returned. Slowly, she approached Aval and Maverick. The creatures scented her. Three of them turned towards her, circling her, lurking closer.

The time had come. Liya opened her mind completely, offering free passage to the magic within her, allowing it to reach the limits of the ban or go beyond. The witch's spell that suppressed her gift seemed weaker. Was this possible? Her opponents moved slow and ponderously, while she exceeded all physical limits. She grabbed the swords on the ground, one in each hand, and danced quickly, rhythmically, and elegantly around the monsters, effortlessly parrying all attacks, striking them down. Her opponents had no escape. One by one, they all fell. The last sparks of life left their mighty bodies as she stood in the middle of their battlefield.

She turned her attention to the immediate edge of the forest. Aval crashed into a tree, while Maverick parried an attack. She drove forward with full force and whirled her sword around. She fought alongside Maverick, metal meeting metal, until the last attacker went down.

A strange silence settled over them. The scattered bodies seemed much smaller than before. Sweat and blood clung to Liya. Her sharpened perception faded, and an unbelievable tiredness seized her. The fight was over; they had survived.

"Where the hell did you learn to fight like that?" Maverick groaned, straightening up with difficulty.

The admiration in his voice did not escape her. She only hoped that they hadn't noticed her gift.

"We have to leave," Aval said.

With the greatest of difficulty, he dragged himself to them. Maverick whistled loudly. The horses trotted out of the woods. Maverick helped Aval mount, then took the rope from the saddlebag.

Liya stared him down with disbelief. "Thanks to me, you're still alive."

"That doesn't change the fact that you are our prisoner."

"She can ride with me—without shackles," Aval interjected.

"If she runs, you'll have to answer for it," Maverick growled.

He sounded less grumpy, though. He helped her onto the horse. Exhausted, she leaned against Aval's chest. This time, she didn't even try to fight her tiredness.

Liya awoke with a groan. She stared at the tent blanket stretched over her. Her body ached, and her throat felt scratchy and dry. Soft voices reached her and, jerkily, she sat up.

"Awake again, sunshine?" Maverick grinned at her.

He and Aval sat in the middle of the tent with another man. The stranger had dark hair and black eyes. His face reminded her of a bird of prey. He grinned, then politely lowered his head.

"My name is Folnar," he introduced himself.

Someone lifted the tent cover from outside and entered. Her heart stopped: Haydn! His blue eyes twinkled with amusement. She couldn't help but stare at him in disbelief. Fate did not mean well for her. With slow steps, he approached and handed her a cup. She drank greedily.

"What brings King Louis' master spy to my country?" he asked.

She choked. What had Haydn just said? Feverishly, her mind tried to grasp what his words meant.

"Your country?" she choked out.

Maverick suppressed a snort.

"My kingdom."

When she realized the connections, she fought down all her emotions and built a wall around herself. She knew that her face was devoid of emotions. After the ball, she had suspected that Haydn was not a simple soldier, but an emissary with connections to the ruling house of Dar'Angaar. Far from her perception, Haydn *was* this ruler, who had probably been crowned king and was to marry Lady Beth. How much all this pained her, she must not show.

"Let me go, and I'll leave your country."

"I'm afraid I can't do that. Trespassing is punishable by death."

Her pulse quickened. Maverick had already hinted at something like that.

"I saved your men's lives," she attempted.

"That's what they reported. But now answer my question: what are you doing here?"

"Since you already called me a spy, that should be obvious, right?"

"What are you looking for?"

"You're good at guessing, aren't you? Keep guessing." If looks could kill, she was in for it now. "You can't intimidate me. I killed those monsters, so your 'I'm the evil king, I can kill you' doesn't mean anything to me. You'll have to do better than that," she groaned angrily.

A surprised expression spread across his face. Out of the corner of her eye, she saw Aval struggling to suppress a laugh.

"Usually, just my presence is enough to intimidate people," Haydn replied with a sheepish smile.

She snorted contemptuously. His expression darkened again, and inwardly she cheered.

"My men are indebted to you, but I am not. Besides, Aval brought you here on his horse and saved your life. The claws of those monsters secrete lethal poison. Without our antidote, you would have been dead long ago."

Stunned, she stared at him, her thoughts racing. She was the best not only because she had the gift; she could read people without magic— recognize their intentions and motives. This ability, along with her gift, made her the best. Had he told the truth? Did the claws secrete poison? She had sensed nothing.

"You could have saved yourself the antidote if you were going to kill me anyway," she hissed.

"Then I wouldn't have been able to question you."

She rolled her eyes. "We both know that's not what you're about. What do you want?"

"You think I want something from you?" Haydn's teeth flashed like those of a predator.

"I do."

He laughed out loud.

"Still looking for the crystal?" she said casually.

Suddenly, she had the full attention of all the men in the tent. she groaned inwardly. Her mouth had been too fast again; she had let herself be provoked.

Haydn bent down so far that his nose almost touched hers. "You are either very brave or very stupid."

She had to hand it to him. He seemed truly threatening, but she was not impressed. "How fast are your men when I put my throwing star to your neck?" she replied with a smile.

For whatever reason, they hadn't taken it from her. His face contorted, then he laughed. She watched him with disbelief. *The idiot is actually laughing at me*, she thought, clenching her hands into fists.

"Leave us alone," Haydn instructed his men.

Without argument, they left the tent. He moved away from her a little.

"I'm sorry for what happened in Qilon. I didn't mean for that to happen."

"Of course. You used magic by mistake."

"I really had no intention of using illusion magic."

"Then why did you do it?"

"I guess I was a little insecure. I didn't know how you would react to our reunion."

"Oh, please, Haydn! That was three years ago. What did you believe? That I weep for you because you changed your mind overnight and sent me away?"

"No, of course not. I don't know what I was thinking either."

He seemed contrite, but she ignored it. The memory flared up. She had taken the path across the Lor'sul Mountains in search of her father. Haydn had saved her from bear-like ice beasts. These creatures were much larger than bears and capable of turning other beings into ice. Even then, at just eighteen years old, his illusion magic had been amazingly powerful.

"You haven't changed, Haydn. You still conceal the truth."

His penetrating eyes scrutinized her. "For you, it didn't matter what status I had. Only I, as a person, counted. This was new for me. I wanted to tell you who I was, but there was never a good moment."

"When you brought me back to the border, that would have been a good time."

"It wouldn't have changed anything."

"You presented me with a fait accompli. I've often wondered what mistake I made. Do you think I couldn't have handled the truth?" She knew she would have, even though she had been in love with him.

"Maybe I chose the easiest way for me," he said softly.

She ignored the pain spreading through her chest. "All that is in the past. Tell me what you want from me now."

He raised his eyebrows. He looked undecided. Instead of answering her question, he explained again, "Anyone who crosses the border into Dar'Angaar without express permission risks the death penalty."

"You are the king!"

"Even as king, I must abide by the laws of my country. What kind of ruler would I be if I put myself above the law?"

"Am I right in thinking that there is a way for me to save my head?"

"I have to get something. You've already picked that up. If you cooperate, I'd be inclined to override the death penalty due to special circumstances."

With his head tilted, he looked deep into her eyes. She withstood his gaze until she felt uneasy.

"It's that simple? I help you, and you let me go?"

"I'll let you go, but it won't be easy."

"What's the deal with this crystal?"

"A relic from the Ancient Era. That's all you need to know. I want it. Help me, and we'll be even."

His facial expression was serious and surreptitious, but his eyes told her that he spoke the truth. He meant every word he said. What else could she do but accept the deal?

"I agree," she pressed out.

Should an escape opportunity arise, she would take it! Until then, she had to play along.

Haydn patted his thighs. "Get ready. We leave in half an hour."

He rose and left her alone in the tent.

The afternoon sun burned unbearably on her face. Hunger gnawed at her. Out of the corner of her eye, she kept noticing Haydn looking at her. If it annoyed him that she rode with Aval, he didn't show it.

Maverick directed his stallion next to Aval's horse. "Why can an emissary of King Louis fight like a warrior?"

She turned to him, looking at him closely for the first time. His dark hair was razor short. A fine scar stretched across his tanned left cheek. His green eyes sparkled curiously.

"Guess my parents wanted to make sure I could fight back," she replied, her face glowing.

"Having a man by your side should keep you safe."

Pah! She snorted contemptuously. "I can take care of myself."

Maverick laughed. "That's why you're enjoying our company now, because you did so well."

"Who told you I didn't mean to do that? Master spy for the king—remember?" She smirked at his befuddled face. Served him right.

Her satisfaction did not escape him. His eyes lit up. "Of course, sweetheart, you seem quite eager to sacrifice yourself for our king."

Sacrifice? "We have a deal. That's why I'm helping you."

"Like you helped us in the battle?" Now it was he who smirked.

She gave him an evil look. "Next time, I'll let you die."

"You've already taken us into your heart, you just won't admit it," he said with amusement.

He laughed out loud, and she sensed that Aval was also trying to suppress a laugh. Maverick winked at her and rode back to Haydn. She would find a way to escape. After all, they trusted her enough that her hands were no longer tied.

After what felt like an eternity, they reached a forest that looked like a city wall made of tall trees and dense leaves. She took a deep breath of the fresh, cool air.

"We are not far from a stream. There we will rest. The sun will set soon," said Aval.

After about half an hour, they reached a shady clearing. A stream babbled on the opposite side. Aval, Maverick, and Folnar dismounted and walked to the water.

She was just considering the possibility of grabbing the reins and riding away when she felt Haydn's hands on her waist. He lifted her off the horse. Even when she had solid ground under her feet, he did not let go.

A shiver ran down her spine. She hastily detached from him. "I don't need your help."

"A simple 'thank you' would have sufficed," he replied. "You belong to us now."

"Wrong. I'm only going along with this because I'm your prisoner, and I have no choice."

"Don't make me regret my decision. You need me more than I need you. Your life is at stake, *Kardia mou.*"

His words squeezed the air from her lungs. "Don't ever call me that again!" she hissed.

He eyed her carefully as he leaned forward. "Because of our shared past, you are still alive." His voice sounded deeper, softer.

"We agreed to put the past behind us. Stick to it."

She left him standing alone and marched towards the stream.

Her head was pounding, and her breathing was shallow. She looked for a spot far away from the men and splashed cold water on her face. What a relief! She peeled her clothes off and sat down in the stream. It was wonderfully invigorating.

Wistfully, she got out of the water after a while. There was blood on her dusty leather armor. She took the dark green tunic and black riding pants out of her bag. After she had dressed and combed her wet hair, she washed her clothes in the stream, taking her time. When she was finished, she leaned her head back. The sun colored the sky red, announcing the end of the day. She couldn't put it off any longer, so she returned to the camp. Everyone stared at her as she joined them at the fire.

"What?" she asked sullenly.

"You're a lot prettier than I thought," Maverick said. "I almost didn't recognize you without all the dirt and blood."

She grimaced and stuck her tongue out at him. "A bath would do you good, too. It would be a relief for my nose."

Aval patted Maverick on the shoulder. "True words."

The men had not only built a fire but had also unsaddled the horses and prepared sleeping blankets. She counted only four.

"I'm afraid we don't have any more blankets," Aval said.

"I'm sharing my sleeping space with you," Haydn declared.

No! was Liya's first thought. She looked around for another solution. She really didn't want to be that close to him. She felt him watching her closely, but she ignored it. She sighed; the only option would be to share with one of his companions. And that was strange, too.

Folnar handed her a piece of bread with cheese. Gratefully, she took it and bit off with relish.

"So, what's the plan? What do I have to do?" she asked.

Maverick crossed his hands behind his head. "We'll march into Ebra's palace, steal the crystal, and leave."

"Ebra?" she asked.

"My uncle," Haydn replied. "He stole it a long time ago. We're going to get it back."

"Now that you are king, why can't you just order him to surrender?"

Haydn's face showed no emotion. "Only a few know that the crystal is in Ebra's principality. I want to keep it that way. I want as little as possible to get out about the crystal. We'll steal it quietly. Ebra will notice, but he won't catch us. Besides, he can't go after his king without a lot of ado."

"Why shouldn't your people know about it? "

"Because I said so."

"Of course, *Your Majesty*."

Folnar cleared his throat. "The device that holds the crystal is secured with a mechanism from the Ancient Era. It won't be that easy to steal. I will practice with you."

"A mechanism?"

"Beams of light that burn your skin as soon as they hit you. It also sets off alarms. There's a secret shaft that you can use to get into the room."

"How would you have stolen the crystal if I hadn't run into you?"

"There probably would have been more blood, sweetheart. But now, our king thinks it will be a better idea to make use of a skilled little thief," Maverick said.

"How are you going to smuggle me in?"

"Not at all. You accompany us and play a role," Maverick replied.

Surprised, she looked from one to the other. What was that supposed to mean?

She wanted to ask Maverick what he thought it meant, but Haydn rose and said, "I suggest we go to sleep now and discuss the rest tomorrow. It's going to be a long day. I'll take the first watch."

She breathed a sigh of relief. Before she fell asleep, she would not have to lie next to him. Wordlessly, all but Haydn wrapped themselves in their blankets. Silence fell in the camp. She stared up at the night sky.

Why is this crystal so important? She pondered the situation. Sakima had mentioned the gates that King Keldor had opened. The Guardians would have prevented him from passing through. Did the crystal have something to do with it? Was it, in the end, the key to opening the gates?

Goosebumps formed on her arms. She would not flee; instead, she'd steal that crystal and find out what all this was about. Haydn obviously had exactly the information King Louis needed.

Shortly before sunrise, Liya woke up. Haydn had his arm around her waist. Her heart began racing. She tried to free herself from his embrace. As soon as she moved, his grip tightened, and he pulled her closer to him. His warm breath tickled her neck.

"I like the way your hair smells," he murmured sleepily.

She ignored the pleasant warmth that his proximity gave her. With a jerk, she freed herself, jumped up, and fled to the creek. The cool water drove away the last signs of fatigue.

"You must be an early riser?" asked Folnar.

She hadn't noticed him. "Actually, no," she pressed out.

"Is it true that you are King Louis' spy?"

"Yes."

"I wonder to what extent we can trust you. Louis is our enemy, after all. And the action at Ebra's palace is delicate."

"What do you want? I'm helping you because Haydn promised to release me afterward. That's a good reason."

He looked at her urgently, as if weighing her words. At last, he said, more to himself, "You're actually too young for this kind of assignment."

"You're not much older."

"I was trained for this."

"Maybe it's the same with me."

His gaze wandered over her body. "You're a girl—a petite girl."

"Underestimating me would be a big mistake."

"Maverick and Aval told me about your fighting skills. But other talents are needed in a theft."

"What part do you play in this funny ensemble?" She made a sweeping hand gesture toward the camp.

"I'm an assassin."

Had she heard wrong? Folnar—an assassin, a contract killer? Images of murdered families came to her mind.

"I don't kill innocent people." He'd noticed her bewilderment.

"Isn't that what all *assassins* claim?" She focused on the magic inside her, directed a touch of it at him, and detected no hint of a lie. What she sensed was concern, excitement, and joy. *Interesting*, she thought.

"I don't have to justify myself to you, *spy*," he replied.

This conversation was getting nowhere. "Show me how to get past those beams of light!" she demanded, changing the subject.

A grin replaced the harshness of his expression. He went to the horses and took something out of his saddlebag. He returned with several ropes that he stretched between tree trunks, some higher, some lower. In some places, they crossed each other. In the end, the mesh was a maze.

"What is this?" she asked as he smiled at his artwork.

"Just like these ropes, the rays of light run in the room where the crystal is kept. You must pass through this tangle. However, you cannot see the light rays, so you must memorize this pattern. Every movement, every sequence, you will learn *by heart*."

Her gaze oscillated between the labyrinth and Folnar. "You mean that?"

"Absolutely. If you don't make it, we're left with Maverick's bloody variant."

"If you already know the pattern, why do you need me to do it?"

"The issue is getting into the room where the crystal is. That's why we need help—the funnel is too small for us. The way through the labyrinth of light beams is divided into fifteen movements. I will teach them to you. Watch!"

With disbelief, she watched him roll, pike, jump, and seal. He was incredibly fast. *I'll never be able to do that.* Then she remembered something. "When do we leave for the palace?"

"In three days."

That can't be true. "Haydn wants me to do this in three days? Is he crazy?"

"Good morning, sunshine," called Maverick, who was still a few steps away from them. "Do you have to make such a racket?" He yawned heartily.

The horses neighed. Worried, she looked around.

Maverick joined them. "Everything is fine," he said. "Haydn and Sonaris are riding to the next village. They'll be back in three days. You'd better start practicing, honey."

She rolled her eyes. "Haydn is clearly crazy. You're all crazy."

The next two days flew by. Folnar did his best to drive her insane. Liya discovered muscles she had never known existed. In the evenings, she ran through the sequences, over and over again, before falling asleep. Until that afternoon, she had only made it once, and she had only half a day left. Deeply frustrated, she trotted to the river. Her tunic clung to her like a second skin, and her hair had developed a life of its own.

"Don't take too much time. Soon there will be dinner—hot dinner!" Folnar called after her cheerfully.

Maverick and Folnar had been fishing for a while. Judging by their comments, they had been successful. Her stomach growled suspiciously at the thought of food. She couldn't complain, though. The rations were not large, but they were sufficient.

Without thinking, she took off her clothes and jumped into the stream. Her heated body relaxed in the cool water. When the smell of fried fish reached her, her stomach growled. She left the water and put on Folnar's shirt, which he had left for her. After all, she didn't want to sleep in her leather armor. The shirt reached her knees. She quickly washed her tunic and hurried back to the camp.

"Don't you dare eat it all, Maverick!" she shouted boisterously as she hung her tunic on a long branch.

"Then you'd better hurry, honey. The fish tastes delicious!" Maverick yelled back.

She smirked. He would save some for her, all right. The only question was how much. In a cheerful mood, she turned around and bumped into Haydn. She staggered, and he grabbed her arms.

His blue eyes, framed by long, dark lashes, shone brighter from one second to the next. He pulled her close to him.

"You! " She managed to look scornful, whereupon Haydn immediately let her go.

His eyes wandered along her body, and his expression darkened. "Are you having fun?" he pressed out.

"So far, yes!"

A muscle twitched in his jaw. She had no idea why he was mad, but she didn't care. Without waiting for a reply, she walked past him.

Maverick grinned mischievously at her. "Just in time."

She sat down with him and took the plate from his hand. Aval sat down next to Folnar. Not for the first time, she noticed the looks they gave each other, almost tender.

"Did they treat you well?" asked Haydn.

"Folnar always drives me crazy with his maze. And Maverick, well, Maverick is just the way he is. It's a wonder he's survived this long."

The men burst out laughing. The corners of her mouth twitched as well. But something was wrong. How could she have fun with them? She was facing the death penalty, and Haydn was taking advantage of her. These were her enemies. Only, it didn't feel that way.

"How are the exercises going?" inquired Aval.

"She'll be fine," Folnar replied.

"Honestly," she countered, shaking her head, "I'd need a lot of luck to get out of that room alive."

"You'll be fine. We believe in you," Maverick snorted.

Grinning, she slapped the flat of her hand against her forehead. "What did you put in the fish, Folnar? Maverick is complimenting me. He must have gone crazy."

"My general went crazy?" Haydn's voice sounded right next to her ear. "What on earth happened in my absence?"

"There's nothing wrong with me. After all, I caught three fish with my bare hands," Maverick said proudly and began to explain his fishing technique.

"Should I ask why you're wearing Folnar's shirt?" Haydn whispered.

She turned to him. "No, because it's none of your business."

He laughed softly. "That hits me hard." He clutched his chest theatrically.

"You'd have to have a heart for that."

His eyes flashed with amusement. With a gallant gesture, he took her hand and guided it to his chest. "Do you hear it beating, *Kardia mou*?"

She quickly withdrew her hand and turned her attention back to her fish. Fortunately, it was already dark, so no one saw her heated cheeks.

"When do we leave?" inquired Folnar.

"Tomorrow in the morning. Ebra is expecting us," Haydn replied.

Aval stretched out his feet. "We have beautiful clothes for you, Liya."

"What do I need that for? I'm supposed to crawl through a shaft and steal the crystal."

Haydn's eyes rested on her. "That can only be done once you're inside. You will enter my uncle's palace by my side."

"What exactly does 'by your side' mean?"

"You're going to take… well… Beth's role."

Had she heard wrong? What an absurd idea.

"We have no resemblance at all," she groaned.

"Ebra doesn't know what my intended looks like."

Well, well, she thought, *this whole idea is absurd.* Besides, she had her own plans. She just needed to play along.

"How should I act to make it seem real?" she asked. "What's Beth like?"

"She is very caring and in love with me, and she doesn't contradict me. It's all very simple for you."

Maverick slapped his mouth to stifle a laugh.

"You can't be serious. I can't."

"What, exactly? Agree with me or act enamored?"

She threw her hands in the air. "I'm surrounded by crazy people."

"A little illusion magic will help," Haydn explained cheerfully. "I'll give you the appearance of a docile, well-mannered princess."

That too! "We're all going to die!" she exclaimed.

"Like Maverick said, we believe in you."

"Then, Haydn, you're all idiots."

With that, she stood up and marched to her blanket. Never in her life had she embarked on a mission so ill-prepared. Eryon was teeming with spies. It would not surprise her if Ebra also used the same means. What exactly did Haydn's uncle know? They had no idea. Hopelessness spread through her. All she'd needed was information—how could she have gotten herself into this mess?

After a while, she felt movement at her back and pretended to be asleep.

Looking out of the carriage window, Liya studied the mighty Lor'sul mountain range. Snow-capped peaks rose high into the sky, serene and peaceful. Maverick had arranged for the carriage in the small village, while Aval had stayed at the inn. Haydn had whispered to him at breakfast, and they had parted ways. Would they really reach Ebra's palace at sunset? Haydn eyed her carefully but did not say a word.

She avoided looking at him, concentrating instead on the surroundings. The closer they got to the mountains, the wider the path became, and the rocky ground was replaced by gravel.

She spotted a vast city in the distance. The snow-white wall of the city would probably glow even in the dark. It stretched as far as the eye could see, to the hills toward the west and the plain toward the east. A massive castle perched on a hill above the city. Spellbound, she stared at the magnificent structure.

They passed the imposing gate in the white city wall. The two guards on duty saluted them. Although Haydn had explained to her that his stay with Ebra would not be made public, the soldiers were informed about the king's unofficial visit. Cursing softly, Maverick rummaged through his leather pouch.

"Ah!" He took out a box the size of Liya's palm, opened it, and pulled something out. "Here it is." He handed her a small transparent ball.

"What am I supposed to do with this?"

"You put it in your ear, and then we can talk."

With her mouth open, she stared at Maverick. Was he making fun of her again? Grinning, he put a bullet in his ear and took two more out of the box. Haydn and Folnar took them from him and did the same. Haydn turned his wrist and tapped it twice. A green band with numbers on it appeared.

"I'm connecting us. I'm one, you're two, Maverick's three, and Folnar's four. If you want to talk to one of us, you just tap the number to your ear."

Maverick leaned forward. "Of course, Haydn can invite us all in for a chat."

Curious, she looked at the object. "Is this from the Ancient Era?"

"Yes, we found it by accident. It's extremely useful," Haydn confirmed.

She hesitated briefly, then put the ball in her ear and tapped three times.

"Yes, sweetie?" Maverick's voice rang in her ear.

"How can I end the conversation?" She grinned.

"By pressing on it longer with your finger."

Fascinated, she watched Haydn do something with his finger on his wrist.

She heard him say, "Test."

"I hear you," Folnar said.

"Me, too," Maverick said.

She confirmed too.

"Please keep these bullets in your ear at all times. No one can see them. When you use them, take good care. No one must notice anything," Haydn said and ended the contact.

Mockingly, she raised her eyebrow and looked directly at him. His face darkened.

"Your freedom is at hand," he said tersely. "Soon, you'll have it."

When she looked out the window again, the carriage was already at the foot of the hill on which the castle stood. It stopped in front of a massive gate. Maverick got out and spoke to a guard.

"What about the illusion spell?" She looked at Haydn.

"I changed my mind."

"What does that mean?" she hissed.

"You will act as my mistress. Because you're right. We have no information about Ebra's level of knowledge regarding Beth."

"You're just telling me this now?"

"I changed my mind a few minutes ago."

She glowered at him. "You just got engaged, and you bring a mistress? He'll never buy that."

"Let me worry about that. You play your part; I'll play mine."

A guard opened the carriage door, and they got out. Only with the greatest effort did Liya manage to control her emotions. She had to concentrate now. She would play her role, commit a theft, and then return to Namoor—with the crystal in her luggage.

Four guards led them through the ornate iron gate into a huge courtyard. Soldiers were posted everywhere in front of the three-story, light-colored stone castle. She especially noticed the colorful windows. The towers rising far into the sky seemed to touch the glistening afternoon sun. In front of the entrance portal, two uniformed men stood on each side. They wore gray robes and silver breastplates. Inside, a fluffy carpet led to two massive, richly decorated wooden doors. Here, too, soldiers stood guard.

Fear seized Liya. Her instincts sounded an alarm, and her stomach rebelled. This place was cold; there was no warmth. She could always sense danger, and this place cried out for it. She never doubted her sense.

When the soldiers opened the doors, she sought eye contact with Haydn. His expression was impenetrable. For a brief moment, she saw the gentleness in his eyes. Then, with Haydn, she entered the largest hall she had ever seen. Maverick and Folnar followed. The floor was of the purest marble. They walked in front of an entire wall front made of glass, into which were set colorful pictures of various scenes. Purple curtains dimmed the light.

"My nephew—our new king!" someone shouted in a subdued voice.

The way they said it made her blood run cold. The voice sounded disparaging, without any warmth. Instinctively, she wanted to back away. For a brief moment, the thought of grabbing Haydn's hand and turning back crossed her mind.

A middle-aged man with a few graying strands in his pitch-black hair came toward them. He was not much shorter than Haydn, but somewhat stronger built.

"Uncle!" Haydn said curtly.

Exuberantly, Ebra hugged him and patted him on the shoulder. "Who did you bring?"

"This woman I met at a ball. She makes for a pleasurable trip. You already know Maverick and Folnar, part of my bodyguard." Haydn's voice sounded hard and cold. He played his role brilliantly.

With a smug smile, Ebra extended his hand to her. "Welcome to my city, *my lady*."

The mocking undertone did not escape her. She performed a curtsy. "I'm glad to be here."

While Ebra kissed the back of her hand, he did not take his eyes off her. Without making a face, she withstood his gaze.

She noticed a slight smirk before he continued, turning to Haydn, "Come now! The evening games will soon begin. For the next three days, I have come up with something special, dear nephew, to celebrate your visit—which is now truly historic."

Haydn nodded to his uncle. She wondered what was going on in his mind. They followed the prince. Involuntarily, Liya tensed her shoulders. Ebra amplified the uneasy feeling.

"We don't plan to stay long. We are expected back the day after tomorrow," Haydn said.

Abruptly, Ebra stopped and looked at him. His expression was inscrutable. "I'm sure you'll agree that we should put the past behind us. My wretched brother has finally passed away; I open my kingdom to you. But do not make a fool of me! This offer is unique. It's up to you whether you accept it or not. Participating in the games would be a good start."

The warning undertone of Ebra's voice sent an icy shiver down Liya's spine. Without waiting for an answer, he continued his way through the hall. Why hadn't Haydn defended his father? The whole thing seemed strange to her. At the end of the hall, an oval table was set, at which several people were already seated. A lady with dark circles under her eyes but a gentle look to her face rose to her feet.

"My dear nephew!" Her voice sounded warm. She kissed Haydn on the cheek and smiled.

"You will surely remember Yara, the mother of my children," said Ebra. Sweeping, he pointed to the young people and a little girl sitting next to the princess. "Ebradis—my second eldest son, Ithos, and Rhimor." He grinned. "My youngest daughter Mayra had her fifth birthday yesterday."

Ebradis was the spitting image of his father. Ithos and Rhimor, with their brown hair and green eyes, resembled Yara. Judging by Ebra's nonchalant hand gestures, she understood that his sons only played the role of his subordinates. Liya was still undecided about whom Mayra resembled. She clearly had the darker skin tint of her father, but she could not find more similarities.

Ebra pressed a kiss on the forehead of a young woman, around the same age as Liya, and continued, "You will remember Tafriani best, my dear Haydn." His lips twisted mockingly.

Liya felt a stab in the region of her heart. Why did this remark bother her? Tafriani was a dark-haired beauty with almond-shaped eyes. Her auburn hair was braided back, and the eye patch she wore did nothing to diminish her radiance. Her skin was a little paler than her siblings. One black eye fixed Haydn as she nodded briefly at him. Unlike her mother and sister, she wore gray pants and a wine-red leather short coat.

"I am happy to see you again. It's been a long time. May I introduce you to Liya?" Haydn took her hand. "She is my companion for the next few days."

The way he said it left no doubt as to what he meant. She suppressed the desire to hit him or yell at him. Instead, she lowered her eyelids and played the shy lover.

Haydn pointed to Maverick and Folnar. "My officers will ensure our safety on this trip."

If this bothered Ebra, he didn't show it. He clapped his hands in glee. "Let's go outside. The games are waiting for us, and the hall still needs to be prepared for tonight."

He snapped, and a group of guards rushed over. Two soldiers went ahead. The princely family and Haydn's entourage followed. Two more guards brought up the rear. Through a small door behind the panel, they entered a narrow corridor. There were no windows, and it smelled musty. Lamps, however, provided enough light.

Liya couldn't shake the feeling that this was a secret path and wondered why Ebra was revealing it. They turned several times before reaching a gallery.

"We are now in the east wing. This is where our theater is located," Ebra explained proudly.

The elliptical reception hall led to a spacious terrace. From there, loud noises and laughter reached them. Ebra directed them to elevated, gold-backed seats. All around, conversations fell silent, and guests bowed.

The guards lined up behind their chairs. Ebra had assigned his nephew and her the seats in the middle. He himself took a seat next to Haydn, while Ebradis sat next to Liya. Yara and her daughters joined Ebra, and the other two sons joined Ebradis. Maverick and Folnar remained behind Haydn and her. In front of the terrace, a theater with awnings stretched out over an oval arena. From their elevated position, they had a good view of all the action. Theater was perhaps not the most appropriate term. The floor was sandy, and the spectators were seated on marble benches, each row slightly higher than the one in front, ensuring a clear view of the arena.

Liya estimated the number of visitors at about a hundred. She was overcome by the oppressive feeling that perhaps the theater performances were not the only thing taking place here. She looked at the gilded railing in front of her with some trepidation. When Ebra rose, trumpets sounded. The audience fell silent. He strode forward to the railing.

"Dear friends, dear people! I am pleased to announce a new era. My nephew, our king, is the first visitor from the capital in many years. In his honor, we will hold these games for three days and bring the legends to life."

He turned to Haydn with shining eyes. His face beamed with joy. He must be up to something. He gave Haydn a broad grin before turning his attention back to the spectators.

"Today, we will tell the legend of the origin of our kingdom. Hardly anyone knows all the legends of the time when magic overshadowed everything, until our ancestor, King Eirik, put an end to it." He raised his hand. "Sal, come join us."

A rotund older man hurried over and bowed to Ebra, who took his seat. Sal went to the railing, spread his arms, and waited. There was a tense silence.

"Once upon a time, there existed a kingdom that had the magic of the Elders." His voice echoed through the hall. "Elladur! Hardly anyone dared to speak the name. Allyria, the princess of Elladur, was the high priestess. She combined perfect beauty and magic in her being."

Liya held her breath. A few days ago, Sakima had told her about Elladur. She did not believe in coincidences.

Thunderous applause erupted. A woman in a floor-length white dress entered the arena. Her blond hair reached her waist, and a sword shone in her hand.

"The princess fell in love with a boy named El'Orim."

A man appeared on the other side of the arena. His muscular, naked torso was covered with tattoos of black ink. The audience applauded loudly, and Liya's pulse quickened at the sight of him. She felt heat rising in her cheeks and dared not look at Haydn. Out of the corner of her eye, she noticed Ebradis watching her. Nervously, she hoped that her face did not betray her thoughts.

With a raised hand, the storyteller urged silence. "They were young and in love. Allyria decided to run away from home to start a new life with El'Orim after her father forbade the relationship. For El'Orim was no ordinary man—he was a dragon! But fate had something else in mind."

With a creaking sound, another door opened. Soldiers rushed toward El'Orim. He deftly dodged the first attacks, but he had no weapon, only a shield to defend himself. One soldier pierced his shoulder with his sword. Another threw a net over him. The white sand turned red while the audience applauded in wild rapture.

Liya froze. These were not games. People were getting hurt, possibly even dying, but no one seemed to mind. On the contrary, the audience clapped more and more euphorically. Her heart raced, and her stomach tightened. Haydn had not exaggerated. Ebra was a monster. She saw Folnar clench his hand into a fist, while Maverick's face showed no emotion.

Sal raised his hand, and a short trumpet blast sounded.

"When Allyria arrived at the agreed meeting place, she caught sight of her wounded lover. Soldiers held him down. Using her magic, which dated back to the days of the Elders, she tried to free El'Orim."

The sky above the arena slowly turned reddish, as if announcing the battle. Allyria ran screaming to the dozen soldiers. One by one, they struggled with her, the only sound in the arena the clanging of metal. She dodged the attacks, whirled her sword, and managed to hit the first man in the neck. Blood splattered on her dress as she delivered the death blow. The second attacker seemed to be in shock, and the woman killed him with two blows. The soldiers attacked individually, not daring to attack as a group. Only when half of them were dead did they launch a three-pronged attack. A punch knocked the princess to the ground. The men kicked her, but her screams were drowned out by the raging crowd.

Liya's breathing quickened. Whoever this woman was, she was being publicly flogged.

"Don't worry, the actors are prisoners who deserve to die," Ebra said, leaning over to Haydn and her.

One of the men grabbed the woman's head and dragged her by the hair to the wounded El'Orim.

Sal raised his voice again. "Despite her magic, Allyria suffered severe injuries."

One of the bloodied soldiers dragged her away, kissed her brutally, and punched her in the face. She fell to the ground.

Liya would have liked to get up and leave the stands, but she had to continue watching Ebra's death game. She could not rebel against him without risking all their lives. She knew that she would not last three days of this brutality. She had to get to the crystal as soon as possible. A loud blast from the trumpet silenced the crowd.

Sal shouted, "But El'Orim freed himself from the net. When he touched Allyria, he combined his dragon power with her magic. Despite their injuries, they managed to kill all of their attackers."

Liya felt a brief, faint spark of magic.

Ebradis rose and went to the railing. Fireballs shot from his hands at the soldiers, sparing Allyria and El'Orim. Their bodies lit up like kindling, and the screams of the men went through Liya's spine. Ebradis was delivering the crushing blow of Allyria and El'Orim. This prince's son disgusted her deeply. Even the audience fell silent in the face of the burning men. Ebradis fired until the screaming died away.

Liya felt the fear of the people around her—this was what Ebradis had intended. He wanted to be feared. Men in black appeared to extinguish the burning bodies. She felt sick. She looked at Haydn and noted the horror that flickered briefly in his eyes.

After Ebradis sat down, Sal cleared his throat and continued. "They defeated the attackers, but his beloved was fighting for her life. When

El'Orim's companions, the Dragon Men, appeared, he asked them to save Allyria. Unanimously, an alliance was formed between Elladur and the Empire of Dragons. This blood alliance would stand the test of time, but it would bring about the most terrible war the world has yet known—the Great War."

Thunderous applause echoed in the theater as a jeering audience celebrated the prelude to the cruelest play Liya had ever seen. The charred bodies left on stretchers as Ebra's soldiers entered the arena. They formed a circle around the woman and the man.

Ebra turned to Liya and Haydn. "Now comes the climax." He rose, strode to the railing, silenced the crowd with a wave of his hand, and shouted, "El'Orim is no longer with us, but one of his descendants lives—a descendant of the Dragon Beings. We were led to believe they were extinct."

Dragon beings? Ebra could not seriously believe that they actually existed. In Namoor, children were told stories of creatures that looked like humans but could transform into dragons. In this form, they flew around and took naughty children. There were no limits to the imagination of storytellers.

With his index finger, Ebra performed a few strange movements. She lost her breath when she felt strong magic resonating around her.

Someone roared, "Show us your wings, dragon!" The crowd went wild.

Desperately, Liya shook her head, trying to sort out her confused thoughts. She struggled for breath, everything in her screaming, *No!* At that very moment, the man in the arena raised his head. She felt his gaze rest on her, though he was much too far away.

"Show us your wings, dragon!" the crowd chanted.

The surroundings blurred before her eyes. some pieces of the puzzle came together, and she realized something. Ebra knew about the gates.

Just like Keldor, he wanted to open them. She had no idea what lay behind the gates, nor did she understand exactly what Sakima meant by the bond between the worlds, but it was about power and magic; there was no doubt about that. What role did the crystal play? Perhaps it *was* the key to opening the gates. She did not believe that Ebra had invited the son of his unloved dead brother to improve family relations. No! Haydn possessed something that Ebra needed. Feverishly, she tried to clear her head.

"Show us your wings!" hissed Ebra. With another wave of his hand, he forced the man to his knees. The audience roared.

As the performer playing El'Orim struggled to get up, Ebra drew more signs in the air. He became more and more impatient, and then he cursed softly. When he turned to Haydn and Liya, his face was dark red with anger. This man was clearly crazy, and that frightened her.

"I'll teach him a lesson," Ebra muttered. "Then his healing skills won't help him either." With a devilish smile, he turned to Mayra. "My darling, would you like to watch your father?"

The little girl jumped up. "Yes, I'll come with you."

Yara rose as well. "Ebra, she has seen enough for today."

The look Ebra gave his wife made Liya's blood run cold. His eyes were full of hatred and disgust.

"She is not like you—she is *my* daughter. Take care of the banquet hall. Rhimar and Ithos will go with you. Ebradis and Tafriani, you accompany Mayra and me!"

Although Liya was afraid of further cruelty, she needed to know what happened next and what it was about descendants of dragons and their magic. She rose to her feet. "I don't want to miss this either." Her voice sounded firm in her ears, though she trembled inside.

Haydn rose. "An excellent idea. Let's go!" To Maverick and Folnar, he said, "You wait here." His face revealed nothing.

Surprised, Ebra raised his eyebrow, then laughed. "Your *company* seems to like my games."

He patted Haydn on the shoulder, then took Mayra by the hand and motioned for them to follow. Ebradis and Tafriani joined them. While Ebra talked in detail about the reconstruction of his palace planned for the summer, Liya tried to sort out her feelings. Under no circumstances could she show weakness. Whatever Ebra had in mind, it would be terrible, she was sure of that.

They reached a staircase, in front of which was a door leading to a vaulted corridor. There were no windows. Torches in wall sconces lit the way in intervals. Haydn let Tafriani go first and took Liya's hand. The corrosive smell of burnt flesh assailed her nostrils. Her stomach turned. Via a narrow staircase, they reached a cellar with cells. She heard the moans of the prisoners. Silently they walked on.

At last, light appeared at the end of the tunnel. The smell of clammy, damp earth replaced the stench. Men in dark robes blocked the way through a massive open door. When they saw Ebra, they bowed their heads respectfully and stepped aside.

Her heart pounded as they entered the arena. The spectators were still sitting in the stands, watching the spectacle. The circle of soldiers around the man who represented El'Orim opened to let the prince through. Ebra stood before the unfortunate man. His little daughter held his hand, her large eyes reflecting sheer terror. Ebradis and Tafriani stayed behind, while Haydn and Liya stood next to Ebra.

El'Orim got to his feet. His eyes rested on her. Among his many tattoos, the image of a dragon caught her attention. The dragon's head was emblazoned on his chest, its mouth wide open over his heart. Blood dripped from the man's shoulder. She noticed bandages on his leg.

"Do you really think you can stand up to me?" asked Ebra in anger. When the man remained silent, he slapped him. "Kaldru, I'm talking to you!"

"I am not afraid to die," Kaldru replied in a calm, low voice, turning his gaze to Ebra.

"We had an agreement," the prince pressed out. "You were to show your wings."

"Dragons exist only in legends."

Ebra let go of his daughter's hand, who moved closer to Liya. Trembling with anger, Ebra gestured to a soldier, who handed him his sword.

Liya took Mayra's hand and leaned down to her. "If it gets to be too much, just close your eyes. I won't tell anyone, not even your father," she whispered.

The girl nodded and clung to her arm.

Kaldru looked at Liya again. "Something in my head said no," he breathed.

"Kaldru, perhaps you are not afraid to die. But most become weak when death or suffering threatens someone they care about. Your friend seems suitable in our case."

The sound of metal whizzed through the air. Allyria, standing next to Kaldru, cried out as he severed her hand. Crying, she fell to the ground, holding her stump.

"I don't have any friends," Kaldru groaned. "You should know that." He spat at Ebra's feet.

But she had seen something else in his dark eyes. He had feelings for this woman. Allyria started laughing softly, getting louder and louder.

"What do you think is funny?" cried Ebra.

"You! You are pathetic and weak. We will never give up. We will fight you with every fiber until we defeat you and free the slaves."

Liya held her breath. This woman was ready to die. Allyria's gaze pleaded with Kaldru not to intervene. Then something happened that Liya would not have thought possible. She watched in disbelief as a hand slowly grew back from the stump. Humans did not have such self-healing powers!

Ebra raised the sword, but Haydn stepped forward and put a hand on his shoulder. "Uncle, you actually want to kill the leading lady? The healers had better take care of her wounds so she can perform again. I would be terribly disappointed if I couldn't see this story through to the end. After all, this is being done in my honor, isn't it?"

Liya's stomach tightened with nervousness.

"He has not kept to the agreement and must be punished," Ebra replied in a dangerously low voice.

"I think that has been sufficient. Liya and I would like to freshen up before the feast. Dusk has already set in." Even though Haydn pretended to be friendly, it was not a request.

Her heart threatened to burst. Would Ebra dare contradict the king? In recent years, he had ruled his principality like an autocrat. But the coronation had changed the political circumstances and his status. The word of a king was law.

Ebra's eyes flashed, but he nodded. Liya sensed that he obeyed only reluctantly. When Ebra turned to her, she shuddered at his expression. The brief moment of relief was wiped away. The games had just begun. And Liya realized that they were not only taking place in the arena.

Liya looked in the mirror and was startled by the tense expression on her face as she looked at herself. The floor-length burgundy dress with the heart neckline clung perfectly to her body. It was by no means too tight, yet she felt uncomfortable without her leather armor. A V-shaped stripe of tiny crystals sparkled on the top. Fortunately, the dress had no train. Sighing, she put her hair up.

She flinched at a knock on the door. Tafriani entered.

"We should get going—the first guests will be arriving soon." Ebra's daughter's dress was also burgundy, but it was off-the-shoulder with a swinging, wide skirt. A ruby necklace completed her appearance. How beautiful she was!

"Shouldn't we wait for Haydn?" asked Liya.

"He is already in the hall. My father wanted to discuss something with him."

Somewhat puzzled, she followed Tafriani down the hallway and down a spiral staircase. Laughter reached them through the wide-open doors. At the other end of the spacious hall stood a festively decorated rectangular table. Small round tables dotted the room. Although the decorations were perfectly coordinated with the colorful windows and the red and black roses, nothing could mitigate the lurking air of heartlessness.

Liya shivered, and she found it difficult to walk. The further she moved away from the door, the stiffer her legs became. Out of the corner of her eye, she noticed girls hurriedly distributing carafes of water and wine to the tables.

In front of the large table, several armed men were talking, Haydn among them. He turned around as if he had sensed her presence. A sparkle lit up in his eyes, but it went out almost instantly. He looked at Liya, from her upswept hair to her burgundy sandals, flashing briefly from under her skirt with each step.

"Welcome, my lady," a tall man beside him greeted her.

He had hazel hair and bright turquoise eyes. During his insolent scrutiny, she showed no emotion.

Haydn followed the man's gaze. "A feast for the eyes, isn't it, cousin!"

She fought the urge to give Haydn a suitable answer and only looked at him indifferently.

"Liya, may I introduce Arlandth, Ebra's eldest son." Haydn pointed to the man with one hand.

She nodded to Arlandth. When he took her hand and breathed a kiss on her fingertips, she forced herself to smile. Arlandth gave a wave to the men in the group, whereupon they spread out among the tables in the room.

"I'm afraid you missed the round of introductions," he told her. "Let's make ourselves comfortable—dinner is about to be served. I'd be honored to sit next to you."

"Of course!" she pressed out.

What choice do I have? She let the curious looks pass over her without reaction. They were probably interested in the color of her hair, since all the others were dark-haired. She took a seat at the large table with the princely family, Haydn, and his officers. Soon after, dinner was served.

Haydn talked mostly with Ebra, who sat next to him, while Arlandth devoted himself to her.

"My father has invited his royal brother only once before," he told her good-humoredly. "I was just a little boy then. When they fell out, my father's principality was considered a renegade enclave. I guess the only reason my uncle didn't invade was because my father had quite a large army. The fact that my cousin, the new king, is being received is a historic event for the people here. You must not resent their curious glances. And what about your hair! It shines like the sun."

She listened attentively. This information was vital. "You were not present at the opening of the games in the afternoon," she asked with a smile. Maybe this way, she would learn even more without showing her interest too clearly.

Arlandth laughed. "I am no friend of this spectacle." He leaned towards her. "I much prefer to give my attention to beautiful things."

She studiously ignored his remark. "Tell me something about Aughdar. I couldn't see much because the curtains of our carriage were drawn."

"It is not very different from other capitals. However, our slaves give us a decisive advantage. There are no run-down neighborhoods in Aughdar, and we always have enough workers to cultivate the fields."

"Slaves?"

"Yes! Prisoners." He took a big gulp of wine. "Would you like to see the city?"

"Now?" A queasy feeling spread through her.

"Yeah? Why not? We could do something useful."

"I don't think this is the appropriate time," she replied, shaking her head.

"All right, later then. I'm going to stretch my legs for a minute." He grinned, got up, and went to his men, who stood in front of the window.

"Are you having a good time?" Haydn asked softly.

"It's keeping within bounds."

"Arlandth is very fond of you. Maybe we can take advantage of that."

"You want me to respond to his advances to get something out of him?"

"No, of course not. However, I would be very interested in information about the conditions here and my uncle's plans. I would only ask you to listen carefully."

He couldn't be serious. *I'm supposed to spy for* him? She couldn't answer, however, because Ebra again engaged Haydn in conversation.

While dessert was being served, she looked around the table, bored. She noticed that all the women were dressed in extremely noble fabrics and hung with expensive jewelry. She watched as the musicians entered the hall and began to play.

Arlandth returned. "Did I miss something?"

"No, there's still cake."

"I'd rather dance," he said, offering his arm.

"Gladly." She was surprised how easily the lie came from her lips.

Arlandth was by no means unattractive, but there was something wild about him that deeply troubled her. She noticed that Ebra narrowed his eyes when he saw his son leading her to the dance floor.

"Lord Ebra does not seem pleased," she whispered.

"I probably beat Ebradis to it, and he's Father's favorite," Arlandth replied. "That makes it even more fun for me to dance with you." He gently put an arm around her waist. "Ready, my lady?" he asked with a broad grin.

Arlandth proved to be an exceptional dancer. His flowing movements were one with the music.

"Surprised?" he asked.

"Is it that obvious?"

Briefly, he laughed. "Your body betrays you. At first, you were tense, and now you're not."

"How come you can dance so well?"

"My mother taught me. But we had to stop the lessons when my father found out."

"Why? Dancing is part of noble life."

He pulled her closer. "There is no reasonable explanation for it. My father has always made life difficult for me. He used to beat the crap out of me for dancing. Since my mother died, our relationship has cooled even more," he whispered.

"I'm sorry about that."

She hadn't known that Yara was Ebra's second wife. Haydn's family seemed far more complicated than she had thought.

"It doesn't matter; I would surely do it again. Some things are worth the risk." A strange expression appeared in his eyes.

"Even if it means putting your life on the line?"

"Then even more so." His expression became serious. "Wouldn't you put yourself in danger, too, if you were convinced of something?"

"I would not make such a decision lightly."

"You're in a strange city. Some would call it a reckless decision to follow a man you don't know well."

"Haydn invited me." She knew this reply made no sense.

He winked at her. When the music ended, he asked, "Can you manage one more dance? I just warmed up."

"Isn't he upset enough yet?"

He poked her nose with his index finger. "Maybe I just like dancing with you."

"Of course."

He spun her around. "You know what I really like about you?"

Playfully, she rolled her eyes. "No!"

He laughed again.

She felt a tingle on the back of her neck as an arm wrapped around her waist. "It's time for a dance."

Smiling, Arlandth released her, and Haydn pulled her close.

"You should not forget what role you are playing," he whispered.

"Can you make up your mind? You said not long ago that you wanted me to find out more."

"You don't have to make eyes at him."

Their bodies touched. His warm breath brushed her cheek as he murmured in her ear, "You belong to me."

"I get it," she pressed out.

Servants brought more wine as women in light robes appeared, walking around the hall, smiling.

"What's happening now?" she asked in wonder.

"My uncle is bringing out all the guns. He wants the female slaves to take care of the men. Wine helps with that."

"And the wives of the men who are gratified in this way just let that happen?"

Haydn squeezed her hand for a brief moment. "My aunt Yara does not rebel against it, so what chance would other women have? Aughdar is known for oppressing the female sex—more than usual."

"Terrible. These are young girls."

"Liya, I can't change everything at once in my kingdom."

She reluctantly agreed with him.

When the piece of music ended, Ebradis stood behind Haydn. "May I ask for the next dance?" Without waiting for an answer, he took Liya's hand. After Haydn reluctantly moved away, he whispered to her, "My father was very upset."

She held his gaze. "I thought you wanted to dance?"

"You obviously had a great time with my brother." His grip tightened.

"You're hurting me!"

"I think you need a strong man by your side," he replied spitefully.

She stopped and stood on her tiptoes. "I have a strong man by my side, and he doesn't like it when someone else causes me pain!" she murmured in his ear.

"Are you threatening me?"

At that moment, Yara stepped up to them. "Liya, I hope you won't be angry with me if I dance with my son one more time before I retire?"

"No, of course not," she replied with relief.

Reluctantly, Ebradis released her. Having no desire to return to the table, she meandered past the dancers to one of the large columns. Sighing, she leaned her head against the cool marble.

"Ready to look at Aughdar now?" asked Arlandth.

"I guess you won't leave my side."

"You need to be taken good care of."

"Ebradis is pretty annoyed."

"Did he say that?"

"Something like that."

"Good, my brother needs to learn his place."

She scanned the room quickly, looking for Haydn. He was standing on the other side, talking to some men who were toasting him.

"How long have you kept slaves?" she asked Arlandth.

"For seven years," he replied impassively. "Now it's my turn. Why are you here?"

"Haydn accepted his uncle's invitation. I knew nothing about the difficult family circumstances." As he eyed her curiously, she wondered if that remark might have been a mistake.

"Haydn thinks you should freshen up," Tafriani said, joining in.

"Of course," Liya replied quickly.

"I'll show you the way," she offered.

She smiled at Arlandth, who shrugged regretfully. Then she left the hall with Tafriani, breathing a sigh of relief as the doors closed behind them.

"There are washrooms up ahead," Tafriani said. She seemed to be in a hurry.

"Where are you going, ladies?"

She noticed Tafriani's body tense for a brief moment before she turned around. *What's that about?* Liya wondered as she turned and eyed the three men coming toward them. The one who had spoken devoured Tafriani with his gaze. There was no warmth in his eyes. He had short, light brown hair, and his angular face emphasized the hardness in his facial expression.

"Balrath, what do you want?" Tafriani asked coolly.

"You know." With one hand, he clasped her chin and pressed a kiss to her mouth.

Although Tafriani did not resist, her entire posture stiffened. *She detests this man.*

"Come with me, I don't want to wait anymore," he said in a hoarse voice.

"I'll escort Liya to the washroom. I'll be with you in a few minutes."

"No! My lady will find the way on her own. I have a right to you. Your father promised me."

Liya felt nauseous. Before she could say anything, Tafriani turned to her. "The washrooms are not far, the third door on the left."

She watched in disbelief as Tafriani moved away with Balrath and his men. Her mind told her it would be better to turn around and move on, to not to interfere in other people's affairs, but her gut feeling disagreed. How could Ebra rule over his daughter in this way?

"Wait!" She hurried after them. "Tafriani has orders to accompany me. I insist on it," she heard herself say.

"You will find the washrooms on your own. I have waited long enough. Now I will take what is rightfully mine," Balrath replied, narrowing his eyes.

"None less than your king has ordered Tafriani to accompany me. Will you defy him?" she purred.

"It is touching how much you care for Tafriani," Balrath grimaced. "So I will tell you something about your friend. The king did not order her to do anything. Before she lured you out of the hall, she put something in his wine. The poison probably won't kill him, but it'll weaken him. One of Ebra's sons will ask him to fight, and your officers are not in the hall. What a happy coincidence!" He laughed maliciously. "And you want to help this traitor?"

She felt herself turn pale. She stared at Tafriani with wide-open eyes. She looked past her with a blank face. Liya ran away. Her heart was beating wildly. With a trembling finger, she tapped her ear three times.

"Maverick!" she whispered, out of breath.

"Liya, what's wrong?"

"Where are you?"

"We're on our way back to the ballroom right now. We found the shaft."

"Haydn was poisoned."

"Damn you! You can't be left alone!" he hissed. "We'll be right there."

Without waiting for Maverick and Folnar, she opened the heavy door. Jeering men had gathered in front of the hall. Her pulse quickened and her stomach contracted painfully as she walked towards the group. Under no circumstances could she show any fear.

"What's going on here?" she cried cheerfully.

The men turned around. Haydn stood swaying in the circle with a pale, chalky face. Ebradis, not two meters away from him, had already raised his sword.

She giggled and hoped fervently that it sounded real. "Men! No sooner do you leave them alone for a moment than they unwrap their favorite toy." With a slight sway to her hips, she sauntered over to Haydn. "But now you will play with me, my king."

Someone whistled, others laughed loudly, and still others applauded.

"You can't just interrupt a fight." Ebra took a step forward.

"Do you want to deny your nephew this...?" Liya raised her hand and posed as her palm ran along her body. "I think we both know which game Haydn prefers."

Jeering, the men agreed with her. Ebradis came dangerously close to her, then turned to the roaring crowd.

"Look at Haydn. He won't be able to serve you today. You'd better leave him here and find a replacement."

His laughter sounded fake. His eyes looked clear and cool, as if he could sense her fear. Desperately, she tried to control her terror. But with each passing second, it spread inside her. She took a deep breath, and a surge of power and anger displaced the wave of panic.

"Let's see," she murmured and strode towards Haydn. Her heart was beating like crazy. Not only would she have to use her magic again, hoping no one would notice, she would also have to kiss Haydn. She wasn't sure what worried her more. She clasped his face with both hands, gathered her magic, and concentrated on removing at least part of the poison from his body to snap him out of his daze. As she kissed him passionately and gently, her energy flooded into his body. His eyes widened. She felt him open his mind as he returned her kiss, intimately and wildly. Panting, she broke away from him. Her cheeks burned.

"Well, I'd say that was clear!" Smiling, she took Haydn's hand and pulled him along.

Laughing, the men opened the circle. Fighting the rising nausea, she quickened her steps. She had ingested too much poison, making her weak. Not enough to cause real trouble, but enough to risk falling over. She needed to get to bed; her healing magic would be able to flush the poison from her body while she slept.

"Wait!" thundered Ebra.

Her body began to tremble. Soon, her entire dinner would make its way upstairs.

"Father, let them go!" intervened Arlandth. "Our cousin would never forgive us if we robbed him of this night. I certainly wouldn't."

She would not forget that. With the last of her strength, she continued on her way. As soon as the door closed behind them, she exhaled deeply. Maverick and Folnar hurried toward her. Luckily! They communicated with glances. They still had to be careful, because the walls had ears.

"The king wishes to retire with me," she said emphatically, calmly, and formally. "Take us to our chamber!"

As soon as they were in the room, she ran to the sink and vomited. Haydn staggered to the bed.

"Liya," he murmured.

She rinsed her mouth quickly, then sat on the edge of the bed with him. He was shaking all over, though she could see his aura glowing.

"Fight it, Haydn. Use your magic!" she whispered.

"Why doesn't he heal himself?" asked Folnar, staring at Haydn from the foot of the bed. "He has that power."

"I don't know," she replied.

"Damn! Sonaris isn't here. With his magic, he could flush this stuff out." Maverick cursed. "What do we do now?"

"Aval has the gift?" she asked in disbelief.

"Yes, but his is…complicated," Folnar replied.

Haydn was breathing shallowly, his body cooling slowly.

She couldn't believe how often she had to rely on her gift. She hated it. The memories, the pull—all of it. And now, she was forced to use her power again.

"Swear you won't tell him!" she said, wrestling with herself.

The men looked at her, confused. "What do you mean?" asked Folnar.

Hopefully, I won't make a mistake now, she prayed silently. She replied softly, "Aval is not the only one with the gift of magic."

Silence reigned.

"That's wonderful!" declared Maverick.

He sounded a little surprised, but mostly relieved. Folnar gave her an encouraging look. Of course, they had no idea. Things were different in Dar'Angaar when it came to magic.

"It's not that simple," she whispered. "In my country, magic is frowned upon. Only members of the Mages' Guild are allowed to engage in it, and they must abide by strict rules. No one must know of my gift. You must swear to me not to tell anyone, not even Haydn."

She read in their faces that they were beginning to understand.

"I swear on my life," Maverick said with finality.

"I, too, swear to you on my life." Folnar put a hand over his heart.

Gently, she channeled her magic into Haydn's body, his mind barely resisting. Dark clouds of mist appeared in the room. She absorbed the haze like air. Her breathing quickened; her heart raced; she began to sweat. No matter how much she took in, new mist kept pouring out. Her stomach churned. At last, the clouds dissipated. Heart pounding, she returned to the outside world, blinking, and saw Maverick's worried face before her.

"Take me to bed," she whispered with the last of her strength.

She enjoyed the warmth enveloping her body. *Just don't wake up!* The gentle caress on her back felt too good.

"Liya," someone whispered.

A few more minutes...

"Liya!"

Reluctantly, she opened her eyes. Haydn was lying next to her. When she realized that she had snuggled against his arm, her cheeks burned. Abruptly, she sat up.

"What are you doing in my bed?" she asked indignantly.

"You were screaming and shaking in the night."

"I don't understand," she pressed out.

The memory slowly returned. Ebra and his brood had poisoned Haydn. To save him, she had used magic. She was disgusted with herself.

"I guess my uncle's hospitality, those games, and all that wine were too much for me," he remarked.

"What do you remember?" She moved away from him a little.

"I had some wine. After that, everything blurred, but I felt incredibly strong, almost winged. Ebradis started fighting, and I wanted to fight with him." He ran his hand through his hair and grinned. "But you stopped me with a kiss. Guess I fell asleep at some point and only woke up to your scream."

Inwardly, she breathed a sigh of relief.

"You gave me quite a scare," he continued. "What was the matter with you? And why are you still wearing your dress?"

"It was probably too much for me, too."

He eyed her intently. "Liya, look at me." His soft voice made her shiver pleasantly. With one finger, he lifted her chin, his blue eyes looking directly at her. "We can stop this at any time."

"What about the crystal?"

"I'll find another way." His voice sounded rough.

"We have an agreement. The crystal against my freedom. Remember?"

"I'm not going to kill you. You know that."

As she saw the storm that raged in his eyes, her breath hitched. Everything inside her felt warm. Her heart tightened. She was far too close to him!

"We should get up," she gasped, but her body did not obey.

"We should," he replied hoarsely.

Then she felt his lips on her mouth, like a bolt of lightning. *No!* She pushed him away. "Don't ever do that again!"

"Should I wait until you kiss me?" he asked with a grin on his face.

"Not going to happen," she hissed, standing up quickly and disappearing behind the screen.

"You can't know that."

"You bet I do." She dressed hastily.

There was a knock at the door. Without waiting, Maverick entered, followed by Folnar.

"Breakfast for the lovers," Maverick chirped.

What was she to make of *that*?

"All over the palace, they tell of our lady's passion," Maverick continued.

Haydn winked at her as she stepped out from behind the screen. She felt herself blush.

Folnar sat down at the table and motioned for them to take a seat. "We found the shaft," he explained matter-of-factly. "It's in the west wing."

Maverick set the tray down, took a seat, and popped a piece of bacon into his mouth. "Right now, there is a small reception with Ebra's family. Yara has sent an invitation to tea," he reported with his mouth full. "I suggest you two pose as lovers to distract everyone and then retire. Then, while Liya has to get some rest, the Royal Majesty will distract his uncle."

"Sounds like a plan." Something occurred to her. "What about Tafriani? She poisoned Haydn's wine. I don't think she did it of her own free will, though. She seems at the mercy of her father. I find it hard to believe that Ebra promised to give his daughter to that creep, Barlath."

Maverick frowned. "She made an attempt on the king's life."

"We have no evidence of that," Haydn said.

Maverick clicked his tongue. "Barlath said it, and Liya heard it."

"Barlath will surely deny the accusation, and then it will be his word against Liya's," Folnar sighed.

Liya realized how absurd her situation was. Haydn, the new king of Dar'Angaar, had threatened her with the death penalty because she had no business snooping around in his country. Then, he'd declared that he would not kill her. The relationship between their countries was more than strained, and she was working with the enemies of Namoor. To make matters worse, she felt good in the company of these men. As for the crystal, she would still pursue plans of her own. *What's wrong with me?* she wondered. She should not care that the renegade, traitorous prince of Aughdar was trying to kill his royal nephew.

"I am the enemy," she groaned. The men stared at her.

Folnar shook his head. "No, you are one of us."

"I am King Louis' best spy. And it is, after all, possible that war will break out between our countries." She didn't know why she'd said that.

Maverick shrugged. "Still, you're here now."

He didn't believe her. No one in the room did. "You're idiots."

Folnar grinned. "You've said that already."

She rolled her eyes and looked from one to the other. There was no point. "Let's go to this reception," she finally said.

As soon as they left the room, Haydn reached for her hand. He was playing a role, she knew that, and yet she couldn't stop the cozy feeling that spread through her stomach.

The reception was held in a small room with yellow walls. Rays of sun fell through the open patio door, giving extra warmth to the room. She saw Ebradis, Yara, Tafriani, Arlandth, and Ithos; Ebra was missing.

When she entered the room with Haydn, Tafriani lowered her eyes to their clasped hands. Haydn greeted his aunt warmly, then exchanged greetings with the others.

Ebradis' greedy gaze lingered on Liya for a moment before turning to his cousin. "I hope you had your fun."

Haydn smirked and pulled her closer to him. She felt herself blush.

Ebradis looked her straight in the eye and laughed coldly. "After yesterday's performance, I didn't think you could feel anything like shame."

"What can I say? Your cousin has conquered me."

"Enjoy your love affair while you can, for soon the wedding bells will be ringing for Haydn." Ebradis' words stung in her ears.

"Since when have you been so concerned about my welfare?" inquired Haydn, gently squeezing her hand.

"We just want to make sure Liya doesn't get her hopes up. The alliance with Eryon comes first," Ithos spat. His face contorted into a vicious grimace.

Arlandth yawned exaggeratedly. "As exhilarating as our royal cousin's love life may be, I'm getting bored with it." He looked at Haydn. "Is it true that you have given up hunting?"

She was grateful for the change of subject. Yara took the opportunity and joined her. "Let's leave the men alone and go outside," she said kindly.

She followed the princess, somewhat taken aback when Tafriani joined them too. Yara led her to a beautiful terrace with a sweeping view of the garden. Even in this place, where life was supposed to bloom, everything seemed cold. No flowers, a few scattered shrubs, and a barren meadow stretched as far as she could see. Yara took a seat and motioned for her to sit next to her. Tafriani also settled down.

Furtively, she eyed the prince's daughter. Tafriani really had some nerve! After all, Liya knew what she'd done. No matter the circumstances, she had poisoned Haydn.

"How did you two meet?" inquired Yara.

"At a ball."

"I find it amazing that Haydn just took you along. That's not like him at all," Tafriani murmured.

Her stomach twinged, but she didn't respond.

Undaunted, she continued, "His love affairs are usually very short-lived."

With an apologetic smile, Yara handed her a cup. "Please, my dear— jasmine tea." Liya gave Tafriani a dirty look. "I hope there are no *extras* in my tea."

Yara looked surprised. "What do you mean?"

Tafriani blanched. "We drink our tea with honey. There's nothing else in it."

Yara smiled. "I am so happy about Haydn's visit. A long time ago, our families were very close. Two years ago, after his successful return from the Lor'sul Mountains, Haydn spent some time with us. I was hoping that he and Tafriani would get married, and that this would bring the brothers close again. Unfortunately, instead, the situation escalated, and the enmity intensified." She looked dreamily into the distance before continuing, "You must know that Tafriani is not Ebra's daughter. She's not related to Haydn. Her father died when she was a baby."

For a moment, her eyes went black. This could not be! After their time together in the Lor'sul Mountains, Haydn had visited his uncle's court and replaced her with Tafriani. She quickly suppressed the thought, for it took her breath away. Fortunately, the two women seemed oblivious to her inner struggle.

"That was a long time ago," Tafriani replied. Her longing look did not escape Liya.

"Why haven't the brothers been in contact?" she asked.

Yara rubbed her arms and looked up at the sky, which was growing darker. It looked like it might rain.

"Ebra is the elder. His father's decision to favor the younger son and leave him in charge of the country was a slap in his face. Two years ago, quite surprisingly, Ebra visited his brother. An argument ensued. We don't know what it was about, but Ebra was seriously injured."

"They actually got into a fight?"

"We owe it to Haydn that Ebra survived. He found his gravely injured uncle and took him to a healer." Yara sighed. "A lot has happened since then. We've all changed. But enough about our family drama. Tell us something about yourself. Where do your parents live?"

"They're dead."

"I'm sorry to hear that." The princess looked genuinely dismayed.

"It's been a long time since I lost them."

"But who takes care of you?"

"I'm eighteen. No one has to worry about me." She smiled at Yara. *How could this warm, friendly woman put up with such a monster?*

"Haydn is a good man," Yara added abruptly.

Tafriani cleared her throat. "You shouldn't have come here, Liya."

Yara patted her daughter's arm. "Don't say that."

Tafriani pushed her mother away. "It's the truth. She doesn't belong here."

Now Liya was convinced that Tafriani still had feelings for Haydn. So why on earth had she poisoned him? Who was pressuring her? What was going on here? At that moment, Haydn and Arlandth appeared on the terrace.

"Are you having a good time?" Haydn lovingly wrapped his arm around her waist.

"It's always nice to chat over a good cup of tea," Yara replied with a smile.

Liya felt Haydn's lips against her ear. "It's about time," he whispered.

With a coquettish flick of her eyes, she turned to him, hoping everyone would buy into the spectacle. His bright eyes roamed over her face, and her heart began to beat faster. He lifted his hand and gently stroked her cheek with his thumb.

"We should go back inside," Arlandth remarked.

Moments later, the first raindrops fell. With an elegant movement of his hand, Haydn beckoned the family to go ahead. When she was about to follow Yara, he pulled her to him and kissed her.

"Let yourself fall," he murmured. She felt his lips on hers. Fortunately, the others were already out of sight. Haydn released her. "Now we can disappear into the room."

The warm feeling disappeared as quickly as it had come. *Of course! That's all it is for him.* She pulled away and ran after the others.

Back in the reception room, Haydn quickly said goodbye, took Liya's hand, and left the room with her. In the hallway, she freed herself and marched purposefully to the room. Maverick and Folnar waited for them.

Mischief flashed in Maverick's green eyes. "I guess you guys were convincing."

She gave Maverick a scowl. "*Master spy.* Remember? I can play pretty much any role." She disappeared behind the screen. Shedding her dress, she slipped into her leather armor.

"Maverick, did you find out how many guards are deployed in the housing wing?" Haydn asked.

"No, we can only guess—probably half a dozen. Through the rooms, we get to the secret passages, which serve as escape routes for the princely family in case of danger. I saw the duty roster; we should be undisturbed. However, there might be a problem on the way back. Your uncle usually returns to his study shortly before noon. That's where the shaft is. That's about when Liya will come out."

"While you are doing this, I have a meeting with Ebra and his sons. I will insist on lunch together. That should give Liya some extra time," Haydn replied.

Folnar frowned. "Good, she won't be noticed in the hallway since there'll be enough servants around, busy cleaning."

Haydn mumbled something that she couldn't understand.

"We don't know anything specific about the room where the crystal is kept," Folnar added.

"What are you trying to say?" Haydn inquired.

"We have to consider the fact she may not make it back in time."

"That is not an option. Liya must steal the crystal and return within the allotted time. Ebra must not notice the theft while we are still here. Once you've taken Liya to the shaft, you'll return. Then I'll go and meet up with Ebra. You and Maverick will position yourselves in front of Liya's door and deny anyone entry. Liya will keep us informed via the communicator. Once she has the crystal, you and Folnar will make your way back to help her out of the shaft."

Annoyed, she rolled her eyes. Haydn's commanding tone was unbearable. She stepped out from behind the screen. "I'm ready, *your majesty*. Now, how about some illusion magic?"

Haydn nodded and came toward her. His eyes shone even brighter than usual, and his gaze was highly concentrated. She thought she saw a kind of dark shadow briefly surround him, but it was gone so fast that she couldn't say.

Maverick suppressed a laugh. "You look cute, Liya, like an innocent maid."

"Maybe I'll hit you with the crystal as soon as I get it," she replied.

But he was right. An inconspicuous brown-haired servant looked back at her from the mirror. "Really amazing," she had to admit.

A moment later, Folnar also looked like one of the many servants that belonged to the castle. "One last test!" he demanded.

Haydn did something to his wrist. Immediately, a murmur sounded in her ear, followed by voices.

"Seems to be working," Maverick said.

Folnar nodded. "Then we'll go get the crystal now."

With a serious face, Haydn turned to her. "Recall everything we discussed on the carriage ride. I would like to repeat a few things. This crystal is magic! We don't know exactly how its magic works. What we do know is, in the ancient times, it was used for research. It might be a weapon. You must touch it only with gloves and immediately wrap it in a cloth."

"All right," she agreed.

Haydn reached for her hand. "Liya?"

"Be careful. "

"Don't worry."

She left the room with Folnar. They walked down the hall to the west wing.

"There are surprisingly few people here," she noted with disbelief. Thanks to the communicators in their ears, they were able to whisper.

"We are not yet in the residential wing of Ebra's family. At this time of the day, the rooms are being cleaned. Wrapped in Haydn's illusion, we won't attract attention," Folnar's voice sounded in her ear. "In the family wing, we'll go immediately to Tafriani's room. From there, a narrow corridor used by the servants leads to the rest of the manorial rooms."

She grinned. Folnar, like Haydn, obviously had an urgent need to go over everything they had already discussed.

"The servants' passage is the only way for us to get into Ebra's chambers unnoticed," he continued. "The entrance to the shaft is in a small chamber next to Ebra's private study."

She already knew that. The residential wing was teeming with servants, all of whom seemed to be in a hurry. They adapted, running fast and acting busy. The fact that they entered Tafriani's bedchamber did not bother anyone.

"There must be an opening here," Folnar said, tapping the wall.

She looked around. The room, with surprisingly few pieces of furniture, had a simple elegance.

"Ah—here!" With a broad grin on his face, he pushed open a narrow door without a handle. It was covered with the same wallpaper as the walls, so it was hardly noticeable. "I'll have to close the door behind us. We'll have to feel our way forward," he added.

"You go ahead, I'll close the door," she replied.

She preferred to follow Folnar. After all, he had hatched the plan. The door closed quietly, and darkness surrounded them. Without hesitation, Folnar took her hand. They crept along the narrow corridor. After what felt like an eternity, he let go of her hand and scanned the wall again. On the other side was probably Ebra's study.

"I counted the steps. The entrance must be here somewhere," he whispered.

And indeed! Not five steps further, the wall gave way, and shortly thereafter, they stood in Ebra's study. They heard voices coming from the hallway.

"Quick!" Hastily, Folnar pulled her behind a huge desk. She almost tripped.

Someone entered the room. "All clean," said a man.

"You expect anything else? Ebra's paranoid," another replied.

"Shh! Are you crazy? Do you want them to hang us?"

The door closed.

Relieved, Folnar exhaled. "That was close."

"What do we do now?" she asked, aghast. "Ebra posted guards outside his room. That wasn't part of the plan. On our way back, you'll have to distract them somehow, since we'll be using the hallway."

"We'll figure something out."

She didn't like that at all. "Maybe I should use the secret passage for the way back after all."

"No, absolutely not. We can't predict Tafriani's movements. Regardless of what Haydn wants or even orders, she does what she wants. She may return to her room."

"What do you suggest?"

"You take care of the crystal. We'll figure out how to get you out."

She pressed her lips together. Of course! The crystal was important, and she should take the risk, but she felt used and despondent. "We don't even know what awaits me in the room with the crystal. And Aval is not with us in case I get hurt," she hissed.

"Sonaris has to take care of the girl we originally chose for the job. We won't let you down."

"*Of course not!*" She heard for herself how mocking she sounded. "That reminds me… What does the crystal even look like?"

"We don't know that for sure, but you will recognize it. Let's go. The grate in front of the opening at the other end of the shaft may be locked. Do you have your dagger with you?"

"I do."

"All right!" He took a deep breath. "Here's the most important thing: there are two pedestals. You tap one of them four times with your finger. That has to be done first. On the other one, there's a button you have to press. A door should open somewhere in the wall. Behind it, we believe, you will find the crystal."

"All right," she murmured. She didn't feel very confident, though. She was aware that Haydn's knowledge of the crystal was poor.

The entrance to the shaft was in a corner about two meters above the ground. It looked like a vent. Folnar helped her up, and she crawled inside. After a few minutes, her eyes became accustomed to the darkness. In her mind, she repeated the movements. On all fours, she kept crawling until she felt the wind blowing directly into her face. There, she turned. More and more light fell into the shaft.

A few minutes later, she reached an opening. Carefully, she tried to lift the grate, but it did not move. She stroked the edges with her finger, felt for the screws, and slowly turned them with her dagger. After an eternity, she loosened the four screws, removed the grate, and peered down. At the end of the room were two pedestals; between them was a block of white stone, no more than a meter high. Two busts—a woman and a man—stood on the block. She would never have suspected an elaborate security system here; the small room seemed completely inconspicuous. A large bookshelf was set up on one of the walls, and oil paintings hung on the other.

The time had come. She put on the gloves and jumped down. She waited. Nothing happened. For a moment, she closed her eyes, breathing deeply and slowly. The exercise ropes appeared in her mind's eye. She went through each movement once again. Then she was ready. Side jump. Duck. A roll. She felt the rays without seeing anything. Adrenaline flooded her body. Duck again, walk under an imaginary rope, stand up, dodge. She slid a bit across the floor toward the pedestal.

Stunned, she realized that she had made it—at least this far. With trembling fingers, she stroked along the pedestal, but found no button. So here, she had to tap four times against the stone. Then she turned to the other one and scanned the lower area. No sooner had she pressed the button than she heard something shifting. Less than five meters behind the busts, a door hidden in the wall opened. Cautiously, she crept closer and peered inside.

"I'm through," she informed Folnar on the communicator. "The opening in the wall is just behind the pedestals."

"What exactly do you see in this opening?" asked Folnar.

"A long hallway."

"Nothing else?" That was Haydn's voice. When had he connected with them?

"No, I'm going in now." Now came the part of their mission they knew virtually nothing about. Neither Haydn, Folnar, nor Maverick had any information, only guesses. With each step, her body tensed. The hairs on the back of her neck stood up. She sensed danger with every inch of her body. "Oh."

"Oh! What does that mean?" hissed Maverick.

"Remember when I told you guys we were in danger? That *oh*."

Maverick cursed. The door behind her closed, but one opened in front of her. A vicious growl reached her ear.

"Turn back immediately," Haydn said.

"It's too late for that."

"What do you mean?" He sounded panicked.

"The door behind me is closed."

"Damn it!" exclaimed Folnar.

The rectangular room she entered was dimly lit. A pedestal rose in the middle, on which stood a glass box with the crystal. Black. Sparkling. No bigger than her hand. It radiated a strange energy. *Attractive. Gloomy. Powerful.* Unconsciously, she moved to the center.

A ferocious growl brought her back to reality. A black, bear-like creature with red eyes, standing on its hind legs, stared back at her. She held her throwing stars at the ready. The creature circled her.

A fresh soul. The voice in her head sent a cold shiver down her spine. *Today you die, human.*

"Why does everyone always threaten me with death?" she cried, throwing the first star.

Faster than expected, the creature attacked. Liya's throwing star protruded from its shoulder, but it drew a sword and leaped forward. At the last second, Liya deflected the blow with Maverick's short sword. The force of the attack sent her staggering back. The creature sensed its chance and lunged again, this time even harder, even faster.

With all her effort, Liya fought it off. Her arms ached. Up close, she saw that the beast, which at first had looked like an upright bear, had human-like features. The face, however, was disfigured, the lower jaw thrust too far forward. It had enormously broad shoulders and arms. The hands had no fingers, only claws. And this thing wore a robe! As it circled Liya, she counterattacked, charging at her opponent in a flash. The creature parried her offensive effortlessly. Liya lunged and struck, but to no avail. The more she tried, the more skillfully this creature dodged.

Tired? it asked.

She pressed her lips tightly together. With her next attack, she screamed her rage. A fist hit her back with a crash and slammed her to the floor.

Pathetic.

Liya tasted blood. Her breathing was fast. She scrambled to her feet and lunged at the monster, but every blow missed. It circled her again before grabbing her and hurling her across the floor. Gasping, she crashed against the pedestal. With the last of her strength, she struggled to her feet.

"Not enough yet?" The harsh, cruel voice of her opponent sounded aloud and in her head.

"I never lose," she replied, grinning as best as she could.

Quick as a flash, she turned around and hit the glass with her fist. To her surprise, it broke. She had expected magical protection. She darted for the crystal, gripping it tightly.

"*No!*" the creature screamed. "*You are not worthy of him. No human is!*"

The room shook. She had felt enormous energy when she entered, but nothing could compare to the power now enveloping her body, penetrating her, forging a path through every vein. The magic befuddled her senses and gave her extraordinary strength. If she had ever doubted it, now she knew: the crystal was a relic from the Ancient Era! Incredible feelings intoxicated Liya. She was invincible—immortal.

Laughing, she looked the creature in the eye, jumped forward, and drove her sword into its chest. Shrieking, the monster struck at her with full force. Its claws dug deep into her flesh, but she felt nothing. Her hands grabbed him. Fire flowed through her body, ready to destroy.

A shrill scream filled the air. Embers covered the creature's skin like flowing lava. It slumped, whole body still glowing. Liya stared at the beast in astonishment. Charred, lifeless remains coated the floor. She couldn't make sense of what had just happened. Completely exhausted, she sank to the ground, despite the power vibrating inside her. She took the cloth from her pocket and wrapped the crystal in it, then scanned the floor. Somewhere near the base, she had lost the earplug. Countless shards of glass glittered dangerously on the tile. A thousand cuts later, she found what she was looking for.

Her hands shook. She tapped once—nothing. She tried Maverick, and then Folnar, but no one answered.

Clinging to the pedestal, she pulled herself up. Each step took more air from her. Her lungs ached. She reached the entrance to the hallway and was relieved to find that the door on the opposite side was open again. The corners of her vision blurred black. She stood, dazed, one foot in front of the other... Somewhere, blood dripped. She could almost hear it plopping. All she felt was pain—pain everywhere. Gritting her teeth, she entered the anteroom. How on earth was she supposed to manage the movement sequences in this state?

The crystal! She must use it once again. Trembling with fear but aching for the irrepressible power, she took out the cloth, unwound it, and reached for the sparkling rock. *Intoxicating. Dark. Consuming.* The pain vanished and, without thinking, she started the maze. A blink of an eye later, she found herself on the other side of the room, leaping up and grabbing the edge of the shaft.

Something inside her tugged at her soul. Her magic stirred. How liberating! Warmth flowed through her. Veils of mist lifted, and her mind cleared. She shimmied herself up with one hand. In the shaft, she grabbed the crystal again and crawled forward.

Soon she saw the opening; below her was the chamber. She landed on the floor just as the door was torn open.

Haydn stared at her in disbelief. His gaze was dark. Maverick and Folnar rushed past him. She groaned as Maverick embraced her.

"The last time you called was two hours ago! Folnar has been here several times to pick you up," Maverick blurted out.

With a shaky hand, Liya took out the cloth and handed it to Haydn. "The crystal—as agreed."

"We're leaving now. Liya's wounds need to be tended to," Haydn said dully. "You take the secret passage. I'll lure Tafriani out of her room if she's there." He turned to Maverick. "As soon as you get to Ebra's study, let me know."

How exactly they made it back to Haydn's room, she did not know. Trembling, she sat down on the bed.

"We need to look at her wounds," Folnar said quietly.

"It isn't just my blood," she murmured.

Folnar helped her take her jacket off. His worried look did not escape her.

"That bad?" she croaked.

Haydn pushed the door open and hurried in with long strides. "You can start the diversion," he ordered. "Maverick, have you prepared enough bottles?"

"The fire will be enough to cause panic. In any case, it will give us a reason to leave the palace early," Maverick replied.

"Won't Ebra suspect anything?"

"I don't think so. Besides, we need Sonaris to heal you."

Reluctantly, she shook her head. "I just need rest. My body will heal on its own."

She snuggled against the warm body.

"Liya?"

She opened her eyes and jolted upright. A tent was stretched above her, and Haydn lay next to her. Her throat felt dry. She wanted to say something, but could only croak.

"Here, drink water."

Gratefully, she accepted the bottle. After she drank, she lay back down and closed her eyes. "Where are we?"

"Near the village where you stayed with Sonaris."

"I just remember us talking in the room about fire and leaving early."

"You've only been awake once briefly."

"How long was I asleep?"

"Five days."

"I guess my body isn't going to heal itself after all."

"No, it won't."

"Did you change my clothes?"

"Yes, and I cleaned your wounds." He stroked her arm.

"But how did we get away?"

"You forget that I am a master of illusion magic. Folnar took over your role for a few hours. I gave him a sickly appearance. Since you're small, you fit into a large travel bag. No one noticed that one of my officers was missing. Men like him were everywhere in the melee. When the fire broke out, Ebra had other things to worry about than his guests. He was even happy that we were leaving. If something happened to the king in his palace, he'd have a serious problem. No one suspected a thing."

"What about the crystal? Have they noticed the theft?"

"No. In a way, it amazes me, too. But I think Ebra considers it impossible that someone could pass through the protective measures and get access to the crystal. I don't think it's checked regularly. He probably also has great reverence for his treasure, and certainly, very few people know about it. And you didn't set off any alarms."

She examined him more closely. His face looked narrower, and he had not shaved in a long time. Dark circles under his eyes intensified his tired expression.

"You look the way I feel right now."

He laughed softly. "If that's how you talk to me, then there's hope."

"I have to go home." Saying this felt strange. Besides, there was still something she had to do. She had to get to the crystal. The thought of stealing it caused a strange feeling. *Don't kid yourself*, she scolded herself, *you feel guilty.*

"I know," he replied softly. "Are you hungry?"

"Yeah, kind of."

"Kind of?"

"As exhausted as I am, I don't know if I have the strength to eat. But my stomach is growling."

"I'll help you. Try to stand up!"

He rose and took her hand to pull her up. How infinitely sluggish she felt.

Aval lifted the tent cover and entered. "Liya, you're awake!"

He rushed to her, followed by Maverick and Folnar. They almost embraced Liya, but Haydn interposed himself. "She's still weak."

"Emphasis on *still*," she explained with a smile.

Maverick grinned. "At least you're talking in complete sentences. That's progress."

"You look like how I feel."

Now it was Folnar who grinned. "You've kept us on our toes, especially Haydn."

"Is the stew still warm? Bring Liya a bowl. She has to eat something," Haydn ordered.

Black dots flickered through the air as she tried to rise further. She grabbed Haydn's arm. After Folnar brought her a bowl of food, Haydn told his men to leave the tent.

"Now, we don't have to play our parts." She sighed.

Haydn mumbled something unintelligible. When she held out her hands, he shook his head. "I'll feed you."

She saw deep concern in his eyes. Her chest constricted. "Only today because I'm still tired," she explained. "Tomorrow, I'll eat alone." After the fifth spoonful, she raised her hand. "Enough! I can't take any more."

"Maybe later." He set the bowl down and joined her in bed. He leaned back and opened his arm so she could lay her head against his chest.

"What are you doing?" she asked softly.

"Sonaris said you can't lie on your back. The elevated sleeping position is better for your circulation. That's how you've been sleeping the last few days."

"Thank you for saving me."

"We saved each other."

She rested her head on his chest, breathing in the scent of the forest and fresh rain before her eyes fell shut again.

The next morning, she awoke in his embrace. His beard scratched her cheek. Carefully, she lifted his arm to get up.

"Good morning," he murmured.

She felt his warm breath on her neck.

"I didn't mean to wake you."

"It's okay."

For a moment, she felt comfortable and satisfied. Then she remembered she had only two days left to reach the meeting point with Mojak. How was she going to manage? She felt a lump in her throat.

"I need to get some fresh air," she panted.

"I'll come with you."

"No, go back to sleep. I'll be fine."

He straightened up and looked at her carefully. "You've been lying down for five days. Your muscles are weak." He stood up and took her hand.

They left the tent together. Outside, she took a deep breath and felt blood pumping through her body.

"Good morning, sunshine," Maverick called to her. "Breakfast will be ready in a minute."

Haydn led them to the campfire, where they sat down with the others. She turned to Aval. "Did you heal me?"

Haydn cleared his throat. "Yes, he did."

Haydn and Aval exchanged a glance. This silent exchange worried her. Maverick held out a plate of bread, fried egg, and cheese to her. It smelled wonderful. She bit into the fresh bread, closed her eyes, and savored the taste.

"I've never seen anyone look so happy while eating bread," Maverick remarked with a grin.

"You were out of action for five days."

"What exactly happened?" Maverick inquired seriously.

She reported on the room, the creature, and the battle. At the end, she said, "I had no choice but to use the crystal."

"You touched the crystal?" cried Aval, deeply startled.

"Yes," she replied. "The crystal probably saved my life."

Stunned, Haydn shook his head. "It's amazing that you survived direct contact with the crystal," he said tonelessly.

"As if I had a choice!" She snorted. "I take it from your remarks that others *didn't* survive."

"We assume so," Haydn admitted. "Otherwise, Ebra would have used it long ago." He thought for a while before asking, "What did the crystal do to you?"

"I felt stronger—significantly stronger, almost invincible. I felt no pain at all. The second time, the crystal drained my strength. It was very strange. While I felt strong, my magic started to feel weaker."

Haydn's gaze darkened. "You used the magic of the crystal twice?"

"Would you have preferred I set off the alarm?"

Even though he fixed her sternly with his eyes, he probably realized how thin the ice he was heading toward was.

"Crystal against my freedom. I had no choice," she continued in a biting tone.

Folnar interjected, "What did this creature look like?"

"It had some resemblance to the attackers from the forest, but it was much stronger and less human."

"I don't think Ebra has anything to do with it. These creatures have only been showing up for a few months. Maybe it was trying to do the same thing we were, steal the crystal?" Maverick said.

"That's one possibility. It said that no human deserved it." She shook off the thought. She couldn't bear that right now.

"Where is the crystal anyway?" she inquired.

"Safely stored," Haydn replied.

He had it. That was all she needed to hear. Now, she knew where to look. She gazed at each of the men in turn. They were enemies of Namoor. Haydn had threatened her with death and used her to steal the crystal. But then they had saved her life. As she thought of the day ahead and having to say goodbye, her heart contracted painfully. She liked these men and felt comfortable with them. Over the past few days, something close to a friendship had developed between them. And yet, she could not allow this feeling to overcome her rational thinking. It wasn't right. She stood up and went to the tent.

Restlessly, Liya walked up and down. She was in the service of her king. How could she feel sympathy for Namoor's enemy? Besides that, she had a mission here. Her job was to find out more.

❧

Nervously, Liya paced the tent. She had avoided being alone with Haydn all day. But now, he had asked her to talk to him. She had to banish all the feelings that swirled wildly inside her. Dar'Angaar was the enemy! She had no choice but to steal the crystal.

Haydn lifted the tent cover and entered. His hair was still wet, and it stood up in all directions.

"Were you just going to disappear into the night?" he asked.

Her cheeks began to glow. That was exactly what she'd intended to do, leave the camp with the crystal.

"I can't believe it, you really thought about it," he said in disbelief.

"What's the point? I fulfilled my part of the bargain." Defiantly, she crossed her arms in front of her chest. "You have the crystal."

"That's not the point." He tilted his head and eyed her.

"But?"

"You are the spy of my enemy. And you now possess important information. That poses a danger."

"A danger?" she repeated. Her voice sounded higher than usual. "I risked my life. For the enemy of my king."

"*Your king* put you at great risk when he sent you here." He rubbed his face. "It wasn't planned that way. I'm sorry. All right?"

"No, nothing is all right!" she hissed, unable to hold back her pent-up anger. "You gave me your word. Let me go! I'm done with you."

"But I'm not with *you*," he rumbled.

"Surely Tafriani can comfort you," she sneered back. The words just bubbled out of her.

"If I didn't know better, I'd think you were jealous," he replied with a grin on his face.

What was he thinking? She would say nothing.

"Liya...," he whispered.

What was this guy doing to her? She had to leave—immediately. Slowly, he raised his hand and put it against her cheek.

"You should let me go," she pressed out. She didn't mean keeping his word for her freedom.

"Yeah," he muttered. "I probably should."

A pained expression flitted across his face, and the next moment she felt his lips, warm and firm. It was tempting to let herself fall, to allow this feeling, to forget everything. Her pulse pounded. Before she could push him away, he broke away from her.

"I'm sorry for what I just said," he breathed in a raspy voice. "I'm a man of my word. You can leave this country."

He took a few steps back, increasing their distance. "However, I ask you not to mention the crystal." Before she could say anything, he continued, "I realize what I am asking of you. But before you decide, listen to what I have to say." Sighing, he sat down on the bed and motioned for her to take a seat as well. "More than five hundred years ago, there were bigger and richer cities than today. The people of those days had more knowledge than we can imagine. Today, not much of that progress has remained."

"Just relics from the Ancient Era—like the crystal."

"It's not just about artifacts. In those days, research was done not only on objects but also on people. We owe our gift to the Ancient Era. They couldn't undo or destroy that *achievement*."

"Maybe they didn't want to."

"Possibly. They also created magical portals with their technology to cross great distances in seconds. Some of them still work today."

This kind of information was exactly what she needed. But she could not show her interest too clearly.

"Based on the knowledge of the portals, however, the ancients created something far greater."

"The Gates."

"Right, the gates to another world. I believe that something has been banished to the world beyond the gate, something exceedingly powerful and dangerous. And contrary to the assumption that knowledge of it no longer exists, I assume that it has long since fallen into the wrong hands."

She widened her eyes in disbelief. "Who has this knowledge?"

"That's what I'm trying to figure out."

"What is the role of the crystal?"

"It has something to do with the gates. The power you described could be the key to opening them, but that is only a guess. I need more time to figure everything out. One thing is certain, however. Knowledge of the gates can prove exceedingly dangerous in the wrong hands. If, somehow, these people got the possession of the crystal, it would be a disaster."

"Louis wouldn't—"

You don't know what people are capable of when they feel the power. I've seen how people I thought I knew well can change." For a moment, pain flared in his eyes.

"If we are all in such danger, shouldn't the king of Namoor know?"

"What are you going to tell him? You can't possibly tell him that you stole the crystal for us. He won't understand."

Haydn was right. She didn't understand it herself. "Why did you bring me along? You already had someone for this task."

"Sonaris trusts you."

"Aval?" She shook her head. "What's he got to do with it?"

Briefly, Haydn closed his eyes. "Everything." Then he took her hand. "All I can tell you is that I trust these three men implicitly. And Sonaris wanted you to steal the crystal."

He would say nothing more on this subject. She heard that clearly. What could she do? She was beholden to her king, but Louis would not understand her behavior, and worse, he would no longer trust her. What she had learned in Dar'Angaar was exactly what the king was interested in, but she could barely tell him anything. She didn't even *want* to. That was her real problem.

"I'll think about it," she said softly. "That's all I can promise you."

If this answer disappointed him, he did not show it. From outside, she heard Maverick calling. Dinner was ready. She rose, and Haydn followed her.

At the exit, he whispered in her ear, "I didn't replace you with her." Without waiting for a reply, he left the tent.

She was grateful for that, because otherwise, he would have heard the drumming of her heart.

She listened to Haydn's steady breathing. Could she dare get up? Mojak would be waiting for her tonight. Carefully she rose from the mattress, slipped quickly into her boots, and took the leather bundle. Her heart contracted at the sight of Haydn.

She tiptoed through the tent and rummaged through his things. Her pulse quickened when she felt something round wrapped in a cloth, power radiating through it. Cautiously, she took the wrapped crystal, stowed it in her pocket, and left the tent.

All was quiet in the camp. No wonder! She had stumbled upon sweet yellow clovers on the shore and added it to the food. Although the fresh herb was not as effective as a tincture, it served its purpose. She crept past the sleeping men and headed toward the path. She wanted to avoid any kind of confrontation.

Her heart raced at an unhealthy speed. The farther she went from the camp, the heavier her steps became. She was doing the right thing! She could not doubt that. Even if she liked the men, they were Namoor's enemies. She could not leave the crystal to them under any circumstances.

But she was powerless against her thoughts. *They saved your life. They could have left you dying there. You stole from them. They won't forgive you for that.* She moaned. It was almost unbearable. *I told them not to trust me,* she reminded herself. She pushed away further thoughts and concentrated on the path.

The full moon shone brightly in the twinkling starry sky. When a shadow appeared in front of her, she suppressed a cry.

"Wouldn't have thought you were a coward," Maverick said softly.

"You scared me," she hissed. "What are you doing here anyway? Are you tailing me?"

"I knew something was wrong. You've been acting so strange all day, not even arguing with Haydn."

She bit her lower lip. Obviously, he had not eaten anything for dinner.

Maverick folded his arms in front of his chest. "I didn't want to believe Haydn. He warned us you were about to disappear."

Tears almost rushed to her eyes when she heard the disappointment in his voice.

"But like you said." He laughed bitterly. "You are the master spy. Trusting you is a mistake. Well, I guess we are the idiots."

Her throat tightened. Water gathered in her eyes. "It's not like that. I'm not going to say anything. No one will know anything. I swear that on my life."

"Save it. Our paths part here." He turned and marched back to the camp.

She watched him walk away until she couldn't see him any longer. *Why does the right thing feel so wrong?* As she ran on, tears ran down her cheeks.

Mojak was sitting in front of the tree, already transformed. She wiped her face.

"I was beginning to think you weren't coming," he greeted her.

"Let's get out of here quickly," she whispered hoarsely.

They took off. During the flight, he told her that there had only been a brief commotion about the boat. However, Mojak believed that Sakima suspected something. She was relieved—she didn't want Mojak to get into trouble.

At her request, he flew directly to Namoor. Near the palace city, there was an abandoned hut in the forest where she had often met with Ewan as a child. The hut was run down, but it was well hidden from the paths.

Mojak did not ask any questions, and she was grateful for that. He promised to bring her a bow and sword from his village. After he had done that, he left her for good.

She decided not to contact Ewan right away. This was standard procedure for very delicate missions. She reported to him as agreed with the king, and he initiated everything else.

She needed distance. Besides, she had to hide the crystal.

The mountain range behind the palace city provided cool air, and would even in the approaching summer. Liya crept through the palace city, feeling queasy. Although dawn had already broken, it was still dark. She knew the city well enough to find her way without a torch. She enjoyed the silence of the night.

After two days in the hut, she had sought out Ewan last evening, wrapped in a dark hooded cloak. He had been relieved, and they had agreed to meet on the observation deck this afternoon. Then, they would seek out the king together.

Before meeting her friend, she had something to do. Her destination was the military academy, which was located on open ground near the city walls.

After a few minutes, she passed the stables and the archers' practice facilities. When she reached the forecourt, she heard voices from the dining hall to the left.

Classes would begin just in time for sunrise. It was important that she caught Brath before then. She quickened her steps and hurried through the large archway. Behind the main buildings and the library were smaller practice facilities. The great arena of the swordsmen was behind those. The circular fighting area was surrounded by seating spread out over four steps. She suspected Brath was there; her former teacher used to practice alone at this early hour. And right! As she walked toward the arena, she saw him.

His body was wrapped in a black tunic; his powerful arms threatened to tear the fabric. His tall stature still looked frightening—he had hardly changed. Strands of gray shone in his black hair. He caught sight of her when she passed the lowest row of seats.

"By the gods, Liya," he groaned. His bass boomed across the square. "What are you doing here?" Shaking his head, he lowered his sword.

"On the way here, I tried to think of something, but now I don't know what to say. Nothing seems adequate." She shrugged. "It's been a long time."

"You've grown up to look more like your mother," Brath noted. "Except for the eyes. The gods must have given you those."

She smiled. "That's what father used to say."

"He was a good man."

"I miss him." Her heart grew heavy. She shook off the memories. "They say you stole a woman's heart."

"More like the other way around!" He beamed.

"I'm very happy for you."

"She puts up with my grumpy moods. I guess I'm lucky in that regard. And you?"

"Even Ewan's mother has finally given up on introducing me to any earls," she replied with a smile.

"Who knows where the road will take us."

"True enough," she agreed.

"Everyone is talking about the bad news you brought back from Qilon and wondering what will happen next. A coronation in Dar'Angaar and Eryon goes rogue..." He frowned. "Does your unexpected visit have anything to do with it?"

"I have to get back to training," she answered evasively. "That's why I'm here. I'd be happy to make myself available to your students. And if you could spare a little time, I'd be grateful."

"Then I guess the rumor is true. There will be war."

"I don't know about that, but I think it's better to be prepared for anything." She forced a smile.

Brath used these words when his pupils complained about the hours of practice. He was a strict teacher, who made them drill until they were too tired even to eat. But over time, she had realized that under the hard shell lurked a soft core.

Brath's gaze slid over her shoulder. A broad grin spread across his face, his angular chin thrusting slightly forward. "What are you doing here? Are you coming to practice, too?" he called out.

She turned around and caught sight of Ewan. His sudden appearance surprised her. Judging by his facial expression, he had not expected to see her either.

Brath laughed out loud. "When things get serious, the sheep come back to the fold," he said good-humouredly. "So, my boy, what brings you to me?" He patted Ewan warmly on the shoulder.

"I need to speak with you privately, Brath," Ewan replied, giving her a regretful look.

"I see. Top secret." She rolled her eyes exaggeratedly.

"Go change, Liya, and get a practice sword. My students will be here in a few minutes. I won't be the one sweating then," Brath said.

She hugged him and pressed a kiss to his cheek. "Thank you."

"That's all right. Don't embarrass an old man like that."

Grinning, Ewan held his cheek out to her. "You're welcome to embarrass me."

"He's incorrigible." She winked at Brath, threw Ewan an exaggerated kiss on the hand, and headed for the equipment room.

Half an hour later, dressed in a black tunic and pants, she stood by Brath's side. She suppressed a smirk as he greeted his students with a roar.

"Today, we have a volunteer who is available to fight with you. Stand at attention! You fools! Liya attacks, you defend. We'll keep doing that until one of you manages to parry." The swordmaster raised his arm and pointed to the first one in line. "You start."

The recruit stepped out of line and positioned himself. Her wooden sword jerked forward and struck the boy in the chest before he had even raised his weapon. He fell.

"Pathetic," Brath judged brusquely. "Next."

She knew that Brath intentionally let the weaker ones compete first. That way, the better fighters, who might learn something from her, got more time to study her moves. Her fourth opponent seemed older and more experienced. He managed to dodge the attack but missed Liya's sword. She spun, hit him in the chest, and he went down gasping for air. She effortlessly defeated the next two as well.

"The first row goes to the posts and practices the shots. The second row is up," Brath thundered. "Liya continues to attack. You guys try to put her on the defensive."

She took her time to examine these students a little more closely. She could tell by their brown clothing that they belonged to the fourth year. The younger students wore gray, and from the fifth year on, the clothing was black. Most children were sent to the academy between their eighth and tenth birthdays, though her father had brought her here shortly after her sixth birthday.

The sun glistened from the sky. The light wind failed to soothe her burning face. Her black robe soaked up the heat.

Relieved, she wiped the sweat from her brow when Brath sent the second row to the posts. These students had parried better, but none successfully executed an attack. They lacked the speed and experience they would acquire in the years to come. Gratefully, she took the water Brath offered her before he left.

After half an hour, he reappeared. "Let's see what else you've got." Her former teacher circled his arms to warm up his shoulders.

That too! Inwardly she groaned, took up her position in front of him, and waited. He stepped back and raised his sword as he readied himself for the attack.

She parried the first blow, but she had not prepared for its force. She staggered back a few steps. Brath would not give her any leeway—just like before. He attacked again, leaving her no time for a counterattack.

"You better concentrate! Didn't I teach you that?" he rebuked her.

And then—she felt it. A tingling in her stomach and a warmth flooding through her. Brath's movements slowed down. She reacted without thinking, took an alternating step, bounced off his sword with a loud crack, stepped back, then brought her sword into a favorable position. Instead of parrying the blow, he gave her a blocking thrust. Immediately she stopped using her gift. The more often she used it, the more natural it became.

He lowered his sword. "That's better. Your movements are becoming more fluid."

He increased the pace and difficulty. Despite the sun, his strength did not diminish.

Someone clapped. "Bravo, swordmaster, but you should take care of your students. They're bored out of their minds. I'm happy to take over."

"Hemmet," Brath hissed. His eyebrows drew together.

Somewhat irritated, she looked at Hemmet. His face seemed familiar. Short brown hair waved over amused green eyes. His posture portrayed tension, even if his facial expressions revealed nothing. His full lips were twisted into a smug smile as he approached them.

"Rarely do we get a visit from a pretty lady who is also good at fighting." Ignoring Brath's scowl, Hemmet gave her a broad smile, took her hand, and breathed a kiss on it. "I remember you. You came to the academy a year after me."

Although she thought hard, she could not place him.

"Hemmet Aquilia. It's been a long time."

"Yes, I remember," she groaned.

The son of the lord of Relerin! Unlike his father, he looked quite attractive. He was two years older than Liya, tall, and athletically built. His face was lightly tanned, and his sea-green eyes and flawless teeth shone in the sun.

Grinning, he turned to their teacher. "I'll take over."

Brath merely nodded, gave her an apologetic look, and stood at the edge of the practice field. What was wrong with him? This submissive behavior did not fit the swordmaster she knew.

"My lady, let's get started."

She spent the next half hour fending off his attacks. Something about this man gave her the creeps. During the fight, something kept flaring up in his eyes that deeply disturbed her. *He came here on purpose. I know it. But why?* They were never in touch, and Liya had nothing to do with the academy anymore. Although she hadn't come for just training, she'd also wanted to hear what's going on. Typically, the academy was full of political influence, as the lords were always looking for any kind of information they could obtain.

"I think that's enough for today," she declared as she parried Hemmet's horizontal blow. Her clothes stuck to her body; her hair curled with sweat.

"Too bad, I was just getting warmed up."

"All the students here are available for you to practice."

"Training the aspirants is Brath's job, not mine."

"And what is your job?"

"I have been running the Sword Institute for two years. What do you say we have lunch together?"

"Unfortunately, I have some things to do. Another time."

"I'll take your word for it, Liya. You owe me a meal." With that, he said goodbye.

Brath stepped up to her. "Be on guard; he's dangerous," he said when Hemmet was out of sight.

"How is it that he, of all people, heads one of the institutes?" The heads of the other five institutes were a lot older than Hemmet and had considerably more experience.

"His father got him the position." He sighed. "I don't get involved in politics, not anymore."

That surprised her. "You sound bitter."

"The infighting hasn't lessened since you left us, on the contrary."

She listened. Because of the relative independence of the military in peacetime, not even the king knew in detail what was going on in the academy—what games were being played.

They left the arena. On the way to the shelters, he continued talking. "After Gralin left us, not only was a new academy director elected, but the positions of the six institute directors were also up for election. That I did not apply for the leadership of the Sword Institute at that time was a mistake. Nysa was a good captain and led our institute properly, but he did not recognize the political intrigues. Two years ago, he left the Academy— overnight, and without warning. In order to appoint a successor, the board would have had to meet. But that would have taken months, and we were in the middle of preparing for exams. Someone was appointed to take over his duties until a legitimate election was held."

"Hemmet."

"Correct. In the end, it took eight months for the committee to actually meet. Enough time for Hemmet to make his mark. His father was the influential lord of Relerin, so he was elected. There was no opposing candidate."

"Hemmet was not too young for that? After all, the traditions of the last centuries are supreme."

"How he did it, I'm not sure. Even Sendal voted for him."

"Really?" This surprised Liya. "And that his father supports Prem wasn't an issue at all?"

"No, not even a discussion point."

"That's somehow unbelievable."

"Maybe there's a correlation between Sendal's approval and the significantly lower number of students," Brath murmured.

As they passed the courtyard, they came across students hurrying to their classes.

"Did he take a bribe?" she whispered. That would be hard to believe, but Sendal *had* always used every opportunity to exclude young girls.

"I don't know. One would think there would be a balance of power in our academy and its six institutes, but that's not the case. Warren Hevmeri, our current academy director, seems to be very susceptible to power games. On more than one occasion, he has overturned reforms depending on which institute flattered him more."

She couldn't believe what she was hearing. The six institutes—bow, sword, riding, hand-to-hand combat, alchemy, and officer—had always been in competition, but the welfare of the entire academy had always been the main goal. This was especially true in wartime. Instead, the institutes seemed to be fighting each other.

"Institute leaders are putting up with this from Warren?" she inquired.

"On financial issues, Warren holds the reins. And he is very—well—fickle, distributing money as he sees fit. Hemmet is often the beneficiary. What plays a big role in all this is the military academy's desire to gain more influence in politics. A thorn in the side of our leaders is, above all, the special position of the Mages' Guild at court. The Mages' Guild is repeatedly consulted by the king on political issues or conflicts, while our academy is only consulted for military matters. The participation of the General of the First Legion in the Council of the Wise was no longer enough for them. They want more representatives of the Military Academy in the Council, and these should also be appointed as active advisors to the Court."

"How did Louis react to that?"

"He has granted the Generals of the Second and Third Legions a place on the Council of the Wise."

She recalled that at the meeting she and Ewan had called immediately after their return from Qilon, lieutenants on the council had also been present.

"Yes, I think this was one of the goals of this appointment."

"Are Warren, the institute directors, and their backers happy with that?"

"I think so, at least for a start. The head of the academy and the heads of the institutes now have access to information that they were previously denied. I don't even want to know which lords they're feeding it to in order to profit from it."

"Isn't that what everyone who sits on a board does?" she mused aloud.

The members of the council, lords, mages, and military members were subject to secrecy, but they informed their own people.

"As I said, things have changed." For a brief moment, Brath seemed absent.

"Why does the academy suddenly want more influence? For decades, everyone was happy, right?"

"The question is, who is looking for more power?"

"You think that's why Hemmet was appointed and supported?"

"Yeah. Traditions and rules have been adjusted since he joined. Do I believe in all these strange coincidences? *I don't think so.* They put their henchmen or relatives in appropriate positions and at court. It's all about information. Knowledge means power."

"Surely, King Louis is capable of understanding this strategy. Why does he allow it?"

"Even a king needs the support of the nobility. Apart from that, there is no evidence of my spinning. I'm just an old man who no one pays attention to anymore. Some would go so far as to call me bitter." He smirked.

She needed to have a closer look into the lord of Relerin and his son to figure out whom they were working with. This might be helpful for the issues Louis was having with Prem. She knew the lords had a close relationship, but would Hemmet and his father support Prem? How far would they go to get more power?

"I don't think so. Maybe it's worth getting more information about that."

"Are you now acting as the spy of the king?" he asked with a grin.

"A what? I don't know what you're talking about," she replied with a smile.

He nodded. "You and I, we have so much in common. Little attention is paid to us. Although you have been promoted, you are not talked about at court. Your name is rarely mentioned. Not even an affair with the king is attributed to you. I'm not in the front row either, acting more in secret." After a pause, he added, "There is one thing I always wonder, though. What moves the king to give so much power to a young girl like you?"

She giggled. "An affair it is not."

When he laughed, his crooked teeth flashed. "I thought so."

"What else do they gossip about at court?" she asked.

"Quite a few things. Rumor has it that the queen has moved out of the shared bedroom."

"Is this the most exciting news from the palace?"

"Ah, you're not satisfied with conventional gossip!" Brath's eyes sparkled. "It is also rumored that the king has tangled with Prem and his minions."

"Everyone knows that by now," she replied, frowning. She sensed that her former teacher was keeping something from her. "Do you trust me, Brath? Didn't you just mention that we have so much in common? There's something else. I know it."

"Your direct manner has often gotten you into trouble, my child. You should be more careful in the future. We live in dangerous times." He stopped in front of the shelter. "Will you come to visit us more often now?"

"If you allow it. I need to train more."

"You are welcome, and you know where to find me."

He had dodged her question, though he must know she'd gather her own information, too.

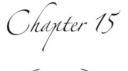

Chapter 15

"Liya, where are your thoughts today?" Ewan inquired as they marched together to the palace. "You seem so changed since your return from Dar'Angaar. Is everything really all right?"

Inwardly, she sighed. Of *course,* Ewan had noticed that she was more silent than usual. She didn't want to lie to him. "I have a lot to think about." To distract him, she asked, "How well do you know Hemmet?"

"Why do you care?"

"He trained with me this morning."

"You better stay away from him. His father supports Prem."

This did not surprise her. Perhaps she had already sensed it. The border between empathy and magical perception was fluid. Sometimes it was hard to say *when* she was using her gift, and not just her intuition and perception. She had to concentrate to feel active emotions, but sensing truth or danger came naturally to her. This also helped to release the magic energy built up from the ban; she had no choice. As for Hemmet, her friend didn't need to know about her intention to accept his offer for a meal.

"Hemmet is Aquilia's eldest son, isn't he?" she asked as casually as she could.

"Yes," he answered guilelessly. "Hemmet now lives permanently in the palace city, while his brother remained in Relerin."

"The family of Relerin are rich, aren't they?"

"Yes, and powerful too. This family has ruled for many decades. Aquilia has requested more soldiers for his city. Louis has agreed, but the cost must be borne by the lord."

"You think this might be a reason for him to support Prem? He can afford the extra cost, after all."

"I have experienced many things, Liya. Greed for power and revenge knows no bounds."

She found the evidence quite thin, but perhaps Ewan was right. It was possible that Aquilia wanted revenge for the support withheld from him.

Arriving at the palace, the guards let them pass unhindered. They walked silently through the corridor leading to the study.

Standing in the open doorway, a picture on the wall briefly diverted Liya's attention—a map of Namoor measuring at least two meters. A few other pictures hung between the shelves full of books. The king sat behind his desk, bent over a roll of parchment that he was writing on with a quill. When the footman announced their arrival, he looked up. They stepped closer and bowed.

"Your Majesty," Ewan greeted formally.

With his left hand, Louis gestured for them to take a seat in the comfortable armchairs on the other side of his desk.

"I'm glad to see you back, Liya," Louis told her. "I would have liked to see you sooner, but I couldn't move my schedule without attracting attention." He poured two glasses of water and asked, "Was your trip successful?"

"The Nirm have been sensing changes for several months now. One of them flew me to Dar'Angaar. In doing so, he defied the council's decision."

She took a deep breath. "I didn't make it to the capital, but I was able to ask around in some villages. The people are fearful. Something's going on. Non-human creatures are attacking innocent people."

"Have you seen these creatures?"

She nodded. "I fought a bunch of them. They are much stronger and faster than humans. Their bodies are covered with fur, and their eyes glow red. Their stature bears a resemblance to a human, but also to a wolf. It's really strange."

Louis leaned back in his armchair. He propped himself on the backrest with one hand, scratching his chin with the other, which disappeared into a thicket of brown beard. "Maybe Amaar is breeding warriors of his own."

"I don't think so. I watched his soldiers fight these creatures."

Lost in thought, Louis nodded. He didn't seem convinced. "Did you notice anything else? Are they using relics from the Ancient Era?"

Now the time had come. She felt a flutter in her stomach. "Relics?"

"I wouldn't be surprised if they had artifacts from the Ancient Era," Louis replied. "After all, the territory of present-day Dar'Angaar was once the stronghold for explorations by the Elders."

"Really?" This was new information for her. What else did the king know?

He waved it off. "What else did you find out?"

"I am sure that Dar'Angaar is well prepared in case of war. There is no doubt about that."

"I'll ask again!" Louis sighed. "What about relics and special equipment that might be from the Ancient Era?"

"The soldiers fight with swords and bows. Magic, however, is used openly. In an emergency, this would give their warriors an advantage."

"We have the Mages' Guild," the king replied.

With difficulty, she suppressed a snort. "We should do everything in our power to prevent a war."

"You think our chances are bad when it comes to a war, don't you?"

"We need more time to upgrade and more knowledge about everything related to the scroll."

"The Council of the Wise sees it differently. They want to send our army to the border to make the first strike if necessary. They believe that Dar'Angaar is reaching for more power to exact revenge."

"Why should they seek revenge? It was their king who betrayed us," she pointed out. What was this all about? After hearing the true story of Keldor, the first king of Namoor, she no longer ruled out anything.

"There are two sides to every story, Liya. Keldor had an alliance with Dar'Angaar and felt betrayed by them. You know the records. Dar'Angaar withdrew its entire army and abandoned us. The fighting in Elladur had still been going on when they changed their strategy. There must have been a reason for this. Perhaps they saw treachery! Ultimately, this discord led Dar'Angaar to isolate itself."

The king's words sounded convincing. She wondered if he knew that Keldor had opened the gates. Was that why Dar'Angaar had withdrawn? If only she could ask Haydn about it. She quickly pushed the thought of him away and concentrated on the conversation.

"I don't think we'll ever know the whole truth," she explained. "Still, I don't think the change in Dar'Angaar's policy has anything to do with revenge."

"Maybe they've found something that will give them the edge."

Discomfort spread through her. It seemed as if Louis suspected something. But that could not be. Deep inside her, something resisted telling him about the crystal. Why?

Louis eyed her, making her more self-conscious. *Why is he doing that?* He knew very well that she had mastered her facial expressions. Did he want to unsettle her? He would not succeed. *Where are these thoughts coming from?* she wondered. He was her king, and she trusted him.

Louis cleared his throat. "I want you to travel to Kapilar and see Prem."

What did that mean? It sounded like a comparatively *normal* order. "Did you find anything out, your majesty?"

"Prem is sealing off his city more and more. That worries me. He's moved the marketplace outside the gates, and the merchants now stay outside the walls. Look around and try to find out what's going on."

"The people in Kapilar are very secretive. I'm afraid they won't tell me much."

"That's why you will go to Prem and talk to him. Thanks to your special ability, you will at least be able to distinguish the truth from the lie."

She felt extremely uncomfortable at the thought of Prem. Every time she had met him, she had felt this emotional coldness, as if he had no feelings.

"You set out the day after tomorrow, for I fear Prem has a spy at court. I want to avoid him finding out about your visit too soon."

She agreed. It might also be helpful to get more information about his alliances.

"How do the Nirm feel about us?" Ewan interfered in the conversation. She was startled; she had almost forgotten him.

"It's a little complicated," she admitted. "The Nirm don't want war. Some of their leaders don't think they should get involved. Others would support us. They haven't made a final decision yet."

Sighing, Louis rose, walked to the window, and looked out. "Be that as it may, we must prepare for the worst." With a jolt, he turned to Ewan. "You will take command of the legions sooner than planned. William's retirement will be brought forward. He will be assembling a small force to carry out special missions for me. I need to make sure the army is not infiltrated. His influence will help me do that. Talk to him, and we'll discuss how to proceed."

His gaze drifted to the door. "The mages should be arriving soon."

Mages? She could not believe her ears. Just as Ewan was about to say something, there was a knock. Involuntarily, she tensed her muscles. Three men in black robes entered the study. One of them had a burgundy collar and silk cuffs. Silently they bowed.

"Thank you for coming," the king greeted them.

With a brisk gesture, he motioned all present to follow him to the oval conference table. After he had sat down at the head of the table, he asked Ewan and Liya to take a seat right next to him.

"Gentlemen," he continued, "you already know Ewan. Liya is First Emissary of our country." He turned to her. "Master Almany is the head of the Mage Council. His companions are Master Darwin and Master Julian." He gestured with his hand to each of the mages.

Darwin looked the oldest with his long white beard and graying hair that spiked from his head in all directions. His full lips twisted into a smirk as he adjusted his small glasses.

Almany took a seat and bunched his bushy eyebrows together. He crossed scrawny arms over an eerily thin figure.

Julian towered over everyone in the room. He eyed her coolly with deep blue eyes. It was probably important for him to keep his distance. Strong, broad shoulders completed his athletic figure, and the slight shadow of a beard on his face softened the hard expression.

With a questioning look, Louis looked from one mage to the other. "I assumed that all the council members would do me the honor?"

Almany cleared his throat. "Master Daniel and Master Rian are busy with research that they cannot interrupt."

With a slightly mocking expression, Louis tapped his fingers on the arm of the chair. "Very well. At our last meeting, I hinted that we must work more closely together, not least because of the dark shadows that are spreading over our world and which you, honored masters of magic, surely sense more clearly than the rest of us. Now you have important news for us, do you not?" His eyes rested on Almany.

The chief magician stroked his chin. "That is so, your majesty. For a long time, we have felt that something is brewing. From the beginning, we suspected that the events had to do with the Ancient Era. Our fears were confirmed. Dar'Angaar is drawing on knowledge from the Ancient Era with the goal of destroying us."

Ewan looked up. "Destroying us?"

"Of course!" Almany looked even grimmer. "Why do you think Keldor founded the Mages' Guild in the first place? To protect our knowledge and gift from those renegade mages in Dar'Angaar who do not abide by any rules or laws. They have never accepted our way of life. Their values, alone, are valid."

Liya's displeasure grew. Almany, of all people, was judging others. The Mages' Guild knew neither mercy nor compassion. Either one followed their internal laws, or one was branded a traitor. She snorted contemptuously. The attention of all present turned to her.

"You doubt my words?" Almany grunted.

His cold gaze and scowling face were probably meant to frighten her, but she felt no fear, only rejection.

Before she could say anything, Julian spoke up. "We have come across a ritual that can open the gates of the worlds."

"*Gates of the worlds?* This is the first time I've heard of that," Ewan said, completely taken aback. "What worlds, then? Surely there's only one."

"There you are mistaken, honored captain. There are at least two." Darwin adjusted his glasses. "You must imagine it as follows. Our worlds are separated from each other by invisible bands. These bands have no fixed shape, are constantly in motion, and—well—one of them has cracks. Since there are no more World Guardians, nobody cares about it. We didn't notice the cracks until they were big enough to threaten the balance of the worlds. Experienced sorcerers sense fluctuations in this balance."

Louis frowned. "What else did you find out?"

Liya found this reaction extremely strange. The king should have been blindsided. Louis knew more than she had assumed.

Julian turned to the king. "We do not yet know how the cracks came about, but we suspect Dar'Angaar's mages are behind it. To what extent Lord Jadmar is involved, we cannot say. However, we believe he has nothing to do with it."

"What is the effect of these cracks?" demanded Louis.

Almany shook his head. "We don't know for sure. However, the records say that if the cracks are big enough, beings from the other world can slip through."

Immediately she thought of the creature in the crystal room. Despite its resemblance to the giants from the forest, it had been different—*unusual, stronger, more powerful.*

"What creatures?" she asked.

Darwin answered, "There are only a few writings, preserved from the Ancient Era. In the illustrations that are available to us, we recognize beings that look like mutated people—a mixture of wolf and human. It seems that they draw light out of people and devour it. We interpret it to mean that these beasts are reaching for souls. That's all we know."

"Have the gates been opened?" the king asked. He sounded somehow threatening.

Nervously, Almany intertwined his long fingers. "No, not yet. But the bigger the cracks get, the easier it will be to open the gates."

Louis nodded to Ewan, who pulled a copy of the scroll from his doublet and unrolled it across the table. "What does this tell you?"

"Where did you get that?" growled Almany.

"May I?" Without waiting for an answer, Darwin stood up. His eyes lit up as he examined the scroll. "The scroll is written in the language of the ancient times. This parchment is exceedingly valuable."

We didn't need an expert for that insight, Liya said to herself. Judging from their facial expressions, Louis and Ewan thought the same thing.

Darwin tapped an icon at the top of the map with his index finger. "Look here. The planets are in a line. In such a constellation, we perceive the elements more intensely because the cosmic energy penetrates to us unfiltered. Water, earth, air, and fire have greater power, and our gift is amplified many times over. This means the energies of the elements can be used to a much greater extent. Theoretically, a group of enormously powerful mages could open the gates without the help of magical artifacts. To put it bluntly, the mages of Dar'Angaar would be able to open the gates and let darkness into our world."

Alarmed, she looked up. "Darkness?"

"On the other side of the ribbon, a mighty army stands ready with a ruler stronger and more powerful than all our kings and princes. His goal is to reorder the worlds."

Ewan frowned. "I've never heard of that before."

Almany gave him a meaningful look. "This is not the kind of knowledge that you pass on outside the guild."

The fact that the king said nothing perplexed Liya. He didn't seem particularly surprised, so he already knew about it. "Where does this ruler come from?" she asked.

"From the Ancient Era. His soul is as dark as his magic," Almany replied.

"How can he still be alive?" she probed.

"His magic is responsible for that. He exists as pure dark energy in the world beyond the ribbon. All beings there are pure energy. However, in the transition to our world, some of them can manifest a physical body for themselves and others," Almany replied.

Incredulous silence filled the room. After a while, Darwin pointed to another sign. Inside a large circle was a smaller one divided by a prong, obviously a lightning bolt. Four thin strokes connected it to the large circle. They reminded her of the legs of a spider.

"The symbol of the World Guardians. We need them to defeat this ruler from the other world. Only the Guardians carry the ancient knowledge, the luminous wisdom of the gods." He sighed. "Hm, do you see the eye with the rays of the sun? I have discovered this symbol in other writings as well. It contains encoded messages. I need a candle or a fire."

Curious, she eyed the sign. The king leaned forward. There were rays of sunlight above his eye and within it, no more than half a finger long.

"I haven't noticed that eye before," Louis said softly.

Ewan went to the mantelpiece, took a candlestick, and made an effort to hand it to Darwin, who demurred. "We must be careful that the paper does not catch fire. It's best if you hold the candle and I hold the scroll," he explained.

"Lights up!" Louis said, agreeing with Darwin.

Everyone looked at the map expectantly.

Darwin held his breath for a moment. "Look," he groaned, "the first signs are appearing below the eye."

Indeed! Letters of black ink formed on the paper.

"*The guardian of light,*" Darwin whispered, "*and the dark knight... strong is the bond... easily broken... in the dark land.*" Closing his eyes, he lowered the scroll and quietly repeated the text. "*The guarding of the light, and the dark knight, strong is the bond, easily broken in the dark land.*" He opened his eyes and looked around. "I have read these words before in an ancient scripture. The message continues: *the day becomes night, and his shadows come into sight. He is the eternal darkness, the remaining stillness. Nothing will be safe anymore; your soul is his forevermore.*"

"What does that mean?" asked Louis.

"We don't know." Darwin took off his glasses and put one of the temples in his mouth.

Something about the text seemed familiar to Liya. Darwin paced up and down the room. He was getting increasingly nervous.

"*The guardian of the light*—meaning the World Guardians or allies of the Guardians," he pondered aloud. "*The dark knight?*" He stopped, looked up briefly with a furrowed brow, then continued. "That's the ruler and his allies in the other world. But I don't understand how the bond can be strong. It doesn't make sense."

Louis took the scroll. "Perhaps the writer of this prophecy means something different than we suspect? Maybe our interpretation is wrong."

Almany's eyebrows formed a continuous line. "There's nothing unclear about the term," he pressed out.

"Light cannot exist without darkness," she replied, not knowing exactly why she had said that.

"Everything is connected," the king said thoughtfully.

"But that doesn't change the facts." Almany clicked his tongue.

"Besides," Ewan spoke up, "there are no World Guardians anymore. Are there?"

Julian nodded. "According to the lore, all of Elladur's people were wiped out, including the Guardians."

"The few who survived the war were persecuted and killed," Almany added.

"I don't see it that way," Darwin said.

Liya's heartbeat stopped for a moment. Like everyone else, she turned to Darwin. The tension in the room was almost palpable.

The tall mage tugged at his beard. "In my opinion, the World Guardians have found a way to protect themselves. The question we should ask is not whether they exist, but whether they will help us."

Silence reigned. *All this roughly fits with what the Nirm said*, Liya thought.

"Do we know when exactly the planets will be in alignment?" asked Louis in a hoarse voice as he stared at the scroll, unblinking.

Darwin nodded, then turned to Julian. "You should look at this. If the Red Brotherhood could calculate the time, then we should be able to do the same. After all, they're already preparing everything for the opening of the gates."

She wheeled around. The Mages' Guild knew about the Brotherhood's plans!

"When exactly were you planning to share this information with us?" the king hissed angrily.

Darwin lowered his eyes. Almany looked at Louis firmly. "We suspect that the Red Brotherhood is making common cause with Dar'Angaar to open the gates. It was not our intention to withhold anything from you. However, we prefer to verify our theory thoroughly before saying anything."

"I will decide if and when information will be further investigated. From now on, you will report any clues, theories, or other knowledge to me immediately."

Almany pressed her lips together, but he seemed to agree. Liya fought against a wave of nausea. This couldn't be. Haydn would not open the gates—or would he? Was the Red Brotherhood really under his command?

"Suppose your theory is correct. What will happen then?" asked Ewan. He looked unusually pale.

"The members of the Red Brotherhood are not so powerful that they could open the gates without magical artifacts. They need this constellation in which earth, water, air, and fire are amplified."

As Almany paused, Liya sensed another secret was about to be revealed. Her heart skipped a beat.

"Only a few members of the royal families descended from the Elders, as well as the Guardians of Elladur, mastered all four elements. In recent decades, I have instructed only a few students who were able to command just two."

Liya swallowed. She saw Louis give the old mage an inscrutable look.

"What if the opening of the gates required not only the power of the four elements but also the blood of a ruler? And that of a ruler who has been crowned *king* in the *ancient ceremony* and has received the *ancient consecrations?*" the king said.

Her heart pounded against her ribs. This simply could not be true!

Darwin's eyes widened. "That's why the coronation," he muttered.

Almany shook his head. "I can't imagine that."

As if through a veil, she perceived Darwin taking a few steps up and down the room. Her breathing became heavier. It made no sense to close herself off to the truth.

At last, Darwin stopped. "Amaar's family ruled long before the war. Why it was decided then to stop holding coronations, I don't know. But that doesn't change the fact that through his veins runs the blood of the Elders." His gaze fixed on Louis. "Just like yours, your majesty."

An eerie silence filled the room. *Another piece of the puzzle.*

The king took a deep breath. "No one outside this room should know about this," he ordered. His tone allowed no contradiction.

Darwin cleared his throat. "Please forgive me. In my zeal, I didn't consider that not everyone in this room knows."

"I trust Liya and Ewan. They will keep my secret."

Ewan shook his head. His face was ashen. It was not long ago that he'd had to cope with the fact that his king had the gift of magic, and now this... "You control the four elements, your majesty, just like Amaar," he whispered in disbelief.

"So it is! Even though my mother's line does not go back to the Elders," Louis confirmed. He turned to Darwin. "I need to know more about Amaar's family tree. Then we can better judge how distinctive his abilities are."

Stunned, she looked around. Ewan was in shock. Almany and Julian could hardly believe their theory was correct down to the last detail. Darwin smiled contentedly to himself.

Everything had changed in the last few minutes. Louis was not only the king, but he was also a descendant of the Elders. The bloodlines of the ruling families from the Ancient Era had been considered extinct since the Great War. It was said that the Elders had possessed incredible knowledge and enormous magical abilities. Why had Louis and Haydn hidden their bloodlines? Why had Haydn stolen the crystal if he didn't need it? It didn't make sense.

With some resentment, she congratulated herself for taking the crystal and keeping it safe. Her decision had been the right one. She closed her eyes to suppress the rising nausea.

"What about the stone tablets?" When Louis broke the silence, she winced and opened her eyes.

She had not given the stone slabs a second thought. For the first time, Almany smiled. These artifacts must be of utmost importance.

"We have found all but one. The messages that were carved are almost completely deciphered and decoded," the chief mage announced proudly. "The tablets show us the way to Elladur."

All eyes were on him. Nervously, he plucked at his thick brows.

"Of course—Elladur!" Louis frowned. "That darn country!"

Almany gave the king a deeply indignant look. "Elladur is the source of magic," he groaned. "If the gates are indeed opened, we will need assistance. We hope to find relics from the Ancient Era in Elladur that will help us." After a moment, he added, "Also, we now know where the last stone tablet is."

Louis looked at him questioningly.

"In Qilon," Almany pressed out.

The mage was hiding something. The king had not missed it either, she knew, but Louis did not inquire further.

"Where exactly in Qilon?" inquired Ewan. His face had gained some color.

Almany put on an expressionless face. "In the mausoleum behind the palace."

Louis turned to Ewan. "We need to organize the withdrawal of our troops. I think this is a task you should take on. It's also a good opportunity to look at the mausoleum."

Ewan grinned. He'd fully composed himself. Judging from Almany's expression, the chief magician agreed.

"It's not easy to get in there, though." Louis' gaze wandered to the mages. "Supposedly, the Grand Duke has protected the mausoleum with a spell. It would be wise for someone to accompany Ewan."

"I'll do that," Julian offered.

"I've made a map that should help you find the stone tablet," Almany explained.

The tension in the room eased.

Louis rose. "Darwin, as soon as you find out anything about the family tree, come to me—immediately." His gaze wandered from one to the other. "What we discussed today is subject to secrecy. If anything gets out, I will know about it. Be aware of that." He took a deep breath before continuing, "That will be all for now. Thank you. Ewan, we will now discuss the troop withdrawal."

With these words, all the others were dismissed. The mages rose, gave a courteous bow, and left the room.

As Liya prepared to follow them, Louis said, "I'll expect your report as soon as you get back. Then contact Ewan immediately."

With a nod, she slipped through the door. Deeply disturbed, she battled dark thoughts on the way out. She could barely grasp the implications of what she had just heard. The order of her world was fading. Everything she believed was being called into question. Where would this lead?

As she walked down the steps to the city, her eyes fell on Hemmet. He was standing at the bottom of the stairs, almost as if he'd been waiting for her. Under no circumstances could she let her inner restlessness show now.

"How did you know where I was?" she inquired.

"I'm on my way to the Bright Star Tavern. Pure coincidence that I met you."

His green eyes twinkled with amusement. He took her hand and deftly maneuvered them through the crowd. At lunchtime, the streets were bustling with activity. People swarmed everywhere.

What he had said didn't quite add up somehow. "Bright Star is that way," she said, stopping and pointing with her chin in another direction.

"Are you really going to make your way through there?" He pointed to the busy street.

"Do you have a better idea?"

"Follow me." He skillfully guided her through the alleys to the city gate.

Puzzled, she looked into the forest. "Are we going berry picking now?"

"You could say that." He pushed her through the gate, led her down the road a bit, and then turned onto a forest path.

A few minutes later, they reached a clearing. A blanket with a basket on top was spread out under a tree.

She raised an eyebrow. "A picnic?"

"I thought it would be more pleasant than going to a crowded tavern."

So, he had known exactly where he would meet her and had prepared everything. They sat down. Hemmet conjured a bottle of wine, bread, cheese, pâté, and grapes from the basket. He shrugged apologetically. "I couldn't find any more in a hurry." He poured the wine. "Cheers."

She sipped from her glass, ignoring his remark and masking her discomfort. He was up to something.

"Unfortunately, I won't be able to train with you for the next few days. I have to go away," Hemmet said.

"I hadn't planned on your assistance with my combat training anyway."

"I know that. Still, it's been fun. We can continue as soon as I get back."

"I'd love to," she replied, smiling. "A few more weeks and I'll be back to my old form."

"Why did you drop out of training then? Your chances of staying in the academy were not bad. At least, that's what I heard."

"You asked about me?" Her uneasiness intensified.

"A little."

"My father insisted on sending me to the academy," she replied, "probably because he had been there himself and served the king. For my fifth birthday, he gave me a wooden sword, and a year later, a bow. But I never intended to stay there."

"You were a son and daughter in one, so to speak."

She was not comfortable with the course of the conversation. She couldn't tell him too much about herself. "How was it with you?" she deflected.

"My choices were limited from birth. It's family tradition for the firstborn to pursue a military career."

"They must be very proud of you; after all, you are the youngest institute director ever at the academy."

"I'm sure my father doesn't see it that way. He'd rather I had Warren's position. But of course—you're right. I've come a considerable way. However, nothing has been given to me; you can believe that, even if some people say so." He frowned. "It's taken a lot out of me. I didn't have time for a wife and children."

Should there be a noble couple who would not have liked Hemmet as their son-in-law! "Your sisters' marriages were arranged."

"Somehow, it's my job in the family to make my father's life miserable." He grinned. "I refused to marry the women who were chosen for me. My father has had his way with me far too often."

His openness amazed her.

"And you, why aren't you married yet?" he followed up.

"Hasn't come up yet, I guess."

"I don't understand. You're smart, pretty, and you can handle a sword. Men should be lining up for you."

"Of course. Most people dream of having a woman like me by their side." She contorted her face.

"Maybe you're a little headstrong... and not exactly a quiet companion. Still, you should have plenty of admirers."

"I'm not worried about that."

His expression became serious. "I'd like to get to know you better."

Something was wrong. She often received advances, but she didn't buy Hemmet's interest in her. "Why?" she asked as guilelessly as possible. "To upset your father when he hears we're seeing each other?"

"What do you think of me?" He pretended to be indignant. Then he laughed. "I'm out of that age. Although I must admit, it would have—now that you mention it—its appeal. But no, I really want to know more about you."

She frowned. "Can we talk openly?"

"I'm asking for it."

"You should spend your time with your own kind. I'm sure it's not hard to find a young noblewoman who appreciates your advances. I'm the wrong person."

"So, you find me attractive?" he replied with a grin. "It's a start."

She gave him an innocent smile. "I wouldn't overstate that if I were you. There are plenty of attractive men out there."

"There's more to you than meets the eye." His smile was as attractive as it was inscrutable.

"You don't know me well enough to judge," she quickly replied.

"I'm trying to change that right now."

"What for?"

As he looked at her closely, he seemed to think about his answer. "You underestimate your person. After all, you are the first emissary of the king. I run an institute of the military academy and have a good connection to some lords. *Politically*, we complement each other perfectly. Our connection would open doors for us. If we spend more time together, you might realize I'm not a bad guy at all. Friendship isn't the worst basis for marriage, and sometimes more can come of it."

Brath had been right. Hemmet belonged to the group of young, ambitious lords who wanted to aim high. He was concerned with expanding his position. She had to be on her guard.

"That may be so," she replied as calmly as possible. "But for my part, I am exactly where I want to be. I would hardly be of any use to you."

"I don't want to upset you." He lowered his eyes. "Should I have been so wrong? After all, you are now part of the king's inner circle of advisors. That goes far beyond your role as an emissary."

"You overestimate me by a long shot. I stumbled into this job. I really have no further ambitions."

"Please, don't be angry. I had a choice to be honest or to flatter you. I chose the truth." He moved closer. "You are beautiful and smart, Liya. I'd really like to get to know you better. Maybe my first impression is wrong, and I'll find I don't like you at all." He laughed briefly. "Who knows what strange habits you have."

Against her will, she had to smile. "You'd be surprised."

"Will you give our friendship a chance if I promise not to talk about our work?"

The ice was getting thin. There was no way she could continue this conversation. "We should be on our way. I already told you I don't have much time."

There was a reason why he was asking for it. Liya had the feeling that there was more behind his approach. What role was Hemmet playing? Was he working with Prem? She needed to figure this out, and he might be useful to get some information. She would play her role and see where it led her. She always trusted her intuition. Nevertheless, she couldn't promise anything. She needed to be careful.

He gave her a disappointed look.

The town had quieted a little. As they strolled down the main street, Hemmet told her about his siblings.

"You seem to care a lot about your brother."

"Yes, I want to bring him to me as soon as possible. Next year he will celebrate his sixteenth birthday. He will complete his two years at the military academy and then assist my father in the administration and government of our principality."

"So, he's going into politics?"

"That's the way it's supposed to be, although my brother would rather write. He's really a good storyteller. But hacks are not welcome in our family."

"Somehow, I thought *you* would follow your father."

"No, my uncle, my father's oldest brother, was a captain in the First Legion. He died six years ago; his heart gave out. So, my future place was in the military. My family strives to be present in all the important areas."

"Doesn't seem so easy with your family."

"Everything has pros and cons."

"Liya!" someone shouted.

When she turned around, she saw Ewan coming toward her, waving. As soon as he caught sight of her companion, his expression darkened.

"Hemmet." Ewan looked past him.

"Ewan." Hemmet smirked.

"I've been looking for you." Ewan stared at the basket in Hemmet's hand.

"I guess that's my cue—regrettably." Hemmet leaned down to her and whispered, "I'd really like it if we could be friends. Take good care of yourself."

She frowned, and he winked at her. "See you soon," he said. He gave Ewan a big grin and left.

"What was that all about?" hissed Ewan.

"I wanted to find out if Hemmet knew anything about Prem. The meeting was not as bad as I'd feared."

"Not so bad? Liya. His father supports Prem. You really should listen to me." Ewan sounded angry. "What did he want? He won't have met with you without a reason."

"He wants to get to know me better." Her annoyance grew as his bad mood rubbed off on her.

"Oh, really? He probably wants to get information from the palace through you. That would be just like him."

"Ewan, let's not get into that. Why were you looking for me?"

"You have to be careful. It could reflect badly on you if you keep seeing him."

She stopped and crossed her arms. "Oh, please! Doesn't it reflect badly on you when you have fun with all the daughters of the nobility?"

"That's different."

"Why?"

"Because these women have no interest in information and don't sound me out about King Louis, his policies, and—state secrets."

"Like I'm giving anything away! You can trust me about that. And maybe he really likes me. After all, I'm a woman."

"I didn't mean it that way, you know that." He took a deep breath. "Why are you defending him? I thought you didn't like him."

Her friend thought she was a naive girl. Annoyed, she bit her lower lip. She didn't care about Hemmet. "Why were you looking for me?" she asked gruffly.

"Julian and I are leaving for Qilon tomorrow. Are you coming with us? We could accompany you as far as Kapilar."

"No, I will travel with the merchants."

"Are you sure?"

"For sure!"

When the towers of Kapilar appeared some distance away, Liya rode a little slower. Exhaustion wore on her bones from the last three weeks. She was looking forward to a break.

However, she wished there was another reason for her stay. The lord of Kapilar had a nasty reputation and was known to be quick-tempered. There was no way around a meeting with him.

According to rumors, Prem hired more mercenaries. His soldiers did not seem to be enough for him. Prem had to be made aware that the king had eyes and ears everywhere. If necessary, Liya should threaten him openly. That thought gave her goosebumps. *Hopefully, I won't have to do that,* she groaned inwardly.

As she progressed on her journey, the mountains on the left flattened, and the outlines of the city became larger and clearer. Some field workers were still working, though dusk was setting in. She rode slowly past the fields. The men and women did not even look up. After a while, she could see that there was an unusually large number of sentries patrolling the city walls. She also made out craftsmen. So Prem was renewing the protective wall.

As she rode through the gray gate, she noticed the mercenaries. They cavorted in the simple wooden huts just behind the city wall, which otherwise served as shelters for the sentries.

It took her a while to realize what exactly irritated her. It was much too quiet. Despite the many people, she heard neither laughter nor loud chatter. Even in the marketplace, bursting with bright colors and smells, it was relatively quiet. The merchants stood with serious expressions, the usual haggling and arguing absent.

In Kapilar, there was no main street, only several alleys of varying length and width. Some were so narrow that no horse could fit, while in others, at least two carts could drive side by side.

The duke's house gleamed in the center of the city. A high, threatening-looking iron gate enclosed the premises. Two guards stood watch. This security measure surprised Liya. Prem seemed afraid. But of what? It did not make sense.

She got off her horse and handed a sealed envelope to a tall soldier on guard. He took the envelope, then went to his comrade. She glanced at the estate. The garden around the three-story mansion of white stone looked well-kept; the flowers and bushes were attractively trimmed. After a while, the guard returned and opened the iron gate. The shorter guard took charge of the horse. The men did not speak a word. The whole procedure had something ghostly about it.

Alone, she walked along the wide, paved path to the marble steps of the mansion. Two dogs lay on the terrace, growling softly. The heavy front door with an ostentatious golden handle opened, and a skinny young woman with black hair stepped out. With her pale face and dark circles under her eyes, she looked sickly. This maid did not speak a word either but gestured for Liya to follow her. The red carpet in the oval entrance hall muffled their footsteps. Liya felt more and more anxious. *What is going on here?* The girl led her through a narrow corridor to Prem's study, knocked briefly, and opened the wooden door.

Prem looked up from his desk, nodded to the maid, and beckoned Liya in.

"Welcome, first advisor to the king." He pointed to the upholstered armchair on the other side of the desk.

She took a seat and hid her surprise that they did not go to the seating area. Nor did her visit seem to surprise the lord.

"May I offer you something to drink?" he inquired, brushing a blond curl away from his face.

"No, thank you," she replied politely.

Emphatically calm, he placed the documents he had been looking at on a pile. "Normally, visits from the capital are announced."

She would not go into that now. "I've seen many mercenaries in the city," she began straightforwardly, feigning surprise.

He laughed. "Ah! Anyone looking for work will find my ears open."

"Well, the work of mercenaries is the craft of war."

His face turned red, and his fingers gripped the desk. "Even if that were the case, why does that concern you?"

She leaned forward slightly. "Everything that is going on in our country concerns the king. Many mercenaries in one city create uncertainty and fear among the population. I am interested in understanding your motives."

"I don't see why I should justify myself to you."

"You have not informed us of this plan, nor have you consulted with us."

He smirked smugly. "As far as I know, I don't need permission to recruit mercenaries."

"Indeed—as long as it is only a *few* mercenaries. However, it seems that you are building a mercenary *army*. King Louis won't be pleased with that."

"Huh, who's talking about building an army?" he countered as he eyed her disparagingly.

She was not impressed by this. "Lord Prem, army or no army, I expect that you will not take any more mercenaries into your service until further notice. Also, I want a list of the names of all mercenaries working for you."

"I don't take orders from a woman!" he shouted angrily, slapping the table with the flat of his hand and threatening her with his index finger. "Who do you think is standing before you? Some servant?"

She stood up, propped herself on the table, and leaned forward. "You serve our king and our country. In my capacity, I speak for the king. Defy my command, and I will see to it that there is a public hearing. Then you may explain to the king and the council why you are building your own army—without your ruler's consent."

When he jumped up, his chair fell backward. He propped himself up against the table and hissed angrily, "Don't mess with me!"

His face was fiery red, and his fists clenched, turning his knuckles white.

"My dear lord, perhaps you can intimidate the people of your city," she put on a superior smile, "but you will not have success with me." She walked around the desk, put a hand on his shoulder, and whispered, "I will protect the king with all the means at my disposal."

To make sure he had understood the message, she looked him directly in the eyes. There, she reflected pure hatred.

"Louis sends his lackey to threaten me? Tell him that he underestimates me. That's all I have to say."

The meeting was over sooner than she'd anticipated.

On her way to the door, she stopped and turned around once more. "I expect the list within three days. Send me a messenger."

As she turned back toward the door, she was jostled rudely. The pale girl almost knocked her over.

Staring at Prem with wide eyes, she stammered, "My lord, please— help us. My sister... Something is—wrong."

"I'll be right there," Prem replied. He looked at Liya. "Our meeting is over. You will find your way out on your own."

She stopped and looked back. Kapilar looked like a toy town. Then she put spurs to her horse and soon reached the mountains. Today or tomorrow, she would come across a troop of traders on their way to Arun.

A hiss twanged through the air. An arrow pierced the neck of her horse. The animal reared up, and she lost her footing. Horsemen appeared out of nowhere, surrounding her.

One of them rode up to her. "My lady!"

A hand held a cloth over her mouth and nose from behind. Everything went pitch black.

Chapter 17

When Liya opened her eyes, she found herself kneeling on the ground. Her hands were tied to a wooden pole behind her. A tent stretched over her, and sparse light fell in through a gap next to a flap at the entrance. She looked around—she was alone.

Judging by the pompous furnishings and magnificent carpets, she gathered that she was in the leader's tent. On a vast four-poster bed, pillows of different sizes shimmered in bright colors. Striking curtains in crimson adorned the sides of the bed. A plain wooden box with a brass lock stood out in the room.

She turned her head as far to the side as she could. A magnificent work table made of nut-brown wood and an upholstered armchair stood in one corner. Simple wooden boxes were stacked next to it—a strange sight in the midst of this neat order.

Hearing voices, she glanced toward the entrance. A tall, broad-shouldered man with black boots entered the tent, followed by a burly guy. The burly guy looked somehow familiar. Bald head, dark skin, brown beard, scarred features—clearly a fighter. He was smaller than the other.

"I see you're awake," said the tall one, whom she thought was the leader.

He knelt down in front of her, put his hand under her chin, and lifted it. The leather gloves were somewhat unusual for the warm spring.

"You are pretty, my lady. Too bad, soon nothing will be seen of your beauty." He spoke with an accent.

"Who are you?" she asked, seeking eye contact.

"We will get to know each other better soon enough," the stranger replied.

The bearded man behind him croaked; it was probably meant to be a laugh.

The face of the tall man shifted closer. No trace of scars, no circles under his eyes, no wrinkles. His eyes, however, as blue as the sky, seemed old and somehow lifeless. His flawless face was beautiful in a strange way. His black hair was short, cut only about a finger-width. A tiny, transparent stone adorned his right ear.

He smiled mischievously at her, flashing white teeth. She got goosebumps; her heart raced wildly. He seemed to possess an unnatural power that made her blood run cold.

He leaned closer to her. "I can almost hear the screaming of your soul."

He looked at her for a moment, then laughed, but nothing moved in his face. Her horror had not escaped him. Finally, he straightened up. Part of a tattoo flashed out from under the edge of his collar. Muscles stood out under his dark shirt, which was tucked into a pair of black trousers. A lush belt wrapped around his waist. The large buckle featured an unusual circular symbol with multiple prongs.

The tent flaps opened. "Our scout has sighted the shipment."

She could not see the speaker; the leader and the bearded man obscured her view. The tall one gave some sign to the burly one. He nodded and left the tent.

The stranger knelt in front of her again, took a cloth out of his pants pocket, and tied her eyes shut. He said softly, "You will now be bathed and dressed. Afterwards, we will have dinner together."

She was pulled up. Someone untied her and dragged her outside. There were at least two of them. She heard crickets chirping; night must have fallen long ago. The men pushed her in front of them. Several times she stumbled, landing ungently on cold earth, only to be dragged up again by rough hands.

Finally, warm, balmy air hit her. She smelled lavender oil. Someone pushed her shoulders down roughly on the floor, and she heard footsteps moving away. Her blindfold was removed.

The interior of this tent was much smaller, with only a wooden tub in the middle. Two old women looked down at her. Both of them had snow-white braids. She couldn't prevent herself from trembling.

"Shh... Nothing's going to happen to you here," whispered one of the old women. She had a small, horizontal scar on the left side of her face.

They began to help her undress.

"Who are you, and where are you from?" asked Liya.

"Shh... Don't talk, keep it down," whispered the other one.

The women's floor-length gray dresses were held together only by a jet-black belt. When Liya looked closer, she noticed that the belts were chains. The women were tied to the posts in the center of the tent. Because of the length of the chains, they could move around in the tent, but they couldn't leave it.

Silently she was bathed and put into a blue-green dress. The velvet nestled against her body. A loop on the middle finger ensured that the sleeves covered her arms. The deep neckline highlighted her breasts.

She tried to cover her cleavage by pulling the dress up. "I would prefer another dress," she mumbled sheepishly.

The woman with the scar shook her head and approached her. "Don't be silly, child. If you're lucky, you'll win a few days. He enjoys the hunt."

Her stomach tightened. She knew what awaited her. Feverishly, she thought about how she could escape. First, she had to get an overview. Instead, she was blindfolded again, and someone led her out of the tent.

The burly man took off her bandage, and a fierce-looking fighter tied her hands to the stake again. She wrinkled her nose at the smell of rum.

"When Arkas is done with you, you'll be a different person." The guy laughed maliciously.

He left the tent with the tribal man. So, the leader's name was Arkas. Desperately, she looked around. She had to escape as quickly as possible.

Gradually, the voices outside the tent fell silent. As time passed, she fought to keep her eyes open, though she still flinched at the quietest noise.

A dark, harsh laugh came from outside, and Arkas entered the tent.

"Still awake?" he asked.

"This environment does not invite restful sleep," she replied.

He twisted his mouth into a grin, loosened her bonds, and pulled her up. Breathing a sigh of relief, she rubbed her aching wrists. Her muscles burned from sitting on the floor for so long, and her legs felt stiff.

Arkas led her to a small circle of seat cushions. She found walking pleasant. Blood pumped through her veins as she felt her muscles slowly relax.

 Five women in cobalt blue robes entered the tent with various dishes. Their floor-length dresses swayed loosely with each step. The women's faces were covered, and only their eyes could be seen. None of them looked up. They began to serve potatoes, rice, meat, and vegetables.

Arkas motioned for her to take a bite, but she shook her head. Although she felt hungry, she couldn't bring herself to eat anything. He shrugged indifferently and tore off a piece of warm bread, then poured himself a glass of red wine. Before he drank, he smelled the wine. Involuntarily, she ran her tongue over her dry lips. Her throat craved liquid, and she stared at the glass of water in front of her.

Out of the corner of her eye, she saw a smile spread across Arkas' face, and that immediately pushed back the thought of the water. Undeterred, he dipped another piece of bread into the bowl of vegetable porridge, visibly enjoying his dinner.

"Liya, you really should try something. It tastes great." He took a sip of wine, then leaned forward a little and murmured, "The food is not poisoned."

His voice was as cold as ice. She felt the power this man possessed radiating from him. His whole appearance left no doubt about it. She reached for the glass, drinking hastily, but dared not touch the food. Instead, she remained stoically silent.

As soon as Arkas was finished, the women came in. How they knew the time, Liya could not comprehend. He had not called for them, nor used a bell. After the women left, he sat down next to Liya. She winced, and he laughed heartlessly.

"Who are you?" she groaned.

"Arkas." He took a strand of her hair in his hand and smelled it. "But you already know that, and probably a little more."

"Where are you from?" she continued, moving a bit away from him.

"I have had a long journey, but I'm slowly getting used to this country," he answered and came closer again.

"Where is your home?"

"Doesn't matter. Now I'm here, that's all that matters."

"What do you want?" her voice trembled slightly. Her pulse quickened when she felt his frigid breath on her neck. His icy lips touched her neck with a gentleness that did not suit him.

"I guess you didn't expect that," he remarked with a sneer.

Her body tensed with disgust. She turned her head away and tried to stand up, but Arkas held her down. His firm grip hurt. He eyed her attentively while he pulled her to him. She wanted to resist, but she felt as if invisible shackles hindered her. Magic—clearly! Her voice no longer obeyed her.

He took a deep breath, his lips still touching her neck, right at the artery. Finally, he loosened his grip.

She took the opportunity and pushed him away. He supported himself with his hand.

"You want to play with me, little hawk," he whispered, looking at her with twinkling eyes.

She straightened her dress and crossed her arms. She wondered if a person's heart could burst if it raced too fast for too long. He not only knew her name, he even knew the nickname her father had given her. He had information that even spies in the king's immediate environment could not provide him. How deeply had his magic penetrated her mind? What else had he found? She had to escape as soon as possible.

When he stood up again, she became afraid. For the first time in her life, she didn't know if her strength would be enough to counter him. He was superior to her, had been able to put her out of action in no time with his gift. Anger boiled inside her. *There's no way I'll give up. He wants to hunt? He'll get his hunt.*

She shook her head. "It will not have escaped your notice that I am different."

The howling of wolves reached them. She heard soft voices outside the entrance.

"My lord," someone said.

It sounded so urgent that Arkas stumbled. He eyed her, then went outside.

She could hardly believe her luck. Hectically, she looked around the tent, hurrying to the desk and rummaging through the boxes. She let her gaze glide through the room. Then she noticed a shimmer at the edge of the carpet and lifted the runner. A broken arrowhead lay beneath it. Her heart leaped. A weapon! Quickly, Liya went back to the seat cushion and hid the tip in her right shoe. When she shifted her weight on it, the end bored into the ball of her foot.

Cursing, Arkas returned, followed by the tribesman, who tied her hands behind her back and put a blindfold on her again. What had happened?

As they left the tent, Arkas whispered to her, "Regrettably, I have an urgent matter to attend to. We will continue our game tomorrow. I look forward to it."

He squeezed her arm so tightly that she groaned. Before darkness enveloped her, she heard another muffled sound.

When Liya opened her eyes, her temple ached. Carefully, she reached a finger to the spot and felt dried blood. Daylight illuminated the inside of the tent only slightly. Many women, including several young girls, were lying or sitting on mattresses. Astonished, she noticed that no one was tied up. A frightening silence weighed on her.

Just as she was about to get up, someone hissed, "Shh, stay seated! Otherwise, they'll come and hurt you."

A girl, no more than eighteen years old, was lying on the mattress next to Liya. Her long blond hair was matted, her narrow face dirty.

She moved a little closer. "Who's coming?"

"His men," the girl whispered.

"How long have you been here?"

"I don't know exactly. Several weeks, I think. When they brought you to the camp, I was with him."

Liya tried to classify this information in order to get an idea of the situation, but her aching head prevented her.

"He's a monster." The girl pointed to the inside of the tent.

She blinked. The light was too dim to make out much.

"They don't have a soul anymore," the young woman continued. Tears rolled down her cheeks.

Liya knew she would not survive a second meeting with Arkas unscathed. It was high time to leave! She slipped from her bed and crawled on all fours. Her way to the exit led between the mattresses.

"They will betray you," the girl chortled and turned to the other side.

With a jerk, the canvas was pulled open. Motionless, she remained on the ground. Her breathing was labored. Muffled footsteps approached. A hand tugged her up by the hair.

In front of her stood the burly man. "Where are you going, bitch?" he growled angrily, then punched her in the face.

She fell to the ground, ran her tongue over her split lip, and tasted blood. "Arkas won't be happy about this," she said, getting to her feet.

With a clenched fist, she glared at her tormentor, whose fat belly spilled over his dirty pants. His no less dirty, formerly white shirt was unbuttoned to the middle, where a densely hairy chest bulged out. His broad grin revealed dark teeth; obviously, he chewed too much tobacco. Disgusted, she averted her eyes and noticed the dagger on his hip.

Two other men, right behind him, held lamps and waved them around. "Ardo, let's get out of here. You can't run," said the taller, lankier of the two. He seemed nervous. So Ardo was not acting on Arkas' orders.

Ardo ignored the man. With a mocking grin, he said to her, "Unfortunately, we're not allowed to play with you yet." His hand clasped her neck and yanked down her crystal necklace. "You won't be needing this piece of jewelry." He looked around with a lurking gaze. "For your misbehavior, I will punish another." With a crazed look on his face, he dragged a young woman by her hair.

She screamed aloud and began to cry. He slapped her across the face. "Stop whining. You shouldn't have angered your master. You forgot who you serve. Now, you belong to us." With a mischievous laugh, he gave the girl another slap.

What is going on here? Liya recognized the young maid from Prem's palace. She had asked him to help her sister. Prem was behind her kidnapping and this cruel camp! Horror paralyzed her, but the sound of tearing cloth brought her back. Ardo was ripping off the young woman's clothes.

The tall man behind him grabbed his head. "Ardo, to hell with you! I'm leaving." He hurried out of the tent. The other stayed behind, looking indecisive.

Liya took a step toward Ardo. "Leave her alone."

"Or what?" He twisted his mouth into a mischievous grin. "Don't worry, you'll be taken care of by the master himself."

When he lashed out again, she grabbed his hand. His other hand moved so fast that even though she saw the next blow coming, she had no time to dodge. His fist crashed into her stomach. Groaning, she fell to her knees. For a brief moment, her breath caught, and tears welled up in her eyes.

She heard him loosen his belt buckle. While she slipped off her shoe and took out the arrowhead, something stirred inside her. Small sparks grew into a fire, blazing within her. Heat flooded her body, from her toes to the tip of her hair. Blood trickled from her palm as she clutched the tip, but she did not perceive the pain. The power intoxicated her body, though her thoughts stayed strangely clear. Silence pressed on her ears. Calmly, she raised her head and looked up at Ardo, who was standing in front of the girl with his pants pulled down.

She lunged at him and rammed the arrowhead into his neck. Warm blood streamed over her hand as she pulled the weapon out. He stared at her with wide eyes before he went down, taking his last breath. She tossed the arrowhead away and took Ardo's dagger. Out of the corner of her eye, she saw a mercenary running toward her. She spun and plunged the blade into his chest. His scream died instantly. She pulled out her weapon as the man toppled forward.

"Get dressed!" she said to the trembling, half-naked maid. She hurried to the entrance and looked around with disbelief.

This was not a small camp, as she had assumed. Tents stretched as far as the eye could see. All of her strength left her. Despondent, she hung her head and suppressed a cry. She had not the slightest idea how she was supposed to leave this place alive. *Pull yourself together*, she ordered herself silently and went back to the maid.

"I have to look around first," she told her.

The girl sobbed.

"What's your name?" she asked softly.

"Vicky."

"All right, Vicky. My name is Liya. I'll be back. I promise."

She crept to the entrance and peeked out again. How could she possibly proceed? Something occurred to her, so she went to the girl who had warned her to keep quiet.

"You're going to die," she whispered.

Liya ignored the words. "You said you were with him when I arrived."

The girl nodded. "I was lying in his bed. Those eyes, that pain. I felt like I was going to die."

"Do you know who he is?"

The girl shook her head.

"What about the other women?" she asked.

The girl shrugged. "I don't know. When they come back from him, they don't have a soul."

"What do you mean?"

"Don't you see that emptiness in their eyes? They're just shells now. He *does* something to them."

"But you're not like that!"

"He pushed me out of his bed when he heard they had seized you and forbade his men to touch you. No one was allowed to play with you, not like they did with us." Her voice sounded bitter.

"He's a monster," Liya whispered.

She looked around indecisively and spotted a bucket of water. This gave her an idea. She cleaned her face, washed the blood off her hands, then arranged her hair. Whatever plan Arkas had for her, it gave her an unexpected advantage. No one would dare disobey his order.

With her head held high, she left the women's tent. Finding Arkas' tent was not difficult, as it was magnificent, larger than all the others, and guarded by two sentries. A fiery red carpet decorated the entrance.

Her eyes wandered further. The camp was in a wide clearing with tall grass. She noticed several tree stumps. The men had cut down the trees to make more room for themselves. She tried to find a landmark, but there was nothing to be seen far and wide except conifers. They were deep in the forest. That didn't help her. Sighing, she started moving. The bathing tent had to be close by. With her head held high and her posture straight, she marched in what she thought was the right direction.

Some soldiers looked at her in surprise but said nothing. She ignored the men and kept her pace. Despite the sprawling camp, she counted only a dozen men. Smoke rose in several places from the camp's dying fires. The grass was still wet from the morning dew, and cool air blew in her face.

One of the guards outside Arkas' tent approached her with heavy steps, blocking her way. "What are you doing here?" He held a spear in his right hand. His gaze was dark and grim.

She raised her head and looked firmly into the man's dark eyes. "What does it look like? I'm going to the bathing tent," she answered, rolling her eyes and pointing at her dress. She stood on her tiptoes. "How do you think Arkas will react when he sees me like this?" she crooned in his ear, breaking away from him again. "One of you left me in the dirt. I'm going to tell Arkas about it. He won't be pleased, will he? His order about me was clear. Isn't that so?"

Seeming unsettled, he cleared his throat. "I'll take you to the bathing tent."

So far, her plan was working. She didn't let her relief show. On the way, she spotted several horses tethered no more than fifty yards from Arkas' tent. The bathing tent was empty.

"I'll get the old broads," the soldier grumbled.

"No need, I can do it by myself."

But the sentry did not tolerate an argument. He left the tent with a stony expression.

After a while, one of the old women came in, nodded to the soldier, and closed the tent flap. "I see you bought yourself some time," she murmured.

"I need a new dress," Liya whispered uncertainly.

The old woman raised her eyebrow. "Our master won't be back until evening. Why are you here already?"

Liya ignored her question. "Do you have a dress for me, a dress made of light fabric?"

The old woman examined her from head to toe. She was standing so close that Liya could feel her breath. "Maybe you can fool the soldiers, but not me, girl. Arkas won't be pleased to see you wandering around the camp," the old woman said softly. She put her hand over her mouth. "You're not planning to escape, are you?"

Liya felt herself turn white as a sheet. She opened her mouth to reply, but the old woman cut her off. "The soldier brought me here to dress you. That's what I'm going to do, nothing more, nothing less."

Silently, the old woman brushed her hair, put it up, and decorated the hairstyle with pearls. The dark blue dress she gave her was long, and the cut emphasized her cleavage, but the fabric was pleasantly light. As the old woman turned to her herb table to look for something, Liya tied the dagger around her lower right leg with a leather strap. Her feelings had not deceived her; the old women still had their own will.

"Ah, here I have it," the woman murmured. "He loves rose scent." She dabbed a few drops on Liya's neck.

"Thank you," Liya whispered.

"The master will find you. He always finds them. There is no escape," breathed the old woman.

Liya was startled for a moment. The woman's voice sounded changed, as if she was far away.

Pushing aside the troubling thoughts, she crept to the back of the tent. Directly in front of her was the coniferous forest. From the tent next door, she heard snoring. She crawled through a tarp, groping her way slowly in a stooped position. On her way to the bathing tent, she had seen an arch in front of the entrance to the neighboring tent. She heard a rustling sound; alarmed, she raised her head. A squirrel sat on a branch, watching her, then ran up the trunk. She breathed a sigh of relief.

She crawled forward, looking around frantically. The shadow of the tent offered little cover. She stretched her hand around the corner and felt the fabric of the bow pocket. She heard a soft rattle. Too late, she realized the danger. A snake was already coiling around her arm. Liya held her breath, pausing in her position. The silver-gray and yellow shining reptile had a dark zigzag band on its back. The snake straightened up. Liya realized that she had disturbed the animal's prey.

She heard voices coming from a short distance away. Panicked, she stared at the snake, which made no effort to move. Either Liya risked a bite, or she would soon be caught trying to escape. Inwardly, she despaired. The soldiers moved closer.

It's now or never! she said to herself.

She clasped the bow pocket with her fingers and took a deep breath. The soldiers' boots clanked. With a jerk, she withdrew her hand, and the snake bit her. Hot pain jerked through her body. Liya rolled onto her side and crawled backward. Only with difficulty did she suppress a scream.

With her free hand, she pulled the reptile from her arm and threw it into the forest. The bite mark glowed red. She tried to suck out the poison, then tore a piece of cloth from her dress and tied off her forearm to stop the poison from spreading.

With the bow bag, she crept on until she reached the last tent and looked around. This could not be right. The horses were quite far—there was no way she could reach them unnoticed.

Out of the corner of her eye, she spotted a cooking fire that still glowed. She took an arrow and used it to cut four pieces of cloth from her dress. Then she filled the pieces of fabric with dry grass, wrapped them together, and skewered them on four arrows.

She tiptoed to the fireplace, lay down on the ground, and crawled forward. When she was sure that there were no soldiers nearby, she left the protection of the tent.

With bated breath, she put the first arrow into the embers. It seemed like an eternity until the cloth finally caught fire. She quickly pulled the arrow back, repeating the process with the other arrows. Finally, all four projectiles burned. Liya straightened the bow and shot the arrows, one after another, at the roofs of the tents opposite her. In a few moments, she heard the first shouts. There was movement in the camp as soldiers discovered the fire. Orders were shouted and curses were uttered as men ran back and forth in panic.

It was time to free Vicky, like she'd promised. This time, in order to make sure she wouldn't get caught, she took the way through the forest. The forest was so densely overgrown that it delayed her, but finally, she spotted the women's tent and crept inside.

Vicky rushed to her. "The other girls don't respond to my words. They just stay seated."

Liya groaned quietly. "We'll come back for them, but we have to escape now," she whispered, and with a curt gesture motioned for Vicky to follow. Outside the tent, she showed the girl where the horses were. "No matter what happens," she said to her, "go to the horses. Don't worry about anything else."

Soldiers with swords and spears appeared, coming toward them.

"Run!" yelled Liya, drawing her bow and shooting. Her arm stung, and she missed her target.

Vicky did not get far. A line of at least thirty soldiers formed in front of them. Liya ran to Vicky's side.

The blonde from before appeared from the line of soldiers. She turned her face toward Liya. Realization struck her like a bolt of lightning. Those eyes! Cold, hard, and lifeless—the same eyes as Arkas'. Her tale of being saved by Liya's arrival was a lie. A smile flitted across the blonde's face. She raised her hand, and the men stopped.

"Did you really think you could escape?" she asked, shaking her head and laughing wickedly.

Liya's hand hurt, and she felt the first signs of paralysis. Her heart raced, and breathing was difficult. She went over everything in her mind. She should have noticed that no one came into the tent, even though she had killed two soldiers. Arkas had taken precautions. He was just playing with her. Everything had been in vain. She no longer felt strong. She lowered her head and let her shoulders droop.

The girl with hard blue eyes smirked. "Arkas saw it coming. I didn't want to believe you were so naive." She grinned. "He didn't expect you to take anyone with you, though."

The blonde strutted to one of the soldiers, took his sword, and strolled back. Her appearance changed from one second to the next. Her blond hair blew silkily in the wind, and her shabby dress transformed into a black, noble robe. Her pale face looked even younger.

"Who are you?" Liya's voice trembled.

"Adriana, his best student and second-in-command." The blonde waved her sword around. Her voice sounded arrogant and haughty. She pointed at Vicky with the sword. "Do you think you can protect that little girl? She's going to die because you tried to escape."

"Please, spare her. It was my idea alone," Liya pressed out.

A loud laugh reached her ears. It sounded sinister, cold, heartless. "Arkas likes to play games. He hasn't had this much fun in quite some time. You'll see... tonight."

Liya reached for her dagger. "She is not to blame, I beg you, spare her life," she repeated.

Chains clanked, and Liya raised her head. Two soldiers dragged the old woman out of the bathing tent. Her lips were bleeding. Without hesitation, Adriana turned and drilled the sword into the woman's chest, pulling it out slowly and with relish. Liya winced.

"There is no escape—for anyone," Adriana said.

Liya's vision blurred, and she was shifting back and forth. For a brief moment, she saw two Adrianas. *The poison!* "I'm so sorry," she whispered to the old woman.

She looked at Liya and smiled weakly. There was no trace of fear or anger in her eyes before she slumped down.

Blood dripped from Adriana's sword as she pranced toward Liya. She was light-footed, as if she floated above the ground.

Liya clasped the dagger tightly with her fingers. When Arkas' student stood directly in front of her, she straightened up. A gentle pulsation overcame her. For a moment, time seemed to stop. The people around her moved infinitely slowly, and all sound faded. She put her left hand around Adriana's shoulder while she rammed the dagger directly into her heart with her right.

"With every fiber of my being, I will fight back," she whispered.

Arkas' best student had simply underestimated her. For a moment, she saw something like recognition in her cold eyes. She held Adriana tightly while she pulled out the dagger. When she let go of her, Adriana slid to the ground.

The soldiers looked at Liya—completely shocked. She had just incapacitated Arkas' second-in-command.

Breathing heavily, she took the sword and raised it in the air, pointing it at the soldiers. "Let us go, and you will be spared."

Clouds passed by, and the sky turned black. There was thunder. The soldiers, however, did not back down. Their uncertainty had been short-lived. Ready to fight, they lined up opposite her.

The budding hope extinguished in an instant. She felt infinitely helpless. Every time she thought to take a step forward, she was thrown back again. The wind whistled louder and louder, the sound mingling with the stamping footsteps of the soldiers, who were, inexorably, approaching.

She turned to Vicky and murmured, "Stay close behind me!"

The first blade came down, and Liya parried. The clashing of swords drowned out the howling of the wind. The first raindrops fell. Her left forearm was numb, and her strength began to fade. The fighters were in no hurry; they attacked one by one.

Of course, she thought. *Arkas wants me alive.*

The soldiers would not hurt them seriously. No one would dare disobey Arkas' orders. Two swordsmen ran toward her, while two soldiers with spears took aim at Vicky. She bit her lower lip, desperation beating in her chest.

"Down, Vicky!" she croaked.

With the last bits of her strength, she raised her weapon, took two steps forward, leaned her upper body backward, and dodged. She turned and rammed the sword into the stomach of the first soldier. The second one made a leap forward and lunged. Vicky knelt directly in front of him.

Anger, despair, and fear flared in Liya. Instinctively, she threw the sword at the soldier and hit him straight in the neck.

Now she stood without a weapon, the two swordsmen slowing their pace in victory. With clenched fists, she roared out in pain. All the emotions that moved her wrestled inside her. Heat fueled her body like a volcano about to erupt. It boiled inside her, and she felt that fire within her, as she had back in the crystal chamber. But this time, she didn't need a crystal to feel her power, to release her gift. Something inside her awoke. Absolute silence returned. Her scream died away as everything around her slowed down. Even the raindrops almost stood in the air.

The white tree appeared in her mind's eye, its bright light turning increasingly red. Another wave of heat flooded through her; a conflagration spread through her body like a volcanic eruption. Never before had she experienced her gift as powerful and terrifying.

Her body craved the sea of flames, but it was difficult to control. Finally, she gave up all resistance and released the tremendous force. Light enveloped her body. She raised her hands—lightning shot out of them.

The earth shook, branches fell to the ground, and trees burst into flames. The sea of fire spread around her, drawing a large circle of almost ten meters. When she realized that there was no more danger, the energy subsided. Exhausted, she fell to the ground, blood dripping from her nose.

Vicky helped her up. Liya looked around in a disbelieving haze. All but one of the fighters lay motionless on the ground. One mercenary stood frozen, his mouth open. He dropped his sword and ran away.

The power she had wielded left a feeling that was as comforting as it was frightening. But at the sight of the dead, Liya tasted bile and vomited. Her magic, which she loathed and which she had banished, had returned. And now, it was more powerful than before. In fact, she was not so concerned with the fact that she had killed her enemies. What frightened her most was the extent of her gift and the impossibility of controlling it.

The thundershower gradually extinguished the fire, clouds of smoke rising everywhere. Silently she went to the horses, accompanied by Vicky. Turning around once more, she caught sight of a petite figure standing in the smoke—Adriana.

Dusk was already turning the sky and clouds purple as they reached the mountains near the town of Corzon. Liya's left arm was completely paralyzed, breathing was difficult, and her head hurt like hell. The adrenaline had washed out of her system long ago, and the images in her head nauseated her.

She saw the faces of the dead before her, terror evident in their wide eyes as they felt Liya's power. She threw up over and over until her stomach was finally empty. For a moment, she felt relieved. She pushed the guilt aside and devoted herself to finding shelter.

They followed the narrow gravel path into the mountains until Liya discovered a cave in a clearing, not particularly large, but dry. Although there were no trees in the clearing to provide shelter, Liya decided to rest here. She had no strength left to search further.

"Get out of those wet clothes," she told Vicky. She rummaged through the saddlebags and found empty water bottles, tinder sponges, and a small knife. She untied the blanket from the saddle and gave it to Vicky. "Keep warm with this. Later, we'll make a fire. I'll get us something to eat."

Tired, she got back on her horse and rode as fast as she could into the forest. Although the city was only half an hour away, she did not dare go there. Prem's power lay like a shadow over it.

She slowed down when she reached the deciduous forest. At a stream, she tied her horse to a tree and filled the water bottles. She didn't have a torch, so she had to find something to eat before it got dark. She picked some blueberries and stowed them in her bag. She heard a rustling sound. Her heart started pounding in time with her aching head. She breathed a sigh of relief when she spotted a rabbit in the undergrowth. One of its paws was stuck in the thicket of roots. She could hardly believe her luck.

Pain went through her like lightning when she killed the animal with an arrow. Beads of sweat formed on her forehead, and she gasped. *I have to do this,* she ordered herself. *Giving up is out of the question.* She struggled to pull herself up and dragged herself to her horse.

On the way back, her thoughts circled around the mercenaries' camp. How had it been possible to escape? This power she'd felt during the fight—that was her gift, her magic! The spell her mother had asked the witch for many years ago seemed to be broken. Maybe it was related to the alignment of the planets, as Darwin explained. She couldn't think of anything else. And she had taken a liking to it. Even now, she felt that power slumbering deep within her, yearning to be released. It both overwhelmed and frightened her.

She could imagine how angry Arkas would be. She shuddered at the thought of him, and fear made her heartbeat faster.

As she approached the cave, Vicky breathed a sigh of relief. *At least she's not afraid of me*, Liya reflected. Vicky took the rabbit from her and made a fire.

"We can't let it burn overnight," Liya said. "I don't know if they're looking for us, I mean, looking for me. I'm sorry."

"You saved my life," Vicky replied.

When she stood up again, she swayed.

"What's wrong with you?" Vicky asked anxiously.

"I'm just exhausted. The best thing for me to do is lie down for a bit. Wake me up as soon as dinner is ready. After that, I'll take over the watch."

She took a sip of water, then took off her wet clothes and wrapped herself in a blanket. Her body shook, and her teeth chattered. When she tried to pull the blanket tighter around her body, a moan escaped her.

Vicky joined her. "You look pale."

"Help me up, please," she whispered, for she lacked the strength to stand. Her forearm was severely swollen.

The horses neighed.

"Quick, into the cave! As deep as you can. Don't come out until I call you," she whispered.

Vicky immediately disappeared into the cave. Liya crawled away from the entrance on all fours and stopped behind a bush. Her thoughts faded in and out. Arkas had probably returned. Voices approached. Any moment now, Arkas' men would appear in front of her.

"Liya!"

She heard someone calling for her, but her senses faded.

Distant voices awakened her. Startled, she opened her eyes and looked around. She was lying alone in the cave under some blankets. Her head hurt as if someone was hitting it with a hammer. Her pulse quickened. Where was Vicky? She struggled up and staggered out.

"Liya!" Julian rushed to her side to support her. "Did we wake you?"

At the fire sat Ewan and Vicky. Thank heaven! Ewan jumped up, hugged her, and gave her a kiss on the cheek.

"You gave me quite a scare. Luckily our friend here," he pointed to Julian, "was able to help."

She looked at her arm. The swelling had a yellow-blue border and had clearly gone down. So, the mage had healed her. She felt uncomfortable at the thought. She didn't want to be indebted to him. Ewan seemed to have put aside his dislike for Julian.

"Thank you," she said meekly.

Julian smiled contentedly.

"I'm glad you're feeling better, my lady," Vicky said shyly.

"Would you like something to eat?" Ewan asked.

"I'd rather not." She still felt a little sick to her stomach. "How did you find us?"

Ewan pointed to Julian. "He's got a rather good sense, I'd say. We were just on our way back from Qilon."

She looked at the mage, but he said nothing.

Ewan took her hand and squeezed it gently. "It was a damn close call, Liya. I thought you were dead."

"You're not getting rid of me that easily."

"It's not funny. My heart stopped when I saw you." He put his arm around her shoulders and pressed another kiss to her temple. "Let's sit down."

They all took a seat by the fire. Ewan handed her the water bottle.

"I'll get us some fresh water," Vicky said and moved away from the group.

"I'm going to look for this camp," Ewan explained. "A squad of my soldiers is on its way to the palace city. I'll intercept him so we can free the other women."

She sighed. "Vicky has already told you about it."

Ewan leaned toward her and said, "And about your fire, too."

"I don't know how I did it." She sensed Julian's attentive gaze. The man had saved her life, yet she didn't trust him.

Ewan smirked. "You always have surprises. The main thing is that you're alive. That's all that matters. And we'll keep your secret." He fixed Julian. "Won't we?"

The magician nodded. "For now, let's keep this to ourselves."

His formulation had not escaped her. *For now*. Something occurred to her. "What about the stone tablet? Did you find it?"

"Oh yes! We had to work with smugglers. The mausoleum has magical protection." Ewan frowned. "Unfortunately, we didn't have enough time to take a closer look. With some luck and unexpected assistance, we managed to escape."

"Was it a trap?"

"I wouldn't call it that. But our mission did not go as undetected as we hoped. A mysterious woman came to our aid. We owe her a favor."

She gave Ewan an incredulous look. The situation must have been hopeless if he had gotten involved in such a deal. "Do you have any guesses as to who she might be?"

"No," he replied carelessly. "But we have the stone tablet. How did it go for you?"

"Prem has actually hired quite a few mercenaries. And this Arkas, the leader in this camp, is extremely powerful. Never before have I felt such fear." Involuntarily, she began to tremble. "I'm sure he's working with Prem. We must report this to the king."

Ewan tensed. "He works with Prem? What makes you think that?"

"There is no doubt about it. In the camp, I recognized one of the mercenaries. He'd been in Kapilar. Prem opposes the king." She shuddered again at the thought of the lord.

Ewan snorted angrily. "That damn dog!"

"Still, we can't take action against him," she said quietly. "We have no evidence to present."

"I ride to meet my soldiers." Ewan rose. "You should be on your way soon, too."

"Two days at the earliest," Julian said. "Liya still needs rest. Her body is dehydrated."

Ewan shrugged and pressed another kiss to Liya's head.

"Please, be careful. Arkas is dangerous," she urged him.

"I always am." He winked and marched to his horse, then rode off.

"When did you awaken?" asked Julian quietly, not looking at her.

She winced. "W-what do you mean?" Her voice quivered.

He turned to her. "Liya, I was only able to find you because you used your gift, and I was close enough to sense it. Once the effects of the poison have completely worn off, you will regain your strength, and your gift will stir. Your awakening is probably related to the events in Dar'Angaar. Never before have I felt the awakening of a gift with such intensity. Your power must be extraordinary."

With her mouth open, she stared at him. "W-what?"

Julian sighed. "The Grand Mages are sensitive to changes in the magical sphere. That's how we manage to find new students. We sense their magical potential. Yet we have overlooked you—until now. That's incredible. There are few people whose gift awakens only in adulthood. And your aura is many times stronger than most magicians."

So, all her efforts had been in vain. The spell should have protected her. Why didn't it work anymore? She must have overridden it, but how was that possible? Thoughts whirled wildly through her head. For the first time, she wished she could talk openly about it with someone. Her mother had initiated the ban from the witch, so there must have been a reason for it. She'd never questioned it, as she'd hated her gift already, and was happy to have limited access. But now? How would she be able to handle this? The awakening of her magic, as Julian named it, was like a dam bursting.

Instinctively, Liya reached for her necklace. But it was not there! She must have lost it in the camp.

"Does anyone know about this?" he asked quietly.

"No."

"Good." A gentle smile flitted across his face. "You must learn to handle this power. Surely the guild has sensed a shift in magic. I'll consult with Darwin about how to proceed."

Vicky returned, and they discussed the trip home.

Two days later, they set out for Arun. They had agreed to take Vicky to Ewan's uncle. She would be safe as a maid at his court. Liya was still weak, but her body had largely recovered. Her appetite had returned. Since Julian did not want to waste any time, they took only a few breaks during the day.

The next three days passed quietly. Julian spoke little with Liya, although she noticed that he often watched her out of the corner of his eye. Vicky also talked little.

On the fourth day, the mighty mountain ranges in front of Arun appeared at some distance. Dark clouds floated in the violet light of dusk.

"We'll be there soon. If we hurry a little, we'll be at Claudius' court before nightfall," Liya told Vicky.

"Are you staying the night?" the girl asked sheepishly.

Julian quickly dismissed the idea. "No, we have to keep going. Liya is feeling better, and we've already lost a lot of time."

She was disappointed but did not reply. "I'll visit you as soon as I can," she promised. "Claudius is very nice, and so is his wife, Marie. You'll be out of danger there."

Inwardly, she sighed. How she would have liked to stay at Claudius' court. She liked Ewan's uncle. He was a cheerful man.

Julian urged them to hurry. As he had predicted, they reached the residence of Ewan's relatives before nightfall. A simple wooden fence enclosed the grounds and the two-story mansion. Several residents were out and about, looking curiously at the visitors. Liya knew some of them.

Claudius stepped out of his house. With a pipe in his mouth, he smiled. His beard had already reached his throat. "Liya, what a surprise!" He turned to the door. "Marie, we have guests. Liya is here."

She got off her horse to greet Claudius and Marie. Ewan's aunt had her cooking apron on, and traces of flour were visible on her narrow face. She'd tied up her red hair, and freckles spread across her cheeks.

Marie hugged Liya, gave her a kiss on the forehead, and asked, "Where is my nephew?"

"He couldn't come with us, unfortunately. I can't stay long either," she replied. "Let me introduce you to Julian and Vicky. Julian is a member of the Mage Council, working closely with Ewan. I met Vicky at Prem's court."

In short sentences, she described how Vicky had been treated at the court of the lord of Kapilar and asked for help. She did not mention the camp. As predicted, Claudius and Marie gladly took the girl in.

"Are you sure you don't want to at least stay for a late dinner?" Ewan's uncle asked.

Ge glanced curiously at Julian, who just nodded politely to the two of them and remained seated on his horse.

"We have to go back to the palace city," she replied regretfully, hugging Vicky goodbye.

Tears rolled down the girl's cheeks. "Thank you for everything," she sobbed.

"You'll be fine here," Liya assured her.

She thanked Claudius and Marie once again, then got back on her horse.

⚮

Julian set a fast pace, but fortunately, the torch stayed lit. He finally slowed down after midnight.

"Are we going to ride all night?" She was fighting against her exhaustion.

"No, we'll rest soon." He looked as if his thoughts were far away.

After a while, he gestured with his head that they should look for a suitable place to sleep in the forest. He chose a small clearing, close to a babbling brook. She felt famished. While Julian tended to the campfire, she took the jerky Ewan had given her out of her bag and broke off a piece of the bread before passing it to him. As she ate, she watched him stare into the fire. The flames lit up his face and hands with orange light, but something seemed off. A pale light flashed. At first, Liya thought it was the fire. As she looked, a line of bright white light flowed around his silhouette, almost hidden by the fire's glow. She gasped softly as realization hit her.

"Do all mages have such a bright aura?" she asked quietly.

Surprised, he raised his head. "You see it?"

At that moment, appearances faded.

"What happened?" she asked.

"I used my protection. The brighter the aura glows, the greater the power. All mages put a protective veil over the glow so a sighted person can't gauge their abilities."

"I see."

His eyebrows drew together. "How do you do it?"

"What do you mean?"

"You are not a trained mage, yet you hide your aura. Your protective wall works perfectly."

"I don't know." Hungrily, she took a bite of the bread, chewing as she looked at Julian.

"At least the other mages won't notice you. That will make it easier for us to keep secrets," he replied.

Despair overcame her. The emptiness she had felt almost constantly since her return from Dar'Angaar felt even worse now. She wished to experience that unbridled power again, along with that strange euphoria. *Where are these thoughts coming from?* She didn't want her gift, even now. She disgusted herself.

He cleared his throat. "Liya, there is something I need to discuss with you."

"That bad?" she joked.

He remained serious.

"In order to release the poison from your body, I had to connect us."

"Connect?"

"My spirit flowed into your body. I gained access to find the poison."

"I don't understand." She pretended ignorance; he had cured her as she had cured Haydn.

He took a deep breath. "This is a complicated process. Your spirit guided me. However, I had to overcome your protective wall first. How did you manage to build such a strong wall around you? Normal people resist for a short time, which is hardly of any importance. Mages' protective walls are stronger, but we can overcome those too, especially if there is an injury."

"What are you getting at?" she asked in a quivering voice. She felt increasingly uncomfortable.

"It took me quite a long time to get through to you. And I only succeeded because you thought I was someone else." Bitterness resonated in his voice. "You thought I was Haydn."

Had she heard correctly? What was she supposed to say to that? As soon as she had taken in his words, she closed her emotions and watched him with an expressionless face. His eyes now seemed distant and cold.

After a while, he cleared his throat. "When you realized the mistake, it was too late. I already had access. While I was getting the poison out of your body, you trusted me. Your mind opened." He took a deep breath. "Are we talking about Haydn here... Haydn Amaar?"

Her heart almost stopped. Using magic was dangerous, but she could pretend that her gift had just awakened. But the thing with Haydn... The consequences were far worse. She lowered her eyes, biting her lip. No matter what she said now, Julian wouldn't understand.

"It's a long story, but yes, it's him," she whispered.

Her voice threatened to fail. She could not remember calling out to Haydn. How stupid of her. What had gotten into her? She hoped she hadn't given away anything else. She had sworn to Maverick. A tremendous restlessness overcame her, and she wrapped her arms around her knees.

"I met Haydn many years ago. It was a long time ago."

"Liya..." Julian shook his head. "I don't care how or when you met him. But you trust him. You can't, no, you *mustn't* trust him. He is our enemy." His voice took on a threatening tone.

When he approached her, she flinched. He squatted in front of her, grabbed her shoulders, and shook her gently.

"Do you understand?" He took her head in his hands and held it tight. "No one must ever know about this. This is treason. *To trust the enemy—*

this is treason. You know that! Lock up your past! You mean a lot to Ewan. Your betrayal would destroy him. For his sake, I'll keep this secret. Make sure I don't regret it." His voice was ice cold.

She nodded and decided not to let anyone get close to her anymore. She would build a wall around her mind that nothing and no one could overcome, not even if her life was in danger. She dug her fingernails into her palms and increased the pressure. Then, she went to her sleeping place.

Chapter 20

Liya was packing her things when someone banged wildly on the door. "I'm coming," she called and hurried down the stairs.

The knocking did not stop.

"Ewan, I told you I was having dinner at home," she cried angrily.

When she opened the door, instead of her friend, two unknown men supporting a third stood in front of her.

"H-Hemmet," she stammered.

"Please forgive me! The gentleman really wanted to be brought to you. He's injured, keeps losing consciousness, but doesn't want to see a doctor," said the man on Hemmet's left, while the one on the right nodded.

She let the men enter and told them to put Hemmet on the sofa by the fireplace.

With shaky hands, Hemmet rummaged in his coat, pulled out a small purse, pressed it into the hand of one of the men, and muttered, "Thank you. And not a word to anyone."

The two men left the house.

"You need a healer," she stated as she gently removed his coat.

His shirt was soaked with blood from a wound on his upper left arm.

"I can't. I don't want to answer any questions," he whispered. His eyes fell shut.

She put his feet up, got a bucket of water, some strips of cloth, and scissors. She cut off the sleeve of his shirt and cleaned the wound first. Fortunately, the cut was not as deep as she had feared, but it ran halfway down his arm. Even as she began to sew, Hemmet remained unconscious.

His condition worried her; his breathing was becoming shallower. She did not understand why. The injury was not life-threatening.

"Hemmet," she said aloud, feeling his forehead. Despite the beads of sweat, it felt ice cold.

After Liya opened his cloak, she managed with difficulty to turn his upper body on its side to look for further injuries. She found a small bloodstain under his left shoulder blade. She cut an opening in the tunic. This injury did not appear to be large, but it was already infected. With her fingers, she carefully felt the spot, felt no residue, and rinsed the wound. Just as she was about to apply a bandage, she discovered tiny black veins at the top of the injury. She quickly covered the area and laid the unconscious man on his back.

"Hemmet!" she addressed him again.

But he did not respond. When she felt his pulse, she was shocked to discover that she could barely feel it. Her heart began to race, and her stomach fluttered with nervousness. She couldn't let him die.

She bent over him, her hands touching his chest. A warm, tingling feeling spread through her body. The aura that surrounded him shimmered slightly. He could barely maintain his protective wall. Without much effort, she gained access and realized that he was fighting for his life.

The feeling that dominated her now was strange and exciting at the same time. How easy it was to access her gift, and how powerful. She had no idea what her skills really meant for all those years. Before, her magic was like a whisper in the wind, and now it was more like a storm, which she was able to guide.

A faint light pulsed in Hemmet's mind. His condition had nothing to do with the arm injury. She had already suspected that. Dark spots were forming around his heart.

She had to penetrate even deeper into him. Would his innermost being, the last wall of resistance, let her, or would his spirit refuse? A fight, she knew, could mean his death.

Her attention was focused on the now jet-black opacity near his heart. The touch of darkness was going to suck up the last of his life energy. Cautiously, she followed the trail. The closer she got to the shoulder blade, the blacker the tunnel became. The small cut looked like a harmless ink stain.

She understood. Hemmet had been poisoned. Briefly, resistance sprouted in her. Hemmet was no follower of King Louis. What exactly he was planning, she did not know. Still, she wanted to help him, and it felt right. She trusted her intuition.

She sent out her light, letting it snake through the paths of darkness. Death touched her gently as the cold flowed toward her. Her intrusion was immediately noticed, and the room narrowed. She discarded her concern for Hemmet's spirit and hurried. She'd just managed to reach the place of pain before his spirit blocked the passage.

Her body was already shivering as she began to absorb the poison. Never before had she cured a poisoning of this magnitude, but intuitively she knew what to do. Her inner light guided her. The more she absorbed the pitch-black liquid, the more violently she froze. Still, she kept going. Her perseverance was rewarded with the first speck of light.

Finally, she had done it, and the node turned bluish. A tremendous wave of power crashed into her. The impact catapulted her spirit out of

Hemmet's body. She cried out in pain, lost her footing, and her spirit fell into the depths, landing hard on the ground of reality.

She felt her head fall against Hemmet's chest before fatigue overcame her.

❦

Liya opened her eyes. Her neck ached. She lifted her head and stretched. Her body was stiff. She was still kneeling in front of the couch while Hemmet slept soundly. Dawn had already broken. Soon, Ewan would come to pick her up.

Hemmet's breathing had returned to normal, though his face was still a little pale. Gently, she shook his shoulder. "Hemmet, you need to wake up."

He did not move. When she lightly pinched his healthy arm, he opened his eyes wide, and she recoiled in fright.

"Two men brought you to me last night," she explained.

"Water," he whispered.

Liya fetched him a glass, then helped him sit up. Greedily, he drank it all.

"Thank you," he breathed.

"I stitched your wound. Let me change the bandage." She fetched fresh water and set to work. "It was reckless of you to come to me."

"Before the last fight, I felt dizzy, nauseous. That's when I knew something was wrong. I don't know where else I could have gone."

"You were poisoned—that's why you were so weak. I'm not skilled in such complicated healings. You're lucky nothing went wrong."

She shuddered at the thought of what she had felt when she was rudely pushed back by Hemmet's ghost.

"I took that risk deliberately," he whispered. "That you had the gift was just an assumption. But I was right."

She felt the color drain from her face. "Where...?"

He leaned back and closed his eyes for a brief moment. "Don't worry, your secret is safe with me."

That did not reassure her.

As if he could read her mind, he continued, "I did some research and went through old procedural transcripts. You were involved in all the sensitive cases, but nowhere did it say that you did any questioning. You just *listened*! What was the point of that? For what reason does King Louis send you to wherever there are the biggest challenges if you do nothing but listen? You are an emissary and a spy at the same time. The events of the last few months made me wonder about it."

She had never looked at these protocols before.

"Then I got it," he followed up. "I've been convinced of your gift ever since I knew you escaped from that camp near Kapilar."

"You know about the camp?" Her pulse quickened.

"Special circumstances led me on this trail. I was looking for something else," he replied. "Instead, I found a burned-down camp and—well— check my jacket pocket, please."

She reached into his pocket and pulled out her necklace. "You found it," she groaned.

"Yes, that's how I knew you had been there. I have sources in Kapilar who told me about that camp." He closed his eyes for a moment. "How did you manage to remove the poison from my body?" He sounded unsettled.

"I was in a panic. Somehow, I managed to use my gift," she replied hesitantly. "Every human being is surrounded by an aura. The more open his mind and the deeper his understanding of this world, the brighter it shines. Our world is full of magic. Because we cannot see it with our eyes, many believe that it does not exist. But it does. With your healing, we were lucky, because I can't control my gift. Well—not really. It just happened. I couldn't even tell you how I did it. In any case, only skilled mages should do healings of this kind."

"The mages of the guild are not among my friends at present," Hemmet muttered.

"Me neither." When she realized that she had actually said it, she was startled.

"I know." He lowered his head. "Sometimes things are different than they seem."

Sighing, she rose. "Please, go now. Ewan will be coming for me soon. He can't see you here. You should change that bandage again tonight."

"Don't you even want to know what happened?" he asked in wonder.

"Of course, I would be interested, but…"

"But you don't trust me, so you want to stay out of my business!"

"How could I trust you?" she asked.

"Rely on your intuition. The king does, too."

She did not feel that he had lied to her so far. However, she wouldn't tell him that.

Sighing, he continued, "Why don't you give me a chance to show you what I'm really like?"

"Maybe I just don't want to!" She looked him in the eye.

"Maybe you're afraid to find out you were wrong about me?"

"This is absurd." Undeterred, she put her hands on her hips. "It's no secret that you're working against the king. I just don't know what your role is in Prem's plan. It's not clear to me how far you'll go."

Somewhat ponderously, he stood up and gently grabbed her by the shoulder. "Make up your own mind—don't listen to the opinions of others! Then I will accept your decision, no matter what conclusion you come to. All I ask is that you give me some time and make your own judgment."

"Why is my opinion so important to you?"

He sat down again. "It's very simple. I need allies."

"You think we could be allies?" She laughed shrilly. "I would never harm the king."

"You wanted an honest answer."

Shaking her head, she crossed her arms. "That doesn't make any sense. But fine, let's leave it at that. Tell me what happened."

"I was making inquiries when I was ambushed by mercenaries."

"What inquiries?"

"Lately, students have been disappearing. When we find them, they're dead or dying."

"Who's kidnapping them? Why?"

"They're strangers! I'm sure of it. That's why I wanted to see you."

Her stomach tightened. "You mean *strangers* from Dar'Angaar?"

"No, I don't think so. For King Amaar, the students and I are of no interest whatsoever." He took a deep breath. "It sounds crazy, but my feeling is that we're giving our attention to the wrong things. The students who are still alive are completely changed. It's hard to describe."

How he tensed his jaw muscles! Obviously, he didn't want to tell her everything. She waited until he was ready to continue.

"Their eyes—they scare me," he finally continued. "All black, absent, and malicious. Like they don't have a conscience anymore." Briefly, he laughed. "You probably think I'm crazy."

"No, I don't," she said softly. "The girls in that camp had a strange look too, lost and empty."

He looked at her thoughtfully. "I can't help feeling like I'm missing something important," he finally explained. "You're closer to the king than I ever could be. Maybe he and Prem are too busy trying to disempower each other, and that's why they're missing the point. You're going to Eryon today. Keep your eyes and ears open. If I'm right in my guess, we've got a lot of trouble other than a war with Dar'Angaar."

She was getting hot. The meaning of his words seeped into her mind. Yet, she knew intuitively that Hemmet was right. She, too, did not think Dar'Angaar was the real threat. The crystal, the portal, a dark ruler, and— Arkas! The shadows were influencing everyday life.

"You're probably right. The puzzle is coming together piece by piece," she whispered.

A knock on the door startled her. "It's Ewan," she groaned. "Quick, go upstairs and hide!"

He stood up. She pressed the bandages into his hand and hurried to the door. When Hemmet was out of sight, she opened it.

Ewan grinned at her. "Good morning! All set?" Briskly, he entered the house. "You look a little worn out, Liya."

"I didn't sleep well. I'll get my things and be right back."

"Can I help?"

She held him back by the arm. "No, there's no need for that. You can get our provisions."

With her chin, she pointed in the direction of the kitchen, then hurried upstairs.

Once on the second floor, she whispered, "Hemmet?"

The door to her room opened. He handed her the luggage.

"Ewan and I will be gone soon. Then you can leave the house, preferably through the garden."

As she turned, he grabbed her hand. "Be careful in Qilon. The wedding is upsetting the political conditions quite a bit. One or the other might take advantage of that for themselves."

He sounded worried. She couldn't figure this man out. She nodded and ran downstairs.

"I've already saddled your horse." With an exaggerated bow, Ewan opened the door. "My lady!"

His good humor was contagious.

Liya breathed a sigh of relief. It was already late afternoon when they approached Qilon; they would reach the capital of Eryon by dusk. The days were getting shorter as summer slowly came to an end.

The last few weeks had been quite exhausting. Because of the queen and the ladies-in-waiting, they'd had to take many breaks.

She still felt uncomfortable in Julian's presence and avoided him as much as possible. She felt like he was always watching her. The closer they got to Qilon, the more often she thought of Haydn. Would the others be there, too? She didn't want to admit it, but she missed Maverick, Folnar, and Aval. Her heart grew heavy at the thought of her *friends*. What a strange word for King Amaar's companions, yet it felt true.

An officer brought his horse to a halt in front of Louis, who rode beside her, and saluted. "Soon, we will reach Qilon, my king."

Louis nodded. "The queen and her maids will be pleased." Smiling, he turned to Liya. "Are you sure you don't want to stay with us at the palace?"

"Yes, I'm sure. Lady Amalia invited me. I'll feel more comfortable in her house."

She returned his smile and studiously ignored Ewan's worried look. He had tried to dissuade her from her plan several times. Safety was his top priority. He could best ensure it if they were all in one place.

As she looked at Ewan, her thoughts drifted to Hemmet. *How ironic,* she thought. Hemmet was not a magician, but he had realized that there was much more to all the recent events than others assumed. He had confirmed her suspicions.

Arkas was by far the more dangerous enemy, regardless of Prem's role. Ewan had not been able to find any clues in the camp. There had been only a few burned tents, nothing else—no dead soldiers, no women. How was that possible?

Prem's goal was to depose the king, but she was in the dark about Arkas. The military and the Council of the Wise put their focus on the wedding and the related political changes. This was not surprising, but Ewan, the king, and the council of mages paid too little attention to recent events. Certainly, the mages knew more, but they kept much to themselves.

She dropped back until she rode next to the queen's carriage and nodded to Gerard, who was looking out the window. The king's first advisor seemed quite nervous.

"I'll be glad when we go home again," he said quietly.

"Everything will be fine. We'll take care of the king and queen," she replied in a firm voice, trying hard to sound convincing.

She shared Gerard's concern—after all, the king had forbidden his sons to come along. The heirs to the throne were to remain in the palace city.

"I hope so," Gerard whispered.

As the column passed the city gate, trumpets announced the arrival of the king of Namoor. Curiously, the inhabitants watched the arrivals. Some waved at them, and others whispered or laughed. A pleasant welcome!

The town seemed to be looking forward to the event of the year. Lanterns hung everywhere, and flowers littered the streets. Dusk bathed everything in atmospheric colors.

The entire city teemed with busy people. Merchants rushed to the side entrance of the palace with their goods for the great feast. The guards oversaw everything; everyone was strictly controlled. She had her doubts about whether Jadmar's concern was solely for the king's safety and not for his own. Sighing, she got off her horse and quickly said goodbye to the king and Ewan.

One of Amalia's servants was already waiting for her. He led her to the duchess' carriage. She enjoyed the short ride herself. The house of the princely couple was not far from the palace. In contrast to other princely estates, the three-story building seemed almost plain. It wasn't ostentatiously decorated, and there was no fence or guards, only a delightful little garden.

Liya got out and walked along the path to the house. An elderly woman opened the door, inviting her in. Liya looked at the servant. She was small and petite, with glasses hanging from a thin silver chain. She wore her gray hair tied at the nape of her neck.

"Lady Amalia sends her apologies. She would have liked to greet you personally." Her voice sounded powerful and was unusually deep for a woman. "My name is Elsa," she added. Then, with a curt gesture, she signaled Liya to follow her.

Footsteps echoed on the white-gray marble floor. No ancestral gallery adorned the staircase, as Amalia preferred landscape paintings. Only the narrow crimson carpet testified to the wealth of the heads of household. On the second floor, the sconces were already burning. Elsa showed her to her room, where she admired the elegant furnishings and the pastel yellow walls.

"The bathroom is next door," Elsa explained. "You can enter it from your room. I'll run a bath for you." She disappeared through a yellow door in the wall next to the bed.

Looking at the big four-poster bed with the thin mosquito net, Liya noticed how tired she was. The large glass door was closed; it was still too warm outside to ventilate. Fresh roses provided a pleasant fragrance.

A precious-looking fruit bowl with dark blue decorations rested on a small table—probably an old heirloom. She was surprised that Amalia used it for the guest room.

Elsa came back. "Everything is ready. If you need anything else, send for me."

"Thank you, Elsa."

"In an hour, I will come and help you dress," Elsa continued. "A carriage will take you to the palace."

"Will I be riding with Lady Amalia?"

Elsa shook her head. "No, m'lord and m'lady are not attending the reception today. They are still on the road. Unfortunately, there was an unforeseen delay, but we expect them back tonight. The princely couple will not attend the wedding festivities until tomorrow."

Amalia was not there at all! Liya didn't quite know what to make of that. A young man brought her luggage, so she thanked him and closed the door.

❧

As promised, Elsa returned an hour later to help her get ready. Liya wore an elegant, dark blue silk dress. The sleeves were made of transparent fabric with delicate floral embroidery. Small gemstones completed the successful arrangement.

She looked at her face in the mirror. The light summer tan made her blue eyes appear brighter. Elsa had put her hair up and decorated it with pearls. Her necklace, with its black jewelry, looked clunky, but Liya couldn't bear to part with it. She touched it, remembering her mother. Absorbed in the sight of her reflection, she put on pearl earrings, then looked at herself with satisfaction.

When she boarded the carriage a little later, her nervousness grew. Her stomach tingled; her fingers went ice cold.

All too soon, they reached the palace. When the door opened in front of her, she took a deep breath. A burgundy carpet, at least two hundred meters long, led into the palace. Soldiers in white uniforms stood less than five steps away from the entrance, while servants greeted the arrivals and escorted them inside. They made sure that there was enough distance between the guests, and when they entered, their names were checked against a list.

The sight of the reception hall and the beguiling fragrance overwhelmed her. Red, white, and yellow roses decorated the banister. Pink blossoms were scattered on the floor, and green ivy entwined along the thick marble columns. White silk scarves reaching to the floor covered the tables. Small bowls of water with two floating rose heads adorned every surface. Despite the wall lanterns, there were flickering candles on every table. After all, this was a romantic event. When she realized this, she felt a twinge in her heart.

A man in a black suit asked her name and checked a list. Her nervousness intensified. She hoped for a seat further back, but she was seated about halfway down the hall. Gerard waved at her from the table when he spotted her. Unlike the masked ball, the women were not seated separately from the men.

"Would you like a glass of wine?" Gerard asked as she sat down.

Gratefully, she nodded and hastily took a large gulp. The tension in her grew from minute to minute. Alternately she became hot and cold—only her fingers remained icy. She breathed a little warmth into them, but it didn't help.

Slowly, the hall filled. She spotted Julian at the officers' table; he was pretending to be one of them since he didn't want to be exposed as a mage. Ewan sat with the generals at the next table. Many men from King Louis' entourage had not brought their wives. They didn't trust the whole thing, and she understood all too well. Three pairs of princes from Qilon took seats at their table.

Silence returned as Grand Duke Jadmar now rose and tapped his wine glass with a spoon. He cleared his throat.

"My dear guests!" the Grand Duke called into the hall. "I am pleased that so many of you have come to join this evening's celebration. I am especially pleased to welcome King Louis and Queen Cecile, as well as the lords from Dar'Angaar. It is my special honor to be able to welcome them." He raised his glass in the air. "Let us now toast to the bride and groom, to a beautiful evening, and to a new age."

He toasted, and the guests raised their glasses. A commotion arose at the entrance. All heads turned to the door.

There they stood, bride and groom. Liya held her breath. Haydn towered over Lady Beth by at least two heads. She wore a long, dark red silk dress. Small roses adorned her high hairdo. She stared ahead with a serious, otherwise expressionless face. Haydn looked confident, his gaze wandering through the rows. A black silk shirt shone beneath his black jacket. A red sash hung over his shoulder.

She swallowed hard. Just as she was about to avert her gaze, Haydn looked at her. A small smile played around his mouth. Her stomach tingled, and she wished she was far away.

Haydn and Beth took their seats at Jadmar's table. There sat all the high nobles, including, of course, King Louis and Queen Cecile.

The appetizer was served. Liya could hardly follow the table conversation. She pretended to listen attentively, though she would have liked to get up and leave. She barely touched anything, not even the delicious main course.

When the dessert was served, the musicians began to play. Grand Duke Jadmar and his wife opened the dance. As time passed, the dance floor filled, and the mood became more boisterous. Servants distributed bottles of wine. Most of the guests seemed to enjoy the party, although many were worried about the occasion for this celebration.

"My lady, may I request the next dance?"

Startled, she looked up. "Maverick!" She forced a smile and stood up. She would have liked to hug him. As always, mischievousness flashed from his green eyes.

"Enjoying the party, little thief?" he inquired after the first turn.

With her eyebrows drawn together, she replied, "I think we both know the answer, don't we? You know I had no choice."

"You didn't trust us. What did you do with the crystal?" he murmured in her ear.

"Well hidden."

He sighed. "You're not staying in the palace. We were surprised and disappointed about that."

"I thought it was the better option," she replied reservedly.

"It makes a meeting difficult," he whispered.

Her heart pounded. "It's difficult anyway. I'm under constant observation."

"I understand," he said quietly. "It's a pity that Lady Amalia is not with us today."

How does he know that? She didn't let her surprise show.

"You must pay close attention," she whispered.

"What do you know?" he replied just as quietly.

Had he really asked that? "Really now? What don't I know, General?"

"Humble as ever." He grinned at her.

"Let's dance in front of the wall next to the terrace. There are fewer people there," she suggested.

She could talk to him reasonably undisturbed there. They had to be careful. Julian worried her, and she also felt the presence of other mages. Maverick agreed and elegantly maneuvered them near the terrace exit.

"Our delegation, especially King Louis, must leave Qilon unharmed," she whispered.

"Haydn has no intention of attacking your king," he murmured. "Do you still have no confidence in us?"

"That Haydn will not arrange this is clear to me. But it could be that others will do it and want to blame it on him. Do you understand?"

For a moment, he fell out of step, then quickly regained his composure. "Let's see what we can find out."

The song ended. He accompanied her back to her table, kissed her hand, and thanked her for the dance.

"I don't know if I can stop him from meeting you," he murmured to her before turning to leave.

No sooner had Maverick disappeared than Julian stood in front of her. On the dance floor, he pulled her much too close. She tried to break away, but he held her tight.

"What are you doing?" she asked indignantly.

"What do you mean?"

"You're barely letting me breathe."

"A lot of women like that." Mockingly, he grinned at her. "Interesting dance partners you have."

"I'm afraid I can't choose who asks me to dance," she replied indignantly.

She didn't feel like talking to Julian about Maverick. Annoyed, she pushed him further away and glared at him.

"You were careless," he continued.

"Excuse me?"

"You guys were whispering in the back corner. That gets attention. After all, Maverick is Amaar's general."

"I understand that you care, but maybe you should have a little faith in me."

"We both know why this is hard for me."

He was really getting on her nerves! She rolled her eyes.

"Don't forget our deal!" he hissed.

"You mean your demand," she corrected. Her annoyance grew by the minute. Since the conversation in the forest, when Julian had demanded that she forget Haydn, he had not broached the subject.

Smiling, he danced with her to the windows. When the music came to an end, he bent down to her. His lips brushed her neck, then approached her ear. She tried to pull away, but he held her tight.

"What are you doing?" she hissed.

He raised his head and came so close to her face that she could feel his breath. "I'll make sure things are clear." His tone sounded cool, and his eyes looked at her coldly.

She got goosebumps. Julian's right hand gripped her waist tightly, while his left hand pushed her head forward. Her body stiffened as she tried to free herself from his grip without attracting attention. That was the last thing she needed tonight.

"You're welcome to make a scene and keep all eyes on us." With a strange look in his eyes, he broke away from her.

She pressed her lips together. He performed the last turns and danced back to the center.

"What are you trying to accomplish?" she hissed.

His features tightened. "I'm not the only one keeping an eye on you. Or why do you think Maverick was dancing with you?"

What was he thinking? He pretended a familiarity between them that did not exist. As if Haydn would react to that! Julian's behavior was arrogant and unreasonable. She felt heat rising inside her. She struggled to restrain her anger.

"I can't believe how childish you're acting," she pressed out. His suspicious look irritated her to the core.

"Liya," he whispered in a rough voice. Shaking his head, he heaved a deep sigh.

With her head held high, she rushed past him. Julian treated her like an inexperienced child who needed to be reminded what was right and what was wrong. But it was not that simple. He knew only black and white. Haydn was the enemy for him, but that did not give him the right to treat her like a traitor.

For the rest of the evening, she declined dance offers and listened to boring table conversation. At least that helped her calm down.

Around midnight, the first guests left. She waited a few more minutes before saying goodbye to Gerard. Then she went outside and asked a servant to bring her carriage.

The lamps were still burning on the first floor of the princely residence. Quietly, Liya opened the door. Elsa had promised she wouldn't lock the door tonight.

"You're still up?" she asked, surprised.

Elsa came up to her. "Yes, of course. I was waiting for you. Do you need anything else?"

Gratefully, she declined and wished the servant a good night, then climbed the stairs and opened the door to her room. The room was pitch black. She felt her way along the wall, turned on the oil lamp, and jumped in surprise.

"What are you doing here?" she groaned.

Haydn grinned at her. "I'm glad to see you, too."

"You scared me." As if the evening hadn't been exhausting enough.

Haydn had drawn the curtains and leaned casually against the wall next to the window. He walked over, obviously wanting to embrace her, but she evaded him.

"Haydn, please leave," she said coolly.

Keeping him at a distance, she walked back to the sitting area.

"Does that mage mean anything to you? You seemed very familiar."

Puzzled, she looked at him. Then, she laughed. "That's why you're here?" What irony, Julian had achieved precisely the opposite of what he'd intended.

"Maverick told you I wanted to meet you." He strolled over to her in a very casual manner.

"If anyone sees you here, I will be charged with treason."

He changed the subject. "You didn't give the crystal to your king, did you?"

"No, it's safe with me."

"You could have talked to me about it instead of sneaking off like a thief."

She snorted. "As if you'd let me have the crystal."

"Probably not. And now I'd like my property back."

"Do you think I carry it around with me? I've hidden it. For now, no one gets it."

Annoyed, he groaned. "You really make life difficult."

"You, of all people, say that! The power of the crystal is dangerous. What do you need it for?"

"I can't tell you that."

"Then I can't give it to you." She crossed her arms in front of her chest.

He sighed and turned his head to the window. She could almost feel how hard he concentrated. *What's he up to?* He looked at her so insistently that she felt dizzy.

"Do you swear not to give the crystal to anyone?" There was a threatening undertone in his voice.

"Yes," she pressed out.

"You shouldn't underestimate me." Something lurked in his gaze. "If I put my mind to it, I'll find the crystal. However, I also think it's best left with you *for now.*"

She had not expected this concession on his part. "You should go now," she remarked pointedly. "Surely you want to say yes to your *future queen* without bags under your eyes."

"I don't feel anything for Beth." He smirked.

She withstood his gaze. Though her anger began to waver, she braced her hands on her hips. "Just go!"

"How stubborn and intransigent you are. Think about it! You're supposed to protect a man you don't know as well as you think you do. As his spy, he used you for his own purposes." His blue eyes were fixed on her. "A king with many secrets!"

"I helped my king gather information about potential enemies. After all, it's his job to protect his people and his country."

"Does that justify the fact that he endangered your life twice—first on the mission in Dar'Angaar, and then in Kapilar?"

Heat rose in her face. What was he imagining? "Your actions speak for themselves. Stop accusing my king! I know about the Red Brotherhood and the Gate. Louis is not the one planning to bring a dark army into our world."

His jaw muscles tightened. "If you're not going to listen to me, at least don't keep putting yourself in danger. Louis has enough soldiers to guard him."

"No, that's my job too."

"You were lucky in Kapilar. The mercenaries in the camp didn't count on your magic."

She stumbled. "How do you know about the camp?"

"Why aren't you being instructed in magic? Maybe they're afraid of your gift. How can you trust them?" he hurled at her.

"How can I trust you when *you're the one* who wants to open the gates?" she hissed.

He sighed. "It's better for you to stay away from your king."

"Really? Or is it better for *you*?"

A low growl escaped his throat. His eyes darkened. "You're driving me crazy."

"Then you should finally leave my room."

After two steps, he was with her. She cried out briefly when he pressed her against the wall.

"What are you doing?" she gasped.

"I'm not sure about that yet," he pressed out.

She braced her hands against his chest, whirled around, and pushed him off her with all her might. Briefly, he staggered, but in the next moment, his strong arms grabbed her. He pressed his mouth on hers. His lips were warm, and his hand slid to her lower back. She melted into it, letting it happen.

"Stop it!" Gasping, she pushed him off her.

"Why?" he murmured hoarsely. His eyes glowed.

It cost her tremendous strength to resist him. "Because you are my enemy," she whispered.

"Physical attraction has nothing to do with political circumstances," he replied coldly. His voice was so icy that she shivered. But what had she expected? She was the one who had just called him an enemy—her enemy. Still, his reaction hurt.

"You should leave now and give your attention to your intended." Her voice did not betray how agitated she was.

"Can't you just accept it?"

"What exactly am I supposed to accept?" Angrily, she put her hands on her hips. "That you are plunging our world into war?"

"Liya, it's not that simple...!"

With a wave of her hand, she interrupted him. "As if that weren't enough, you're also marrying another woman." *Did I really say that?*

His gaze softened. "Let's put it this way: Beth and I have an agreement that satisfies both sides." He sounded conciliatory. "And you shouldn't underestimate Beth. She knows exactly what she's getting into."

Slowly, the meaning of his words seeped into her mind. "Really?" She snorted. "Does Beth know what you're planning?"

"Of course not." He reached his hand out to her.

"Go!" she breathed.

He looked at the window. Something changed in the room, as if they were in a bubble. He was weaving exceptionally fine magic. This was about much more than politics.

"Soon, you will travel to Dar'Angaar again, and I will be waiting for you," he whispered. "Whatever your mission will be, it doesn't matter. What matters is that you comply and bring the crystal with you."

She'd known he would say that. "There's something between you and me, isn't there?" she breathed.

He nodded. The bubble dissolved, and the outer world captured them again.

"I wish things were different," he whispered. "Please, Liya, take good care of yourself."

He disappeared through the window.

Liya strode down the stairs to the open garden door. Lady Amalia and Ewan were standing in front of the house, talking. The duchess held an umbrella, and her green dress shimmered in the sunlight.

"Good morning, Liya. It seems we don't have time to chat. Ewan just told me that he has to take you away right now," she said regretfully.

"Good morning, Amalia," she replied. "I hope you had a pleasant trip." She gave Ewan a questioning look. What was going on?

"We must go to the palace. I'm afraid it can't wait."

"Shall I have a carriage brought forward?" Amalia asked.

"No, thanks, we'll walk." Ewan seemed to be in a hurry.

She turned to Amalia. "Perhaps we can catch up later. Thank you so much for your hospitality. Elsa has taken wonderful care of me."

"It's my pleasure. See you later, my dear." The duchess smiled pleasantly.

Ewan bowed. Amalia gave him a smile, then returned to the house, and they set off on their way. Although the sun had not yet reached its peak, oppressive heat weighed down on them.

"What's so important that you're picking me up already?"

"We received a message."

"Yeah, so what?" His secrecy was getting on her nerves.

"It's about an assassination attempt on the king."

He spoke so softly that she could hardly understand him. Only after a few seconds did the words make sense. She stopped. "How do you know that, and what are we going to do now?"

"Louis requires your presence," he replied curtly. His facial expression told her he would say nothing more on the subject.

The guards outside the palace nodded at them. Ewan led them to a ground-level building at the far edge of the princely estate, hidden behind trees. It must have been unused for some time—the originally white stone shone a grayish hue. Ewan opened the door, and they went inside. The cracked wooden floor creaked with their every step.

On the opposite side of the spacious hallway, they entered a large room. Brown curtains covered some of the tall windows, blocking the sunlight. She saw books, card games, and chess boards nestled on the shelves. Perhaps they were in a servants' lounge—that would also explain the distance from the palace. King Louis sat on a sofa in the far corner with a decidedly serious expression. Julian and Gerard stood behind him.

"My king," Liya greeted him, dipping her head. She nodded to the mage and the advisor.

With an inscrutable expression, Julian walked up to her and held out a paper. "We are being warned of an attack that will, allegedly, take place at lunch."

"Allegedly? You aren't certain yet?"

Louis rose and walked up and down the room. "So far, we haven't been able to find out anything about it," he said quietly.

"Maybe Dar'Angaar is behind this," Ewan opined, dropping down on the sofa.

"What would be the point?" she asked, sitting down next to him and crossing her legs.

Julian and Gerard sat down on two armchairs opposite them. Both eyed Liya.

"Why do you say that?" Gerard frowned.

She drew her eyebrows together and leaned forward a bit. "So far, there have been no hostile acts on the part of Dar'Angaar. And to use the festivities, of all times, for an attack would be extremely unwise. The Grand Duke of Eryon does not want war either. Amaar would risk losing allies."

"By assassinating King Louis, he could weaken Eryon and Namoor from within," Julian pointed out.

She pretended to think about it for a moment. "It doesn't match his previous behavior. Besides, he thinks he's the greatest."

Julian eyed her disparagingly.

Louis took a seat next to Gerard. "I agree with Liya," he declared. "The young ruler is confident and arrogant. He won't see any point in trying to get me out of the way."

"This morning, after all, you spoke with him," Gerard interjected. "We haven't had a chance to talk about it yet. What impression did Amaar make on you, Your Majesty?"

"Hm... He was polite and charming. Even when Jadmar mentioned the withdrawal of the troops, he held back. I have a hard time believing he's out for war." Louis heaved a deep sigh.

"He keeps up appearances well," Julian said quietly, not taking his eyes off Liya.

"How are we going to deal with this anonymous warning?" Ewan asked, somewhat impatiently.

"We have to take it seriously." She guessed that the message came from Haydn. His people had found out something.

"I suggest we cancel our attendance at today's luncheon," Gerard spoke up.

The king folded his arms. "We can't do that."

"We'll choose another location for the luncheon," she suggested.

"There are too many people. We can't change it on such short notice," Louis explained. "Besides, it would give the assassin a heads-up."

Silence filled the room.

Liya looked at the king. "What if I join you?"

"All nobles, including the high princes and, even, I, are allowed only one companion." Louis looked doubtful. "You *could* accompany me instead of the queen."

Silence.

The king frowned, ran his tongue over his lips, and added, "No one will suspect anything if Liya came along, and I would be doing Cecile a great favor. The heat in Qilon is getting to her."

Julian jumped up. "I don't think this will work out!" he shouted angrily. "Liya can't protect you!"

She started to answer, but Ewan was quicker.

"Of course she can! She's one of the best warriors I know. And, few people are aware—an added advantage. I would trust her with my life."

Louis tapped his hands on his thighs and stood up. "Then it's decided. Gerard, do you have the attendance list? We can go over everything on the way to the palace."

The first advisor rose, and he and the king left the room.

"I'm meeting with one of our spies—he's been looking around the city," Ewan explained. "Maybe he could find out something."

She nodded. "Sorry that you have to go alone."

Julian sat next to her on the sofa. "Do you have a few more minutes?"

Ewan looked at them, raised his eyebrows, and disappeared.

"What are you doing?" groaned Julian, holding her by the arm. "What makes you think you can protect the king?"

"Are there any alternatives?" Undeterred, she freed herself from his grip.

"No," he growled. "You seem changed, Liya."

She said nothing.

"Why are you so convinced that Haydn will not make an attempt on the king's life?" he asked.

"The king is of the same opinion."

"That's not the answer to my question."

"I just know."

"Did you meet with him?" he inquired with a threatening undertone.

Now she was tired of it. She stood up and looked down at him. "I don't owe you an account."

He rose and grabbed her arm. "We have a deal," he hissed.

He went too far. "Let go of me," she snorted. "You're hurting me. We have no deal!"

"You will plunge us all into darkness," he said softly.

His pained look startled her.

"I won't," she replied.

"I just can't understand how this is possible. How can you feel affection for an enemy, for someone who will wage war against us? You wonder why I have a trust problem?"

His facial muscles tightened; his eyes sparkled. It seemed to her as if his figure were getting bigger. She backed away, afraid.

With one giant step, he was close to her again. Although his hands did not touch her, she felt as if they were on her neck, choking her.

"Are you a lost soul who craves love so much that you can no longer distinguish between good and evil?" he roared.

She lost her balance and staggered. "Maybe you're wrong," she said in a choked voice. Julian had used magic against her. The anger left her, leaving only disappointment.

There was nothing more to say, so Liya left the room.

⇛

The midday sun burned Liya's face as she approached the palace. Ewan's parting words circled in her head.

"You cannot fail."

She'd not had time to look for her necklace. She must have lost it again. The last time she remembered having it was before her argument with Julian.

Louis waited for them at the entrance to the palace. Guards escorted them through the foyer and the empty banquet hall. The parquet floor shone in the sunlight falling through the windows. The soldiers led them down the terrace stairs. They walked in the shadow of the wall until they reached the other side of the palace. A small yard with a pond stretched in front of them, and a large white canopy arched over the trimmed lawn. Under it stood a long table, covered with a white cloth and surrounded by posh chairs. Of the invited guests, they were the last to arrive. Conversations fell silent as they approached the table.

Liya looked around. No sentries. Jadmar did not expect an attack. She felt Prem's gaze and flicked her eyes to him. A chill ran down her spine. His pale face lacked emotion.

Jadmar rose and bowed his head to the king. The lords did the same.

"Have thanks, honored Jadmar," Louis said good-humoredly. "My queen is not feeling well, so I have brought my advisor, Liya, to this dinner."

If Jadmar found this strange, he did not let on. None of the other guests paid her any mind.

She was relieved that only the lords from Eryon and Namoor were invited to this lunch, but the table order displeased her. Louis, of course, sat next to Jadmar; she herself had the seat on the other side of the king with the palace at her back. No doubt Jadmar wanted to enjoy the beautiful view of the garden while eating, but how could she see anything suspicious from this angle? How could she prevent an attack? She doubted anyway that she would actually be able to protect Louis, despite her confidence from yesterday. The silence at the table matched her subdued mood.

Jadmar rose and clasped his hands in front of his stomach. "I know the relationship between our countries is somewhat strained. Your worries, Honored King Louis, Honored Lords of Namoor, I can understand. But I assure you, there is no cause for concern." He cleared his throat. "With this wedding, we can secure peace once and for all. A fantastic future awaits us."

Some lords of Eryon agreed with Jadmar, but Liya saw some doubtful faces.

"Dar'Angaar is rich in raw materials that will benefit both our countries. We can expand our trade agreements and finally bury the old enmity," Jadmar continued.

"You have lifted the border protection. Dar'Angaar could descend on us at any time," Lord Mattern said.

His dark brown hair curled in the heat, and beads of sweat formed on his forehead. She knew him from the annual council meetings. She remembered well the battle of words between him and Jadmar the last time.

"Why would they do that? The king of Dar'Angaar is marrying my daughter," Jadmar replied, slightly annoyed.

"You should be wondering *why* he's marrying her," Mattern hissed.

Jadmar gave him an angry look, and the lord lowered his head. This surprised Liya. Jadmar had to have something on the belligerent lord if he backed down.

The appetizer was served, and the Grand Duke steered the topic to the trade agreements. The atmosphere surrounding the table remained quiet. Even during the main course, Liya had the impression that everyone involved wanted to be done with the lunch as quickly as possible.

Finally, Jadmar's wife, Lady Elira, took the floor. Her narrow, pale face was framed by dark waves that fell gently on her shoulders.

"I can't believe yet that our daughter is actually getting married," she said in a friendly, chatty tone. "How was that for you, Mattern and Rosa? Your Marie got married last year, didn't she?"

Mattern's wife smiled and told her of the hectic wedding preparations. Other duchesses joined in on the conversation. The tense situation among the ladies relaxed. In the end, the gentlemen also found a topic—hunting. Nevertheless, the relaxed conversation was merely a façade.

While Liya poked listlessly at her food, a strange feeling came over her. She felt sick to her stomach, and her heart began to race. A chill spread through her body despite the heat. The cold came from inside the palace. Magic!

Mumbling an apology, she stood up. Princess Sara whispered the way to the ladies' guest bathroom for her. As she walked back along the palace wall, she shivered. Something was very wrong. Panting, she dragged herself up the steps. At the top, she looked around. Everything seemed quiet.

The ballroom was empty, but the icy cold she felt came from a corner in the back. She tiptoed through the hall. Shivering, she stood in front of an inconspicuous narrow door and hesitantly reached for the knob.

As she reached through, she perceived a cloud of mist enveloping the door. She snatched her hand back and stood still. Strong magic was at work here! She tried to hold back the panic. She wished she'd spent more time with Darwin.

She cursed inwardly. What had possessed her to accompany the king? What an irony of fate! For years, she had suppressed her gift. She'd reveled in the witch's spell to ban her magic. And now? She'd weakened or possibly even broken this spell while fighting for her life. Again and again, she was forced to fall back on her gift.

Calm down, breathe slowly, she said to herself. If only it weren't for this cold air that spread around her like an icy winter night! She was so miserably cold, she could hardly form a clear thought.

Intuitively, she called for her inner light, but the white tree was pale. She barely managed to concentrate. Why she had chosen the white tree as a symbol, she did not know. Perhaps because her parents had always told her the legends about the tree before she went to sleep. She was grateful for Sakima, who'd advised her to have an image in mind for meditation and concentration. That helped her block everything else out.

The white tree began to glow. With it, she found it much easier to let her energy flow through her body. She imagined the branches growing longer and spreading through her body. The more intensely she felt this, the brighter her inner light shone.

She no longer trembled. Reddish, shimmering mist appeared in front of her. When she looked more closely, she saw that it consisted of thin threads. She realized they were crackling branches, countless, tiny, glowing flashes. Cautiously, she sifted through the mist. She was searching for something, but she didn't know what. And she almost missed it! A delicate golden glow flickered behind the red thicket—a small sphere, enclosed in a web of red threads. The key to this door!

She directed all her strength to the sphere. She sensed that she had little time before her presence would be noticed. The sparks in the mist crackled more powerfully, and the energy in the air increased. The feeling of being pushed back almost overwhelmed her. A red wall built up around her, drawing ever closer.

She thought she would suffocate, but she suppressed her fear and turned her attention back to the weave. It seemed to be inching away. She couldn't reach the orb and knew instinctively that she had to be careful with this red magic. She had to think of something quickly. The branches of the white tree that had reared up in front of the sphere lost power. Her inner light was weakening.

Involuntarily, she channeled her life energy through the white tree and its branches. A force as powerful as a wave crashing against a rock flooded her body. The beam of energy that now shot out of her was strong but barely visible. It hit the golden sphere. The sphere grew larger, then burst from its prison. Quickly, she reached for the key.

The fog dissipated, and the door opened. A gust of cold wind caught Liya's breath as she peered through the open crack. A shadow flitted by before a hand grabbed her, dragged her inside, and hurled her against the wall. She cried out, but no sound came.

The shadow muttered something unintelligible. The room sank into darkness. Footsteps moved away, and she struggled to her feet, groping along the wall. Every minute counted. She knew the mage would go to the window. He had little time left—he had to attack the king now. She heard voices—Jadmar's company. Someone had opened the window.

She could see nothing, but she knew the sound that now reached her ears. The mage was putting on a bow. She heard him draw the arrow.

As she crept in the direction of the sound, she took out her dagger. The voices from outside grew louder. She had almost reached the open window. With a leap, she threw herself forward, hoping to catch the assassin. Her dagger missed its target, grazing the mage only on the shoulder. He took a step to the side. The arrow clattered on the ground.

The shadow man cursed. A hand grasped her neck and pulled her upward. Her fingers clawed into the hand, deeper and deeper. Finally, the stranger let go of her, and she gasped for air. A blow hit her in the face, and she went down.

The mage mumbled to himself again, but she knew what to do now. She quickly created a protective shield that flickered around her with a bluish glow. Her mother's words came to mind. *Your consciousness flows into the energy. Your thoughts form the magic.* Dimly, she now perceived the mage in the darkness. His aura flickered with a grayish hue.

She rammed her clenched fists into his stomach. He reacted as fast as lightning, with an arrow in his hand. The tip drilled into her stomach, and she sank to the ground.

The assassin laughed hoarsely and crouched in front of her. Before he pulled the arrow out, he twisted it in her womb. She writhed in pain, opened her mouth to scream, but failed to make a sound. Tears ran down her cheeks. When she pressed her hands on the wound, warm liquid flowed over her fingers.

She heard the bow being drawn. Hastily, she scanned the ground for her dagger, found it, and closed her fingers tightly around the hilt. On all fours, she crawled in the direction from which warm air was blowing. She struggled to pull herself up. Gritting her teeth, she reached out as far as she could and plunged the dagger into the mage's back. Immediately, she pulled the weapon out and attacked again.

The darkness faded; light crawled into the room. The man, wearing a black cloak and hood, which was pulled far over his face, turned to her. Again, she stabbed. The mage knocked the dagger out of her hand. Injured and weakened as she was, she had no chance against him.

So, this is the end, she said to herself. For the first time, she was aware of the responsibility that weighed on her. Only then did she understand the implications, but it was too late.

A cold hand clasped her neck and pressed her against the wall. He lifted her so they were at eye level, but the shadow of his hood obscured his face.

Haydn! she cried out. The light inside her faded. Her magic withdrew, and life energy flowed out of her body.

Black emptiness spread out. A deep abyss opened before her, and she fell until there was no warmth, no light—nothing.

Chapter 23

She awoke in a large bed in a darkened room. As she tried to sit up slowly, a sting reminded her of the wound in her stomach. She had survived, but where was she? Seeking help, she looked around. Despite the darkness, she could tell the room was spacious. Dark curtains shielded her from the bright daylight.

When she heard a noise, she looked up and spotted a figure. She held her breath, panicked. The shadow came closer—she recognized Julian. A wave of relief overcame her, which was immediately replaced by disappointment. She remembered her last conversation with him.

"Liya, you're awake," he whispered. He lit the lantern on the round table next to the bed.

"Where am I?"

"At the guild. We've been back for two days."

"I missed the return trip?" Her mouth was dry.

He nodded, took a glass of water from the table, supported her head, and gave her a drink. "You've been asleep most of the time."

She looked at him more closely. He looked tired. A slight beard framed the lower part of his face, and deep circles under his eyes made him look years older.

"Was the injury that bad?" Discomfort rose in her. "Did you heal me like you did then?"

The mage ran his fingers through his hair. "I tried to, but you'd put up a blockade."

"I don't understand."

He sat down at her bedside. "Neither I nor Darwin could get access to you. Even though you were asleep, your mind was awake. No one could reach you."

Liya nodded, unsurprised. Her wall worked.

"More water—please!" she croaked.

She drank greedily, trying to quench this seemingly never-ending thirst.

"We don't know exactly what happened. Your life energy was low. That's all we could tell."

Before he could speak further, the door opened, and Darwin entered. "Liya, how wonderful!" he exclaimed enthusiastically. With quick steps, he approached the bed, then turned to Julian. "Perhaps you are ready to lie down now?"

Darwin went to the window and pulled the curtain a crack to the side, so daylight softly illuminated the room. She had to blink. Immediately after, he was standing next to the bed again.

"Julian, I'm serious. Go now, at least treat yourself to a bath and lunch. I'll stay with her."

"As you command, master." Julian grinned, then left the room.

Darwin sat on a simple wooden chair and adjusted his glasses. "How do you feel, my child?"

"Good, but exhausted."

"You'll be fine. I'm sure Julian will bring you something to eat soon."

"Is this his room?"

He nodded. "My house is too close to the main building. Do you mind if I open the window? This room badly needs fresh air."

She shook her head. He stood up, pushed the curtain completely aside, and opened the window. Gradually her memory returned, and fear seized her.

"The king—is he all right?" she asked.

"Yes. He will return in the next few days. We left with you and Gerard immediately. Gerard probably encountered the assassin as well, but his injury was far less serious."

She didn't quite understand what Darwin meant. What did Gerard have to do with all this? But the king was alive, so she had fulfilled her mission.

"We were starting to think you weren't going to make it. You lost a lot of blood."

Carefully, she felt for the thick bandage around her belly.

"Your wound healed quickly, yet you didn't wake up. A few days ago, we felt your life energy become stronger; that gave us hope."

Her eyelids felt heavy. Darwin was talking about the return trip, but his voice was getting quieter and quieter. She startled when the door was pushed open. Julian came in with a tray full of food. Behind him, Ewan rushed into the room. He hurried past Julian and hugged her.

"Slow down, you're hurting me," she panted.

"Liya, I'm so glad you're alive. We were so worried," he said, helping her up and leading her to the table.

She chewed on a grape. "What happened to the mage?"

The three men stared at her.

"Mage?" Ewan asked.

"What mage?" added Darwin.

What was that all about? She didn't understand anything at all. The men sat down at the table with her.

"Let's start from the beginning," she said. "How did you find me?"

"A servant reported that you were lying in the palace annex, in the lounge, on the big brown sofa," Julian replied. "Do you remember?"

Her gaze shuttled between Julian and Ewan. "That's where we had our meeting with Louis. But I don't remember revisiting the room." She crossed her arms. "Who took me there?"

Silence. "We don't know," Darwin replied tonelessly. "That's where you were found."

"Liya," Julian said in a determined tone. "Tell us exactly what happened."

She took a big sip of water, then told them about the strange mist in front of the door, how she had dissolved it with the help of her inner light, and about the fight with the mage. That she had had death in front of her eyes, she left out. After she finished, Ewan shook his head in bewilderment. Darwin stared at her with widened eyes. Julian looked at her thoughtfully.

"You didn't save me?" she whispered. *Haydn!* Of course, he and Maverick had known about the assassination. "Where's my necklace?"

Julian stood up. "Don't worry. I found it."

He went to the small shelf on the wall and took it out of a basket. Gratefully, she accepted her necklace.

"Do you have any idea who saved you?" Ewan asked.

When she looked at Julian, she realized he shared her suspicions. He knew. But this time, there was no anger in his eyes. Dejectedly, she shook her head. The memories of Haydn were too painful.

"Liya, do you know what you have done?" asked Darwin. He sounded concerned and surprised at the same time.

"What do you mean?" She didn't like his tone.

He scratched his head. "Few sorcerers have the ability to access the source of magic within them—without years of training." Nervously, he tugged at his beard. "The gift must be extraordinarily strong to be able to work such a thing. I don't know what to say. Both events are extraordinary. You have, with the help of your gift, which has drawn enough energy from your life essence, reached a depth of magic that should not be possible. Not just that, the mage you fought must also have an extraordinary gift. That kind of magic hasn't been used since the Great War!"

"This is extremely dangerous," Julian added.

"Thank goodness everything turned out all right," Ewan interjected.

"That's true," Darwin grumbled.

Tiredness overcame her. For a moment, she closed her eyes. When she looked up again, she was in Ewan's arms.

"You fell off your chair," he said.

Gently, he laid her on the bed, helped her out of her robe, and tucked her in.

"Thank you," she whispered.

Liya looked around once more. She pulled her hood further over her face before turning quickly to the right to leave the palace city. The guards at the gate paid no attention to her. In a few minutes, the sun would rise on the horizon and announce the new day.

"I see you've recovered well in the last few weeks." Hemmet appeared next to her out of nowhere.

She winced. "I didn't even notice you," she replied and looked around.

"Don't worry, Liya, no one is around. I was standing in the shadow of the wall when you came through the gate. Far be it from me to frighten you." He gestured down the hill. "Let's go there. I'm sure there's breakfast for us in the little marketplace."

"A marketplace outside the city?"

"A walking marketplace," he corrected with a wink.

She noticed his stubble. He had not shaved for several days, and his sea-green eyes looked tired.

"While I kept seeing Ewan at the academy, you dropped off the face of the earth," he continued. "That's when I was sure something was going on in Qilon. I couldn't inquire without getting suspicious. After all, you wouldn't want anyone to know about our meetings. Even Brath had no information."

"You went to see Brath?" She wondered what she had missed in the last few weeks.

Hemmet gave her a mischievous look.

"How's *your* wound?" she said, changing the subject.

"All healed well, though I'll have a scar."

Silently, they took one of the field paths. The pleasant smell of freshly baked bread and bacon rose to her nose as she descended the hill with Hemmet.

A dozen tents stood in a small clearing among the cornfields. Goods of all kinds, ranging from knives and food to clothing, were displayed on wooden tables—a black market. The guards often turned a blind eye to such enterprises. She watched the many people milling around the small compound, haggling with each other. In contrast to the market in the city, it was quiet. No one paid attention to Liya and Hemmet.

"How about eggs, bacon, and bread for breakfast?" he asked, pulling her to a slightly out-of-the-way booth.

"Sounds wonderful."

Hemmet nodded at the round man with a cooking apron, then pointed to the inside of the tent with an inviting gesture. A few tables had been set up there, but there were no guests except for an elderly couple.

"The usual?" the cook inquired.

"Yes, twice, please," Hemmet replied, and the man left.

"You seem to be here a lot," she noted.

"Now and then. It doesn't hurt to keep your eyes and ears open. But it isn't always easy to figure out the current location of the market."

"Why did you want to meet me?" she asked.

"What happened in Qilon?"

"Is that why you showed me this place? You put your trust in me, and I'm supposed to do the same?"

"Well—not only. I also wanted to show you that sometimes, the good is hidden."

"Whether I approve of this, I really don't know. Without implying anything about the merchants, we can both imagine where most of these goods come from. And that you, as the head of a military academy institute, would take advantage of this *offer* surprises me."

"Still, I'll take the risk. Even though I know Ewan has his people on me."

Her ears perked up, but she was not surprised. "I don't know who Ewan has under surveillance," she explained, and that was true.

"Doesn't matter, either. Your injury must have been severe if they kept you hidden in the guild for so long."

So, he already knew that, too. Could he be helpful to her after all?

"A strange mage attacked me." She didn't feel like mincing words.

"From Dar'Angaar?"

"I don't think so," she replied, silently wondering why she believed that. Haydn had saved her life, after all. She suspected that the mage had something to do with Arkas.

Hemmet's face showed no movement.

"You're not surprised?" she asked. "How come?"

The cook came in to serve them breakfast, interrupting their conversation. She bit into the warm bread with relish.

"After your recovery, I would have expected you at Brath's, but you didn't come," he said after a while.

"Honestly, I had quite a while to go with my recovery." Something occurred to her. "You and Brath should get along better. Your relationship is weird." She remembered exactly how disparagingly her former master had spoken of Hemmet.

"If you know me better, I'm not so bad," he replied evasively, grinning.

Theatrically, she rolled her eyes. "How could I have missed that?"

During the meal, Hemmet revealed that he had been attacked two days after Liya's departure. The wound had burst open again in the fight, and in desperation, he had sought out Brath at home.

"I had lost a lot of blood, and the wound needed stitches. I couldn't go to the healers because I didn't want to answer any questions. So, I ran to Brath." With that, he finished his remarks, drank his tea, and rose. "Let's go for a walk."

On the way out, he slipped the cook a few coins. They left the clearing and followed a narrow path through the cornfields.

"Who were the attackers?" she inquired.

"I don't know. It was dark, and they were wearing hoods. When some drunken soldiers approached, they let go of me."

"Why would anyone attack you? That doesn't make any sense." The king certainly had nothing to do with it, she was sure of that.

"You don't have to speak softly here. If we get visitors, I'll know about it. Some of my people are watching over us." Hemmet folded his arms behind his back as they slowly walked along. "Finding those who are behind the attack is proving extremely difficult, even for me. I don't completely rule out Dar'Angaar, though I think it unlikely. Whatever the new king is planning, a war with Namoor is obviously not it."

Had she heard right? "You're the only one who sees it that way," she groaned.

"If he wants war, he doesn't need Eryon. His force could simply overrun Qilon. Even though we know his army is ready at all times, he sends—

well—rather peaceful signals." He stopped. "You think the same, don't you, or am I mistaken?"

"Whatever Haydn Amaar is up to..." When she spoke his name, her heart grew heavy. "...He is not the greatest danger to us; I am sure of that. Nevertheless, we must not underestimate him. "

"I'm curious to see what Jadmar will do now that the wedding is off."

It took her a moment to realize what he had just said. She stopped. "There was no marriage?"

He shook his head. "You've been back for weeks and no one told you? How strange! The bride got separated from her companions while riding. They searched for her for days—in vain. Her horse was found near a ravine. She probably fell."

She pondered this. Why didn't she know about it until now? Ewan had visited her only once just after she woke up because he'd had to ride to a meeting with the former General Adesson. Julian had withheld this information from her. That mage! She suppressed her anger and turned back to Hemmet. "What about the alliance?"

"It will remain. They will honor everything in contract, even without the marriage."

"This is definitely not what Jadmar had in mind."

"True enough." Lost in thought, he stroked his chin. "Who was that wizard in Qilon?"

"I'd like to know that, too. His gift was incredibly strong, and I'm sure he wasn't from Dar'Angaar."

"Why were you alone with him? Where were the others?"

"Only a small circle attended the lunch." She was aware of how flimsy that sounded.

She had also asked herself several times why only she had sensed something. The king also had the gift, yet he had perceived nothing. What kind of magic flowed through her veins, and why was her power becoming stronger? She had many questions but no answers.

She sighed. "None of us expected a mage." What else could she say to that?

"Were you able to interrogate him?"

"No, he got away. When I was found, I was unconscious and alone. I told them about the attacker."

He furrowed his brow and seemed to ponder this for a while. "The question is, who benefits from an assassination of King Louis and then an inevitable war between Namoor and Dar'Angaar?"

"Good question. " She felt it would be better not to talk about it now. "Have you found anything out about the students yet?"

"No, I'm afraid not. I could use some help with that, perhaps from a spy with magical abilities. Would you be interested?" He grinned.

"My services are not cheap; you should be aware of that," she replied with a smirk.

Hemmet laughed and led them back to the city.

Darwin was cleaning his room when she stepped through the open door. "Liya! I'm glad you're here. I wanted to tidy up a bit while I was waiting for you," he confessed, adjusting his glasses.

This elicited a smile from her. The room looked exactly the same as before—she couldn't tell the difference. Books and scrolls were piled everywhere. She spotted her face in the mirror next to a bookshelf and realized that her eyes were bright blue—no green anymore. They hadn't changed since her awakening after meeting Arkas.

"Today, we're going to go over the four elements of magic," he explained as he searched for something on his desk.

"Could we also do hands-on training?" she asked.

Surprised, he looked at her. "You lack the basic knowledge of magic. You need to master that first."

"I don't think our enemy will give me the time to acquire theoretical knowledge first." Of course, she could not tell him that she had this knowledge from long ago.

"That's just the way the rules are. There's nothing I can do about it. Though the gift is from the Elders, we need to keep the rules. What would happen if we didn't? Chaos would ensue." He opened a dusty book.

"Rules? They are already being circumvented. Why not work around them in my favor? No one needs to know about it."

"You want me to lie?"

"No, Darwin, of course not. But who's going to ask about it? No one asked about me when I was lying around badly injured, did they?"

"Liya, you're acting strange today. What's wrong?"

"Nothing. I just want to be prepared."

"That's exactly what we're concerned with. How are you going to work with magic if you don't understand the connections? For example, you have to understand where the power comes from and how to realize your own limits in order to avoid serious injury. This is important information. Don't you think?"

"Of course. But I also need to practice in order to get better." She wanted to explore her capabilities, see how strong she was. After the fight in Qilon, she'd realized that she was not prepared at all.

"Be patient."

His voice sounded soothing. Not wanting to argue with him, she agreed. While Darwin was teaching her, her mind wandered. She listened with one ear and thought about Haydn's words. He was probably right. The mages would not share their knowledge in its entirety with her, for she was not a student of the guild.

Darwin did his best, there was no doubt about that. But he belonged to the guild and would only pass on what the community of mages approved. Besides, he was a theorist, more of a researcher than a mage. Who would teach her what she really needed? She *needed* to master her magic. It was dangerous to react impulsively.

"Liya, are you listening to me?"

She looked at him blankly. "How do I know what to do without having practiced first?" she inquired, feigning interest. It made her feel guilty to lie to him, but he belonged to the guild.

"I can't tell you that either. Your case is extraordinary. Normally, one is born with the gift and grows into it. We take the gifted ones into the guild to train them. As the years go by, our students acquire both the knowledge of the connections and the ability to use their magic. " He closed his eyes for a moment before continuing, "Our legs carry us through the world, and we were born with them. Nevertheless, we have to practice walking. It is similar with magic. The gift is a part of us. We have everything we need, but we must use it."

He cleared his throat. "As I said, your case is more unusual, Liya. Perhaps your gift was blocked. Sometimes, it's possible to suppress magic in infancy—we have seen that many times. Parents don't want to bring their children to us. But the abilities are hard to control, especially as children get older and more emotionally unstable. That's why education is so important. It's a mystery to me how your gift could have remained hidden for such a long period of time."

Her heart was beating wildly. *Because I worked on it every day*, she answered his question silently. She had built a wall inside, strengthened by the spell, and buried her magic behind it. Until now.

Something occurred to her. "The mage in Qilon—you said the extent of his magic was also unusual."

"We shouldn't talk about it here," Darwin replied quietly. "We don't practice that kind of magic because it is inevitable that people will be harmed. After all, *that* magician needs energy from other living beings."

"Why didn't the king sense any of this?" she asked.

His eyes widened as he looked at her with concern. He inhaled sharply. "You must never ask that question again, nor tell anyone about it. Were you asked why you left the table?"

She shook her head.

"Good, you can't even tell Julian that you felt anything. Do you understand?" He stood up and leaned toward her. "Mages like this guy, who use their gift in this way, cannot be sensed by us. We do not sense them because they have *dark magic*. We are not able to locate dark magic," he whispered in her ear.

She felt sick.

"We should return our attention to the lesson," he stated calmly and sat down again.

That was the end of the subject for him; he continued talking about the elements. But her thoughts were racing. What did all of this mean?

At last, he said, "We'll continue tomorrow, at the same time."

"I have a few things to do first. I won't make it tomorrow," she fibbed. This was a waste of time, and she needed to meet Hemmet.

"It's important that we continue with the lessons."

She nodded, said goodbye, left the room with quick steps, and hurried to the first floor. The bright sunlight blinded her as she stepped out of the building. Students swarmed outside. She weaved her way through the crowd. At a small stall, she stopped to pick up a patty filled with feta cheese. Someone grabbed her by the arm.

"Julian, you scared me!" she hissed.

"Why are you in a hurry?" he replied. "This afternoon, we have to see the king. We've put off the meeting for a long time."

"I didn't put anything off. I had to recover first," she retorted angrily.

"King Louis is eager to thank you and discuss next steps."

She lowered her head. "Yes, of course."

With his index finger, he lifted her chin. "Is everything all right?"

She shrugged. "You're right, I guess. I probably don't want to be reminded of the event in Qilon."

She did *not* want to be the center of attention. She didn't want to be questioned by Ewan, Julian, and the king. Her counterpart looked at her thoughtfully.

"Very well, then, I'll see you at the king's," he finally said.

She said goodbye, passed the control at the end of the bridge, and left the quarter of the mages.

She left behind the murmur of voices in the street as she entered the palace. Her head ached, a gentle pounding that had accompanied her since early afternoon. She had no desire to meet the king and the others; she felt dejected.

So many things were going around in her head. Haydn was not the only problem. What was it about Arkas, the autocratic mercenary leader?

Where did he come from? There was no doubt in her mind that Prem had hired him to capture her. But still, no one seemed to care about investigating him.

Her attempts to talk to Julian or Darwin about it had failed. Louis had put Julian to work on other tasks. Darwin was devoting his time to the planetary constellation puzzles. She didn't understand. The longer she thought about it, the more she was convinced that Louis was wasting time on useless matters.

She made her way to the fireplace room, took a deep breath, and opened the door. The chaos in the room surprised her. The dark wooden desk could only be guessed at because papers, books, and scrolls were scattered all over the place. It smelled a little musty; the king had probably not aired the room for some time. The curtains were drawn, and several lamps flickered in the room, but it was still dim.

Louis was sitting with Julian and Ewan on the worn sofa by the fireplace. The king got up, grabbed her by the shoulders, and kissed her forehead.

"I finally have a chance to thank you." He looked tired, and he seemed to have aged by years. His beard was unusually long.

"I was just doing my duty," she replied, smiling tentatively. She found his behavior rather strange.

With an inviting motion, he gestured for her to take a seat. He sat down with Ewan.

"How are you, Liya?"

"I have recovered well, your majesty."

"Darwin is yet to join us, but we're going to get started." Louis glanced at the door before continuing. "The scouts returned today. Soldiers from Dar'Angaar are gathering on the border with Eryon."

"How many?" exclaimed Ewan.

"It's hard to say. They've set up a camp with, probably, a thousand soldiers."

Ewan jumped up. "I knew it. He will send the soldiers through Eryon to attack us." Reaching the fireplace, he turned. "We should position our army on the border. Prem is gathering mercenaries around him. If we don't get our soldiers there in time, he will praise himself as a savior whether he wins or not. We cannot allow that to happen. We must protect the people of Namoor, not the lord of Kapilar."

Somewhat ponderously, Louis stood up, took a map from a shelf, and spread it out on the table in front of them. "William has gathered a small force of a hundred men near Corzon," he explained. He turned to Ewan. "Your brother is stationed with his men near Averin. I want both units to head for the forests of Relerin. From there, it is not far to the border. In case of an emergency, it would only take them a day. We have soldiers close to the border but hidden from Eryon's eyes for the time being." He tapped Averin. "Ewan, how many men does your brother have under his command?"

"Two hundred at the most. "

"They are too few," the king replied thoughtfully. "We should also send the Third Legion to Relerin. That would give us close to six hundred men near the border."

When Liya noticed the looks of the men, she realized that she had sighed loudly. The third legion was led by an aggressive commander whom she remembered as extremely brutal and simple-minded.

Ewan fixed her. "I guess you don't agree with that!"

She waved it off. "Never mind."

"Liya, I've known you long enough to recognize when something is bothering you. Speak up." He sounded testy.

"I don't think we should just focus on Dar'Angaar."

Julian gave her an incensed look. "Oh, really?" he snorted.

The displeasure that Julian and Ewan showed her washed over her like a wave. This was the first time she had felt it with such intensity. *Very strange*, she thought.

"If Amaar's only goal was to invade Namoor and increase his power, he could overrun our border with or without Eryon's consent," she said as calmly as possible. "Maybe we should ask ourselves what his real goal is."

Ewan stared at her with disbelief. "Dar'Angaar has wanted to rule over us ever since I can remember. What makes you think that anything has changed? The only thing that is new is the matter of the gates and the mighty army on the other side, in this other world. The gates are the key to power, and Amaar wants to open them. Then he will strengthen his own army with the soldiers from this dark ruler. Everything points to it."

Of course, Ewan believed that. She herself had only realized in the last few days that preparations had been made in Dar'Angaar for a long time in secret. Hemmet had confirmed her suspicions. This was about something other than war, she was sure.

She looked at Ewan urgently. "Have you wondered who this Arkas is? Where he comes from? Who he's working for?"

"That's what you told us. Prem."

"It may be that Arkas accepted Prem's order to eliminate me because it suited him." She paused. "But Arkas is too powerful to take orders from someone like Prem."

Ewan frowned. "Maybe Amaar is behind this. That would make sense."

"No, I don't think so," she replied firmly.

She noticed that Julian was looking at her tensely.

"Your faith is not enough, Liya. This is not a game. We are facing a war. We must protect our people!" Ewan thundered.

"And how are you going to do that? By positioning a few hundred soldiers at the border? Do you think that will be enough?"

Quickly, she stood up, walked up and down the room, took a few deep breaths, and finally turned back to the men. "I know that Arkas was not acting on behalf of Amaar." She took another deep breath. "Dar'Angaar is not the only danger we face, and certainly not the greatest."

"How can you say that?" asked Julian with a grim face.

"This Arkas is not from here, and by that, I mean—*not from this world!* Whoever sent him is the real threat." She brought her voice down. "Events have been set in motion that we can no longer stop. We must *not* close our eyes to this. All of this was planned long ago. The assassination of King Louis was meant to provoke a war to divert attention from something else."

Louis shook his head energetically. Before he could say anything, Julian took the floor. "We have neither proof nor evidence for your theory. We can't chase a phantom; we have to prepare for the immediate threat. Besides..."

Louis raised his hand, silencing Julian. The king looked her straight in the eye. "Liya, listen to me carefully! Darwin believes that you are a World Guardian. It will be your task to prevent Amaar from opening the gates."

She had thought it couldn't get any worse, but now she was proven wrong.

"What are you saying?" she stammered.

The door opened, and Darwin came in. He bowed to the king and nodded to the group.

Louis searched his gaze. "I just told Liya about your theory."

Darwin sat down. "I have already told you, Your Majesty, that we believe the World Guardians still exist and live in secret to protect themselves. After all, they were once hunted. Now to you, Liya. Your gift, which you suppressed for years, is tremendously strong. What magical abilities you still possess, we can only guess. At least one of your ancestors must have come from Elladur and been a Guardian. The Guardian heritage is passed down from generation to generation."

"That's not possible," she whispered.

She was seething inside. She felt like she was on the verge of a volcanic eruption. Her mother was from Elladur, this was true, but she was *not* a Guardian. *This can't be true*, she thought. Fortunately, he assumed that she had not known about her gift and had suppressed it. And nobody was asking about her mother, either.

Darwin adjusted his glasses. "Of course, I don't have any definite proof. Only one thing is clear: none of us has such a source of energy. Liya is able to sense things in an extraordinary way. Intuitively, she uses magic in the right way. I've always wondered how the Guardians managed to pass on the knowledge and handling of their incredible abilities to the next generation in such a comparatively short lifetime." He looked meaningfully from one to the other. "Now, I understand. All this knowledge is embedded in their genes. Something like this, such a manipulation of the human genetic makeup, only the scientists and mages of the Ancient Era were capable of."

Now she felt sick—really sick.

Her mother's words came to mind. *Magic has flowed in our family since the beginning. We were chosen to protect all life. There is no escape from our responsibility. I tried, but the past catches up with us. Nevertheless, you shall have a normal childhood. Take good care of yourself, my child, and trust only your father. Guard the secret of your heritage. Tell no one that my lineage originated in Elladur. Only your father knows. He will protect you with his life.* The next morning, she was gone.

"I could take a blood sample from Liya and test it," Darwin suggested.

"Liya is not an experimental subject to be researched!" Ewan exclaimed indignantly.

Darwin's cheeks turned red. "Of course, she isn't. I didn't mean it that way."

Breathing heavily, the king rose. "This information will not leave this room. Liya's life would be in danger."

Ewan looked at him in amazement. "You believe it too, your majesty?"

Louis nodded. "I've suspected it for a long time, but it doesn't matter now." He looked around the room. His eyes lingered on her. "Liya, I want you to travel to Dar'Angaar. I need you to stop Amaar from opening the gates. Do whatever is necessary."

It was not a request but an irrevocable command.

"Ewan," the king continued, "what about your search for the traitor in our ranks? Who is informing Prem?"

"There are indications that Lord Nekoda or your nephew Joseph have passed on important information."

She did not miss the eye contact between Ewan and Julian. Ewan trusted the mage. At that moment, she felt incredibly alone. Her chest tightened.

Louis folded his arms. "What about Philip?"

"Once a week, your son secretly leaves the palace. His trail vanishes as soon as he leaves the premises. That's why we assume a mage is helping him. We can't tell who he meets or where he goes."

For a moment, pain flared in Louis' eyes. "I understand. You're going to keep a watch on all these people." He stroked his beard thoughtfully. "I have already ordered the covert deployment. Also, we'll send part of the Second Legion to the border officially. The remaining troops will be stationed directly in Relerin. Prem will be anything but pleased about this. I want him to believe that Relerin has betrayed him. This will put an end to the alliance between Relerin and Kapilar. "

Ewan nodded. "Our enemies will think we are also struggling with domestic problems. The traitor in the palace city may become careless."

"That's exactly how I see it," Louis replied. "Your brother should reinforce his troops in secret, as much as possible. The woods near Averin offer sufficient protection."

"Will Aquilia join in?" asked Julian.

Louis waved it off. "I'll take care of that. At the end of the day, he wants to survive." He turned to Darwin. "What about the planetary constellation?"

"In about eight weeks, the planets will be lined up. I expect the Red Brotherhood will try to open the gates then."

"Maybe this is linked to Arkas. We need to get more information about him. Even if we find that he's really just working for Prem, it's better to know. It's too risky to ignore him. He's too powerful, and I believe Prem just fit into his plans. There's more going on here."

With an inscrutable expression, Louis turned to her. "We don't have enough proof, and our resources are limited. Liya, Julian and Darwin will accompany you to Dar'Angaar! Ask the Nirm for help again. We need the stone shifters at our side when our enemies invade Namoor." His gaze was so intense now that it almost hurt. "You must close the gates. Do whatever is necessary!" he added quietly.

Liya ground her teeth. They were not listening. Not everything was about Dar'Angaar.

Louis closed his eyes for a moment. "Let me repeat. Everything we discussed today will remain between us. As of now, the council will not be consulted. What I decide after our discussions will be communicated to the council," he stated.

"Your Majesty, you are putting yourself above the law," Darwin pointed out.

Louis ran his fingers through his hair. "I know, but I have no choice. Decisions have to be made quickly. Nothing more can get out."

Ewan nodded. "What are we going to do about Prem?"

"For now, we focus on weakening his alliance with Relerin and wait."

With that, the king ended the meeting.

Liya sat in front of the fireplace. Lost in her thoughts, she looked out the window. The sun had long since departed from the sky, and the half-moon now shone brightly in the starry night.

"Are you hiding?" asked Ewan, stepping up to her.

"I didn't hear you at all," she replied.

"How are you, Liya?"

"Darwin is right about everything he said about me."

He was silent for a moment. "I think it's hasty to send you back to Dar'Angaar so soon," he finally said, sitting down with her. "I don't care if you have the gift or not. You are Liya, *my* Liya, my best friend."

"Hold back judgment! "

Surprised, he raised his eyebrow. "You say that so seriously."

She took a deep breath. "My mother was from Elladur—not all of them died in the war. The surviving residents rebuilt Elladur. My mother was pregnant when she fled. She met my father while she was on the run. I'm not sure if he even knew I wasn't his child."

Despite Ewan's shocked expression, she continued. "She didn't tell me about any Guardians. But the night before she disappeared, she talked about our family's heritage. My mother explained to me how extraordinary our gift was and how great was the responsibility that came with it." She sighed. "I was twelve years old then. I sensed something. That night, I got up several times to make sure she was still there. Eventually, I fell asleep, and the next morning she was gone."

Ewan's gaze darkened. "You knew all along that you had the gift."

"Before you judge me, wait for the end of my tragic story. I looked for her everywhere. I couldn't understand why she had left us. My father just accepted it. I investigated, checked her every move, and found out that she had been meeting with a mage for a few weeks before she disappeared."

"I don't understand that. How could you figure that out? "

"In the past, my *intuition* was much more developed. I could access people's memories. When they thought of something, I saw it in my mind. During my search, I came across a tavern in the lower quarter. The innkeeper remembered my mother. I saw everything clearly in front of me."

Ewan blanched. "What exactly did you see?" he pressed out.

"I saw a quarrel between my mother and a mage. I couldn't recognize the man's face. My mother yelled at him that he had betrayed her and thus put her life at risk. He yelled back that she could no longer run away and would have to face her responsibilities. My mother had been crying. As she walked away with him, she told him that he had not only destroyed her life, but now she would have to go back to protect the people she loved." Liya shrugged. "I guess she meant my father and me."

"Why didn't you ever tell me about this?" Ewan groaned.

"I would have put you in danger. You would be bound to report it. Keeping such a secret is treason. I couldn't let that happen," she explained. "My father was a different person after my mother disappeared. He even forgot my thirteenth birthday. That's why we had a terrible fight; out of anger, I almost set our house on fire. He said, 'You are like her—you'll also leave me. But I will protect you.' I will never forget the look in his eyes when he said that." The painful memory crashed down on Liya. She closed her eyes. She opened her eyes and took out her necklace. "This jewelry is from Elladur. With it, I suppress my magic. Aqua taught me how to repress my gift into my innermost being. I asked her for a spell so my gift would not grow stronger."

"That still doesn't explain why you didn't trust me."

"Magic is like a curse, a curse that I can't get rid of. It destroys everything and everyone. You're all I have left. King Louis' nurse, Hermione, took me in when I was a child. She took good care of me and has always been kind to me, but she's not family. I didn't want to put you in danger. You shouldn't have to keep this secret. And under no circumstances did I want to go to the mages. You heard what Darwin said. They would have treated me like an interesting object and locked me up for the rest of my life."

"That's intense, Liya. What do you want me to say? You lied to me—kind of. I'm not even sure I know who you are. I always admired you for how quickly you could slip into different roles. Sometimes a countess, then a farmer's wife, then a counselor. Now I wonder what role you played for me."

He looked upset and hurt. She reached for his hand. "I kept my gift from you, that's all."

"Actually, I just wanted to check on you for a minute because I was worried. " He stood up. "I've got to go. Julian's already waiting for me."

"I'm so sorry."

Liya could not blame him for his reaction, but it took her a while to calm down. She got up and quickly changed her clothes; Hemmet had sent her a message saying he wanted to meet her. Because she could not risk being discovered, she slipped into the uniform of a young soldier that she had procured. Hopefully, Hemmet had news.

As soon as she was out in the fresh air, she took a deep breath and headed for the north gate. Arriving at the clearing, she noticed movement under the shade of a tree.

She walked closer and whispered, "Hemmet! "

"Liya! "

Hemmet came out from behind the oak, sword drawn. "I didn't recognize you right away," he said. "Why the disguise?" Grinning, he put his sword away.

"I don't want to take any chances."

"Who's shadowing you?" he asked.

Surprised, she raised her eyebrows. Hemmet's powers of deduction were admirable. She had suspected that Julian was having her watched. However, she didn't want to voice her suspicions. So she just shook her head.

He laughed softly. "You're late, and you look like a young student of mine."

He had a point there. "So, Hemmet, how can I help you?"

"I wasn't sure you would comply with my request." He loosed a whistle, and a horse trotted toward them. He mounted and held out his arm. "Come, I want to show you something." Then he helped her up, and they rode into the nearby forest for less than an hour before Hemmet stopped. "Let's dismount and walk the rest of the way. "

Her pulse quickened. Adrenaline pumped through her body. She liked the excitement.

"You'll meet some people—good, brave men. We won't reveal our names—we will use aliases."

"What's yours?" she asked curiously.

"Wolf."

Silently, she followed him through the thicket of the forest. In the darkness, she could hardly see anything, but Hemmet didn't seem to mind. He marched on without stopping. Someone whistled, he answered. They turned left and, after a while, came upon a small camp. Five men were sitting around a fire, talking quietly.

Hemmet greeted everyone with a handshake and introduced them to Liya: "Coyote, Owl, Weasel, Raven, and Eagle. "

She found the aliases interesting and amusing at the same time.

At a nod from Hemmet, the lanky man, Owl, took the floor. "The prison camp is still in this clearing in the forest. We counted about a dozen men with two prisoners."

"Students?" she asked.

"We don't know that for sure. The prisoners are in a tent. We've been tracking this group for two weeks. They never stay in one place for long."

Right next to her sat the young man they called Eagle. He was hardly older than she was. His black hair hung over the right side of his face, while the other side was closely shaved. His hands were large and, judging from his tunic, he had an athletic build. Weasel, his neighbor, was smaller by two heads and a little rounder, yet still athletic. His bulky upper arms barely had enough room to fit in the sleeves of this shirt, and his full beard covered half of his neck.

Before Liya could even look at the next fighter, Weasel took the floor. "Are you sure this girl can help us?" His voice was unusually low.

"We've already discussed that, Weasel. There's nothing more to say about it."

She didn't dare look at Hemmet. His words were curt and revealed a side of him she hadn't seen.

Owl rose to his feet. "We should leave immediately."

Hemmet nodded. Wordlessly, the men packed their things and saddled the horses.

Coyote, a balding man shorter than Liya, approached her. "I've never met a female mage before. We're all extremely excited."

Had she heard wrong? Her angry glance pierced Hemmet's back.

He turned around. "Go pack your things, Coyote. We can talk later."

The bald man laughed, but it sounded more like a grunt. "Judging by the look on your face, maybe you should talk, Wolf."

Hemmet growled something unintelligible and pulled Liya to his horse.

"You told them. Have you lost your mind?" she hissed angrily.

"There was no other way. I needed their approval to take you with me."

"You should have asked me."

"Would you have come then?" He leaned down to her. "I really need your help. We need you to track down the mages for us. Last time we were caught off-guard by them, and we lost half our men."

"I don't know if I can help you track them down. And what are you going to do if there are any today?"

"I don't know. We'll see." He swung himself onto his horse and helped Liya mount.

"You've really gone crazy," she said, stunned.

"Owl, ride ahead!" he ordered the lanky man.

The moon gave so little light that Liya had no idea where they were. The small group rode off the trail without torches. She admired the men who were able to find their way in the darkness. She wondered if this was Owl's special skill. The lanky one led the troop. The horses trotted in single file. After about an hour, Owl stopped. The fighters dismounted and tied their horses to trees.

"We have to go down the slope, then to the left. Not fifty meters from here is the camp. Be quiet and follow in my footsteps," Owl said softly.

"I don't have a good feeling," Liya whispered.

"You'll be fine," Hemmet replied.

Sighing inwardly, she followed the men, Hemmet walking behind her. She felt his gaze on her back. Finally, she saw the flicker of a fire further ahead among the trees. They stopped. Hemmet motioned for her to follow him. They joined Owl behind a thick tree trunk. Owl made a few hand signals, and Hemmet nodded. He tugged on her arm and pulled her down to him.

"Nothing has changed. Try to find out if there are any mages among them. The prisoners are in the tent with two guards."

She agreed, her heart beating wildly. Deeply, she breathed in and out, trying to calm herself. Finally, she murmured to the two, "I need to get closer."

Owl made a sign to her. She followed him to the other side. After a short time, he stopped, tugging at her sleeve. She felt his breath on her cheek. He took her head and turned it so that she caught a glimpse of the camp between the leaves of a bush.

The mercenaries were not twenty meters away. *I can do this*, she told herself. But nothing happened. Her body did not react. After a while, she touched Owl on the shoulder. They made their way back.

"So?" whispered Hemmet.

"I don't feel any magic. "

"Are you sure?" interjected Eagle.

"However, I don't know what abilities the mages might have. In Qilon, I could clearly feel the presence of magic. We'd better get out of here," she said, turning to Hemmet.

"Absolutely not," he replied. "No mages! We attack. Who knows when we'll get the next opportunity?"

With a wave of his hand, he issued instructions, and the men swarmed out. "Stay close behind me," he said to Liya and pressed a short sword into her hand.

Silently, they approached the camp. The call of an owl pierced through the silence as arrows flew into the air. The men at the fire jumped up, and others ran from the tents.

His two swords raised, Hemmet quickly charged. She heard metal clanking, along with screams and shouts. At first, she saw an expression of relief on the faces of the mercenaries. Moments later, they looked baffled, desperately fighting for their lives. A wild scream tore her from her thoughts. She saw a swordsman running straight at her. He attacked her, but she quickly parried. While she was light on her feet and fast, her opponent moved much slower. He was strong but sluggish and would not cause her much trouble.

She deftly dodged his attacks, whirling around him, performing spin after spin. While he was still dodging the thrusts of her sword, she stabbed her dagger into his stomach. Stunned, he stared at her. Then he collapsed, trying, at the same time, to stop the flow of blood with his hands.

The fight was over quickly. Six mercenaries were dead, four surrendered. None of Hemmet's men were seriously injured, though some had suffered a few cuts.

Hemmet rushed toward the tent where he suspected the prisoners were. When she entered the tent behind him, a foul odor met her nose. Deeply horrified, she stared at three fragile figures squatting on the ground. They were bound. Liya noticed the ribs protruding from their naked torsos; they were starving. Only with difficulty was she able to suppress the rage that built up inside her. She knelt down in front of a boy who was no more than sixteen years old and began to loosen the bonds.

"We'll save you," she whispered.

Owl entered the tent with a torch. "Look at their eyes," he said. "They no longer dwell among us. "

When she lifted her head, she looked into the lifeless eyes of the young boy. Whether or not he registered that he had just been freed, she could not say with certainty.

"It's coming," he breathed. A crooked grin spread across his face, and rotten teeth flashed. She jumped up and took a step back from the beastly stench.

"We'll take them with us," Hemmet hissed. "Maybe they can still be saved."

Owl shook his head. "We should leave them here. They're lost. "

"We have to try. See if you can find a cot," Hemmet ordered.

With a curt nod, Owl left the tent. She helped Hemmet wrap the emaciated bodies in blankets. They took one boy after the other, they pulled them outside.

Owl and Eagle returned with a large cart. "We couldn't find anything better." Owl shrugged apologetically.

There was a kind of cage in the loading area. Bloodstains covered the wooden floor and bars. It stank of urine.

"This will have to do." Hemmet sighed. "Put some blankets in it. Then we should leave quickly."

Coyote stepped up to him. "What do we do with those?" He pointed at the mercenaries who had surrendered.

"We'll take those, too. Get them on the wagon." Hemmet turned to Liya. "What do you think about all of this?"

"I don't know. That blank look is scary." She thought about it. "Something's giving me a headache. You spoke of two prisoners."

"When we tracked the camp three days ago, we only discovered two. We missed the third boy, or perhaps he joined in later."

She should have been satisfied with this explanation, but the uneasy feeling remained. Right now, it was important to get away from here as quickly as possible.

"Where are you taking the mercenaries?"

"Good question," Hemmet replied. "We need to hide them so I can question them in peace."

Eagle and Coyote harnessed their horses and hitched them to the cart, and the troop started to move. Eagle muttered angrily to himself about taking the road, but the cart was too big for the narrow forest paths. For a while, they rode in silence.

Suddenly, Liya became restless. She thought she perceived something dark, something incredibly old, but the next moment it was gone.

"What's wrong?" asked Hemmet, who was right behind her.

"I feel like we're being watched."

"Mercenaries are not around; otherwise, Coyote and Owl would have discovered them long ago," he replied quietly. He kept his voice calm and soothing.

Does he think I'm scared? "I'm not afraid. Whatever it is, it's been following us for some time," she hissed.

The hairs on the back of her neck stood up, and icy cold seized her body. Her gift stirred like a raging river. Instinctively, she jumped off her horse and peered into the dark forest.

"Liya! "Hemmet dismounted and hurried to her.

"It's getting closer," she said quietly as she drew her bow.

The men gathered around Hemmet and Liya, looking from one to the other, shifting on their horses.

"What the hell is going on?" asked Eagle, sliding out of his saddle.

"Look at the students," Owl whispered.

The rickety figures were standing, grinning. The next moment, they attacked the mercenaries. Like wild animals gone rogue, they bit and clawed at the men.

"They're going to kill them," Coyote remarked.

The mercenaries could hardly defend themselves since their hands and feet were tied. Their desperate cries gave Liya goosebumps. Quickly, all her comrades-in-arms got off their horses.

"Either we kill the students right now, or we won't have any prisoners in a few minutes," Coyote stated in disgust.

"They're our people," Weasel said softly.

The usually silent fighter looked pleadingly at Hemmet. Liya clearly read the pained expression in Weasel's eyes.

"We'll help the mercenaries," Hemmet decided, taking a big step toward the cart.

A creature jumped out of the darkness and mauled one of the horses in front of the cart. The beast was about the size of a brown bear, but its body resembled that of a wolf.

Liya shot several arrows in succession. Although she aimed well, the projectiles bounced off the creature's black fur. It turned toward her, its fiery red eyes glowing. The horses neighed in panic; the men tried to calm them. Eagle led the horses to a tree while the others gathered around Liya. Hemmet began throwing knives at the creature; they fell ineffectively to the ground.

"This thing smells like rotten eggs," Owl muttered.

The creature stumbled toward them. When it was less than ten meters away from them, Liya noticed a sticky substance shimmering in its fur. The beast of darkness stopped and howled. The horses galloped away. Eagle ran up to them.

The beast stood up on its hind legs. It stretched out paws with curved, sharp claws. Soon, they would pierce their next victim. At that moment, she remembered. She had met such a creature once before—in Dar'Angaar.

"Don't let the claws get you. They're poisonous!" she shouted to the men.

A cruel scream escaped from the being of darkness. She felt it inside her. A strange coldness spread through her, but then a familiar feeling set in. Time seemed to stand still; all sounds faded into the background. Liya breathed calmly. Now her thoughts were clear; only her heart was racing.

This time, she didn't have to speak; her mind formed the lava flow inside her. Her entire body vibrated as her gift took control. As much as Liya feared this power, she enjoyed the hot, thrumming sensation. This magic was many times more intense and powerful than it had been before.

Boldly, she took a step forward. Fully immersed in her gift, she withstood the evil gaze. The fiery red eyes were fixed on her, and the wide-open mouth approached her.

When she raised her hands, the fire exploded out of her. The first hot jet bounced off the monster's fur, but she did not give up. The volcano that had been dormant within her awoke. As she increased the flame, she felt light and floating, intoxicated.

Something detached itself from her body and looked down on what was happening from above. The fire did not make the creature's fur burn, but it caused it pain and weakened it. Still, it approached the beast steadily, and then she heard a cruel roar leave its throat. Liya noted that the creature in Dar'Angaar had looked somehow human, but this one did not.

It jumped. She took a step to the side, clawed at its fur with both hands, and pulled herself onto its back.

She realized that the sticky substance on the creature's fur had been a shield. Now it had melted from the heat. The monster howled agitatedly. Its fur wouldn't burn, but lava slowly flowed over it. It jumped wildly until, finally, it lost its footing, was flung away, and crashed into a tree. Her eyes rested on the monster. Although weakened, it staggered toward her. She rose, clenching her fists. Under no circumstances would she give up.

Then something unexpected happened. Horrified, she wrenched her eyes open as the creature's head, pale and somewhat indistinct—dream-like—appeared directly in front of her, though the beast was still at least fifteen paces away.

It was trying to gain access to her mind! How was that possible? What magic did it possess? A sharp pain flashed through her, and her body froze. Cold started at her legs and crept upward. She couldn't let it reach her heart! Liya had no idea how she knew this.

She needed warmth. With a deep breath, she envisioned a sea of flames and stepped into the middle of it. She concentrated on the protective wall she had built around her gift and burned it down for good. From afar, she heard screams. A roar sounded, then all was silent.

Dazed, she opened her eyes. In front of her lay the huge, lifeless body of the creature. Blood dripped on her lips—from her nose. She breathed out cold air. Her body trembled.

"Hemmet!" she whispered.

Everything spun. The last thing she saw was Hemmet's horrified face. The world went dark.

"**S**low down," Hemmet said, helping her sit up.

Liya looked around. The large room was sparsely furnished with a long table, three armchairs, and two old chests of drawers. Owl and Weasel sat in front of the fireplace on a woolen rug. When she looked over at them, the men quickly averted their eyes.

"Where are we, Hemmet?" she asked.

"At Weasel's house," he whispered.

She wanted to say something, but he shook his head.

"We're going to go collect wood," Owl declared. The two got up and left the house.

Startled, she realized it was already daytime. "I have to go back to the palace city."

Gently, he placed a hand on her shoulder. "Slowly," he said.

Somewhat unwillingly, she waved him off and freed herself from the many blankets. Hemmet handed her a glass of water.

"Thank you. How long have I been here?"

"We brought you here last night. Now it's noon."

"I guess I underestimated this fight."

"You moved so fast. I've never seen anything like it," he groaned.

"That's not all, is it?" She felt uncomfortable. Hemmet seemed changed to her.

"This creature was covered in lava. It must have burned from the inside out. Nothing remained but a stinking coat, the underside of which was charred." He looked her straight in the eye. "You didn't move a foot from the spot. Your eyes..." He hesitated briefly before continuing, "At first, they glowed sapphire blue, then they shone white, like the sun." Sighing, he sat down beside her. "I had no idea how powerful you were, Liya."

"Because I am untrained, I misjudged my strength," she replied quietly.

"This is not your fault. The mages have to help you."

"Maybe so." She didn't want to talk about that with him. "Have you seen a creature like this before?" she asked, trying to change the subject.

"No, never before. So far, in our search for the kidnapped students, we've only come across mercenary camps, and once they had mages with them," he replied. "How about you?"

"I have fought with such a creature before. But the one from yesterday was stronger and faster."

This did not seem to surprise Hemmet. "Who could possibly make use of such a creature?" he asked.

"Those who kidnapped your students."

"I keep thinking, 'what do they want from the students?'" He exhaled deeply. "In any case, the kidnappers are being fed information. These attacks are planned and targeted."

She agreed.

"Our first guess was that some kind of experiments were being conducted on the young men."

"That would make sense. Probably, the experiments failed, and they were released knowing that they wouldn't survive."

The door opened, and Weasel and Owl entered with a pile of wood.

"We should eat, then take Liya to town," Owl said. "I'm sure she's already missing it. "

Hemmet nodded and helped her up. Gratefully, she grabbed his elbow. Everyone took a seat at the table.

"I'm surprised that Ewan and Julian aren't already looking for me," she remarked, sipping some deliciously fragrant vegetable soup.

"Ewan is a permanent guest of Brath," Hemmet explained. "And Brath is privy to our excursions. He told your friend that you were accompanying Edna in search of herbs, at his request."

"Ewan believed him?"

Hemmet grinned. "Not at first. But Brath can be very convincing. Besides, Ewan knows that Brath is very cautious when it comes to his wife's safety."

"Where is Edna now?" she inquired.

Owl answered, "Not far from here, in our camp. She tried to heal the soldiers, but there was nothing she could do. The bite wounds were poisoned."

"And the students?"

"Well," Weasel interjected, "they died along with the creature."

"Edna should be here soon," Owl said, taking another ladleful of soup.

He had barely finished speaking when the door opened. Brath's wife grinned broadly. She arranged her unruly copper-red curls, embraced Liya warmly.

"Brath will be glad to see you again." Her scrutinizing gaze slid over Liya's face and body. "Can you ride yet? You look pretty weak."

"I'm fine. But even if it were different, I have to go back."

Edna sighed. "I'm afraid you're right. Your friend already has someone looking for you."

As soon as Liya finished eating, she helped Weasel clear the table. Despite his resistance, she felt the urge to move.

When she had washed the last plate, she turned directly to Weasel. "Thank you for the shelter. I know anonymity is important to you."

"I owe you my life. And after all, we know your name." Wolf blabbed.

She gave him a smile. "That's true, though."

"My name is Dahur," he whispered.

"Thank you," she replied softly. She was happy he trusted her.

"We have to go," Edna called from the doorway.

Everyone hurried outside to where the horses stood, already saddled.

"Liya and I will walk a bit so she can warm up her muscles before she gets on a horse. She then rides with me," Hemmet ordered. "The rest of you, ride to camp and get the rest of our party. We'll meet at the clearing outside town."

Weasel, Owl, and Edna galloped away. Hemmet attached a short rope to his horse's halter, then they marched off.

"How are you feeling?" he inquired.

"A little tired, but overall good."

He offered her his arm, which she accepted gratefully.

"Are your people afraid of me?" she asked hesitantly.

"No."

"I'm relieved, then."

"You gave them hope."

"What do you mean?" she asked, surprised.

"We've been fighting mercenaries for several months. Weasel's son was also kidnapped. He was already dead when we found him."

"How awful." Her heart constricted as she thought of the little man with the long beard.

Hemmet closed his eyes before returning her gaze. His green eyes glowed in the sunlight. "We don't know who's abducting the students or what experiments are being done on them. We lost half of our men in the last operation. Now, we have hope again. With you by our side, we could defeat the mercenaries and find out who is behind this."

"So now you're wondering if I'm going to keep helping, aren't you?"

"That's right. I would understand if you—"

"If what?" she interrupted. "If I would stop fighting? I'm not afraid to accompany you." She thought of her upcoming trip to Dar'Angaar. She *was* afraid of that. "I will support you whenever I can."

"Thank you."

Hemmet stopped and got on the horse. With a smile, he extended his arm. "I was worried." He helped her mount. "Hold on tight."

She wrapped her arms around his waist. When he galloped off, she tightened her grip.

❧

"Ready?" Edna looked at Liya intently. "Everything will be fine, don't worry. If Ewan catches us before we get to Brath's house, just act surprised. You'll be fine. "

However, her concern was not the acting but Ewan's distrust. That was why he'd searched for her. Surely Julian had encouraged him. After her confession yesterday, their friendship was on a knife's edge.

Hemmet approached with his stallion and leaned over to her. "If, for whatever reason, he doesn't believe you, don't try to change that. Let time play out for you. True friendship lasts even through the most difficult times."

If only he knew!

Her eyes glazed over. The loss of Ewan's friendship would hurt her deeply. She pulled herself together and said, "I don't know when I'll be able to join you again. Ewan will be having me watched."

"I could come visit you," Hemmet suggested.

"To further fuel the distrust." She frowned. "Even if I help you, I haven't forgotten who your family is attached to."

His face darkened. She wanted to add something, but he galloped away. Sighing, she set her mare in motion.

"Do you have the herbs?" she asked Edna.

"Of course." Brath's wife pointed to the leather bags on her saddle.

Half an hour later, they rode through the open gate of the city. Liya breathed a sigh of relief when she didn't spot Ewan and Julian anywhere.

"Let's go straight to my husband—he's already waiting," Edna said.

"We should first turn in the horses to the stable master. That would be the usual procedure after a ride to find herbs."

"Right, of course."

They put the horses in the paddock and headed for the academy.

"I saw Ewan just ahead of us," Edna whispered, pointing her head to the right. "Don't look. A tall man is escorting him." She winked. "We should talk casually. Do you know how I met Brath?"

She began to tell the story, trying to sound relaxed and cheerful.

"Liya!" Ewan grabbed her arm. Before she could say anything, he snapped, "I've already sent out a search for you. Where have you been?" His black eyes glared with anger.

"Search party? What for? I was accompanying Edna. Didn't Brath tell you?"

"Yes, he did."

"Then why are you looking for me?" she asked, equally irritated.

He narrowed his eyes and turned to Edna. "I guess you'll find your way to your husband on your own."

Edna gave her an uncertain look.

"It's all right," she said quickly. "You go ahead, I'll catch up with you later."

As soon as Brath's wife was out of earshot, she put her hands on her hips. "Have you lost your mind?"

Julian stepped up to them and murmured, "Not here."

Angrily, she pointed her index finger at Julian. "Did you do this? What are you two making a fuss about? What is this nonsense?"

Ewan took her arm and pushed her in front of him. "We're going to the palace."

"Before that, I want to freshen up," she nagged.

"You can do that later," Julian said. His voice sounded hard.

"Let go of me," she hissed, shaking Ewan off. "What do you think you're doing? I'm not under your command." She looked at Ewan, then Julian. "Or yours. You can't give me orders."

"Liya, I was really worried."

She raised her hand. "No, you're going too far. I can take care of myself. You know that. You have doubts, I understand that. Still, you can't boss me around."

"After we talked, you just disappeared," he hissed.

"Am I accountable to you now?" Her voice sounded shrill.

"We're in a delicate situation," he countered. "We have to work together."

"We? This is not collaboration." Dark spots danced before her eyes.

"What's the matter? You're all white in the face." Ewan sounded worried.

"I knew it." Julian cursed softly.

Frowning, Ewan looked at him. "What are you talking about?"

"Herbs, my ass."

"You've done enough damage already," she hissed in Julian's direction.

"Me?" The mage laughed out, sounding cold and fake. "You think we're buying that story? You're still weakened from using your magic recently."

"I don't care what you believe," she countered.

"Let's go to the palace. There, we can talk undisturbed," Ewan intervened.

"I'm not going anywhere with you guys. I want to go home."

The next moment, soldiers appeared around them. A group rushed toward Ewan, their leader whispering something to him.

"We must go to the palace at once," he said in response. "There is no other way, Liya."

When she realized how desperate he was, she complied.

When they reached near the entrance of the palace, Gerard was already hurrying toward them. "Follow me, quickly!" he said urgently.

"What's going on?" asked Julian.

They rushed to the palace without an answer.

Liya noticed Gerard's shaking hands when he opened the door to the king's fireplace room a little later. "Master Darwin is already here," he said.

The room was completely darkened. Darwin knelt on the floor in front of the desk, muttering incessantly to himself. Two candlesticks flickered beside him.

Behind Ewan and Julian, she hurried into the room. Gerard followed. Darwin was bent over a motionless body. Her heartbeat stopped. The king lay on his back in a pool of blood. He was gasping. Blood poured from his torn shirt.

"Sire!" Ewan cried in horror.

"A creature attacked him," Darwin said without taking his eyes off Louis.

Julian looked around. "Did you kill it?"

"When I approached it, it disappeared." Darwin sighed. "I can't manage to heal him. Whatever the creature thrust into the king's chest was poisoned."

Julian knelt down and put his hands on Louis' stomach, then closed his eyes. Silence filled the room.

After a while, Julian shook his head. "I can't get through to him either."

"Should we get more healers?" Gerard, who stood immediately behind them, asked in a trembling voice.

"I'm afraid they'll be just as powerless." Julian slumped down.

Never before had she seen the mage so desperate. As he looked at her now, his face darkened and his jaws creaked. "Are you still convinced that your lover poses no danger to our king?"

Fearlessly, she looked at him but said nothing, hoping Julian would leave it at that. Instead, she turned to Louis. Her heart clenched.

"Answer me!" Julian yelled angrily.

"We should discuss this another time," she said as calmly as she could.

He stood up, grabbed her rudely by the upper arm, and pushed her to the floor. "Explain to King Louis why he was attacked."

"I don't know."

"Julian, what are you doing? We're all worried, including Liya!" Ewan shouted indignantly and put a hand on the mage's shoulder.

Julian shook him off. "I hope you're not mistaken about that! Our dear Liya knows the new king of Dar'Angaar well. I doubt her judgment."

"What's he talking about?" Ewan turned to her.

Full of anger, she sparked at Julian. "This is neither the place nor the time. Your anger is blinding you."

The mage grabbed her with both hands and held her tightly. "You defend him over and over again!"

"What are you doing, Liya?" whispered Ewan.

Before she could answer, the king clutched her arm and coughed. She felt cornered, like a deer facing its attacker. Several things happened at once. As she breathed faster and faster, her headache intensified, and the voices around her grew quieter. A bright light shot out from her hand and pushed Julian away. She registered that he was trying to reach for her again, but he could not.

Flowing energy caressed her. The infinite power of the sky and the earth became part of her. She thought she was leaving the world she knew. What a liberating feeling. Green mist spread out around her, and the outer world disappeared. A crushing weight fell from her, and she could breathe again. In front of her, in this green world, lay Louis. He was still holding her hand. The look he gave her was pained and fearful. For a tiny moment, it seemed as if he was afraid of *her*.

A black spike protruded from the center of his belly. She did not see blood in the green world, but she felt a dark energy, almost as if the spike was fighting for its life. Gently, she put her hands around it. Sparks of light danced in the air, then spun in a vortex around the spike.

The resistance of the spike was immense. Like a living creature, it tried to free itself from the net of ever-brighter light, but she would not allow it. Her palms singed as she increased the pressure. The now-white light nearly obscured her hands. Carefully, she felt around the thorn until she found the area that pulsed the most. She sent her energy to the spot, and almost effortlessly, the darkness receded, and the spike dissolved.

All her strength drained out of her. A sharp pain ran through her body, and she toppled to the side, unable to move. The fog dissipated; she could see her surroundings again. The trepidation she had not felt in the green world returned. Her breaths heaved in her chest, rapid and choppy. She could not stop shivering.

342

Coughing, Louis tried to sit up. Everyone stood and stared, paralyzed. "Help him!" she whispered.

Ewan and Julian were startled. Together, they supported the king and dragged him to the sofa. Louis was also shaking all over. Gerard picked up the blankets from the floor and spread them over him.

Darwin knelt by her. "Your gift!" he murmured. "It is extraordinary."

Groaning, she turned her head and looked at Ewan, who was standing in front of the sofa with Julian and Gerard. "Nothing will ever be the same again," she breathed.

The king mumbled something. Darwin helped her up and led her to the sofa.

"Now you've saved my life for the second time," Louis said in a hoarse voice.

She squatted in front of the sofa so their eyes were level.

"I don't know how to thank you for that," Louis continued. He took her hand. "Still, I can't just let Julian's accusations stand. I heard it all." He closed his eyes.

A stifling silence followed. Gerard handed the king a glass of water.

Gratefully, Louis took a few sips. "Liya, do you understand?" he asked.

Before she could answer, Ewan took the floor. "We shouldn't make decisions we might regret later."

"Wise words! However, time is short, and the enemy is right at our door. I must act," Louis replied.

Gerard whispered to her, "Say no more now." He bent down to Louis. "My king," he began, "I propose that Liya resign her position, effective immediately, for personal reasons. And please consider, you have been seriously injured and have lost consciousness frequently since then. Who can say what you have heard!"

Her heart tightened painfully at Gerard's proposal. She was aware of the precarious situation—Julian had accused her of treason, which was punishable by death. But the king trusted him, didn't even question him? *After all these years and everything I've done for him?* She could not believe it. Disappointment spread through her. Was he going to accept it?

With a barely perceptible nod, Louis closed his eyes again. "I will accept the resignation. Prepare everything!"

"I'll take care of it," Gerard affirmed, gesturing for her to leave the room.

Liya pressed her lips tightly together and suppressed her anger. She clenched her fists, but she could not prevent her emotions from affecting her magic. A hurricane raged inside her, but in the eye of the storm, she realized that she had just been given her freedom.

⁂

Liya walked through the dark corridors of the palace. Five days had passed since the attack on the king. She could not get out of her mind the way he had looked at her. Today, she would sign her resignation. Louis insisted that they do it in his study.

She knocked on the door and entered the darkened room. The curtains were drawn to block the midday sun. A few candles glowed with a soft light.

Philip, the king's eldest son, nodded to her and left the room. Louis, who was sitting behind his desk, beckoned her closer without lifting his head. After a while, he put the pen aside and looked up. The encounter with death had changed him. His eyes sunk deep into his angular face, like two stones pressed into a cake, and his pale skin was faintly grayish.

"How is the wound healing?" she inquired.

He motioned for her to take a seat across from him.

"I'm still in pain, but it's getting better." Louis stroked his graying beard as he eyed her intently. "Gerard has already spoken with you, I guess?"

"Yes. Immediately after this meeting, I will leave town."

The days when she held intimate conversations with the king seemed long gone. Louis even wore the red, fur-trimmed cloak he reserved for official business.

"Gerard was so kind, he prepared everything." He handed her the parchment that declared her resignation. She'd reviewed it with Gerard as he wrote it.

She took the pen and signed. She held no grudge against the king.

"Officially, you have been relieved of all duties. We announced that you have resigned for personal reasons. Gerard indicated that you wanted to think about your future. No one will suspect a thing." He sighed. "I know you would never do something against me or Namoor. Don't think I don't know that. But if someone finds out about your relationship with the king of Dar'Angaar..." He shook his head. "My country is not stable enough at the moment."

Liya didn't respond. He was saying that *his* position was not stable enough, and he needed to avoid any further issues. Even though it hurt, she agreed. The situation could cause difficulties given the mages in Namoor and their opinions about magic. It would be worse to keep her position.

He leaned forward and added, "Still, I want to ask you for one last—shall we say—*favor.*"

An uneasy feeling spread through her.

"Prem is on his way here with a group of mercenaries. The lords who support him already arrived this morning. "

She looked at him in disbelief. Was Prem planning to overthrow the king? "How many mercenaries?"

"According to my scouts, around fifty."

"That's not enough to take the city."

"You're right, of course." He looked calm and determined. He leaned back, interlacing his fingers. "But something is afoot. You must know that my deceitful son is after my throne. He knows I will never make him king. He's no strategist, but he *is* greedy and easily influenced. The kingdom would fall into chaos. Prem has taken advantage of that."

"What could they be up to?" she asked.

"Well." He drank from the glass of water in front of him. "Prem's mercenaries, and the few men the lords have in their retinue, can't do anything against my soldiers. But they are planning something. Prem and my son are the masterminds. They think they have a trump card against me, so I have to find out what it is. That's why I'm not doing anything against Philip yet."

His eyes narrowed. She felt sick. What did he want from her?

"Wouldn't it be unfortunate," he remarked in a conversational tone, "if something were to happen to Prem?"

Had she heard wrong? "You want me to get rid of Prem? So, you don't want him to be held accountable?" She pressed her lips together.

"That's right." He frowned. "There's no way he can get into the city. I don't want to put the inhabitants in danger! If you capture him in my name, he will neither surrender nor be reasonable. A fight is inevitable. He could die in the process..." His gray eyes sparkled dangerously.

She remembered the anxious look the king had given her in the mist. "There's something else, isn't there?" she groaned.

He had been afraid of her because she was able to discover his secret. She had found something else inside him, but he'd immediately suppressed it. Now the realization hit her with full force. "You knew about my gift from the beginning. How?"

"Your father told me before he left, Liya. I regret that he did not return. "

"My father let you in on his plans!"

"Well, my captain told me that he was going to Dar'Angaar to follow up on clues related to your mother's disappearance. In case something happened to him, he asked me to take care of you and protect you. It was vital to him that you finish your education. He mentioned that his trip would be for your protection." He paused. "I didn't inquire further at the time, but he made me curious. What makes a man leave a child alone, and what did he mean by protecting you? So, I supported his preparations. After he left, I began doing my own research. Over the years, I ferreted out relics from the Ancient Era." His eyes shone. "What a loss! All that great knowledge—destroyed! At the time, I had no idea of the implications."

Her underlying nausea intensified. "What did you find?"

"An object of immense power. I had to involve the mages and let them do further research for me." He smiled. "I am convinced that Elladur still exists. We need to find that city. There are more of these, well, *items* there."

Her stomach lifted. He possessed a crystal; she was sure of it. Was history really going to repeat itself?

"The old knowledge was lost for a reason."

"You are still young, Liya. I'm tired and I'm sick of all these intrigues."

This could not be true. Had the king gone mad? "Do you really want to use magical relics to stop political intrigue? Where is this going?"

"You tell me."

Many things she didn't understand before now made sense. "Thanks to you, I was able to take the academy exam two years early. You bypassed the rules."

"You had to stay close to me. Your abilities were unique even then. To hold the position of First Emissary, you must have completed the academy's training. " A sad expression entered his eyes. "Two years ago, we came across a parchment with information about the World Guardians. Only then did I understand the true extent of your gift. Only the Guardians have these special magical abilities, only they have these extraordinary eyes—blue green. After the magic has fully unfolded, the green disappears. After your return from Dar'Angaar, I noticed a small difference, but I wasn't sure. However, after your return from Kapilar, your eyes glowed blue, and my suspicions were confirmed."

"Who did the research for you?" she asked, but she already knew.

"I commissioned Almany. He and his mages found more than I'd dared to hope. The stone tablets will soon be fully deciphered and will, hopefully, show us the way to the desert city. With what we find there, I will defeat all my enemies."

"What do you expect to find in Elladur?" she prodded. *A weapon?*

"There are few records about it. It is mentioned in legends and folk songs. Supposedly, the Guardians of Elladur were able to combine their gift with a certain extraordinary metal. In this way, they created an incredible weapon that could only be used by mages."

It had only been a guess, but she had hit the mark. She perceived a blinding headache that felt like a sudden rush. The king had spoken the truth, she had no doubt about that. However, the way he eyed her as he spoke troubled her deeply. She tried to block out the realization that was taking shape in her mind.

"Who is your enemy, your majesty?" she pressed out.

"The gates cannot be opened. We agree on that." Louis leaned across the table, his eyes taking on a sinister expression. "It's too dangerous."

That wasn't the answer to her question, but what he meant was clear. He didn't trust her anymore.

"I'll do anything to protect my country."

"And what will you do if the gates remain closed? Will you still need the weapon?"

He stood up somewhat heavily, leaning on his black cane. His smile was fake.

"Walking is more comfortable with the cane. Less pain," he explained in a gentle tone. With one foot, he pushed an armchair right in front of her and sat down. "One thing at a time, Liya. First, we have to stop Prem. I'm not asking anything impossible of you. And know this: Prem will take every opportunity to kill you." He put the walking stick aside and took her hand. "As soon as this mission is over, I expect a scout. You will not return to my court. Ride directly to the Nirm. There, you will wait for Darwin and Julian, who will accompany you to Dar'Angaar. The Nirm will support you, I am sure of it. Whatever is necessary has to be done to prevent the opening of the gates."

He smiled again, and she shivered. What had happened to the king she knew?

"Do we have a deal?"

"As if I have a choice," she muttered.

He had not said it, but she knew that the success of this mission was the price of her freedom. She wasn't sure if the king had just ordered the murder of Haydn. In any case, murder was one of the means to which he had expressly referred.

"Good, Ewan's putting together a small squad. They'll be waiting for you at the north gate." Slowly, he stood up and walked back to his desk.

The conversation was over. She left the room feeling strange. She wasn't angry, but rather sad and disappointed. As if she had lost a friend. *What an illusion!* she thought. Louis had never been her friend; he was the king.

They had left the palace city a day ago. Liya let her eyes wander over the wide grassy landscape that stretched beyond Lake Smutny. In the darkness, the few bushes were barely visible. The light of the full moon showed them the way. Ever since Liya had left the palace city, she'd felt the pulsation of her gift, tantalizing her. When they'd set up camp the night before, it had suddenly become stronger. Occasionally, her whole body seemed to tingle. She wasn't sure if it was related to the crystal hidden in her side pocket. She wasn't sure if she would need it for the gates, so she'd taken it with her.

Ewan had banned fires so as not to attract attention. He commanded a group of eighteen soldiers, including three former comrades from the military academy. Mina was a dark-haired beauty who had hardly changed since their days at the military academy. Her black eyes almost always twinkled with amusement when she spoke. She was a good archer, but she was even better with her throwing skills. Keo and Joi, the twin brothers, were excellent hand-to-hand fighters.

Liya's thoughts drifted to Hemmet. She shuddered as the images of the soulless students appeared in her inner eye. Hemmet was searching for more camps with his troop. He firmly believed that somewhere, there was a larger camp where the experiments were being conducted. She knew exactly how much he was tormented by the question of who was doing such a thing to the young people and, above all, *why*.

"The scout should be back soon." Ewan snapped her out of her thoughts. He had not mentioned the last conversation with the king, though he'd distanced himself from her.

"How many mercenaries do you think are accompanying Prem?" asked Keo, who was riding beside Liya.

"I expect they'll be at least twice as many as we are."

At that moment, they heard the stamping of hooves. A horse was approaching at a breakneck pace. Ewan raised his fist, and the group stopped. Out of the corner of her eye, she saw Mina reach for her bow. She was relieved when she realized it was the scout. His horse neighed loudly as he yanked back on the reins to stop.

"General," Kanto greeted. "I have sighted the enemy force. Their camp is not far from here at the edge of the forest, not far from here."

She felt sick to her stomach. Tomorrow, they would be meeting Prem's people. And, if the lord of Relerin remained intransigent, they would be left with no choice but to fight for their lives.

"How many are there?" Ewan asked curtly.

"I can't say exactly. I'd guess fifty to sixty men."

Ewan turned his horse around. "I suspect they will take the path through the forest to avoid being seen." He clicked his tongue. "Prem's people are in the camp now. We'll ride through the forest and should be close in a few hours."

❧

In the morning, blue haze hung over the fields, waiting to be carried away by the autumn wind. She sat down by the campfire with Ewan. Silently, they ate their breakfast.

"How do we proceed?" Mina finally inquired.

Everyone looked at Ewan, almost like back in the academy, when they had tested combat situations and had to prove themselves against other groups. Even then, Ewan had always been their leader. Only the serious faces of those present made the danger they were in clear.

"We launch a surprise attack. We have to break up the force before it can form," Ewan explained.

"Shouldn't we try to talk to Prem?" Liya objected though she knew full well that wasn't the point. *Prem must die.* That was probably the king's order for Ewan.

"Considering their troop strength, relying on negotiations is too risky. Prem won't surrender easily. He's most likely to do so if we surprise him with an attack and gain the upper hand." As he spoke, he did not look at her. He hadn't made eye contact this whole trip.

"Ewan is right," Keo agreed. "They outnumber us. Our chances are extremely low anyway."

Thoughtfully, Ewan looked around. "Keo, you take the rear guard. Take seven men and ride into the mountains. Wait for my signal. We will wait for them at the fork in the mountains near the forest and attack from the rear. As soon as you hear the trumpet, ride out. We can only hope they are expecting far more soldiers than we have. Mina, you take an archer and cover us. Find a spot back there." He pointed to the hills that fronted the mountain range. "Pack everything up, we leave in ten minutes."

As she was about to leave, Ewan held her by the arm. "Don't use your magic. I only want the fighter, not the mage. You are not yet in Dar'Angaar to have a free hand."

"I'm just wondering how the king is different from Prem. He, too, attacks without provocation."

"Anyone who attacks our kingdom is an enemy. We are at war. The king protects his people."

"So, it's that simple."

"Yes, Liya, it's that simple." He leaned toward her. "You should be the last one to criticize this course of action. You are friends with the enemy."

He left her standing there. His words cut through her and left a dull, empty feeling. She had closed her heart, but the wall was crumbling.

Ewan was now speaking to each soldier personally. She suspected he was giving them words of encouragement. None of them had the kind of combat experience they needed—they knew wars only from books. Involuntarily, she shuddered as she thought of Arkas.

Her thoughts were interrupted when Ewan rode past her. She also swung herself into the saddle and joined his group while Keo led his people into the mountains. Her heart pounded with fear.

Ewan, the general, led them into the forest. The colorful foliage swirled on the ground and swallowed the sound of galloping horses.

After a while, Ewan stopped and formed his men into a line, facing the mountains. Her horse stood next to Ewan's. Minutes seemed like an eternity to her, but her pulse rate calmed slightly.

They heard a noise. Horsemen in blue uniforms with silver breastplates approached closer. Their faces were hidden behind hoods pulled deep over their faces. They were looking for a way through the narrow mountain pass in rows of two.

All her courage left her when she saw that none of the soldiers on foot. *Does the king know what he is asking of us?* There were twenty of them in total, facing a mounted unit of at least fifty mercenaries. The king could have informed the Council of the Wise. For an official operation, he could have assigned far more soldiers. But, of course, he wanted to carry out this action secretly.

When the troop finally rode past them, Ewan raised his hand. He waited until the dust cloud cleared, then gave the signal. Their horses galloped after the mercenaries at a fast pace. Liya prayed that none of them in the rear ranks turned around. The stomping of their horses was lost in the noise made by the far larger group of their opponents. Ewan raised his sword, the metal tip glinting in the sunlight.

They formed up, two archers riding on the left side while Liya took the right flank with another. She drew her bow and held it so tightly that her knuckles stood out white.

The mercenaries were less than a hundred meters away when Ewan gave the signal to attack. The first riders fell. One arrow after another was shot, and the horses of the opponents reared up. The men turned around, the line of two confused for a moment.

"An ambush! We're under attack! Turn around!" an order rang out.

The mercenaries drove their animals in all directions. When the first steel blades clashed, the archers who were hiding on the hill fired their arrows. The rear ranks of the mercenaries were once again torn apart, the front line fighting their attackers.

The first person Liya fought was a strong, brown-skinned man with an eye patch. The wind had blown his hood off his head, and she found herself looking into an angry face. He was an excellent rider, nimbly pulling his horse around, dashing off with his sword drawn. She severed his arm above the elbow. The man fell out of the saddle and disappeared under the hooves of his panicked horse.

The next rider galloped toward her with a lance without a trace of fear. Just in time, she brought her mare to a halt and turned in the saddle. The lance missed her by a few centimeters. Without thinking, she raised her sword and brought it down on the horse's neck. The soldier jumped off as the animal went down, covered in blood. With an angry cry, he drew his sword, thrust, and—fell silent. Several arrows had pierced his back. He took a few more steps before sinking to his knees.

Short trumpet blasts sounded. She looked around. The soldiers had regained their formation. These men were no ordinary mercenaries; they had mastered strategy and military discipline.

"They're trying to surround us. Break through their front!" shouted Ewan.

Along with the others, she rode towards the troop, which thundered toward her like a mighty fist. Battle axes and swords clashed again; screams ripped the air. Keo's group rushed up. She spotted Joi, who was already without a horse and striking at any mercenary who came near him. As she ran to him, she overlooked a rider who rammed into her at full speed. She fell from her horse. The mare staggered to the side, then went down as well. The attacker jumped out of the saddle and took a swing.

She sat up and parried at the last second. However, she did not have much strength to counter the force of the blow. Her sword flew over her head. With eyes filled with hatred, the man clasped his longsword with both hands and raised it. He jerked when a sword tip protruded from his chest. Stunned, he looked at the metal tip, which immediately disappeared. Ewan stood behind him.

"Hurry up and get your sword!" he shouted to her, then was again swallowed up in the tumult of battle.

Out of breath, she kept a lookout for Prem. She had to find him soon, or none of them would survive. Although they had already killed some of their opponents, they were still vastly outnumbered.

A mercenary came riding toward her, his lance tearing up the earth. Liya hacked it in two, spun around, and rammed her sword into the man's leg. When the rider fell out of the saddle with a scream, she grabbed the horse's reins, tried to steady the stallion, and swung herself onto its back.

Where was Prem? He would not fight, that much was clear. However, he should be watching the action. There! On a small hill near the battlefield. He sat on his magnificent steed, his blond curls blowing in the wind. His golden breastplate shimmered from underneath a white cloak.

As she struggled to reach him, she breathed calmly and evenly. She nodded to Keo and pointed to Prem. Without further words, he formed a small group and helped her find a way through the melee. She was not fifty meters from Prem when he caught sight of her. His face colored with anger, and he reached for his sword. He was almost ready to attack her.

He stopped when a strikingly tall man rode up to him. His dark blue uniform was covered by a silver breastplate. Unlike the others, this mercenary had a saber in his hand. He wore no helmet, his head showing only a thin line of fuzz. His unusually long brown beard protruded a hand's breadth above his chin. Prem talked to the man until he turned his horse and rode directly toward her. She saw anger burning in his eyes.

Her father's words suddenly came to her mind. Once, during a combat exercise, she had been truly angry because her father had proved to be an insurmountable opponent. No matter what blow she threw, she had failed miserably. A painful lesson! *Anger is the worst and most dangerous tactic in a fight because it makes you blind.* The strong man with the saber had already signed his death warrant.

She waited until her opponent was only an arm's length away. She grasped her sword with one hand, the metal tip pointing back. With the other hand, she held the reins. As the man charged, she deftly dodged to the right, her face almost touching his horse, then thrust her sword backward with a jerk and rammed it into the man's back. He lost his balance but managed to land on his feet.

She pulled the reins firmly to the right, swung her sword forward, and struck at him again. He dodged at the last moment. Her weapon left only a scratch on his arm. He stared at her, muttering under his breath.

As if he was not in pain, he raised his sword, shouted, "Ultio!" and ran for her.

Just before he reached the horse, she jumped off, rolled to the right, and stabbed. The man cried out. She pulled her sword out and struck again. He had no time to react, and this time she caught the carotid artery. Blood spurted in all directions. He grabbed his neck before he collapsed.

She wiped the blood from her face and looked at Prem. His pale face was filled with horror. He turned his horse, but on the hill, not fifty meters away, Mina and another archer stood with their arrows aimed at him.

"Your leader is dead, and Laurus Prem is in captivity," Ewan shouted. "Surrender! Then we will let you live."

Confused, the mercenaries looked around, not knowing what to do.

"You fight to the bitter end! We are superior, and we will not give up!" Prem roared.

Of course, he was right. They could not win this fight based on numbers. The pulsing inside her grew stronger as she sauntered toward Prem. Silence returned.

"I'll get you." Irritated, she looked around. No one but she seemed to have heard the whisper.

Prem stared at her. She thought she saw a twitch at the corner of his mouth. Her magic lurked inside, waiting to be released. Her head began to pound.

"Only a few have the necessary awareness for the power of creation. Allow the connection!" The voice sounded hoarse.

She stopped two arm's lengths from Prem, his black eyes scrutinizing her in a strange way. For a moment, she had the feeling that not Prem, but another very old and wise being was watching her.

"Call your men back!" Her voice was calm, her heart beating at normal speed.

Prem laughed mischievously. "What are you going to do, girl? Throw me off my horse and kill me?" He brushed a curl from his face, then leaned forward slightly. "Do you think I care if they die?" he said quietly.

She believed him. He would sacrifice everyone if he had to. Black clouds darkened the blue sky. Thunder sounded; wind came up. Prem jumped off the horse, then she felt his hand on her throat. *How did he move that fast?*

His laugh sounded rough, and his face changed. That strange expression came into his eyes. "You really believed you could defeat me."

Grinning, he tilted his head and squeezed her throat harder. She gasped.

"Let her go, or an arrow will pierce you!" Mina shouted.

The next moment, a dagger pressed into Liya's neck, and Prem turned in Mina's direction. "Get out of there and take your friend with you. Your arrow is no faster than my knife. Liya dies first."

She felt the knife carve her skin. Mina and the archer crept back.

"There—reinforcements...," she gasped, which of course was not true.

But Prem turned around, loosening his grip. She used this moment to hit his nose with her head. The blade dug into her wound for a moment, but Prem was distracted. Groaning, she escaped his grip and pushed him back. He staggered two steps backward, blood dripping onto his white shirt from his nose.

"You think that changes anything?" He laughed. Blood ran down his lips and teeth. With his dagger raised, he rushed toward her.

She crossed her arms and fended off the first attack. She made a half turn and rammed her fist into Prem's stomach. He doubled over, so she grabbed for the dagger. He swung at her, trying to get the weapon. She rolled to the side, and he jumped ahead, but he landed right on top of her. She held the handle tightly as the blade bored into his chest. Finally, with the last of her strength, she pushed him aside.

"I'm dying," he whispered, stunned.

"If you pull it out, you will bleed to death," she said coldly, getting to her feet.

He pulled the blade out of his body, stood up, and lunged at her.

"You die with me, you cursed woman," he hissed.

However, his movements were much slower, and blood poured from his wound incessantly.

Without much effort, she dodged. "Give up, you've lost."

Again, he stumbled towards her. She raised her hands, drew a circle in the air, and with the other hand, hit him on the chest. Gasping, he collapsed, coughing up blood.

She knelt beside him and murmured, "You should have left the king alone."

"Silly girl. It's just begun, and it won't end with me." He was still gasping when he finally closed his eyes.

Only now did she notice the silence on the battlefield. Then she heard Ewan instructing his troops to collect the weapons and tie up the prisoners.

Ewan stepped up to her and looked at Prem's body. "Did you use your gift?" he whispered.

"No, what makes you think that?" she asked.

"Your movements were very fast."

"I am well-trained," she replied. But she wondered if she had unconsciously used magic without even noticing. *Was that even possible?* She shifted uncomfortably at the thought.

"Good." Ewan waved two soldiers over, who picked Prem up and put him on a horse. The animal neighed and galloped away.

Keo wanted to follow, but Ewan raised his hand. "The horse won't get far. First, we'll take care of the wounded and the prisoners."

The moon shone peacefully in the calm night sky. Almost nothing of the morning battle remained—even the smoke from the burning corpses had cleared. Their group had dwindled, as eight soldiers had fallen in the fight. Liya entered the tent. Ewan, Mina, Keo, and Joi stood around a small table studying a map.

Ewan tapped the sketched forest and mountain range near the town. "One of the mercenaries told us where more units are hiding. They've set up camp near Kapilar."

"There are only twelve of us left," Keo pointed out. "We can't attack."

"My brother Rhos will join us with his troop in two days at the latest."

A murmur went through the small group. So, they *would* get reinforcements.

"Kanto is already on his way to the king to give him the news of Prem's attack and death," Ewan explained. "Now that it's official, we can call for reinforcements. As soon as Rhos arrives, we'll leave. Get some rest, it's been a long day."

Liya noticed the change in his behavior. He had led his squad into battle, and soon, the First Legion would follow him.

"Liya, I need to talk to you for a minute," he said. He signaled to the others that they were dismissed and waited for them to leave. "I have a favor to ask of you. Can you postpone your departure for the Nirm, just until Rhos has joined us?" A pained smile flitted across his face.

It amazed her how hard it was for him to ask her. "Of course," she replied.

"I hope we don't have to resort to your gift."

She would not respond to that. Instead, she said, "I guess the others don't know yet that I'm leaving you."

He shook his head. "No, I'll let them know as soon as Rhos arrives."

She hesitated. "There's something I need to talk to you about."

Surprised, he looked at her.

"The Prem thing was strange," she continued. "He was a politician, he never actively intervened in a fight before. Yet he did today. He also seemed like a leader, even though we both know he's not one. The mercenaries obeyed him, even when they had long been defeated. It seemed to me that he was getting stronger as his opponent got weaker."

"They're mercenaries, they get paid for it."

"Maybe, but my gut tells me there's more. The men were afraid of Prem, I saw it in their eyes." She sighed. "Be on your guard when you visit this camp."

They were silent for a while. "You seemed unsettled today," he finally said.

"Who wouldn't be? Does that surprise you? After all, we *were* outnumbered," she replied indignantly. "Besides, none of us had any real combat experience."

"Liya!" he burst out. "You're my friend, my family. I thought I knew you. So much has changed, but you don't seem to realize it. You're blind."

"What do you mean?"

"In these times, despite everything, you must be a leader. You are not allowed weakness. Ever. Whether you like it or not."

"Oh?"

"You can't allow yourself to look insecure or show fear. People like you and me are not afraid. We push ahead, and others follow us." He exhaled loudly. "Even if Joi and Keo joke with you, they respect you, especially after what happened today. In the morning, I felt their uncertainty, but now I see hope in their eyes. We give them hope."

"I know that," she murmured.

"People will look up to you even more when they find out you're a World Guardian."

What was she supposed to say to that?

"No one knows yet," he continued. "But that will change. Then people will talk about it, tell each other stories. Everyone will see you with completely different eyes. Your opponents will look for weaknesses." Reluctantly, he shook his head. "Damn it—you're already a living legend." Nervously, he stroked his fingers through his hair. "Haydn Amaar is a problem. If anyone finds out the connection between you and him, it will be considered treason, no matter what exactly it is. No one will be able to protect you then."

"How can you doubt me like that? I would give my life for you," she whispered.

Affected, he lowered his gaze. "You must kill Amaar. He is not allowed to open the gates. He must die."

She stared at him, thunderstruck. He had always been able to analyze tactical and strategic situations quickly, thanks to his excellent instincts. That's why they had won every flag game at the academy. He had honed this skill during his years of service. What he was asking was strategically smart, but it didn't match the Ewan she knew. He wouldn't have ordered a murder. The scales fell from her eyes.

"Julian! He put that nonsense in your head."

"He's not the only one who sees it that way. The king is also of this opinion."

"Pah! The king! He's using us all!"

"Do you hear yourself?" Ewan shouted at her. "You doubt your king and your friends!"

She looked directly at him. "With every breath I take, I will protect those I love. Trust me, as you did before."

He reached for her hands and held them tightly. "I'd like to. It tears me up inside to lose you. But that's the way it's going to be. I realized that when I talked to Julian."

"Ewan..."

With a wave of his hand, he interrupted her. "Whatever. Julian will get rid of him if you don't."

She closed her eyes briefly and tried to push the image of Haydn out of her mind. Then a loud scream rang out. Startled, she opened her eyes. With his sword drawn, Ewan ran outside, and she followed him. All the soldiers were standing near the prisoners' tent. Mina came towards them. She looked exceptionally pale.

"What's going on?" Ewan asked.

"I've never seen anything like it," Mina stammered.

With a scowl on his face, Ewan marched past her, Liya on his heels. When he pulled back the tent cover, she grabbed her nose. The smell of decay hit the back of her throat. All the mercenaries rotted lifelessly on the ground as if they had been dead for several days. But that was impossible.

"What happened?" asked Ewan.

Keo's eyes narrowed. "We don't know. They slumped, writhed, and—died. Most of them didn't even scream, they just whimpered. I tried to talk to them, but they didn't seem to understand me. The whole thing lasted only a few minutes. There was nothing I could do."

Ewan patted him on the shoulder.

"Wait, there's something on their heads." Liya approached a corpse and knelt. The smell of decay almost robbed her of her senses.

"Looks like a metal spiral behind the ear." Ewan squatted down next to her.

"A left-handed spiral, it goes inward."

"Maybe you're right, Liya. There's more to this than kidnapping and war." Ewan straightened up. "We burn the tent with the bodies."

Her stomach growled as they reached the swamp area around noon. After the conversation in the prisoners' tent, Ewan had not spoken to her. He'd stayed out of her way. The death of the mercenaries, and especially the circumstances of their deaths, had tested the morale of their troops. The comrades had been frightened and at a loss. Only when Rhos joined them with his men had the tension eased. Through Mina, Ewan had wished her a safe journey and assigned two soldiers to accompany her.

The loss of his trust hurt Liya deeply. She suppressed the urge to cry and got off the horse.

"We'll have to walk from here," she told the two soldiers.

The younger one, a handsome fellow, dismounted. The older one, with graying hair, got off his horse and wrinkled his nose.

"Don't dream, Emris," he drove at the boy.

"All right, all right. You're an old grumbler, Nelar," Emris teased him.

Liya pushed the reeds aside, they took the reins of their horses and set off. Strangely, it was very quiet. She looked around attentively, but she couldn't see anything wrong. When they entered the clearing in front of the Nirm village, she was sure something happened. There were no children to welcome her. There was nothing but this uneasy silence.

"Something's wrong here," she whispered, taking her bow and leading her horse to the pasture. The men followed.

They ran across the clearing in a crouch. Soon, they reached the village and squatted behind the first house. Liya carefully scanned the area. There was no one around. Presumably, the Nirm were in the mountains.

"Let's move slowly," she said softly.

They crossed the main square, and Liya headed for the largest house in the village. A foul smell greeted them—rottenness, her mind registered. She stumbled. In front of the entrance lay two corpses, completely unrecognizable and as black as night. Cautiously, she approached closer. Nausea rose in her. Her heart became heavy.

"There's something stuck to their arms and upper bodies," Emris said tonelessly.

She swallowed. She knew this viscous substance.

"We'd better not touch anything until we know what's going on," Nelar whispered in a trembling voice.

"You're right." She knew that long ago. The wolf-like creatures were responsible for this. But why the Nirm? They lived entirely apart and had not interfered until now.

They crept on. Smoke rose from the ancestral house. Her legs almost fell off in relief when a dozen Nirm warriors stepped out. Sakima was among them.

"Iishuhah, Sakima, wisdom on your way," she greeted him.

"Iishuhah, Miakoda, wisdom on your way."

"Sakima, what happened?"

"We were attacked—by a horrible beast," Ahiga said from behind him. "As I prophesied, you brought misfortune upon us. "

Mojak stepped forward and grabbed Ahiga by the shoulder. "Don't say that. We can use all the help we can get."

Ahiga shook off his hand rudely, and Mojak staggered back a few steps.

"She's our problem." Ahiga turned to the other Nirm warriors. "Because of her, these creatures are attacking us. I told you, strangers bring disaster."

Nelar and Emris stepped forward and stood behind Liya.

"Maybe we should leave," Nelar whispered.

She shook her head and turned to Ahiga. "These creatures didn't attack only you. We have to stick together."

The Nirm's face turned red. "You are responsible for all of this! We should never have taken you in. Come to think of it, Sakima is to blame for accepting you. Perhaps we should banish him as well!" he shouted.

The fire inside her began to bubble. When she looked down at herself, she noticed that her body was surrounded by a bright glow.

She fixed her eyes on the angry Nirm. "Don't challenge me, Ahiga!"

"Enough!" Sakima interfered. "We all feel the changes and the shadows. All of this has nothing to do with Miakoda. We have to stand together."

❦

Leaning against a post of Sakima's house, she watched the dark gray clouds mar the shimmering red sunset. Emris and Nelar were already on their way back to the combined force of Ewan and Rhos. Darwin and Julian were supposed to arrive soon.

An inner restlessness seized her, and with good reason. She carried the crystal with her, but she would not give it to Haydn. If necessary, she would use it herself.

Sakima stepped out of the house. "When do you expect your friends?" he asked.

"Soon enough."

"Will they go with you to Dar'Angaar?" he inquired.

"Yes, the king insists. Besides, he has instructed me to ask for your help."

"What do you want from us?"

She sighed. From now on, she was going to follow her own plan. What the king or anyone else asked of her was no longer important. There was another task waiting for her, even if she didn't know what it was yet. "Just a boat," she replied.

"You let yourself be accompanied by two mages you obviously don't trust, and yet you don't expect me to support you?"

In a split second, she decided to reveal something to Sakima. "The king of Dar'Angaar is expecting me to show up. There is no danger to me from him. I possess something he wants." For a moment, she closed her eyes. "What exactly will happen, no one can say. I assume that we will be taken to the king, but whether we will make it back is another question. Dar'Angaar's soldiers will probably join us at the border between Eryon and Namoor. Louis has also sent troops to the border region. Who knows how long it will take before a fight breaks out. Your people need you here. You must prepare yourselves."

"Our destinies are closely linked. I believe you have a special task to fulfill, and it is my duty to help you."

"I don't feel comfortable taking you with me. It's too risky."

"You think it's too risky for me, but you have no fear for yourself?" He laughed softly. "My people can be some time without me, no worries. I'm going with you."

She knew Sakima believed in having a destiny, so there was no sense in discussing it further. He was stubborn and wouldn't change his opinion.

As she let her gaze wander, she spotted the two mages riding across the clearing. They approached quickly. Darwin waved at her, but Julian's expression remained icy.

Sakima left the porch. "Mia—Liya has informed me of your arrival," he said kindly. "We will dine at my son-in-law's house."

The mages dismounted. "Thank you for your hospitality," Darwin replied, cleaning his glasses with a cloth.

Sakima smiled. "I'll show you the way."

As they followed the Nirm, Darwin said, "Unfortunately, I bring bad news. Philip has attempted a coup and narrowly failed."

"Attempted a coup?" She stared at him in disbelief. "He called a meeting of the Council of the Wise. All the lords except Prem showed up. He told them of losing your position, your contact with Dar'Angaar, and of the king's refusal to open negotiations. He almost got away with it. Fortunately, Louis has enough allies who demanded solid evidence."

"That's good, isn't it?" Sakima interjected.

Darwin shrugged. "It's hard to say, because that's not all. A few hours later, the king disappeared. Gerard was dead in his study. His eyes were black, completely black. Someone or something had taken possession of him. We suspect he was the traitor."

"Gerard?" She would never have suspected him.

"Yeah, we believe whatever happened to him happened in Qilon, when you were attacked by that mage."

Only slowly did she realize what it all meant. What had happened to the king? How would all this affect the already difficult situation? What did this mean for her mission?

"I still can't believe about Philip. He and Prem—unbelievable," she said.

In Taima's hut, they were received by Pohawe and Isi. The two women nodded to the mages and embraced Liya. Taima raised his hand in greeting. Then they all took their seats at the table.

"When will you leave?" Sakima inquired.

"After dinner," Liya replied quickly. Turning to Darwin and Julian, she added, "We'll take a boat."

Julian didn't seem pleased about that. "That way, we will run a risk of being captured. Wouldn't it be better to try to make it over the mountains on foot? With a little magic, we'd have a chance. We need to get to his castle. We can't make the journey from the coast to the castle without being noticed."

She frowned. "Getting into Amaar's castle unseen is difficult anyway. Since there'll be many soldiers either way, it's almost impossible."

She looked around the room. Julian looked thoughtful. Darwin raised his brows. The Nirm showed no movement. She already had a plan.

"Apart from that," she continued, "our arrival is expected. So, why take on an arduous march?"

"What makes you think we're expected?" Darwin asked in wonder.

Inwardly, she smirked. This was exactly the reaction she had hoped for. "You shouldn't forget the role I played for the king. Information is my business," she replied coolly.

"Amaar will put us all in the dungeon!" Darwin reasoned aloud.

"No, I don't think so," she quickly replied.

For a moment, she detected doubt in Julian's eyes.

"I will accompany you, Liya," Sakima repeated. "On this journey, you need my help."

She looked questioningly at Julian and Darwin. The mages nodded. Of course, it was an advantage to have a Nirm with them.

The men rose without further words and went outside, while Pohawe and Isi cleared the table. Liya packed the provisions for the journey before she left the house. Taima, Pohawe, and Isi accompanied her to the jetty.

"Aren't you taking any weapons?" Taima wondered as he watched Sakima, who was the first to board the boat.

Sakima shook his head. "No, Liya said they know we're coming. It shows that we are arriving peacefully, as expected."

Pohawe pulled Liya aside. "No matter what happens, trust your gut. Don't let anyone talk you into anything."

"Why do you say that?"

Her brown eyes regarded Liya carefully. "Because you possess more knowledge and have deeper magic than the rest of us. The source of our gift is our soul. Your soul is great and deep and old. Do you understand?"

"I'm not sure," she whispered. Pohawe's words touched her deep inside.

"Fear ignorance, but even more fear false knowledge." Pohawe embraced her.

Liya was the last one to board the fishing boat.

They left the towers of Aylvim behind and approached the territorial waters of Dar'Angaar. The moon was reflected in the sea, and clear skies showed that morning would approach shortly. Sakima and Julian had taken over the rowing, while Darwin and Liya kept an eye on their surroundings.

Darwin nudged them and pointed his head forward. A short distance away, three massive warships were heading for them.

"They've spotted us," Liya noted. *Sooner than expected*, she added silently. If they were lucky, Aval was on one of those ships. After all, he was a captain.

"We don't have a chance. We'll be dead before we reach Threng," Darwin declared.

Threng was the only port city. The rest of the coastal area of Dar'Angaar was mountainous and covered by dense forest.

"Put your hoods on," she said softly, "so your faces remain covered."

She gave Sakima an encouraging look. The Nirm frequently complained about the unfamiliar garment.

"I hope your plan works," Julian muttered.

"It will."

The ship that was heading straight for them was at least twenty meters long and had probably six dozen rowers. A ramming spur stretched in front of the bow. She held her breath. It did look as if the warship was about to ram them, but soon it turned to stop beside them. Several archers aimed at the fishing boat, and a black-clad soldier with a silver breastplate stepped up to the railing—probably the captain.

"You are in the waters of Dar'Angaar," he shouted. "If you don't want an arrow in your chest, I suggest you board voluntarily."

He spoke their language with an accent that seemed familiar. She could almost physically feel the looks of her companions, especially Julian's. A ladder was lowered.

She went first. Despite having four slits, her dress proved extremely impractical for climbing. Several times, she had to stop to avoid stepping on the hem or slipping off. Sakima, Julian, and Darwin followed.

Once at the top, she was dragged into the ship. Her companions fared the same. At a nod from the captain, two archers shot incendiary arrows at the fishing boat. Just as she was about to say something, the captain raised his hand and signaled to his men. The archers broke away and scattered to the sides of the ship.

"Shall we tie them up, captain?" one of the men inquired.

"No, our guests will kindly take care of their own safety." He looked at Liya. "Find your footing, it could get stormy."

White teeth flashed from under his brown beard. The captain's boots clanked as he strode to the center of the ship. No doubt about it—it was Aval. Briefly, he fixed her out of the corner of his eye and shook his head, barely perceptible. No one could know they knew each other. Inwardly, she breathed a sigh of relief.

"I don't like this," Darwin hissed to her. "There's magic here. Do you feel it too, Liya?"

He was right. Magic was in the air. A dark storm front passed before her inner eye, lightning bolts shooting out of it.

Aval maneuvered the ship to the other two warships. The silence stretched for an eternity. The three boats rocked gently on the water. They formed the front line, while smaller boats lined up behind them at least three hundred meters apart. She found this arrangement strange.

Along with the others, she crouched on the ground by the railing and watched as the soldiers repeatedly checked their ship and changed positions. Aval shouted various orders. It looked like the crew was practicing. No one paid particular attention to the strangers.

"What are we waiting for, anyway?" Julian murmured.

"Better to wait than to die," Sakima replied, gesturing for him to remain seated.

A deep thudding resounded beneath them, quickly growing louder, as if several drums were being beaten underwater, until a massive force rammed into the ship. Julian was just able to catch her before she slid to the left. They clung to the railing as another powerful strike shook the boat.

"What was that?" cried Darwin.

She understood why the crew had had no time for the prisoners. All the men's concentration was on an enemy in the sea.

Arrows whizzed into the water. Minutes later, an even stronger attack blasted them, skewing the ship. Men flew through the air and landed in the sea. Horrible screams rang out.

Whatever dwelled in the water here had enormous power. This ship weighed several tons, and it had almost been tipped over. Water sloshed over the deck. When the boat returned to its original position, the water was several centimeters high.

Stunned, she looked at Aval and saw a hint of despair in his face that was immediately replaced by sheer rage. Angrily, he shouted orders. One of his men ran below deck and soon returned with several ropes. These he distributed to the archers, who tied themselves to the stern.

Waves gently slapped against the bow.

"Has it stopped?" Liya whispered.

"I think this was just the beginning," Sakima muttered.

She got up and hurried to Aval. She had to find out more.

"Go back!" he hissed.

"What are you fighting against?"

He averted his eyes from her.

"I know you don't trust me. But I can help. *Please*." She grabbed his arm. When he turned back to her, she looked him firmly in the eye. "What is this creature?"

"Looks like an octopus," he replied curtly. "But that's impossible. Octopuses live in the deep sea and don't attack over several days like this critter here."

"Strange. "

"Go back to your companions." He walked away, leaving her standing.

The drumming sounded again, getting louder and louder, and the creature rammed them head-on. Although she tried to hold on, she was thrown backward. Her back hit the mast. She cried out in pain and stayed down. Out of the corner of her eye, she saw Sakima and Julian tumble down the steps. Darwin pulled himself up. As she pressed her ear against the ground, she made a discovery. Was that possible?

"Darwin!" she yelled, waving him over.

The old mage had already helped himself to a rope and crawled toward her.

"What do you hear?" she called out, pointing to the ship's planks.

But her words were swallowed up by the thunder beneath them. She pulled Darwin's hand and pointed to her ear.

He understood and pressed his ear to the floor. "A rhythm!" he groaned. "The drums follow a rhythm."

Whatever this meant, it did not bode well.

"I have to warn the captain." She struggled to her feet and hurried to Aval.

"The drumming—those are sounds that repeat," she called out to him. "Probably signals."

"Damn!" Aval reached for his horn and blew into it.

Three long, low notes, a short pause, and the notes again. He stowed the horn. The other warships seemed to be turning.

"Did you call for backup?" she asked.

While looking out to sea, she noticed something. Violent waves raced toward the ship.

"It's coming back," she whispered in a choked voice.

Under the surface of the water moved three, clearly visible, dark masses—huge octopuses. The octopuses swam side by side, heading for the ship on the right. What Liya saw next made her blood run cold.

They attacked from three sides, ramming the ship. A single, deep crack tore through the air. The tremendous force of the attack sent a shockwave through the surrounding water. The ship Liya stood on swayed precariously. Spellbound, she watched the fight. In three places, several arms shot out of the water and broke through the ship's wall, breaking the ship in two. The hail of arrows ceased as men fell into the water. Some saved themselves on floating pieces of wood, and others tried to swim to a neighboring ship.

An eerie silence settled around them. The creatures were nowhere to be seen, as if the sea had dragged them down into the depths.

Aval was right. They weren't dealing with normal octopuses. Octopuses didn't get together, and they certainly weren't capable of *coordinating* an attack. Something was very wrong here.

The morning sun colored the water red, which began to stir again. She clearly felt the fear around her. Nevertheless, the soldiers bravely held their bows and shot dozens of arrows at the command of their captain. Quite a few missed, and the few that stuck in the tentacles didn't seem to bother the creatures.

An octopus rose above the edge of the ship. Liya looked into its emerald green eyes. They were empty, unreal, and not of this world.

She snatched the bow and arrow from the hands of the man to her left and aimed at the beast's head. While the tentacles shattered the wooden floor next to her, she shot several arrows. Terrifying sounds escaped from the creature, and the tentacles headed toward her.

She threw the bow aside, grabbed a rope, and tied it around her hips. Her hand was shaking so bad she couldn't tie a double knot. *Damn!* Aval ran up to her, nodded, and looped the knot for her.

"They will attack us from below," he shouted.

Her heart was beating in her throat. She closed her eyes to calm herself, then noticed something she'd never seen before. She felt the power of the water, like a whisper in the wind. It was so close, like all she had to do was reach out and grab it. So she did! The flow of energy inside her connected with the water, and she became a part of the sea. Her mind guided her; her thoughts gave the orders.

Her magic commanded the water. She had never tried to control this element before, but her gift was strong. Liya felt that she had not nearly reached her limits. She reached out and created a shield of pure energy that surrounded the entire ship, leaving a gap at the bow. She would lure the creatures to her.

Her mind scanned the bottom of the sea. Slowly, she raised her hands toward the sky and formed a wall of water that grew higher by the second and surrounded the ship just behind the energy shield, still leaving that gap at the bow.

Her senses heightened. The energy flooding her body overwhelmed and frightened her. Her heart raced with exertion. She felt as if the water gushed directly from her body until, finally, she could marvel at her handiwork in the outside world. The wall of water towered at least half a meter above her head.

Through the noise surrounding her, she heard Julian calling out to her, but she was afraid to turn around. She stared steadfastly ahead. It seemed like an eternity until the creatures spotted the gap and moved toward it on the surface of the water. Dumbfounded, Liya realized they were waiting.

She felt a gentle pounding in her head, and blood dripped from her nose. She was not used to this kind of magic—concentrating was difficult.

She felt someone trying to gain access to her mind. The shield collapsed like a house of cards, leaving the ship at the mercy of the monsters.

She suppressed her fear, gathered herself, and tried again. When she plunged into the infinite silence of her gift, it showed her what she had to do.

"Lower the rowboat, and hurry," she said to Aval calmly.

"What are you going to do?" he asked.

"Give me your sword."

"You're crazy. The octopus will swallow you."

"So little confidence in my abilities, Captain!"

"Humble as ever." Smiling, he handed her his sword.

"If things get tight, I don't mind being rescued," she remarked.

He grinned, his teeth flashing. "If I tell the others, they won't believe me."

She climbed into the small boat and rowed away. She had to gain distance from the ship. Suddenly, time stood still. An iridescent glow surrounded her, and a shadowy world appeared behind her. She invoked the element of water to sense the source of the enemy's magic. *Gods*! She could sense the gift, similar to reaching out for emotions. It wasn't as difficult as she thought it would be, but what she felt here was unnatural; the creatures had no magic of their own. They had long since lost their souls—they possessed no inner light, no aura, and were only empty, dead shells. Another had taken control.

Why aren't you afraid, human? The voice sounded distant and almost childlike.

The further she rowed out, the more horribly the air reeked of decay, of death.

Why can she hear us? A colossal head appeared, green eyes staring at her. This creature saw no danger; its movements were slow, relaxed. *There must be a powerful mage behind all this.* Liya was sure of that.

The octopus was right next to her. Quick as a flash, she grabbed the sword with both hands and tried to decapitate it. Her magic helped her, extending along the blade with a beam of pure energy. The head flew meters away as the body sank to the bottom. She jumped into the water just in time to avoid the attack of the other two octopuses. A bright shimmer nestled around her body like velvet.

How is that possible? A voice echoed through her mind.

Her gift stretched like the wings of an eagle and flew through the silence of time, as if she were flying home. The power that now awoke deep within her and was capable of so much more. She created cold from the energy of water to form blades of ice. An icy shiver crept through her veins. Temptation beset her mind like a living creature, wishing to dive deeper into magic, but giving in would cost her life. She would freeze to death.

She needed a new plan! A muffled murmur reached her ears. Someone called her name, over and over again. Finally, she swung the swords of ice through the water, decapitating the creatures.

Strong arms wrapped around her shoulders, hoisting her out of the water.

"I didn't think I'd actually have to save you," Aval said, hugging her tightly.

Her teeth chattered while her body trembled incessantly. Aval put his coat around her shoulders and rowed back to the ship. With the last of her strength, she managed to climb up the ladder in front of him. Aval barked orders, instructing his men to head for the harbor and take Liya's companions to the crew quarters. Her legs gave way, but Aval caught her and carried her to his cabin, where warm blankets waited for her.

Somewhat dazed, she looked around. The chamber was quite large, with a round table for at least six people and a narrow wooden bed. The lamp above the table swayed back and forth. She immediately felt at home, though everything seemed a little strange.

Gently, he laid her on the bed, then rummaged in a wooden box before taking out a dress.

"Take off your wet clothes, we have some things to discuss urgently," he said kindly.

He left. With trembling hands, she undressed and dried herself. The turquoise dress sat a little loose and was not nearly warm enough, so she wrapped herself in a blanket and sat down on the bed.

A knock startled her, and a moment later, Aval entered.

"What a mess," he said, walking over to his desk, pulling out a bottle, and taking a swig. "I had to take your companions into custody. Anything else would be too suspicious, even if my people are simply happy to be alive."

He pushed an armchair to the bed. "You should take one too, it'll warm you." He scratched his beard. "We've been holding down the fort here for two days, and none of us expected to get home alive. You saved the lives of me and my men."

"Don't make a habit of it," she said. "Every time I see you, you're in trouble."

"Last time, it was the other way around," he returned with a grin.

"Right. How are Folnar and Maverick?"

"Do you really care?"

"Of course." She lowered her eyes uneasily. "As I told Maverick, I had no choice. I had to take the crystal."

"It's not just about the theft. We know about it, Liya."

"What do you mean?"

"Your mission—what your king sent you for. I like you, I really do. But don't make me choose between you and my king."

"He has only recently become king." She knew how nonsensical this statement was.

"He is much more, and you know it."

"I can't let him open the gates," she groaned.

"Still so loyal to your king?"

"This has nothing to do with Louis. Opening the gates is dangerous."

"It's not my place to talk to you about this, Liya."

"Of course. It would be *Haydn's* thing."

"A great responsibility rests on his shoulders."

She eyed Aval, a man who clearly had more experience than his age indicated. His large hands played with the bottle.

"Haydn was expecting you. That's why I was on patrol with my men."

"Did he also send someone to the mountains?"

Aval shook his head. "No, he was convinced that you would come across the sea."

"Which wasn't particularly hard to guess. Let's also not forget that he needs me."

"My job was to wait for you and then take you to him."

"I get it."

"My men don't know whether to thank you or curse you. Being saved by a strange mage is frowned upon." Mischief flashed briefly in his eyes.

"I'd prefer thanks," she replied, grimacing. "What happens now?"

"We aren't expecting any more people. Actually, no one can know about your arrival. But modesty isn't your strong point. The other ship will reach the port before us, and the men will tell everything."

"They didn't even realize what I was doing. My companions can disembark as crew members. No one will pay attention if everyone's celebrating the victory." She inclined her head. "You could swear your men to secrecy."

"With my soldiers, I'm not worried. But the rowers are only indirectly under my command."

"Then threaten them. Say I'll curse them if they spill the beans." Liya took a sip. Her throat burned for a moment before comforting warmth spread through her body.

"Now tell me!" she urged him. "Are you taking us into custody or smuggling us out?"

"I will take you to Haydn. On the ship, however, you will remain in custody."

She smirked. "I guess we don't have a choice." Aval's uneasy look didn't escape her. "There's something else you're worried about. What is it?"

"Not that important." He took the glass from her. "Get some rest now. I'll come get you as soon as we approach the harbor."

When Liya saw the cheering crowd in the harbor, she took a deep breath. The fact that it was already night did not stop the people from welcoming their heroes. The light of lanterns and torches flickered on the rippling shore.

"Put your hood on," Aval whispered to her.

"I don't think it's going to be that easy," she replied softly.

Although Aval had donned a plain robe in order to avoid being recognized as a captain, when he disembarked, they saw doubts in the face of so many people. How were they to smuggle themselves through the crowd undetected?

"We'll be the last off the ship," Aval murmured to her, pulling her aft to the oarsmen. "Your companions will join us later."

She wasn't sure what that meant, but she trusted him. The crew was excited; the men were looking forward to finally being able to set foot on land. The fear they had endured had left its mark.

After half an hour, she and Aval were finally able to disembark. He held her hand and led her through the crowd. In the dense throng of people, their progress was slow. She didn't dare look up and hoped fervently that they would soon leave the waterfront behind. People jostled around them. Girls offered their services to Aval, some quite pushy. His deep voice, however, made them step back.

Gradually, the noise died down. They left the busy neighborhood, and soon the streets were almost deserted. Three hooded figures emerged from a side alley: Sakima, Darwin, and Julian. Behind them, two soldiers—Aval's men, moved away. Her knees almost buckled with relief. They nodded to each other and silently continued their way.

This part of Threng was hugely different from the waterfront. The buildings and streets were spotlessly clean, and the few people on the road wore distinguished clothes. Aval led them through several alleys until they came upon a carriage, in front of which six men in hooded cloaks were waiting.

"These soldiers are part of the king's bodyguard. They will take you to him."

"You're not coming?"

"No, Liya, I have to get back to my men."

With a deep sigh, she embraced him. She didn't care that the others were watching. "Take good care of yourself, Aval. I'm not there to save you every time," she said softly.

"The same goes for you." He winked at her and opened the carriage door.

They passed dozens of fenced villas and many simple stone houses. In the moonlight, she even recognized castles in the hills. This city was prosperous; there was no sign of the alleged economic hardship in Dar'Angaar that Namoor regularly reported.

"How do you know the captain? Also an acquaintance from before?" Julian asked.

"Unlike you, I have friends everywhere," she replied coolly.

"How much further is it?" Sakima interjected.

"It takes four to five days to get to Angaar, the capital."

But to her surprise, they continued along the coast.

"What's wrong?" Darwin hadn't missed her worried look.

"We're going the wrong way." She stuck her head out the window and waved a soldier over.

"Milady?"

"Aren't we going to Angaar?"

"No, my lady, the king ordered us to take you to the monastery of Sion."

She had heard about this monastery. Rumors were rampant that ancient forces were at work there, which strengthened the wall on the border with Eryon.

"Are you worried?" Sakima asked.

"No, not even if I have to deviate from my original plan."

She spent the next few hours looking at the landscape. The fields stretched before them, bare and treeless. The soil seemed dry and barren, despite its proximity to the coast. No matter how rich the port city might be, the inland situation showed that all was not well in Dar'Angaar.

Well after midnight, they reached a massive fortress. She trembled at the sight of the imposing structure. The carriage stopped, and its door opened.

So, this was the mysterious monastery of Sion. A fortress of granite walls that rose into the sky like cliffs above their heads. Dark figures patrolled the battlements.

A gaunt man with a bald head, dressed in a black robe, waited outside the arched gateway.

"My lady, I expected you a bit earlier." He bowed slightly to Liya, ignoring her companions. "My name is Jakyn. Please, follow me."

The building was just as enormous on the inside as the outside. Bricked corridors led in all directions into the darkness; only the entrance hall was illuminated by oil lamps. The priest took a lamp and guided them down a long corridor that ended at a narrow spiral staircase.

They descended carefully, where more corridors waited below. Determined, Jakyn went straight ahead, finally opening an oak door. Behind it was an oval room with piles of sacks. Judging by the smell, they contained flour and grain. Some barrels were stacked against the walls.

When Jakyn turned to her now, she noticed how young the priest actually was. His black eyes stood out in stark contrast to his pale face.

"My king trusts you, milady, at least in a way." With his head, he pointed to her companions. "That is not true of your escorts, however. I'm afraid these men will have to wait for you here."

"That's out of the question." Her voice sounded stern.

"You do not understand. Soon we will reveal our well-kept secret. We are taking a great risk in doing so. My king is confident that you will keep it to yourself. But what about their allegiance?"

"My companions are coming with me; they will keep the secret."

"That is not enough. Two of them are mages, the third one is a Nirm. I sense their gift. It's obvious that they will use this knowledge against us."

Jakyn's eyes took on a strange expression as he eyed Julian and Darwin. She could not blame him for being suspicious.

"There's no way I'm leaving anyone here," she pressed out.

"Then they must make a blood oath. Should they break their word, a curse will strike them."

She felt how much Darwin tense behind her. The blood oath was used exclusively by followers of the Red Brotherhood.

"He can't ask that," the old mage hissed.

Jakyn's face remained expressionless.

"Agreed." Julian took a step forward. Sakima nodded as well. Darwin groaned, then agreed reluctantly.

"Stretch out your hands." Jakyn traced some strange signs in the air, muttering something unintelligible. "You don't need to say or do anything. When you feel my gift, don't fight it, just accept it."

With a mixture of fascination and horror, she watched the young priest, who was sketching the mark on everyone's palm with his index finger. Spellbound, she stared at Sakima's palm, since he was closest to her. To her amazement, a letter, perhaps a symbol, lit up briefly. She could not recognize more, as it faded too quickly. Jakyn mumbled something to himself that she couldn't understand.

"That's it."

Surprised, she looked at Jakyn.

"No blood flows in a blood oath, my lady," he explained, slightly amused. "However, the oath is bound to the blood of the one who made it. If you break it, you burn up inside." He grinned. "You have a lot to learn about our magic."

He turned and pressed forcefully against a barrel that lay directly in front of the wall. A passage opened, and he performed an exaggerated bow. "After you."

When she entered the small room behind it, she was almost disappointed. The archway in the middle, about two meters wide, seemed strange and somehow out of place. It took up nearly the entire room. *This whole building must have been built around this archway.*

Jakyn's eyes shone. "Ancient magic of the Elders," he breathed in awe.

Slowly, he walked to the archway and touched some symbols that were depicted on it, then stood in the middle and made more strange hand movements.

Suddenly, a gray mist spread inside the archway. Violet glowed in its center.

"A portal!" she groaned.

Darwin and Julian stared open-mouthed, and Sakima took a step back.

"Do you know how to build such a portal?" she asked.

"No. Though we've been researching for a long time, we haven't been able to solve the mystery yet." With shining eyes, he looked from one to the other. "But we can *use* the portal."

Sakima's features stiffened while the mages' gazes remained transfixed on the archway.

"I'll go first," she heard herself say. Instinctively, she knew what to do and dropped into the mist.

Glaring light blinded her. The suction was strong, the air cool. Her body was whirled around, and her stomach rebelled until she stumbled into a dark room.

The others followed. Behind them, the gray mist receded into a much smaller archway.

Darwin adjusted his glasses. "This is not a good way to travel for an old man like me."

"You get used to it over time." Grinning, Jakyn motioned for them to follow him.

The air smelled musty—they must be underground. Jakyn led them up a spiral staircase and through several corridors. Finally, they arrived at a wide, bright corridor, where guards were posted at some of the doors.

"Gentlemen, here are your rooms. They will bring you something to eat. You are not allowed to leave your rooms. Tomorrow, you will be taken away. I wish you a pleasant night."

As he was about to leave, Julian held him back. "Where are you taking Liya?"

A guard stepped up to him, and he immediately let go of the priest.

"To her room," Jakyn replied.

"She's not housed near us?" Julian asked.

"That's right. Her room is in the king's residential wing."

Her pulse quickened, but she knew her facial expression wouldn't give anything away.

"I'll see you tomorrow," she said to her companions, turning to follow Jakyn.

"Is the king expecting me today?" she asked after a while.

The priest shook his head. "No, it is already late, and you have had an exhausting journey."

She breathed a sigh of relief.

A knock awakened her. Two maids appeared and pulled aside the dark curtains. Bright light streamed through the oval windows. At first, Liya did not know where she was, but soon, she remembered that she was in the capital city of Amaar, in the king's castle. One of the girls left the room, came back shortly with a tray, and disappeared again.

"How long was I asleep?"

"It's just after sunrise, my lady." The other girl put a water jug on the washstand. Then she went to the oak closet and opened it. "Here, you will find clean clothes. As soon as you are ready, you will be taken to the king."

Liya thanked her. The maid bowed and left the room, and she threw the heavy velvet blanket away. She felt lost in this huge room. A four-poster bed stood in the middle, but despite the decadence, no paintings adorned the pastel-colored walls.

A fire flickered in the fireplace. Judging by the ashes, it had been burning all night. She freshened up and ate a snack. Looking at the fine clothes in the closet, she felt somehow strange. Finest fabrics, from silk to cashmere, worn by kings and high nobility! The sapphire blue dress she finally selected was decorated with a discreet beaded belt. Despite the floor length, it proved comfortable, as the finish was airy and light. She could not normally afford such fine fabrics.

There was a knock at the door, and Maverick and Folnar entered the room. Liya quickly ran over and hugged them.

"Nice to see you unharmed for once," Folnar said, grinning.

Maverick nudged him lightly. "You push her like that again, she'll have a couple of broken ribs." Then he turned to Liya. "Well, sunshine, how do you like your room? It's certainly bigger than mine." Interested, he looked around. "Someone must be trying to impress you."

"As if I could be impressed with this."

Maverick laughed. "No, you're more into dangerous action."

She slapped him lightly on the shoulder. "Idiot."

Laughing, he put his arm around her. "Let's go. Haydn is waiting for you."

Soldiers patrolled the first floor. Instead of the dining room, the two led her outside to the stables. The black walls of the castle still looked imposing in the daylight, but they were less threatening than at night. She counted seven towers in all, two of which served as watchtowers. On one, she discovered a sculpture—a creature with wings and a spear in its hand.

Folnar and Maverick led her into one of the stables. The sweet smell of hay and horses rose to her nose.

Haydn was saddling his horse. As if sensing her gaze, he turned and examined her intently from head to toe. For a moment, she recognized pain and worry in his gaze, but then his blue eyes lit up, and he gave her a broad smile. She returned it, but at the same time, her heart clenched.

"Liya." He nodded, drew her hands to his lips, and breathed a kiss on the tips of her fingers. This touch alone caused her knees to go weak. She could not let that happen, so she quickly withdrew her hands from him.

Folnar rolled his eyes. This did not escape Haydn's notice either. "Do you want to tell me something?" In response, Folnar shook his head, while Maverick grinned broadly.

"Did they behave themselves, Liya, or did they walk all over you?" Haydn asked.

"I would say both. And Aval, once again, I had to save."

"Sonaris is being hailed as a hero," Folnar noted. "Supposedly, he not only defeated three krakens, but also drove away an evil witch." Mischief flashed from his eyes. "Who might that witch have been?"

Haydn gave his men a meaningful look. "Don't you have anything to do?"

Maverick whistled playfully. "It can wait."

Haydn narrowed his eyes.

Folnar slapped Maverick on the shoulder. "My friend, we are not wanted."

"See you later, sunshine," Maverick teased.

They disappeared.

"You've conquered them all," Haydn said. "Only you call Sonaris by his first name. To all the others, he has strictly forbidden it."

"Why?"

"Long story. Let him tell it to you himself."

"You've saddled two horses," she noticed. "Where are we going?"

"Let me surprise you." He swung onto his horse and rode out of the stable. She did the same.

After about an hour, when they left the fields of the capital behind, he reined in his horse so that she could finally catch up.

"Where are my companions?" she asked.

"Don't worry, they're fine."

She examined him out of the corner of her eye. He seemed to have lost some weight—his face looked more angular, but his posture had something majestic about it. He was no longer the man she had once met in the mountains. If he deemed it necessary, he would lead a mighty army mercilessly to war. She had no doubt about that.

"Unfortunately, we don't have much time. I was hoping you'd come sooner." He smirked. "With less attention, though."

"A bizarre situation we find ourselves in," she muttered.

He said nothing.

"Where are we?" she finally inquired.

The area was barren—cracked reddish earth with a few oases of grass. Isolated green bushes fought their way through the dry soil. Towering mountains rose in the distance. Although the mountains were still a good two hours away, she could feel the cold air on her sweat-covered forehead.

"In the Atamarya Desert, the driest part of my country. There used to be a lot of rain here, but the climate has changed. This path leads to Thyron."

"The ruined city?"

"You'll be surprised. People live there."

"Did you rebuild the city?"

"Oh no, that happened long before my time." He heaved a deep sigh. "We'll be there soon, then your curiosity will be satisfied."

She rolled her eyes playfully and galloped off.

"Almost like before," he called after her.

"Not quite. I'm better today."

The sound of hooves and the swirling dust made her forget where she was. Memories of riding trips with Haydn surrounded her in pleasant feelings. Even the wind whipping in her face didn't bother her. This feeling of freedom was intoxicating.

Finally, a vast shadow loomed before them. They were approaching an enormous rectangular black wall with an imposing corner tower. She estimated the height of the wall at three meters. What a sight! She could not imagine that people actually lived there. There was nothing far and wide, not even a stone road. Even the birds seemed to avoid the harsh place. The winds whispered a steady rhythm, and an oppressive feeling came over her. She slowed down and turned her head to Haydn.

"I would have caught up with you in a minute anyway." He winked at her, then abruptly reined in his stallion and jumped off. Somewhat surprised, she dismounted as well.

"What's behind the wall?" she asked, though she had a hunch.

At that moment, a huge cloud of dust rose to her right. Haydn told her to stay behind him.

"Probably not friends," she said.

Their horses broke loose and galloped away when a group of riders was still about twenty meters away. She squinted her eyes until the dust settled, then counted seven men, all in dark green clothing, hair and faces covered. Even their boots were green.

One of them trotted his horse out of line, pointed at Liya, and said to Haydn, "Leave her to us, then you can go. That which was agreed upon long ago should not be broken." The stranger spoke slowly and softly. He leaned forward. "Out here, your gift has little effect. So be reasonable."

"The Thyron Council will honor the agreement." Haydn nodded in Liya's direction. "But you cannot have this woman. I require her services, so she remains with me."

"My instruction is clear. This is not subject to negotiation."

Haydn's hand slid to the hilt of his sword. "She is the heiress."

What was he saying? She felt as if the ground shook beneath her. A murmur went through the group of green riders.

"That's not true," the leader stammered.

"Liya, show them the crystal," Haydn said.

She looked at him in disbelief. How did he know she was carrying it? The crystal was in the locket she wore around her neck. Anger stirred in her; she bit her lower lip. He hadn't told her what was going on—again. When this was over, he had to give her answers.

"How is that possible?" The stranger's deep voice no longer sounded confident. His gaze drifted sideways to a gaunt-looking rider behind him. *He must be the leader.*

"That doesn't mean anything." The rider regained his composure.

Haydn leaned toward her. "Either we succeed in convincing them, or we have to fight," he whispered.

"What do you want me to do?" she asked just as quietly.

"Try to activate the power of the crystal again," he demanded.

"There is no heir. We would know that."

Haydn cleared his throat. "Oh really?"

Now the gaunt man got off his horse and sauntered closer. "The agreement was made at the time between the ruling family of Dar'Angaar and the Jade Brotherhood," he explained in an icy voice. "Leave her to us, and we will depart."

Haydn sighed. "That's not possible."

She did not like the way this conversation had developed. These men were dangerous, and they possessed the gift. For a moment, the gaunt man regarded Liya, then mounted his horse again. Her heart raced, and her stomach clenched painfully with fear. The riders began to murmur to themselves, almost rhythmically, as if they were chanting.

Haydn jumped to the left, drew his sword, and kicked a fighter in the thigh. The man let out a scream, slipped out of the saddle, and parried the next attack with his short sword. The horses formed a circle around Liya and Haydn while the men continued to chant.

Mist rose from the ground, chilling her. The higher the haze rose, the more she shivered. She could still see Haydn dragging the next opponent off his horse and driving his sword through his body when the freezing cold forced her down. She sank to her knees.

"Liya, you have to get up!" Haydn shouted. He sounded panicked. "As soon as the fog covers your face, they'll take you. I won't be able to protect you then. Use the crystal!"

He hurled his sword through the air, but the gaunt man deftly dodged it. What was happening to her? Desperately, she reached for her necklace. Cursing inwardly, she opened the locket, took the crystal in her fist, and squeezed tightly. But nothing happened.

"It's not working!" she shouted to Haydn.

"Try again!" he yelled.

She did as she was told but to no avail. "I don't understand," she moaned.

"Then we'll just have to fight!" he thundered.

Wild shouting broke out somewhere, making her flinch. Archers appeared on the walls, sending arrows flying overhead. The buzzing sounds twanged through the air, mingling with the screams. The yells died away as bodies fell to the ground. Gradually, silence fell. The sun broke through the fog as it drifted away, lighting up the clearing. All the green riders lay dead on the ground.

Liya looked around, stunned. *What...?*

An archer approached. "We'll take care of the bodies, your majesty," he said, inclining his head briefly.

Hastily, Haydn took her hand and pulled her along, heading for the watchtower. Most of the archers followed them. When they arrived at the tower, a wide wooden door opened.

Two young women stood in the doorway and smiled at Haydn. They were beautiful. Their cheeks shimmered slightly reddish in the sun, and black velvet dresses draped their slender bodies. Their hair was tied at the sides, with a flower she had never seen before tucked above their ear. It has long, thin purple petals that spiraled out from the center.

No one spoke a word as they walked behind the women through the narrow tower room, then followed a path that ended some distance away, just before a hill. Above it towered a massive, fortified complex of buildings. A few people and some carts traveled on the path. *The goods must come from the capital.*

Below the fortress, a city stretched across the mountainside: Thyron, the desert city. The houses of gray granite were spread out with no discernible order. The sprawling, constantly intersecting streets resembled an endless labyrinth.

Liya looked around in amazement. Everything was clean. The noble clothes of the inhabitants suggested a certain prosperity, but while the people wore velvet or silk, they dressed in black—no colors. Not even a single flower strayed into the few patches of grass beside the road. A certain sadness lay over the town.

Although several residents greeted Haydn with a nod, they did not address him. When they reached a gravel path that led further up, the young women silently said goodbye and walked back. The archers stayed by their side.

"From here, the path becomes steeper. We have to hurry." Haydn pointed to the path.

When they crested the hill, she was amazed. A wide moat surrounded the fortress, whose red walls were at least ten meters high. At each corner of the huge rectangular complex was a watchtower. *This is where the kings of Dar'Angaar resided long ago.* How she knew that was not clear to her.

They crossed a white bridge and entered the outer courtyard. A river enclosed the next complex of buildings like another moat. Five bridges led to the next gate.

The central courtyard opened onto a large hall built on a three-tiered white stone terrace. The hall itself was constructed of wood and had a hipped roof about twelve meters high with eaves that rose slightly toward the outside. The door stood wide open. Despite its good preservation, she sensed that this structure told a very old story. Reverently, she walked up to it beside Haydn.

The moment they passed through the door, very fine magic struck her. The murmur of thirty or so people fell silent. She looked around in amazement and hid her surprise at seeing several of their auras.

Many hundreds of people could fit in here. Benches of red velvet, armchairs with carved armrests, and round tables of walnut spread through the entire area. But what fascinated her most was the throne at the far end of the room. Carved from white stone, it stood on a podium of jade about two meters high—a symbol of pure power.

Haydn shook hands with some people and exchanged a few words. No one showed any interest in her. She sensed something most peculiar going on here. As if hypnotized, she approached the throne. Five staircases led up to it, one of which was directly in front of her.

A total of eight wooden steles, all about two meters high, surrounded the podium. Behind them was a partition wall with dull gold paneling peeling in many places. The staircase in front of her was adorned with a blue carpet into which a black dragon, as large as Liya herself, was woven.

She climbed the steps slowly. Fascinated, she looked at the carved scenes in the stelae. They showed creatures from the ancient stories. Fire-breathing dragons that destroyed cities, dragons that flew faster than the wind. Were they just fantasy creatures? There was no proof of their existence. At least, that's what they claimed in Namoor. But much of what she had believed had recently been proven false. Maybe the kings of Thyron had had dealings with dragons. The spectacle in Ebra's theater came to her mind.

All this made her feel overwhelmed and uncomfortable. But then the magic intensified, and a feeling of happiness flowed through her body. The chatting people in the hall faded into the background.

The closer she came to the throne, the more intensely she felt the energy, gentle waves touching her body. With her fingers, she stroked the carving of a stele, then took a closer look at each dragon. On the first stele, all were depicted in a fighting stance, wings spread, mouth wide open, neck stretched forward. The other pillars showed smaller dragons standing on their hind feet and looking at each other.

On the last step, the black dragon's red eyes stared at her from the ground. The thick layer of dust barely dimmed the fire red. It almost seemed as if those eyes were watching her. She continued walking, covering the eerie gaze with her feet.

At that moment, the voices behind her fell silent. Scorching heat surrounded her, the stelae and the floor shook, and dust trickled from the ceiling. She fell, her face inches from the dragon's eyes. Her lungs ached, she coughed, and she could hardly breathe. The red eyes seemed to burn. She thought she could see flames in the pupil.

Quickly, she rose. She wanted to call for Haydn, but her voice failed. When she looked back into the room, it was as dark as the deepest night.

Around her, barely an arm's length away, flames blazed up from the floor. Horrified, she realized that the fire was slowly encircling her.

Each breath bored into her lungs like the point of a knife. She grabbed her chest. *Why isn't my gift stirring?* It had to be the strange, old magic in this hall. In her mind's eye, a white beam appeared, streaming from her body and lost in space. The pain made her slump back to the floor. Again, she tried to reach for her magic. Her breathing quickened, her pulse raced. She had to get up and try to get to the throne. With the last of her strength, she crawled forward.

Exhaustion overcame her. How she longed for rest. For a moment, she closed her eyes. Haydn smiled at her. Those sparkling blue eyes, which made even the sky pale, regarded her lovingly. He spread his arms. She felt his love and his strength, but only briefly.

The flames stretched toward her. She gasped. Then she felt something inside her—a gentle rocking. Her gift. The endless flow of energy was still part of her.

She squatted down, looked at the dragon, and placed her left hand on the red eye. Her palm burned, but her energy flowed more freely; her gift no longer felt resistance. Tears rolled down her cheeks, and she bit her lip in pain. She hoped she was right about the throne. Her strength would only be enough for one jump.

She formed a thought and aimed at the throne chair, which was not a meter away from her. Energy blazed within her. Then she let her gift run free. The force of the burst vibrated through her body, causing her to lose her breath completely. The power returned, not slow and gentle, but potent and concentrated. The pain faded into the background.

As she jumped, something enveloped her body, not to protect her, but to prevent her from reaching the throne. Instinctively, she knew that this resistance was formed from ancient magic. Just barely making it, like a drowning woman, she clung to the lowest edge of the throne. With one hand, she scanned the wooden floor, found a crack, and held on to it.

The room returned in full force, voices became loud, and the pain disappeared. Only the wound in her left hand was still throbbing. She lay there, moaning, gradually calming her breathing.

"Liya!" Haydn's horrified voice rang out.

She realized what she had done. She, a stranger, had just touched a *dragon throne*. This was probably forbidden and undoubtedly punishable. But how could she have known that? It seemed like an heirloom from the past, and since there were quite a few people in the hall, Liya hadn't thought anything of being in a restricted area. She remembered the Nirm—she was still not allowed to touch the altar in the ancestral house, even though she had been accepted into the tribe. Panic seized her.

With difficulty, she straightened up and turned around. Eight pairs of eyes looked at her from the front row. All the others must have left. All were completely silent and still, except for the shimmering auras surrounding the people. Completely helpless, she sought eye contact with Haydn. He was standing in front of the blue carpet, his left hand resting on his sword. He gestured with his right hand for her to come to him.

For some reason, he seemed taller than usual. She leaned on the throne to stand up. A fearful murmur went through the crowd so that she pulled her hand back in fright and almost fell again.

"Slow down!" growled Haydn. He turned and ordered loudly, "Leave the room!"

She made a beeline for the dragon's head and dragged herself down the side. With quick steps, Haydn came to her, took her hand, and pulled her to him so fast that she stumbled, hitting her head on his breastplate.

"You just shortened my life by ten years." His voice broke. "As soon as I let you out of my sight for a moment, you put yourself in danger. I thought I'd lost you."

What was he saying? Full of rage, she tore herself away from him. "You're not telling me anything. It would have made sense to tell me about the dragon carpet and the throne. Don't you think? Now the villagers look at me with even more suspicion than before. I probably offended them deeply by touching their sanctuary."

He laughed hoarsely. "That's what you're worried about, *Kardia mou*?"

"Don't call me that! So… I'm not getting my head cut off or anything like that?" She glowered at him.

He circled her face with his hands. "I would never let that happen." As he leaned forward, she felt his breath. Very lightly, he brushed her cheek with his mouth before whispering in her ear, "I felt powerless. I could do nothing for you. That was terrible. Please, don't ever do that to me again."

Her body reacted to his nearness, and she fought with herself.

"Despite my gift, I did not succeed in reaching you," he continued. "I even opened my mind to you, but it didn't help. It's the magic of this place."

"You did what?" Dismayed, she backed away.

He had gained access to her, and he was not even aware of it. She had assumed that it had been a memory. How could he get through to her? A protective net lay over her thoughts day and night. No one could just walk into her head.

"How did you know I was in danger?" she groaned.

"Well, that wasn't hard. The floor and the columns began to shake. A loud roar echoed in the room. Then you were lying on the steps. I felt the ancient magic flare up. No one has touched the throne in a long time."

"What did you say to me when you opened your mind?" she asked.

He frowned. "Not that important, it didn't help."

"I need to know, though," she breathed. "Please!"

He took her hands, and she moaned. Her left hand still hurt. When she looked at her palm, a red burn the size of the dragon's eye was emblazoned on it.

"Your wound needs to be taken care of," he pressed out.

Behind them, someone cleared their throat. An old man with thinning hair had entered the hall unnoticed.

"My king," he declared, "we should be on our way."

Haydn nodded and gently pushed her forward. At first, she was confused, but then she stopped.

"I'm not going anywhere." She straightened her shoulders and jutted her chin. "You owe me answers, Haydn."

"My lady, it really is high time." The old man snorted angrily.

"I'm not stopping you. You can leave the room at any time," she replied sharply. Under no circumstances would she give in.

Haydn sighed. "I will tell you everything, but first, we will go to the courtyard. We must leave the Dragon King's throne room. Magic has been awakened."

Judging by his look, he would carry her out if necessary. Reluctantly, she trotted after the men. Outside, all the people who had been in the hall waited for them. She breathed in the fresh air deeply, the warm sun on her skin awakening her spirits.

The next moment, however, she fought a deep emptiness inside her. A feeling of sadness overcame her. It was hard for her to leave that tremendous power behind. Despite everything, she felt the need to go back. The magic in that room was like a pull that wouldn't let go. When she noticed Haydn's attentive gaze, she did her best to forget the great temptation.

The old man turned and gave her a warm smile. "My lady, please forgive the bumpy beginning. I am Ithen." Without taking his eyes off her, he bowed slightly.

Polite, but not obsequious, she thought. "I'm Liya." She bowed her head a tiny bit.

"May I introduce you to the other members of the City Council?" Haydn asked.

He pointed to three men and four women who had joined them. "These are Leveus, Tinior, and Tofeus. The ladies, who spare neither beauty nor intelligence, are Strella, Selena, Mina, and Shia."

Mina? She had a friend at the academy with the same name. *What an odd coincidence.*

Strella, the oldest of the women, smiled kindly. Selena tugged at her braid and nodded at her. She was middle-aged, her hair showing a few gray streaks. Mina gave Liya a broad grin, while Shia eyed her suspiciously with black eyes.

Tinior grabbed his round belly. "I don't know about you, but I am famished. Let's eat at last. I have to digest all this excitement, and the best way for me to do that is with a meal."

"Put on a hat, your bald head is already all red," Strella said, rolling her eyes.

"These eight people keep order in the city. It's better if you follow their advice," Haydn explained good-humoredly.

Ithen clicked his tongue. "Let's go to the main square."

"Liya and I will be right behind you," Haydn said.

As the council members moved away, everyone else left the square in front of the hall too. Haydn waited a moment, then clasped his hands behind his back and turned to her. "You're very upset, I understand that."

"I am disappointed. You keep too many secrets. You expect me to trust you, but you keep pretty much everything from me that could be important. You want my help? Fine. Then start talking. Otherwise, I'm not helping you. It's just me and my mission." For a moment, she closed her eyes. "I don't know what's coming or what my role is in all of this. Don't exclude me if you want us to work together."

"A lot of things have changed— *we've* changed." He swallowed. "We hardly make time for the important things in life."

"Then take the time—right now, right here. Talk to me."

Sighing, he took her hand and led her through the courtyard. They crossed the first bridge.

"We have plenty of time on the way back," she finally burst out. "What's the story behind this place?"

"It's important for me to know if you can feel the magic in the room. That's why I couldn't tell you," he began. "However, I didn't think you would jump right into the throne."

"Very funny! Now you know that I feel the magic. Explain it to me at last!"

"It'll take a long time," he said quietly.

"Start!" she replied impatiently.

"The king who built this throne was incredibly powerful. He was even followed by the dragons." He flippantly passed over her doubtful look. "Yes, Liya, dragons! There were nine dragon lords, the greatest of whom was Jade Green. We suspect that the dragons were created by the Elders.

Involuntarily, she thought of the Nirm and the spectacle in Ebra's theater. She had also heard about the dubious experiments of the Elders. A monstrous thought formed in her mind. Could this be possible?

"The records and lore are clear," he continued. "In the Ancient Era, they performed many experiments on humans to, shall we say, enhance

the abilities of their species. They altered genes, created shapeshifters…
humans who were also dragons."

He paused. The thought in her head took shape.

"We believe that the dragons turned against their creators, who were
also their tormentors. The rebellion of the dragons must have caused the
civilizations of the Ancient Era to disappear overnight. But there was a
second group of people who had been changed." Abruptly, he stopped and
sought her gaze.

"The gifted ones," she pressed out.

"Yes," he confirmed. "People with high magical potential. Some
survivors of the Great Annihilation founded the kingdom of Elladur.
Most had magic, though to varying degrees."

"I know that," she interrupted him. "Tell me more about the dragons!"

"Patience is truly not your strong suit." A grin flashed across his face.
"Many dragon people survived; they also founded an empire. Elladur, as
well as all the other empires that arose in the course of the first century
after the Annihilation, fought the dragons again and again."

"Did the ruler of Thyron also make war on the dragons?"

"He did, Liya, but *before* he built Thyron. The founder of this city was
Eirik, the king of the still quite young kingdom of Dar'Angaar. He made
a pact with the dragons. This made him incredibly powerful. It took a long
time for us to evaluate the records well enough and understand this. Eirik
made Thyron his seat of power. In a way, he did this to honor the dragons,
or perhaps to seal the pact with them. In the ancient legends, the beauty
of his royal consort is praised."

She listened and wondered what this information could be important
for.

"We figured out," he went on, "that it was Allyria, the princess of
Elladur, who had fled from her father with her great love, the dragon

prince El'Orim." Again, he sighed. "Allyria gave up her heritage to live with El'Orim. Since the dragon prince was no longer welcomed to stay with his father either, they retreated to a remote village in Elladur."

Something didn't add up. "Then how in the world did she end up in Dar'Angaar?"

"That's the point," he agreed. "She left El'Orim and married Eirik."

Irritated, she put a hand on his arm. "What made Allyria do that?"

"The love of a child, Liya. I suspect that she was pregnant. Everything suggests that her father was blackmailing her. Living with a dragon in Elladur wasn't easy. Who knows what Allyria's father was threatening her with? In any case, an alliance with Dar'Angaar was of tremendous strategic advantage to him." A shadow flitted across his face. "My mother spoke of Allyria as if she had known the princess personally. Both were seers."

Then they must have met in a dream or a vision, Liya thought. Silently, they continued their way. "How does the story continue?" she finally asked.

"We are certain that it was Allyria who made it possible for her husband to form an alliance with the dragons."

"This made the pact between Eirik and Allyria's father void," Liya reflected aloud.

"That's right," Haydn confirmed. "Influenced by his wife, Eirik pursued a new strategy. He made secret agreements with Namoor. "

In this way, Allyria had taken revenge on her father. Liya could understand that. "What happened next?"

"The people of Eirik's kingdom lived in peace and prosperity for many years. But then, everything changed. Records show that the nobles and subjects accused the king of losing his mind. Intrigues and power struggles weakened the kingdom."

They reached the gravel path and started making their way down.

"The king began to prepare for war because he expected the attack of a huge army from afar," Haydn continued. "For this purpose, he increased his military, had new soldiers recruited, and sent scouts to the borders of the country. He even subjected the ice animals to his command. But neither the nobles nor the ordinary people felt threatened."

"Why did he think an attack was imminent?"

"As I said, Allyria was a seer. In Thyron, she held the office of high priestess. The ancient writings report that magic was felt everywhere in Thyron. The laws for the priests were extremely strict. They rarely left the temple grounds; their service was to the higher power. Marriages were arranged within the temple."

"We don't know what she saw. But her vision was undoubtedly true," Liya reflected aloud. "Eirik had made a pact with Namoor. It looked like Namoor could attack Elladur, and Dar'Angaar would stay out of it. In return, Dar'Angaar could overrun Eryon scot-free. All of that, I guess, is what happened."

"That is what has been handed down," he replied. "We assume that Keldor of Namoor opened the gates before he attacked Elladur."

"I don't think so. Sakima told me that the Guardians stopped him."

"Why do you think it was possible that Elladur, the land of the gifted, mages, and Guardians, was destroyed?" he replied. "That's where most of the relics from the Ancient Era were. Namoor must have led an army stronger and more powerful than we can imagine. Otherwise, Elladur could never have been defeated."

Haydn's remarks made sense. There was no doubt about it. "Then what happened?"

"The war on Elladur's soil spread to Dar'Angaar. In the end, Eirik's army had to intervene and support Namoor's forces against Elladur. Allyria left the fortress to fight. The king could not talk her out of it. In the end, she

ELLADUR — THE AWAKENING

managed to close the gates with the Guardians. We know that she died in the arms of the man she loved the most."

"El'Orim."

Haydn nodded. "After Allyria left him, it became possible for him to live in his father's realm once again. When Allyria died in his arms, El'Orim was already the new Dragon King. With her last breath, she sent a vision to her eldest daughter to save the kingdom. El'Orim died shortly thereafter."

"Allyria's eldest daughter was the dragon's child, wasn't she?" she breathed.

Haydn nodded.

"What happened to Eirik?"

"As far as we can read and interpret the ancient writings, the Winged Ones blamed him for the death of their Dragon King. He had to pay a high price for this betrayal. His city was cursed." Haydn took a deep breath.

"Cursed? In what way?" On the one hand, the story was becoming more complicated, but on the other hand, pieces of the puzzle were falling into place.

"Well, Liya, maybe you've noticed. There is a deep gloom in this town. One cannot be happy here. The town councilors and another forty people do not age. If they don't die from outside influences, like strong magic, weapons, or forces of nature, they live forever —in this gloom. They have to keep the history and the dragon city alive. They've been doing this for a hundred years. No inhabitant can leave the city, ever. Only the city council is able to do so. Besides, in this place, the gift cannot be used. I thought this would be different with your skills, and with the support of the crystal."

Deep in thought for a while, they left the gravel path and followed the granite road. Only a few people strolled about.

"What happened to Eirik?" she repeated with a pounding heart.

"He died at the hands of El'Orim's son. The latter swore to destroy the people."

A shiver ran down her spine. "Where are the dragons now?"

"I don't know," he replied with a shrug. "We suspect they are on the other side, beyond the band between the worlds. There, they are rallying around their leader."

"Around the *heir*?" Where did this thought come from?

"So it is, the son of El'Orim and his dragon queen." Haydn's voice trembled a little.

"So El'Orim married a dragoness?" In a way, this astonished her.

"Yes," he answered simply.

"What happened in Dar'Angaar after Thyron was cursed, the king died, and the gates were closed?"

"The two children of the royal couple of Dar'Angaar abdicated the throne and moved the capital to Amaar. No one was to reach for the Dragon Throne again."

"What power did I feel?"

"The magic of the dragons that imposed the curse."

"I don't understand. Why do you want to open the gates when you have all this knowledge!" She felt the weight on her shoulders threatening to crush her. What was he thinking? Then, she remembered something else. "The crystal belonged to Allyria, didn't it?"

He nodded. "She hid it well at the time, but my mother found it. Just before she died, it disappeared. For years I have been searching for it."

"What kind of magic does it have?"

"I don't know," he sighed. "My mother told me that her job was to find the crystal, not to use it. She never tried to awaken the power. I promised her I would look for the crystal. In the process, I found clues and messages from the ancient times, but not only that. I also found, well, *technology*."

"Technology?"

"The achievements and inventions of the Elders. All the things that made up their progress, things like the earplugs. But there was much more."

The world she knew had long since ceased to exist. And it had all started with their journey in Qilon, when they found the scroll. Although she slowly solved one puzzle after another, gathering information, the solution still didn't seem to be within her grasp. It was maddening. On the contrary, the more she learned, the more questions she had. They frustrated and overwhelmed her.

"What else is there?" she snapped at him.

Briefly, he hesitated. "It's not me who wants to open the gates, Liya. They are already open."

Her heart stopped for a moment. "How can this be, and when did it happen?" she whispered. "Isn't it true that very few are able to open the gates without this particular planetary constellation?"

He closed his eyes. "Whoever performed the ritual was not strong enough and had to stop the process. In order to close them completely again, they must first be fully opened first."

"Is that what you want to do?"

He looked at her firmly. "Yes, with your help. Maybe we'll also be able to finally break the curse that clings to this city."

Somehow, she had suspected it. She would use this situation, in which he needed her help, to learn as much as possible from him.

"Well...," she began, "who were those green-clad men who attacked us?"

"The Jade Brotherhood. I don't know exactly when it came into being. There is an old contract that entitles them to take gifted girls from time to time. In return, they leave the people of Thyron alone. Before this agreement, they'd been trying to conquer the city for a long time. They consider themselves the rightful heirs of the dragons."

"I sensed their gift," she revealed.

"Yes, and that makes them dangerous. In this cursed place, no one can use their gift. That goes for the city and a radius of many miles. I don't know how they manage to get past the barrier. I thought you might be able to do so as well."

"Because of the history and the crystal. Looks like the spell over this place is still intact. What happens to the women?" She shuddered at the thought.

"They all return, but then, they seem lost. The jade brothers take away their gift."

As they entered the main square, Ithen waved to them.

"Let's eat, Liya. We'll have time to talk later," Haydn said. "The council has waited long enough for us."

"What of all that you have told me do the council members know?" she asked quickly.

"Everything."

The townspeople dodged the intense afternoon sun by setting up tables in the shade. A line of people stood at a lavish buffet. In the center of the square, water gushed from the mouth of a man-sized stone dragon, which lent the place a mystical yet peaceful feeling.

She followed Haydn to the buffet. Vegetable stews, along with potatoes and rice dishes, were offered, but neither meat nor fish was on the menu. Somewhat perplexed, she filled a bowl with stew.

"Please, sit down," Ithen urged them as he took a seat at the head of the table.

Mina joined Liya and offered her a piece of bread.

"We were really excited to meet you," Selena remarked, sitting across from her.

"Really?" She raised an eyebrow in surprise.

"He announced you." Mina shoved a piece of bread into her mouth. "You probably don't know that Haydn is breaking an old tradition."

"Mina, please let Liya eat in peace," Ithen admonished.

Haydn sat down next to her.

"When will the ceremony take place?" Tofeus asked. He ran his hand through thick hair and stroked his crooked nose.

"Soon." Haydn drank from his cup. "The final preparations are already being made."

The panic in her suddenly came back, her breathing became heavy, and her heart thudded against her ribs. She inhaled deeply and tried to cool down, but her stomach rebelled, and everything spun in her head. The whole thing felt like a curse that lay on her. The closeness to Haydn was already hard to bear, but the upcoming events took her breath away. She suppressed the urge to cry.

"To our king!" cried Ithen with conviction. "May his mission be crowned with success and bring us salvation."

The others loudly expressed their approval and toasted each other.

"You weren't surprised to see our auras in the hall. How come?" Leveus inquired.

She stared at the boy with the silver hair. *How did he know she saw them?* His big gray eyes examined her curiously.

"I have seen the aura of a mage before," she explained evasively. "In Namoor, however, magic is not practiced openly. Only mages can exercise the gift."

"Girl, you should eat more, you are way too skinny," Strella stated.

Obviously, she wanted to change the subject, and it worked. Tinior philosophized about food, and Mina teased him about his round belly.

Liya took the opportunity to look more closely at her surroundings. People seemed content, laughing, and discussing. She didn't sense any shadows over the city, but she clearly felt something very strange going on. Then she realized that the table had gone quiet again. All eyes were focused on her.

"How did you do it?" Mina asked. "How were you able to break the spell?"

She wondered what they were talking about.

"None of us ever walked on the blue carpet," Selena continued. "When we were kids, we would throw breadcrumbs on it for fun. They burned right up."

Ah, the spell that surrounded the throne.

"I really don't know what exactly happened. I was able to walk on the carpet. Only when I touched the head of the black dragon did I feel like I was burning alive. I could smell the fire, and the heat was unbearable. It was difficult to breathe."

Surprise and fright, but she also saw something like awe in the looks of the people at her table.

"Did you, well, hear voices?" Ithen asked quietly.

"No." She shook her head. "I heard nothing. There was only darkness and an ancient force that I felt was neither good nor evil. It was very strange."

"Her hand needs to be taken care of," Haydn interjected. "She has a burn from the dragon's eye."

Involuntarily, Liya wondered why he only thought of that now. Her hand had been hurting this whole time. He'd probably been waiting for the right time.

"You touched the eye?" cried Selena, stunned.

Some winced, others groaned.

"Show me your hand!" Strella demanded.

She rose and stretched her hand across the table. The old woman examined the burn, then put her hand over it and closed her eyes. It became pleasantly cool, the burning sensation subsiding somewhat.

After a while, the old woman fixed her with green eyes. "I can't heal this wound completely." Her voice sounded strange. "You must take good care. It will take a long time to heal."

She gave Haydn a look that spoke volumes. Strella was hiding something. The questioning faces all around showed Liya that she was not the only one who noticed this strange behavior.

"Did you see the dragon?" Mina asked, unable to contain her excitement.

"No, no dragons," she replied with a grin.

"You think it's a legend," Tofeus croaked angrily.

"Please, forgive me, I didn't mean it that way." These people were kind to her, and she didn't mean to offend anyone.

What she had heard about the dragons so far, she now took at face value, just like the story about the gates. However, she would not openly admit this.

The somewhat awkward silence that followed was interrupted when Haydn stood up. "Liya," he declared in a determined tone. "I want to show you something else."

She was grateful for that.

"See you later." He nodded to the council members. "We will be able to start the meeting on time."

Then he pulled her along. Silently, they left the now very crowded main square. Liya found the silence that fell as they left it behind pleasant.

Haydn headed for a one-story gray building with large windows. With momentum, he took two steps at a time. Two saddled horses were grazing nearby. Although the house seemed rather modest, rich people probably lived here. She realized she had not seen any animals in the city until now. *An extremely strange place,* she thought again.

When the door opened, she could hardly believe her eyes. In front of her stood Beth, the woman Haydn had almost married. Ewan had told her that she had died in a riding accident.

"Come in," Beth kindly invited them.

Haydn gently pushed Liya into the spacious living room. For the first time, she saw colors other than black and gray. Pictures of flower meadows embellished the walls, and a white sofa stood on a light blue carpet. The smell of peppermint rose to her nostrils.

Another woman, about the same age as Beth, sat at the table pouring tea. She wore her hair loose, a braided pigtail the width of a finger adorning the back of her head.

"Mara," Beth said, "you already know Haydn. And this is Liya, isn't it?" Her voice sounded soft.

"Would you like a cup of tea, too?" inquired Mara.

"I'll gladly take one, thank you," Haydn replied, striding over to the table.

Completely baffled, she followed him and sat down next to him.

"Liya, I'm sorry I didn't tell you sooner. There wasn't a suitable time," he said apologetically.

Beth frowned and gave him a stern look. "You didn't tell her?" Although her voice still sounded gentle, the anger was audible. "I suggest you leave us alone with Liya. Take a walk."

Mara quickly took him by the hand and led him out, then closed the door.

"I remember you. You were at the party." Beth smiled. She didn't seem absent at all, the way Liya remembered her.

"I had no choice."

"What do they say?" Beth took a sip of tea.

"They found your horse and a silk scarf near the gorge. Officially, it is assumed that you fell into the depths. However, there are doubts about this. Some hold Haydn responsible. Others blame your father and think that fate took revenge on him for betraying his country."

"Somehow, people have a point." Beth sighed. "My father wanted to marry me off at any price, to an earl twice my age. A greedy, ruthless old man."

Mara stood up, gave her a kiss on the cheek, and sat down again.

"I don't understand anything at all," Liya groaned, but so much was already dawning on her.

"When my father told me I had to get married, my world collapsed. All my life, I felt imprisoned, but I still had hope for better days. When I happened to run into Haydn and found out who he was, I overheard a conversation between him and my father. That's when I got the idea to offer him marriage. I knew my father would agree immediately. A king is better than an earl, and the future king of Dar'Angaar would be the best choice. My father had me watch his every move. Mara and I met only very rarely. It was a terrible time." For a brief moment, she closed her eyes and took a deep breath. "Haydn and I had an agreement. In order to carry out his plans, a—well—merger with Eryon was important. I just wanted to live somewhere with Mara in peace. In the course of time, Haydn and I even became friends."

This revelation made her happy. Haydn did not love Beth, and the idea of marriage had been pure strategy.

"You're rambling, dear," Mara remarked.

"Of course, everything was in order. We planned our escape for months but had to change our plans several times. As I said, my father had me guarded. We had no choice but to leave on the day of the wedding." Beth faltered, her cheeks reddening. The memory was obviously upsetting her.

Mara patted her hand. "It's over."

Beth smiled forcedly.

"I see." Liya didn't know what else to say.

"Unlike my father, Haydn did not find my love for Mara repulsive." Beth clenched her fist. "That power-hungry old man! He would have sacrificed us all just to spite Louis and restore Eryon to its original greatness."

Yes, Liya agreed.

"Everyone knew I loved horses and preferred spirited breeds. We staged my *accident*. And some people from the, shall we say, *underworld* organized our escape. Haydn led us to this place. The residents are very friendly and open." Beth paused. "Haydn is a good man, even if he sometimes acts foolishly," she added.

Liya felt jealous as she realized the familiarity that existed between Haydn and Beth. Before she could say anything about it, he was standing in the doorway, leaning casually against the frame.

"Ladies, I have to kidnap Liya again. I'm afraid our time is quite short; we have some things to do."

Beth stood up. "Haydn, you never have time. You really should take better care of yourself."

"Even though I saved her life, she keeps nagging me," he replied with a cheeky grin.

Beth waved him off and hugged Liya warmly. "He has a good heart, don't let anyone tell you otherwise," she whispered in her ear. Then she took out a cloth from her robe and placed it in her hand. "Take this! We helped soldiers from Namoor escape from the mausoleum. They owe the bearer of the cloth a favor. Maybe it will help you one day."

Things were getting stranger and stranger. But at the same time, they made a certain sense. Beth had helped Ewan and Julian after the theft of the last stone tablet from the mausoleum in Qilon, she was sure of it.

"Thank you," she breathed.

Like Haydn, she gave Mara a friendly nod, then left the house.

Outside, Haydn took her hand and looked at the burn. "I got some wort oil." Gently, he wrapped a soaked cloth around her hand.

"Do you have any more surprises for me?" she asked softly.

"Let's take a break." He offered her his arm, and she hooked her arm around his.

Not far from Beth's house, there was a garden, which was apparently used by the townspeople to grow fruit and vegetables. A narrow path led through it, which ended near the city wall. There were several olive trees. In the sparse shade of a tree, they looked for a place to sit.

Overwhelmed by the events of the last few days, she wrapped her arms around her legs and rested her head on her knees. "A strange place this is, peaceful and sad, but also beautiful in a special way."

"I knew you would recognize the beauty." He moved a little closer.

She looked into his eyes. He brushed a curl from her face, his fingers touching her cheek. Warmth spread through her. His chest rose slightly—a deep breath. He pulled his hand away.

"I have already told you that I need your help to close the gates for good. You haven't answered yet."

"How do I know I can trust you?"

"You can't know that. That's a risk you have to take."

"Even if I decide to help you, Julian and Darwin will do everything they can to stop me. If we do succeed, they will report my betrayal." Pleadingly, she looked at him. "You're not just asking me to help you, Haydn. You are also asking me to leave everything behind. I will never be able to enter Namoor again. The fact of closing the gates again will be irrelevant. No one will trust me anymore."

She looked into his deep blue eyes. Framed by dark lashes, they were the kind that made the heart beat faster. She swallowed. Haydn troubled her deeply, but he also captivated her. She longed to be near him.

He clasped her fingers firmly. "Do you think I'm not aware of this? I would not ask you if there were any other way. In you flows the blood of Elladur."

He already knew—of course.

"Liya!" His deep blue gaze held her captive. "Since your experience with the Dragon Throne, I know you are a Guardian. I had already suspected because you can use the power of the crystal. In three days, the planets will be in this alignment. Whoever wanted to open the gates will try again. We have to get ahead of them."

"I don't know yet if I'm going to help you," she pressed out. "I need more time to think about it. That's all I can promise. I'll consider it."

Disappointment flashed in his eyes before his expression stiffened. "Let's go to the meeting, they're probably waiting for us," he said coolly.

Liya would help him close the gates, there was no doubt about that, but she needed to think of a plan to make sure Julian wouldn't do anything stupid. Even if she wasn't working for the king, Namoor was her home. She wanted to be able to go home whenever she wanted. Even if the word *home* felt inappropriate.

A few minutes later, they knocked on the door of the meeting house.

Strella opened the door. "Everything is prepared. We shouldn't lose any more time. Dusk is setting in soon," she explained.

"What's going on?" asked Liya. "What's the rush?"

"We'll be right there," Haydn said to Strella, who went back inside. He pulled Liya aside. "The Jade Brotherhood will be looking for their men. I must send soldiers to protect Thyron as soon as possible."

She sighed.

"We're going to ask for you to join the city council now, and then we'll ride off," he followed up.

What was *that* about? "No more secrets," she admonished him. "What's the point of this?"

"When people learn that you are a Guardian, they will not welcome you with open arms everywhere. Some will be very afraid of your gift. The council members might protect you." He ran a hand through his hair. "I'm not sure they'll approve of your inclusion, though."

"You blame me for the Brotherhood incident, don't you?"

"Mostly, they're worried about what happened in the throne room. That worries me."

"I'm good at taking care of myself, I've done it all my life." She pressed her lips tightly together.

"We don't know what the future holds for us. Times are turbulent and uncertain. One day you may need their help."

"Why?"

His loving gaze hit her right in the heart. "I have to be prepared for anything. That's all I can tell you."

"All right," she relented. Today he had let her in on a lot of things. She couldn't press him any further.

He leaned toward her, his breath brushing her cheek. "We'll talk more when we get back," he whispered.

She wanted to pull her hand away, but he held it tightly.

In the meeting room, all the council members were sitting around a round table. Liya felt uncomfortable at the sight of the serious faces. I then motioned them to take their seats.

"Haydn, we hold you in high esteem and trust," he began. "You are not only our friend, you are also our king. But we cannot agree to your proposal. We have guarded this city, its magic, and its secrets with our lives. We cannot make rash decisions." He looked directly at Liya. "We know too little to take you in. If we do, we will be obliged to lay down our lives for you, if necessary."

She heard Haydn grit his teeth.

"This time, you must trust me blindly. My family has never let you down." His voice sounded stern. He spoke to them as a king, not as a friend.

Obviously, they were not used to this behavior. The tension that now spread through the room was almost tangible. She wondered why this city was so special.

"We are very grateful to you for that," Ithen stated coolly. "We know the sacrifice you made to protect our city so that we can fulfill our mission."

"He is the king of Dar'Angaar, and we are residents of this land, despite everything. It is his duty to protect his people," Shia hissed.

"Watch your tongue!" Strella admonished her with a stern look.

"You all know that the council is like a family. Liya is a stranger, and she's not even from Dar'Angaar. That's too much to ask for!"

"This woman ignited a magic that has been dormant for centuries. Each of you knows what that means." Haydn fixed each one.

"But we don't know what set her off," Mina whispered.

"She survived contact with the throne and the slumbering dragon. That is the only proof you need." Haydn's voice was dangerously low.

"We swore long ago to protect this city," Ithen countered. "That weighs more than our promise to follow you."

"All we ask is a little more time." Strella was pleading.

"Time we don't have."

Ithen cleared his throat. "Haydn, your faith in Liya is not enough."

"You refuse my request?" Shaking his head, he looked around. "In the same breath, you ask me to send my soldiers to your gates. You should think of the upcoming event."

This conversation confused Liya more and more. Why couldn't Haydn just give orders to these people? He was the *king*. What was going on here?

"And you shouldn't forget who broke with tradition," Shia finally burst out. "That was you!"

"This tradition is based on wild guesses." Haydn clenched his fists.

"You can't know that," Shia hissed. "Visions aren't always clear in terms of timing, but even your father stuck to it."

"My father didn't even know my mother was one of you."

Shia jumped up, her chair tipping backward and slamming onto the wooden floor. "Still, he respected tradition." With her face contorted in anger, she pointed at Liya. "Why is she able to lift the barrier?"

There was approval in the faces of the others. Obviously, Shia had hit a sore spot.

"Regarding the prophecy that established the tradition, there is no doubt at all. The wife of the king of Dar'Angaar must be from Thyron. Only in this way can this damn curse be lifted," Mina interfered.

It took a while before the meaning of these words became clear to her.

Breathing heavily, Haydn rose. "You should never forget one thing. As a king, I have not only duties but also rights. And maybe the interpretation of the prophecy is wrong."

Shia turned pale. "You can't possibly, seriously believe that," she groaned.

"Now is neither the right time nor the right place to speak of this. Here and now, I demand Liya's admission to the community of Thyron and to the council."

When she realized what he was up to, she held her breath. She still didn't know exactly what it was all about and how everything was connected, but it was certainly not a good idea for the king to impose his will on the council of this city.

Before he could speak further, she stood up and took his hand. "I accept your decision and give you the time you need. I trust that you will come to a just decision." She nodded to Haydn, hoping he would leave it at that.

I then rose. "I thank you for your understanding, but I expect that our king also explicitly accepts our behavior."

"Even though I am deeply disappointed, I do not give you orders," Haydn replied. "But remember, every decision has consequences. Liya and I are leaving now."

They quickly left the building. Their horses were already waiting at the gate.

"I still don't get why this is so important for you," Liya mumbled.

"For your safety," he replied softly.

Liya sighed. "Let's ride back."

"Yeah, time is short," he said with an impenetrable expression.

Freezing rain drizzled down non-stop as Liya walked the last part of the journey on foot. Her leather armor was stuck to her body, and she shivered. Haydn was walking a few steps ahead of her. When she'd asked him to show her where she could practice, she hadn't expected him to join her, and neither was she expecting to have to ride there.

"We'll be right there," he finally said.

A clearing spread out before them, at the end of which a waterfall poured into a small lake. Slowly, the fog lifted. A short distance away, he stopped and turned to her. Despite the rain and the dim light, she didn't miss his watchful gaze.

"Here?" she asked. "A little elaborate, don't you think?

"Not if we want to see your skills. Or did your mage friends train you hands-on?"

She said nothing.

"No one will bother us here." He clasped his hands behind his back. "Attack me."

He hurled a fireball that burned the ground right next to her. Startled, she dodged it and glared at him angrily.

He shrugged his shoulders. "How do you plan to use your magic in a few days, should it become necessary? How are you going to close the gates? The enemy is powerful, and I won't be able to help you."

Liya rolled her eyes in annoyance. "So far, I've been fine without your advice. I can access my gift anytime, and I'll use it when the situation calls for it."

His arrogant expression remained unimpressed. "We cannot rely on your magic to break out because you are afraid or angry. Learn to control your gift! Focus on your inner light! Your thoughts shape the energy. Let's get started!"

"Don't treat me like a child," she countered defiantly.

Another bullet flew toward her. She barely managed to dodge it, but the fire grazed her foot.

"Deflect it, create a shield!" He hurled another fiery red ball.

She jumped to the side, but this time she wasn't fast enough. It hit her upper arm, and she went to her knees. She cried out, "Are you out of your mind? Are you trying to kill me?"

"Defend yourself kindly!"

Full of rage, she straightened up. Despite her training, he drove her crazy. Without thinking, she formed a fireball as big as a man's head and threw it. It bounced off Haydn's shield.

"Is that all?" His sneer infuriated her.

Deeply she breathed in and out, trying to restrain her anger, to direct her rage, to calm down. He was right. This was an ideal place to test her strength. Never before had she consciously tried out what she was capable of.

But something bothered her. "Why can't you help me close the gates?"

"Convince me of your magic, and I will answer you."

She stretched her hands out, directed her energy to the water, and connected with it. It rippled through her body as if the water flowed through her veins. She liked this element much better than fire. Water made her feel stronger. She always felt like fire drained her energy.

Four waves moved before her mind's eye. In the light rain, however, it was difficult for her to keep their shape. She needed air, cold air. She exhaled an icy breath. The waves froze, and weapons of ice shot toward Haydn.

Even though his shield intercepted everything, he gave her an appreciative nod. Beads of sweat shone on his forehead. She smiled.

"I won't be able to help you because I don't have enough power to kill him."

"I don't understand, Haydn."

With a movement of his head, he asked her to continue. With folded hands, she stretched her arms forward, but nothing happened.

"Do I have to make you hiss, *Kardia mou*?" He grinned mischievously.

"Idiot," she muttered, trying again to access her gift. Even though she could feel her magic, she couldn't create anything.

Suddenly he stood behind her and wrapped his arms around her shoulders. The rest of his body did not touch her, yet he was much too close. The scent of forest and rain enveloped her.

"Close your eyes and focus on your inner light!" he demanded softly. Gently, he lifted her arms, stroking them softly before grasping her wrists and circling them. "Can you feel the wind?" he breathed.

"Yes," she whispered.

His breath tickled her ear and left a tingling warmth.

"Imagine dipping your hands into a stream and forming a ball of water."

As he spoke, his fingers enclosed hers. He moved her arms in wave-like motions. She felt his body against her back.

"Open your eyes," he said softly.

A sphere as big as her head floated in front of her.

"Keep the shape in your mind's eye and let it grow." He slowly released his hands from her.

She concentrated. The ball grew larger, and she almost cried out with joy. When he put his hands around her waist, the ball swayed.

"Now form something new out of it!" he ordered quietly.

His lips touched her ear. She held her breath and had considerable trouble keeping the water in the circle. Creating something new seemed almost impossible.

"I can't concentrate if you keep interrupting me," she hissed.

"What exactly is distracting you?" His voice sounded rough. "This, possibly?" Gently, his lips touched her neck below her ear.

The ball splashed on the ground. Furious, she turned to him and braced herself against him. His grip tightened.

"What are you doing?" She hissed. "You said you'd train with me."

"That's what we're doing."

"Really?"

Abruptly, he let go of her, moved a few steps away, and said, "The ability to control the four elements was given to us humans by the Elders."

He had changed his attitude toward her within seconds. It took a moment until she could adjust to the new situation.

"Earth, water, air, and fire," he continued. "The royal families of the realms held power over two elements each. Some members of the royal family of Elladur could control all four elements—even rarer, at the same time. I also control all four elements, can switch back and forth between them, but I never could use all the elements at the same time."

She was getting hot. "I've never heard of that," she replied.

"Of course not. That knowledge is older than this world and long lost."

"Oh, you *all-knowing king*!" she purred and performed an exaggerated bow.

He grinned. "Finally, you see that." Then he motioned for her to try again.

They continued to practice. On the fourth try, she succeeded in forming small ice daggers from a water ball and her breath.

"Well done." His appreciation felt good.

Exuberantly, she dropped the daggers to the earth, only to form a new ball right after. This time she wanted to create larger blades. How easily she could access this element! She drew a thin layer of ice around the edges before they fell to the ground and shattered into a thousand pieces.

A sudden certainty hit her with full force. She could no longer deny it. The gift in her was old, very old; she didn't know nearly enough about its source, but this power urged to burst forth entirely. A relic from the Ancient Era.

For the umpteenth time, she wondered what would happen at the ceremony. Despite everything she had learned so far, an essential piece of the puzzle seemed to be missing. And who could Haydn not kill at the closing of the gates? Was he possibly speaking of that dark king?

"Why did you stop?" he asked, pointing to the splinters on the ground.

"Tell me about the ceremony," she pressed out.

A surprised look met her eyes. "We will open the gates all the way and then close them completely," he said calmly. "Even if we don't agree on everything. You know that!"

"That dark ruler beyond the ribbon…," she replied, wondering where the thought came from, "…won't he try to get into our world? After all, the gates will be wide open for a while. "

"Yes, I suppose he will." He closed his eyes briefly before continuing, "This ruler is only made of energy. He needs a shell so that he can manifest in our world."

She had heard that before but had suppressed the knowledge. However, it was precisely this that concerned her the most. "If a shell is not available to him, then he can't enter our world, right?" She suspected it was not that simple.

"It is better to provide him with a body for a short time; otherwise, his spirit could enter several people and cause great harm. In that case, we won't be able to do anything. If he has a body, we can see our opponent."

That made sense to her—at least in a way. "Who will be willing to provide his body?"

"One of my relatives is standing by." He sighed. "However, there is a problem."

"Another one?" She would have liked to laugh hysterically.

"We assume that Zadron, the leader of the Red Brotherhood, will also offer his body to the dark ruler. We have to prevent that."

She swallowed. She didn't need any further explanations. With full concentration, she lifted her hands and moved them. Sparks floated through the air, and a fire exploded in the clearing. In the next second, ice and water extinguished the flames. Out of the corner of her eye, she caught Haydn's dismayed look.

"I guess that's why you don't share all your secrets with me," she remarked.

From now on, she would look at him with different eyes. For many, the king of Dar'Angaar embodied darkness, but she saw the light in him.

"Maybe," he replied. His voice sounded soft.

⤝

She was freezing. Even the dry clothes and the fireplace could not warm her. The morning had taken all her strength, and she felt tired and drained.

Folnar picked her up and led her to the dining room, where her companions were waiting. Still shivering, she rubbed her hands. Her burn throbbed slightly. Sakima, Julian, and Darwin were sitting at the round table eating a stew when she entered the room.

"Liya!" Sakima exclaimed delightedly. She sat down next to him. Darwin and Julian eyed her silently.

"How are you?" the Nirm asked.

"Good," she replied, hoping she sounded convincing. "How about you guys?"

"We spend most of our time in our rooms," Julian groaned. "Every now and then, we can take short walks in the company of a dozen soldiers. It's only when we eat that we don't see the guards."

"Terrible people," Darwin grumbled into his plate.

"How was your trip?" Julian asked.

"I was just looking at a ruined city. "

"That's it?" Julian probed.

Darwin gave him a warning look.

"What did you expect? That I would get access to all the secrets and plans?" she returned.

Darwin took a sip of wine. "Don't hold it against Julian. He, or rather we, have been worried."

"I saw you early this morning," Sakima interjected. "Judging by your clothes, you didn't visit any ruins. "

She avoided his penetrating gaze.

"Well," her friend continued, "I can move much more freely than your mages, often without guards. They even allow me to pay my respects to my ancestors outdoors. Today I did so on the west side, as it is sheltered from the rain. That's when I saw you."

" I was training."

Surprised, Darwin looked at her. "With the king, perhaps?"

"Yeah, he said it wouldn't hurt to be in good shape when we *close* the gates."

In disbelief, the old mage's eyes widened. "He said that?"

Julian snorted. "Oh, please! You're not going to buy it, are you?"

"I don't want to argue," she snapped at him.

"I don't want to either, but I find the situation we're in extremely troubling. You seem to think otherwise."

"No matter what else may be involved," she replied, "the primary concern is to prevent this army from invading our world from the other side of the ribbon. As far as that is concerned, we fight together."

Julian swallowed a bite. "I hope so."

This conversation tired her almost as much as the exercises. "I'm going to retire and rest a bit." With that, she pushed the plate aside.

Sakima touched her elbow. "Please, stay a little longer!"

Shaking her head, she stood up. "That training session took more energy out of me than I thought."

Julian rose and grabbed her hand. With a cry, Liya tried to pull it back, but he reacted in a flash, held her tightly, turned her hand, and looked at her palm.

"What's that?" he groaned.

"An accident. I touched something. It was my fault." With rising anger, she snatched her hand away.

Sakima stood up as well. "I will see you out, Liya."

With perplexed faces, the mages remained behind. The soldiers let Liya and the Nirm pass unhindered. As soon as the door closed behind them, Sakima nodded to the others and walked with her a few steps further.

"Do you trust the king?" he asked softly.

"Part of me does, but another remains cautious. For now, we're pursuing the same goals. It's complicated." She sighed. "I'm trying to solve the puzzle piece by piece. It helps to have a friend like you."

Her gaze swept the stairs. Folnar was waiting for her there.

"My lady, I will accompany you upstairs," he said loudly, nodding curtly to Sakima.

The Nirm raised his hands. "That's all right. I'll go back." Then he hugged her and whispered, "Have faith and listen to your inner voice, as you always have."

With each step up the stairs, she felt Sakima's eyes at her back. A certainty spread through her that she did not yet fully understand. The Nirm was giving her the time she needed. When the time came, he would follow her, for to him, she was the chosen one.

Three days had passed, and Liya had trained in the clearing every morning. By now, it was easy for her to switch between the elements and maintain her shield.

Haydn had sent soldiers to Thyron, but so far, everything remained quiet. His men had taken up positions in front of the city and were waiting for the Jade Brotherhood to attack. Maverick had informed her about all of this; she had not seen Haydn for the last two days. Now, Maverick and Folnar practiced with her.

Folnar told her that he had started his education at the castle when he was six years old. He did not like to talk about that time. But when he told her about his first trials outside the walls, he blossomed.

She learned from Maverick that he had been Haydn's teacher. He had lost his wife and son to illness when he was just twenty years old.

"Keep your sword neat, little witch."

She rolled her eyes. Ever since the story with the octopuses, Maverick called her that. The next moment he executed a blow on her butt.

"Ouch!"

"And you're slow, too," he exulted.

"You realize I *will* take revenge."

He laughed heartily. "You can try."

She frowned, swung her arm, and when she discovered a puddle of water, she formed a ball of water that she burst right over his head.

Folnar burst out laughing, and she grinned.

Maverick scowled. "You cheated."

"Says who?"

"Me."

"Have you changed the rules?" she replied good-humoredly. "You asked me to try everything. That's exactly what I'm doing, *General*."

"If Haydn doesn't put you over his knee soon, I will." He smiled at these words.

"A storm is coming," Folnar interjected. "We should turn back. Will you have dinner with us tonight?"

"No, it's better if I keep Sakima and our mages company."

"Why are you doing this?" Folnar shrugged. "Just thinking about it makes you tense up."

She spared herself an answer. Things were complicated. They rode back in amicable silence. When they passed the edge of the forest, lighting startled her, and she stopped her horse. Lightning flashed across the sky again. She stumbled. *Had there been a green glow?*

Her body tingled from goosebumps crawling over her skin.

"You see that?" she called out to Folnar and Maverick, who had also stopped.

Folnar looked around. "What do you mean?"

"The lightning bolts."

Maverick looked around as well. "There's nothing here. Are we talking *danger*?" His hand slid to his sword.

The sky above her glowed a deep emerald green, white sparks streaking across the landscape in front of her. She felt a tremendous tremor, as if the earth shook beneath her feet. The wound on her hand began to throb.

Help me! A voice echoed in her head, but those were not her words. *Thyron...!*

She understood immediately. The Jade Brotherhood was marching toward the city. There was no doubt about it.

"Ride back," she commanded. "Tell Haydn it's time. The attack on Thyron has begun."

Their expressions told Liya that they believed her every word.

But Folnar shook his head. "We won't leave you alone."

"Do as I said," she hissed.

"No way," Maverick replied. "You think we're going to let you have all the fun, little witch?" He might as well have cursed in that tone.

Folnar whistled, and a few seconds later, a hawk landed on a rock in front of them. From his saddlebag, Folnar took out a piece of paper and a charcoal pencil. He scribbled something on the paper and wrapped it around the bird's foot.

"Always well prepared, aren't you, *assassin*?" She wouldn't admit it, but she admired him for his prudence.

He grinned broadly. "I am the best, *my lady*. Our king will be informed. That's the way it has to be."

Even a brisk pace wasn't fast enough for her. The hours seemed like an eternity, and she worried if they would make it in time.

The rain whipped Liya in the face, and her horse snorted.

"We're almost there," she whispered, patting the mare's neck reassuringly.

Clouds of smoke drifted toward them through the drizzle, with Thyron looming behind them. As they approached, they saw countless corpses in front of the wall. The wall next to the wooden door was destroyed. A cruel silence lay over the place, interrupted only by the wind, which whistled as if it sang a death song in the rain.

Her horse was still moving when she jumped off and grabbed a short sword lying on the ground. Without turning around, she hurried between the remains of the wall. She heard Folnar and Maverick's footsteps directly behind her. There was no one to be seen.

Palace ... palace! screamed the voice in her head.

The sweet smell that hit her reminded her of something.

"Where is everyone?" Folnar murmured to her.

"At the palace," she replied.

Finally, they reached the gravel path. They ran up and took shelter by the wall, a good distance away from the entrance. Voices came to them, but Liya did not understand a word.

Folnar told them to wait. She watched in amazement as he scanned the wall, then nimbly climbed up. Shortly after, he was back with them and crouched down.

"Men in green robes. Just under a dozen are in front of us. Further back, I couldn't make out anything specific. Part of the view is blocked. They probably have everything covered."

"Can we pass through the passageway?" Maverick asked.

Liya shook her head. "That one is guarded."

Folnar agreed. "Let me go ahead. Wait near the gate."

They did as they were told while Folnar climbed over the wall again. Liya thought she heard a muffled sound, but nothing happened after that. Her heart was pounding, and her hands were ice cold.

Finally, Folnar's head appeared at the entrance. She and Maverick tiptoed to him. At their feet lay four corpses. More men were posted at the bridge further ahead, talking amongst themselves. Folnar pulled on a green coat and put on the hood. Maverick followed suit.

"Take me as your prisoner. They probably won't look at us," Liya whispered.

Folnar tied her hands together with a rope. "If you pull on it, the knot will come undone. We must leave the sword here," he whispered.

The closer they came to the men, the more roughly Folnar and Maverick urged her on. Laughter reached her ears; she gave the soldiers an angry look.

A tall man tapped Folnar on the shoulder with a broad grin. "Well, well, look who we have here!" he blasphemed, devouring Liya with a glance. "Maybe we can have some fun later, little one. But for now, make sure she gets to the others. Her people, that pack, are crammed into the hall of the old palace."

Maverick gave her a push, and she fell. Folnar pulled her up again. Undisturbed, they passed the bridge. The guards at the next crossing hardly noticed them.

It seemed like an eternity until they finally reached the gate to the main courtyard. The gargoyles appeared to watch them. With each step toward the massive hall, she felt the pull of ancient magic.

I dwell here. Memory, knowledge, forgetting. Recognize me, the voice hummed in her head. Her body trembled as the power gently enveloped her.

"Please, none of us can break through the barrier," shouted someone a short distance away. "You've seen it, haven't you? Leave it!" The desperate voice belonged to Strella.

She quickened her steps and untied the rope. "What are you up to?" hissed Folnar.

"This is something only I can do," she said, looking at him firmly. "Blend in with the green riders. Sound out the situation. Then come into the hall. You'll have to hurry."

"She's right," Maverick groaned.

Gratefully, she nodded to him.

"All right," Folnar grumbled.

She moved on slowly, while Folnar and Maverick quickly moved away to disappear inconspicuously into the crowd.

In the great hall, the townspeople were divided into groups guarded by soldiers. Ithen knelt a few feet from the throne; a tall, broad-shouldered man with a bald skull looked down on him. Strella stood beside the man. The bald man raised his hand and struck her in the face. She fell to the ground and remained there. The bald one then dragged Ithen to the stairs leading up to the throne, where a charred corpse lay.

"Wait!" shouted Liya.

All eyes turned to her. Her heart pounded.

Go to the throne, the voice commanded.

"Are you volunteering?" the bald man asked.

Immediately in front of him, she stopped. "You don't have the right to be here," she said calmly.

"We've waited long enough," he hissed. "Now we're going to get what's coming to us."

The pitch-black eyes in the tanned, scarred face eyed her disdainfully. His robe was as sea green as the others', but it was of finer cloth and had gold buttons. A leader!

She caught a glimpse of the throne, and horror gripped her. Three corpses lined the way there, all charred. Her eyes lingered on a small group of men standing off to the side with their heads bowed. She heard a kind of chanting.

Go to the throne. The spell is weakening. The voice in her head had changed. The tone made her listen. It was deep and soft, full of darkness, yet somehow familiar.

"I'll go," she heard herself say and was surprised at how calm she sounded.

The bald man pushed Ithen away with his foot. "I suggest you hurry before I change my mind," he hissed.

With her heart pounding wildly, she walked to the podium and climbed the steps, feeling the carpet beneath her feet.

Do not be afraid, human queen. Put your hand on my eye. Then proceed to the throne.

You burned me last time, she replied dumbly.

This time it will be different.

Her feet grew heavier with each step. As she squatted, her heart threatened to fail. A laugh rang out in her head, rough as a grater's iron. Taking a deep breath, she placed her hand with the scar on the red dragon's eye. The room spun, time stopped, and people faded, and darkness surrounded her. Warmth flowed through her body.

Rise and walk on, the voice demanded.

She stopped directly in front of the golden armchair. She could see the energy emanating from it in her mind's eye.

Use the wound for the blood you need. Place your palm in the opening on the armrest. Press firmly, so your blood flows into it. Whatever happens, it must not be reflected in your face. All eyes of the outside world are on you. Do not allow your facial expressions to betray anything.

She sat down. The chair felt hard and cold. Involuntarily, a shiver ran down her spine. She pressed her thumb into the open wound until it bled. Then she pressed her hand on the round opening in the backrest. The earth shook, and bright light—no, fire—made its way through the darkness.

In her thoughts, the voice whispered, *You have nourished the Dragon Throne with blood. Our bond is strengthened!*

She wanted to swallow, but her throat was too tight. Now she knew who the voice belonged to. A strange euphoria overcame her, which was closely followed by panic. To control her emotions, she searched for a point she could fixate on.

Look at me!

Trembling, she blinked and looked around until she perceived an emerald glow. Her breathing calmed.

More blood, demanded the Dragon King.

She pressed her palm even harder into the opening and almost cried out. The pressure in the wound increased, as if someone was sucking her blood. Desperate, she fought against the rising tears.

Don't cry. We will soon make it.

And indeed, a moment later, it was over. The wound throbbed wildly, but the cruel pain was over. What followed, however, took her breath away. Something incredibly powerful nestled gently against her body and caressed her. Secured in this way, her magic blossomed. She released the flow of energy, and their forces united. Yes, she was the *Guardian!*

The Dragon King laughed harshly. Finally, with deep regret, he commanded, *We must end it. It is not yet the right time.*

The energy retreated. She found herself back in the hall, looking into the horrified eyes of the leader. His soldiers circled the throne with their swords drawn.

Do not be afraid. You are destined to take power, hummed the Dragon King.

While maintaining eye contact with the bald man's gaze, she rose.

"What have you done?" he shouted.

Only now did she notice that chunks of columns were scattered on the floor.

"You had no right to take this city," she repeated. "Leave Thyron and never return."

"We won't. We have been waiting for this moment for a hundred years. When I felt the change in the balance of the worlds, I knew it was time. The Dragon King is returning, and the magic of dragons belongs to the Jade Brotherhood."

In his face, reddened with anger, scars shone white. For a moment, the dark aura that surrounded him revealed itself to her.

"I don't know how you broke the spell, and I don't care. You have cleared the way. That's all that matters. And now you're going to die."

A figure stepped next to him. It was Strella, who had dragged herself there in pain. "Only the rightful heir can break the spell," she said with difficulty.

A murmur went through the groups of prisoners. Glances stayed on her, full of expectation and hope.

"We'll see about that," the bald man thundered, nodding to his men, who then approached her.

Her pulse quickened. A flame blazed in the leader's hands, which were held up like a bowl. His mouth twisted into a wicked grin, and his men turned to the prisoners.

Liya's thoughts raced. *They want to kill everyone!*

Then we will stop them. Something about the Dragon King's tone deeply troubled her.

"Stop!" Liya thundered.

"In this place, you do not have magic," the bald man replied.

"Are you sure?" she returned. Inside of her, her magic blazed. A blue flame played around her hands. "I'll give you some more time. Go!" she said calmly.

"You can't save them all, witch," the man hissed.

Help me, she pleaded. An emerald green veil wrapped around her.

The leader gave a signal. At that moment, Folnar and Maverick pounced on the first soldiers. Shrills and screams reached her ears. She clenched her fists. Her body trembled and her cheeks glowed as the ancient force took possession of her. She allowed it to happen. *Gods!* This level of energy overpowered her, hardly bearable. Ice-blue lightning bolts shot out of her body like tentacles and struck the men. They slumped down. Liya felt every last breath of life fade away. Only darkness and cold remained.

It is finished! the dragon king rejoiced.

Did you kill them all? she asked.

They deserved it. They were traitors.

She felt dizzy.

I must go, human queen.

The connection broke. Emptiness spread through her. In the next moment, she felt her last meal making its way up the stairs. She ran down the steps and out of the hall, propped herself against the wall, and threw up.

"Here!" Folnar handed her a handkerchief.

"Please, take me away," she whispered before darkness once again enveloped her.

⚬

In her dream, Liya was haunted by the dead jade brothers. She woke up sweating and trembling. The sun was shining through the window into her room. It must have been late afternoon.

She was still slightly dizzy when she got up and went to the bowl to wash her face. The cool water refreshed her and got her circulation going a bit, then she trotted back to bed. Her thoughts circled around the black dragon. His power was woven into his image on the carpet, and he had connected with her. Never before had she felt this kind of magic. Although she had barely been able to stand the energy, the emptiness that now filled her ached.

A knock on the door jolted her out of her thoughts. She sat up quickly. "Enter."

Haydn entered, ran to her, and embraced her.

Gently, she broke away from him. "Did you come for me?"

"No, Folnar and Maverick brought you back. After I received the hawk's message, I rode off with my soldiers. Halfway to Thyron, I met you. "

He held her and didn't ask questions. He probably already knew everything anyway. Shortly after, there was another knock, and a servant brought in a tray of food.

"Put it on the table there," Haydn ordered.

The girl did so, lowered her head, and left the room.

"You must find your strength," he said softly. "Dusk will be setting in soon."

"Is it time?"

"The planets will line up tonight," he replied. "Will you help me?"

"I will close the gates. That's all I can promise you."

"That's good enough for me," he whispered.

She felt his warm, soft lips on her mouth. The kiss was intimate, tender, and firm at the same time. The way he breathed her name made her dive into another world, a world full of passion. If only she could make time stand still and extend this moment into infinity! Unexpectedly, he pulled her onto his lap. His lips pressed down on hers again. She buried her fingers in his hair. He clasped her waist and caressed her neck. Fiercely she nestled against him, her body tingling and longing for more.

They were both startled by a loud knock. Groaning, they broke away from each other.

"Haydn, we have to go," Maverick called through the door.

"Bad timing," he murmured, gently stroking her cheek. "We need to get ready. "

Only very slowly did the wave of emotions in her subside. She was grateful to Maverick; he had saved her.

Chapter 32

Liya took a deep breath and stepped out of the room. "In armor today?" she asked.

"You never know," Folnar replied. "And you're wearing a dress!"

His admiring look did not escape her. She stuck her tongue out at him. "Where are my companions?"

"In the library."

"Then let's go."

Folnar nodded, and she followed him down the hall.

"I'll wait outside," he said, opening the door to the library.

The men were standing at the window. They turned to her and stared at her with open mouths. Even Julian was speechless.

"Is it really so extraordinary to see me in a beautiful dress?" she asked, amused.

"Kind of," Sakima replied, laughing heartily.

"You look very pretty, like a nobleman's daughter," Darwin remarked.

"Don't get too used to it."

"What's taking place today? A ball?" Julian's tone sounded a little mocking.

"That's what I want to talk to you about." She motioned for them to take their seats.

It all came down to this. It was clear to her that Julian and Darwin were pursuing different goals than she was. She remembered Julian's words about Haydn very well. the two magicians probably sensed that she had long since gone her own way. But the men needed her. Sakima had a different view of things; the Nirm understood the connections. He would support her.

"Tonight, the planets are in alignment," she began.

Three pairs of eyes hung on her lips. Mechanically, Darwin took off his glasses and cleaned them. Something lurked in Julian's gaze. Sakima nodded imperceptibly. Briefly, she caught his true form, and then he looked like a human again. *Interesting*, she thought. In the past, it was not like a shadow; the transformation was usually like thunder. Another hidden skill of the Nirm?

"It's not what we suspected."

The magicians sucked in their breath sharply. The Nirm raised his chin.

"Someone has already tried to open the gates."

A leaden silence filled the room.

"That means the gates are open a crack," Sakima said quietly.

He thought the same as she did. The dark figures and strange creatures of late—they were not of this world.

"That's right."

"They need to be closed immediately," Julian hissed.

Of course! He knew only half as much about the gates and the world beyond the tape as he pretended to.

"It's not that simple," she countered.

"What do you mean?" asked Darwin quietly.

"Before the gates can be closed again, they must be fully opened."

Julian groaned. "And you're going to stand by and do *what* in your beautiful dress?" he sneered.

She withstood his gaze. "I will stand beside the King of Dar'Angaar for the final closing of the gates." After a pause, she continued, "You will attend the ceremony in priestly garb, in the place you will be assigned. You will not be given weapons. Do exactly as the priests do."

When there was a knock at the door, the mages flinched.

Jakyn entered and placed three priestly robes on a chair. "Change your clothes," he said to the men. "We'll be leaving in a few minutes." And turning to her, he said, "The king awaits you in his study."

She exchanged another glance with Sakima. Then she went on her way to see Haydn.

⚶

The soldiers who were standing with Haydn in front of his study moved away when they saw Liya.

A glint shone in Haydn's eyes. His shoulders and forearms were reinforced with black plate armor, and silver chain mail clung to his shapely body. He wore his crown and black cloak.

With an elegant movement, he took her hand, leaned toward her, and whispered, "You look adorable."

Someone cleared his throat. Jakyn came up to them. "It is prepared," he said gravely. "All the priests have assembled."

He gave her a quick glance. So, her companions were already in the ceremonial hall. With a concerned expression, he turned to Haydn.

"Zadron has increased the number of his retainers." His already pale face was almost white.

"Thank you, Jakyn. " Haydn let go of her hand and patted the young priest on the shoulder. "We'll be ready soon. I'd like to speak with Liya for a moment. Wait, please."

He motioned for her to follow him, and they stood a little apart. "I've shielded us so no one can hear us. Do you have the crystal?"

Liya put her hand on her locket. "Yes."

"If something goes wrong, I want you to leave the room," he said forcefully.

"Excuse me?"

"I have instructed Maverick and Folnar to take you out of the country in that case. Tell me here and now that you will comply."

"I can't make a promise I might not be able to keep." He took a deep breath, muttering something like, "*Stubborn... incorrigible...*" She smirked.

At Haydn's side, she entered a dark, terrifying wing. Evil lurked here, she could feel it. They entered a nondescript room with an old wooden door. The flames of a few lanterns flickered, sparsely illuminating the gray walls of the room.

"Behind this door, there is a path that connects the main building with the tower, the oldest part of the castle, via a fortified stone wall. It has stood since the beginning. You will see symbols and signs on the walls that we don't know nowadays. They're from the Ancient Era. Zadron and his people maintain and study these signs."

A cold breeze blew toward them when Jakyn opened the door. The path over the wall was narrow and long. When they reached the tower, Liya immediately felt the dampness. To her horror, the spiral staircase was on the outer wall. The priests had placed wooden planks over the crumbling stone steps, but they were wet and musty. The descent seemed endless. The lower they got, the steeper it became.

After what felt like an eternity, a deep buzzing sound reached her ears. Her stomach contracted, and her pulse quickened. Finally, they entered the interior of the tower and arrived at a wide corridor illuminated by several lanterns. Briefly, Haydn turned to her. His familiar features looked tense, but his eyes were shining. Her heart hammered up to her throat. Only a few more steps to the room where the future of this world would be decided! She did not have the time to be afraid.

Maverick and Folnar waited outside the entrance. They let Liya and Haydn pass before they caught up with Jakyn behind them.

The corridor rose slightly, almost as if one were entering a grandstand. The walls were white and cold, but the burning torches created little warmth. At the end, the way opened into a surprisingly large round hall with four columns in the middle. Many men in black robes and a few soldiers in armor stood in front of the wall in rows. The ceiling and the wall were littered with symbols; some of them were painted on and colored, while others were carved.

But what Liya saw in the middle of the room caught her attention. She knew she was looking at a piece of ancient history. A circular golden plate about four meters in diameter shone on the floor between the columns.

Beside Haydn, she strode up to this panel. Maverick and Folnar positioned themselves on either side of the entrance, and Jakyn stood by a group of black cowls. She could not tell who belonged to the priests and who to the Red Brotherhood. Was there even a difference? Briefly, her gaze lingered on a strikingly tall man.

The chanting swelled, and the magic in the room intensified. Furtively, Liya looked at the golden plate. Four symbols were engraved on it: a wheel of fire, a kind of spiral, and a star, but she couldn't quite make out the symbol that was furthest away. In the center of the slab was a depression about a meter in diameter. Four fist-sized stones were arranged around the edge of the depression. She instinctively assigned the painted characters to the elements.

The big man stepped forward and raised his voice, saying, "Long have we been working for this moment. Let us begin."

She knew it was Zadron. Haydn stepped up to him. Two priests stood beside him and raised their hands.

Wind rose in this windowless room, then the room became warm, then damp. The stones floated up and paused half a meter above the floor. She glanced at Zadron. His black eyes shone in his white face, sending a shiver down her spine.

Suddenly, rays of light shot out of the element stones. She couldn't believe her eyes, but the light solidified. Shimmering columns, about twice the size of Haydn, circled the hollow. Movement arose at the bottom of the pillars. Water flowed around one of them, and a strong gust blew around another. Small flames played around the next, while the base of the last column stood in a shallow sand dune.

As Haydn walked slowly toward the recess, she trembled. He stopped and turned to face her. At the sight of him, her heartbeat stopped. His eyes were also jet black, looking right through her. Wherever he was, he was not in this room.

She did not manage to suppress the trembling of her body. A fearful question haunted her mind. What if she had misjudged Haydn and everything that was going on here? What if she failed in stopping this dark ruler?

The ground began to shake. A black, viscous liquid, like tar, ran from the bases of the column, flowing upward until a dense, black haze wafted around them.

Haydn, Zadron, and the priests stepped back from the circle. Haydn stood next to them. Their eyes met. His eyes shone a deep blue. The chanting grew quieter until it finally fell silent.

Gray mist billowed out of the recess, rose, and filled the space between the columns of light. Lightning flashed through it. In the next moment, four wolf-like creatures leaped out. These creatures she knew. Fire-red eyes looked around warily as they lined up around the circular plate. They were only the prelude to the real horror.

What followed was almost unbearable. A figure appeared, a man, but only a shadow. He had no clear solid form; he was somehow shapeless. There were spikes on his arms and feet, and they moved almost like feathers. It looked as if he wore a helmet with spikes, but it could also be his head.

"One hundred years... one hundred years...," hissed the shapeless one in a voice like that from a crypt.

Nails clicked on stone; the animals greeted their master.

"Where is the body?" rumbled the shapeless one.

She felt his tremendous anger and the potent magic that surrounded him.

Zadron stepped forward. "My prince, royal blood, as you demand." He pointed to a man standing behind him.

It was Melk, a cousin of Haydn, an inconspicuous young man. This seemed strange to her. She heard soft voices. Jakyn was reciting a prayer with some priests.

The Shapeless One raised his hand, and soldiers of darkness stepped out of the gray mist. She counted half a dozen men lined up behind the Shapeless One. They held their swords in front of them at their navels. Liya wondered how it was possible that they had solid forms.

When the dark ruler took a few steps toward Haydn, panic seized her. She felt the Shapeless One trying to penetrate her mind. For a moment, her head felt empty.

A laugh boomed through the room, strangely familiar to her. She had heard it before, in her mind. The mist changed color to a shimmering emerald green. The magic changed as well, feeling like it did on the throne platform in Thryon. What was going on here? A shadow appeared in the mist.

She held her breath. A gaze from emerald eyes rested on her. The Dragon King, the son of El'Orim, had come. He wore black trousers. His muscular torso was unclothed. At first, he looked like a well-trained human warrior, about as tall as Haydn, but this impression evaporated immediately. A green glow flowed from his heart and spread around his figure like an exceptionally fine cloud. Black wings with a span of about two meters protruded from his back on both sides of his body.

He moved his neck, cracking it, and the wings disappeared. The glimmer also faded, and he looked like a human. Nothing reminded her of a dragon anymore. Brown hair fell into his angular face, which was beautiful despite its hardness. He gazed directly at her.

"Rhynalor! " The surprised voice of the dark ruler cut the silence. "How could you leave the intermediate realm?"

"Why am I here?" asked Rhynalor sharply.

Liya stumbled. The Dragon King existed in an intermediate realm, and he had not come voluntarily? Who was responsible for his appearance? The Shapeless One obviously was not.

She watched Rhynalor, who looked around wildly. A metallic band was emblazoned on his neck, which glowed red for a moment.

The Shapeless One paid no more attention to him. Instead, he turned his attention to Melk, who had stepped forward and now stood there motionless. The still unformed hand of the dark king, which looked like a rag of black liquid, touched Melk's shoulder. Gray-black mist spread through the room.

Melk trembled, became transparent, then slowly lost his shape, while the figure of the dark ruler solidified.

Zadron rushed over. "Take me, Lord of Darkness. My body and my spirit will serve you."

That's exactly what she had to prevent. She wanted to start running, but she couldn't get away from the spot. "Haydn, I can't move," she whispered in despair.

But he did not react. She noticed that no one in the room was moving. All the people in her field of vision remained motionless and stared impassively ahead. With a lot of effort, she managed to turn her head. She tried to take a step, but the resistance was too great. Her feet trembled with the effort of fighting. He was so powerful that she had to catch her breath.

The Shapeless One had succeeded—he had incapacitated everyone except Zadron. Her eyes wandered to the leader of the Red Brotherhood, who was preparing to pull out his dagger. With satisfaction, she observed that he also felt the resistance. He struggled in vain to bring his hand toward the weapon. Had the Shapeless One withdrawn his favor?

Out of the corner of her eye, she perceived a movement. The elements! The bases of the columns were surrounded by their respective elements: water, swirls of air, flames, and sand. She reached for her gift and focused on the water. Each time she reached out for it, the connection broke after a short time. She was unable to focus her magic.

She looked at everything with her spiritual eyes. A labyrinth of black threads tightened around the columns of light. She sent out her magic again. The darkness enveloped her energy flow and engulfed it. It felt like a contest, and time was on darkness's side. Beads of sweat gathered on her forehead, and she tasted blood. Completely exhausted, she paused, lifted one hand with difficulty, and retrieved the crystal from the locket.

Gasping with exertion, she finally connected to the water with the help of the crystal. She channeled her magic into it, forming a liquid spearhead and hardening it into ice with a touch. She directed it at Zadron, who stabbed Melk in slow motion. Haydn's cousin fell to the ground infinitely slowly. The ice spike bored into Zadron's body, but it was too late. Melk coughed up blood, then his body went limp.

A savage roar sounded, and Liya flinched. The wolf-like creatures bared their teeth as the mist in which they stood cleared. The spell was broken. Her feet gave way, and Haydn took her hand.

"Royal blood was the agreement," hissed the Shapeless One. His voice sounded metallic.

He moved toward Liya and Haydn, then stopped immediately in front of them. Haydn looked at his cousin, his jaw muscles tense.

"It seems you are not in control of your followers," the Shapeless One nagged, raising his hand.

Zadron shrieked and slumped down.

"What do you have to offer, King of Dar'Angaar?" the dark ruler asked.

"You could have taken Zadron, it would have been enough for the transformation," Haydn replied. Black mist wafted around his feet.

"Your lady would be enough for me," he whispered.

"What is this?" Haydn groaned. "You rejected Zadron because you want royal blood. "

"I will be gracious and make an exception for her." The dark ruler blatantly eyed Liya.

Fear paralyzed her; icy coldness spread through her. The shapeless man's chest and pelvis were solid, but his shape still melted away on the borders. Clouds of smoke enveloped him.

He put a hand on Haydn's shoulder. "My king, you must make a choice. Your blood or hers."

Instinctively, Liya squeezed her palm tighter and felt the crystal bore into it.

The dark one seemed to notice. "What's going on?" he roared.

He grabbed her by the neck and threw her to the ground. Then he hit her arm so hard on the stone slabs that the bones crunched. Her fingers opened, and the crystal fell out.

"When I'm done with you, you'll wish you'd never been born," he breathed into her face. His foul smell nauseated her.

A glistening flame blazed within her. Anger? Or fear? She did not know. Without thinking, she retrieved the dagger from the inside pocket of her dress and plunged it into the dark one's billowing neck. The weapon drove through absorbent cotton without doing any damage.

A punch hit her in the face. Stars danced before her eyes, and she tasted blood again. One of the wolf-like creatures lunged at her. She rolled to the side, sharp claws cutting into her arm.

She looked to Haydn for help, but his expression was petrified. The Shapeless One had again put a spell over the room. No one could help her now.

"You will not be able to save these people, and I will devour this world," said the dark one, emitting a mirthless laugh.

Her body was lifted into the air and then thrown to the ground with fierce force. She writhed in pain. He would tear her to pieces.

"Human queen!" someone thundered. *"Liya!"*

The Shapeless One hovered over her. "Do you really think a human can stop me?"

Her back arched. Once again, the Dragon King screamed her name. Her eyes went black. When her first rib cracked, she cried out.

Like a shadow, the Dragon King came upon the dark one. After a casual wave of the Shapeless One's hand, the red gem in his metal band lit up, forcing him to his knees.

"Rhynalor! You traitor!" boomed the dark one. "You let yourself be lured here from the intermediate realm! Did you think there was a way out of your damnation?"

She saw Rhynalor hit the ground, then immediately scramble up again. His hands reached for the shackle on his neck. He tugged at it, but he stood no chance. Finally, he looked directly at Liya. The bond between them grew stronger. She had felt something similar in the throne room, but now the feeling was more intense.

The Shapeless One hurled Rhynalor against one of the pillars. The Dragon King lay there, blood flowing from his many wounds onto the ground.

"Stop," she whispered. "Please, stop! "

The shapeless man let go of his victim and strode toward her. "What do you care about him?"

The Dragon King grasped her hand, and warmth gently caressed her body. Her agonizing pain ebbed to a throb. His magic helped her. *This isn't right.*

Sighing, she withdrew her hand from him, rolled away, and directed her gift into the water. Quickly, she built a liquid wall around the Dragon King and froze it to ice.

Furious, the shapeless man grabbed her. When she crashed into one of the pedestals, a corner bored into her hip. The jarring pain faded into the background as she felt a vibration. What was happening now?

She lay in front of the golden plate, her blood dripping into the gutters on the floor in front of it. A light flickered in front of her. She recognized the last symbol, which she wasn't able to see before—a circle with a smaller circle in the middle, connected by four jagged lines that resembled bolts of lightning.

She knew what it was—the Guardian symbol! Breathing heavily, she pulled herself up, picked up the crystal, stood on the symbol, and directed her gift into the pillars of the elements. A flame rose, followed by a wave of water, a whirlwind, and a gush of sand.

The Shapeless One backed away. "Elladur's heir!" he whispered, deeply horrified. "This is not possible!"

The forces of the elements united above her head to form a gigantic whirlpool. Something ancient came to life in her and penetrated through her to the outside. With a casual movement of her hand, she hurled a wolf creature into the wall. Loud yelps reached her ears. She commanded the elements. At the same time, her mind looked down on what was happening. She knew that this would not last forever. The ancient gift was lent to her to fulfill her destiny.

Her hands created an explosion of light. Little sparks sprayed everywhere like tiny stars. She slowed down time, and the Shapeless One moved in slow motion while she maintained her speed. But she could not underestimate the dark king—she had to free the Dragon King. She needed his help.

She rushed to Rhynalor, loosened the ice wall, and touched the metal band.

He held her hand tightly. "No, save your strength for him."

"I need you; I can't do this alone. The others are under his spell." Her fingers burned as she touched the cold metal.

A huge fortress appeared in her mind's eye, black as night with high walls rising into the sky, as if she was going up this fortress piece by piece. Finally, she heard a crack, and the metal band fell to the ground. A burn was emblazoned on Rhynalor's neck, but gratitude and mildness were in his eyes.

"I'll take care of the Shapeless One, you take care of his creatures," she said.

"Your king could help us," he murmured.

She shook her head. "No, he's banished, too."

Mockingly, the Dragon King raised an eyebrow. "How easily deceived you are." His head bent down to her; she felt his warm breath on her ear. "Take good care!"

She felt his mouth on her lips. She resisted, but his arm held her tight. Liya was caught off guard and braced herself against him. Briefly, he let go of her. "Look!" he murmured.

Her gaze wandered to Haydn. He stood there with his eyes wide open and his shoulders tense. She thought she had perceived a movement.

Rhynalor let go of her. "He sees everything, and he can move. He would have let you die."

"That's not true," she gasped.

Her energy collapsed, and the sparks in the air faded. The Shapeless One was only an arm's length away from her.

A roar made the room tremble. Enormous wings sprouted from Rhynalor's back, and he transformed into a gigantic black dragon, whose body was surrounded by a light green glow, with sparkling emerald eyes. He pounced on the wolf creatures.

Liya caught the crystal when she felt the shapeless man's hand in her hair, pulling her back. She turned around. His mouth formed gray puffs of air as his hand clasped her neck.

Firmly, she clutched the crystal and pressed it against his chest. Her gift focused the light and directed it into her fingers. The crystal amplified her magic. The shapeless man grasped her hand, and immediately she felt a chill that froze the blood in her veins. Everything around her blurred— it was only her and the dark ruler now. The elemental pillars pulsated, bathing the room in a faint, ghostly light.

Unable to move, she realized that the dark ruler was weakening his opponents with this gray haze. She tried to breathe as little of it as possible, but the mist entered her through every pore. Her head pounded. Focusing and directing her own magic took tremendous strength. Without the ancient gift that had taken hold of her, she would have been lost long ago.

The ground shook beneath her, and her knees gave way. The Shapeless One had a firm grip on her. The terror she had felt just a moment ago was nothing compared to the horror that rose in her when she noticed the mist creeping up at her feet.

She smelled metal as she was pushed piece by piece into the darkness. She had to touch one of the pillars to warm her body. Spasmodically, she stretched as far as she could and touched the base of the fire with her fingertips.

"How did your bloodline survive?" hissed the Shapeless One.

In pain, she concentrated on directing the heat through every fiber of her being. Slowly, the freezing cold passed, and her strength returned. She broke out in a sweat. Gasping, she stared into the face of darkness that grinned at her.

At last, her fingers lit up, fire and light fully spreading within her. She pressed the crystal into his neck. Fascinated, she watched as the brightness that emerged from her hand merged with the dark crystal, leaving behind a silver haze. She perceived the space around her again, but still with blurred outlines and pale colors. Metal clanged. Men were fighting. The Shapeless One could no longer maintain his spell.

She shook violently, tears burning in her eyes. A horrible pain shot up her arm, and she loosened her grip.

HOLD ON! Don't go down, defeat him,

Rhynalor boomed in her head.

She gathered all her strength. When she looked down at herself, she saw that she was shining in bright light.

Fine white lines crisscrossed the shapeless man's chest, seeking a path to his neck. His eyes blazed angrily.

"No, that's not possible!" he groaned. "Foolish girl. Do you think it ends here?"

Light displaced the darkness, and the solid part of his body lost its form. In the end, only dark smoke remained of him, which was then drawn into a roaring vortex above their heads.

In the next moment, the tremors stopped. The space around them became clear and bright. The Shapeless One had disappeared. Only the gray-black mist that had surrounded him crept across the floor, drawing a circle around her. The elemental columns now looked like ordinary pillars.

Rhynalor stood before her in human form. He helped her up. The dark mist dissipated.

The Dragon King's gentle gaze did not match his pained, tortured expression. "What have you done?" he breathed.

"I don't understand," she muttered. "What's going on?" She had defeated the Shapeless One, hadn't she?

And then she heard it. Jakyn and his priests were singing softly. The sounds created vibrations that wrapped around the Dragon King like invisible shackles.

"Stop it!" she screamed. "Stop it now!"

"You have bound yourself to him and condemned me to perdition again!" Rhynalor hissed.

"It can't be," she gasped. "There is no bond between the Shapeless One and me."

"It was not the Shapeless One who did it, but *your king*," roared the Dragon King. His hand grasped her neck, squeezing lightly. "You humans deserve death. Your greed for power is immeasurable. My father should have wiped you all out when he had the chance. But instead, he helped you. Your treachery cost him his life and condemned me to darkness."

She felt his hatred and pain. Her heart tightened.

"Let go of me," she stammered. "I'll stop them. "

He loosened his grip, but he did not do so voluntarily. He had become weaker.

She tore herself away, raised her hands, and created a vortex of air that she hurled across the room. But Haydn was in front of the priests, and her attack bounced off his magic wall.

"You must stop it, Haydn!" she cried in despair.

"I need him," he replied. "I'm sorry, Liya."

In tears, she turned to Rhynalor. "Please, tell me what to do. How can I help you?"

"It's too late." Something in his eyes went out. "I thought you had summoned me. But it was your king's people, his priests. Tell me, *human queen*, how could you have been so blind?"

The deep despair she felt gave way to a cruel emptiness. Haydn had deceived her about his true intention in this game of powers, and worse, he had used her.

"He risked your life," Rhynalor continued relentlessly. "He would have let you die."

She tasted tears. As he drew closer, a new magical band wrapped around his neck. "He will never release me. Or you. You've long been his prisoner, and you didn't even know it."

"I will force him to let you go. I promise," she whispered.

"You owe it to me." He took her face in his hands.

The emerald green of his eyes brightened for a moment as he gazed at her. "I give you six months. Your king is nowhere near as powerful as the dark one. In his delusion, he does not realize who he has become involved with and what I am capable of."

She nodded.

"Swear it on your life!" He spoke softly and very calmly, but he sounded dangerous.

"I swear it," she breathed.

"This is how it should be. Our alliance holds." Rhynalor put a hand on her back. She tried to back away from the heat, but he held her tight. "Don't forget our bargain. Now go to your king, know the truth, and act!"

The sadness disappeared from his eyes, leaving behind coldness. Giving up his resistance, he let Haydn's men put chains on him. Haydn really believed he could lock him up permanently. Now, as she turned to Haydn, she felt Rhynalor's gaze at her back.

"You made it!" Haydn hugged her.

"Was that your plan?" she asked. "To take control of the Dragon King? Did he exchange one prison for another?"

466

He broke away from her. "Liya, we are facing a threat that we can only survive with his help."

"You used me. Your priests were able to summon the Dragon King. But only I, a Guardian of Elladur, was able to connect with him and guide him through the gate."

He lifted her chin and forced her to look at him. "I have not told you everything, but I have not lied to you."

She didn't want to hear any more. Rhynalor was right. The emptiness inside her gave way. Her heart burst into a thousand pieces, and the pain took her breath away.

"Did Melk know about your plan?" she asked quietly.

"Please, Liya, don't torture yourself with this."

She tore herself away from him. "Answer me!" she screamed.

"Time was running out. I had to act."

Out of the corner of her eye, she saw Maverick and his men approaching, swords drawn. She clenched her fists; the earth began to shake.

"Don't do that!" Haydn said.

She clearly noticed the threatening undertone. "What are you going to do? Put a ribbon around my neck, too?"

"Don't be ridiculous. I will explain everything to you. You will understand me, and we will find a solution."

He reached for her hand, but she fought him off. Grief, anger, and despair fueled her strength. She let out a scream.

"Leave the room!" thundered Haydn. "Now!"

Even as the pillars crumbled, she felt no fear. She wanted to destroy everything, but then her eyes fell on Sakima, Darwin, and Julian. With a wave of her hand, she formed a glittering ball that exploded in space, sending sparks flying. Time stood still. With a few steps, she reached her companions.

"You must leave this place immediately. Go to the port city to Captain Sonaris. Tell him the debt is paid, and he will take you back."

"You are not coming with us!" Sakima said. It was not a question.

"I can't."

Julian took out his dagger and threw it at Haydn. With a wave of her hand, she hurled the dagger against the wall.

"I'll take care of that," she told Julian. "That's my job." She looked at them one by one. "You must go now. Your people need you in these times."

Sakima touched her shoulder. "Peace and power be with you, Miakoda." Then he turned and pushed the mages toward the exit.

"We have to get out of here!" Haydn ordered.

"Liya!" someone called.

Emptiness spread inside her, and darkness surrounded her.

SNEAK PEEK

L iya walked down a dark tunnel. Her heart hammered against her ribs in fear. She felt a dark power, yet she kept walking. The passage widened and ended in a circular cavern. The exit in the rocky alcove was above her, about at eye level. Stars shone through the opening.

Her body tingled; coldness covered her skin, yet she did not freeze. She felt connected but did not know with whom or what.

Then a melodic voice rang out, filling the room: *The guardian of the light, and the dark knight, strong is the bond, easy to destroy in the dark land. The day becomes night, and his shadows come into sight. He is the eternal darkness, the remaining stillness. Nothing will be safe anymore; your soul is his forevermore.*

Those were the words written on the parchment that she and Ewan had bought from the smuggler back in Qilon.

Your soul is his forevermore, the voice repeated. It sounded more somber.

A hum sounded, followed by the singing of many voices in a foreign language. An altar appeared as if from nowhere. Someone knelt in front of it, his hood covering his face.

"Grant me the power of earth, water, fire, and air," said the hooded man. "Come from the depths and purify me. I am your son, your executor, and I lay rightful claim to their souls. " His voice was powerful, cold, and as sharp as a knife.

Everything in her screamed *run,* but she was unable to move. The stranger raised his head, looked at her, and laughed. It was the dark king in his solid form.

"Liya!" Someone grabbed her arm and dragged her back into the hallway. Before she could let out a scream, Haydn covered her mouth with his hand. "Quiet! We don't have much time."

He let go of her, and she backed away. "What are you doing here, and where are we?" she hissed.

His eyes darkened. "Your body lies in the castle, recovering from your injuries. Your spirit is ensnared by the dark ruler."

"I don't understand."

He pulled her further in the direction of the exit, then stopped abruptly and pressed her against him.

"A week has passed since you closed the gates," he murmured. "For several days, you have been dozing. With Jakyn's help, I've finally managed to reach you and get to you."

"Where are we?" she repeated. She broke out in a sweat.

"Your mind is in an intermediate world. Jakyn sensed extraordinary streams of magic in your room. We traced them back to their source, which is how we found you."

"That doesn't change your deception," she hissed. "You used me to get your hands on Rhynalor."

"I'm so sorry," he moaned. "Please, believe me. I couldn't tell you. It was too dangerous."

A noise from the cave made them cringe. Haydn's eyes widened.

"We need to get out of here," he groaned, pulling her along.

A faint light glowed in the distance. They stumbled toward it. It became brighter as they came closer to the exit. The sun painted yellow stripes on the rock walls, and fresh air blew in. Again, he stopped and pulled her to him.

"Whatever you think, Liya, you are everything to me," he whispered.

She did not have time to reply. She lost consciousness. When she awoke in her room, covered in sweat, she could still feel his breath on her neck.

CHARACTERS

Kingdom Namoor
Royal Family
Louis Althydan, King of Namoor
Cecilia Althydan, Queen of Namoor
Philipp Althydan, Prince, first born of Louis & Cecilia
Theo Althydan, Prince, youngest son of Louis und Cecilia

Council of the Wise, Palace City
Louis Althydan, King of Namoor
Philipp Althydan, Prince of Namoor
William Adesson, General of Namooranian Army
Tidon Rava, Lieutenant General 1st Legion
Rith Leon, Lieutenant General 2nd Legion
Zain Clove, Lieutenant General 3rd Legion
Nekoda Lorfin, Cousin of Louis, Lord Palace City
Baldin Saran, Lord Palace City
Ullmar Toris, Lord Palacy City

Council of Namoor
Louis Althydan, King of Namoor
Prem Laurus, Lord of Kapilar
Aquilia Flores, Lord of Relerin, Father of Hemmet Aquilia
Cendric Kalyn, Lord of Averin

Eliseus Venmar, Lord of Ralaren
Anorin Vivius, Lord of Shiel
Rantis Daryll, Lord of Corzon
Loran Koris, Lord of Arun

Eryon
Council
Gavin Jadmar – Grand Duke of Eryon
Julius Mattern – Lord of Loron, married to Amalia Mattern
Clive Ginald – Lord of Qilon, married to Marie Ginald
Haris Rawnye – Lord of Qilon, married to Kare Rawnye
Morris Dancan – Lord of Riyla, widowed
Bradon Winder – Lord of Riluca, unmarried

Dar'Angaar
Royal Family
Erthan Amaar, Grand Duke of Dar'Angaar, Haydn's father, deceased
Nesala Amaar, Duchess of Dar'Angaar, Haydn's mother, deceased
Haydn Amaar, Prince of Dar'Angaar

Ebra Amaar, Haydn's Uncle, Grand Duke of Aughdar
Yara Amaar, Duchess of Aughdar, married to Ebra
Arlandth Amaar, first born, Ebra's son and Yara's stepson
Tafriani Amaar, Yara's daughter and Ebra's stepdaughter
Ebradis Amaar, second eldest, Ebra's and Yara's son
Ithos & Rhimor Amaar, twins, Ebra's and Yara's sons
Mayra Amaar, youngest one, Ebra's and Yara's daughter

Thyron's City Council

4 Men:

Ithen – Council leader

Leveus – member of the council

Tinior – member of the council

Tofeus – member of the council

4 Women:

Strella – deputy leader of the council

Selena – member of the council

Mina – member of the council

Shia – member of the council

ACKNOWLEDGEMENT

Thank you to all my readers who took the time to read my book. I am honored to have you and your support. I owe deep thanks to my sister, who is tireless by my side and always believes in me. I would also like to especially thank my editors, Caroline and Rain – I am grateful that we found each other. My thanks also go to my wonderful parents who prepared my path. I also thank my husband who supported me to be able to write this book. I couldn't have done it without you - thank you all for your trust, inspiration and support.

ABOUT THE AUTHOR

Mystery Stories: Angie Delazi is an Austrian writer. Already as a child she loved the world of myths and legends and quickly became a fantasy and romance lover. But she is also passionate about the world of philosophy and great mysteries.

At thirteen she was already writing stories and finally she made her debut as an author with her novel "Elladur - the Awakening" , the start of a fantasy trilogy.

Today, the author lives with her family in Vienna.